TERRY ODELL

Finding Sarah

Cerridwen Press

What the critics are saying...

※

"Terry Odell out did herself; this book, once it gets started, takes off and never slows down again. It was a wild and suspenseful ride, the ending had me riveted, and Terry Odell kept me guessing until the end."
~ *Fallen Angels Review*

"Terry Odell's FINDING SARAH is an amazing book. The suspense kept me on the edge of my seat and the identity of the criminal took me by complete surprise. [...] Terry Odell has my thanks for writing such a thoroughly enjoyable book. I look forward to reading more of this talented writer." ~ *Romance Junkies Review*

A Cerridwen Press Publication

www.cerridwenpress.com

Finding Sarah

ISBN 9781419956515
ALL RIGHTS RESERVED.
Finding Sarah Copyright © 2007 Terry Odell
Edited by Helen Woodall.
Cover art by Willo.

This book printed in the U.S.A. by Jasmine-Jade Ent., LLC

Electronic book Publication February 2007
Trade paperback Publication June 2007

With the exception of quotes used in reviews, this book may not be reproduced or used in whole or in part by any means existing without written permission from the publisher, Ellora's Cave Publishing Inc., 1056 Home Avenue, Akron, OH 44310-3502.

This book is a work of fiction and any resemblance to persons, living or dead, or places, events or locales is purely coincidental. The characters are productions of the authors' imagination and used fictitiously.

Cerridwen Press is an imprint of Ellora's Cave Publishing, Inc.®

Also by Terry Odell

What's In A Name

About the Author

Terry Odell was born in Los Angeles and now makes her home in central Florida. An avid reader (her parents tell everyone they had to move from their first home because she finished the local library), she always wanted to "fix" stories so the characters did what she wanted, in books, television and the movies. Once she began writing, she found this wasn't always possible, as evidenced when the mystery she intended to write rapidly became a romance.

With her degree in Psychology from UCLA, she loves getting into the minds of her characters. When she's not writing, she's reading. She also volunteers for the Adult Literacy League, training new tutors, and serves as the administrative assistant for a scientific organization devoted to the study of marine mammals.

Terry is a member of RWA. Her manuscripts have won several awards, including the Suzannah and the Gotcha contests, and she has several published short stories. She used to do a lot of needlepoint, but ran out of wall space in the house, which undoubtedly steered her toward writing as a necessary creative outlet. She attributes much of her growth as a writer to her local critique group, the Pregnant Pigs. (bio)

Terry welcomes comments from readers. You can find her website and email address on her author bio page at www.cerridwenpress.com.

Tell Us What You Think
We appreciate hearing reader opinions about our books. You can email us at Comments@EllorasCave.com.

Finding Sarah

Dedication

There are countless people deserving thanks for their help in creating this work. To Sandra McDonald, who got me started. To my editor, Helen Woodall, who's seeing me through to the finish. The Short Story Group at iVillage whose weekly prompt led to a full-blown novel. To the Yahoo Novel Construction group, for their crits and feedback. And love to the Pregnant Pigs, who insisted I never give up writing and submitting. To Wally Lind and the gang at crimescenewriter, and to Detective Tom Bennett for the law enforcement and forensics advice. To Dr. Randy Ferrance for the medical consults and Amy Daraghy for keeping me straight on Oregon flora and fauna. And, of course, to all the wonderful people at the Central Florida Romance Writers, who are there for you no matter what. Thanks to Jessica, Nicole and Jason for their parts, and to Dan, my favorite research assistant, especially for always being willing to accept "scrounge" as the answer to "What's for dinner?"

Trademarks Acknowledgement

The author acknowledges the trademarked status and trademark owners of the following wordmarks mentioned in this work of fiction:

Big Red: Wm. Wrigley Jr. Company
"Bridge Over Troubled Water": Simon and Garfunkel
Eclipse: Mitsubishi Motors
ESPN: ESPN, Inc.
Hallmark: Hallmark Licensing, Inc.
Jameson's: Irish Distillers Limited
Looney Tunes: Warner Bros. Inc.
Peter Max: Via Max, Inc.
The Mousetrap: Agatha Christie
Polaroid: Polaroid Corporation
Rolodex: Berol Corporation
Snickers: Mars, Inc.
Starsky & Hutch: Columbia Pictures Industries, Inc.
"Sweet Caroline": Neil Diamond
Thriftway: Thriftway Stores, Inc.
Tilt-A-Whirl: Selner Manufacturing Company, Inc.
Toyota: Toyota Motor Corp.
Tums: SmithKline Beecham Corporation
U2: Not Us Limited
Valium: Hoffmann-La Roche Inc.

Chapter One

Sarah Tucker's hands shook with anger as she fumbled the keys into her gift boutique's lock. Bad enough the bus driver stopped beside a puddle the size of Crater Lake, which she cleared despite the restrictions of her skirt and pumps, thank you very much. But when that headbanger in the heavy metal-blasting SUV had sped through the muddy water, any satisfaction at her nimble footwork disappeared in a dousing of muddy water.

The cheerful jingle of the door chimes did nothing for her mood. Sarah rushed to her small office behind the glass sales counter and shrugged out of her coat to assess the damage. She dampened some paper towels and daubed at her mud-spattered shoes and stockings. She couldn't go home and change and the last thing she wanted was to appear at the bank this afternoon looking like she needed a loan. If you needed money, you couldn't get it, but if you had it, they'd give you whatever you asked for.

Enough negative thoughts. Sarah hung up her keys and tossed her instant soup packet into the basket by her coffeepot. Another gourmet lunch. At a knock on the door, she checked her watch. It wasn't quite ten, but she'd open for a possible sale. Patting her windblown hair into place, she hurried to the front door.

Christopher Westmoreland stood there, looking impeccable as always. No headbanger would dare splash water on his perfectly creased black trousers. His strawberry blond hair wouldn't dare blow in the wind.

"Chris. What brings you to town?" She stepped back into the store and toward the register. "I'm getting ready to open, but if you need anything, I'll be glad to get it for you." As if he'd actually buy something.

"Not today. I've got some appointments over in Salem. Thought I'd say hello before I head out." He strolled to the counter and leaned over its glass top, close enough for Sarah to smell his sandalwood aftershave and the cinnamon gum he chewed. "You haven't returned any of my calls. I know things have been tough since David…died. I only want to help. Why won't you let me? For old times' sake, if nothing else."

Memories of David flooded back. It had been over a year, but the pain lay just beneath the surface, waiting to engulf her. She shoved her emotions back into that metal strongbox in her brain, slammed the lid and turned the key. She was no longer Sarah, David's wife. Or Sarah the daughter, or Sarah the high school sweetheart. She was Just Plain Sarah.

Sarah met his pale green eyes, the ones she'd found so irresistible in high school. "We've been through all this before. I need to do it on my own. I can manage without your money." Even though he'd promised "no strings", Sarah knew if she took a dime from him, she'd be attached with monofilament line. The kind that cut when you tried to break it.

"Are you sure? You look like you haven't slept in a month. And your hair. Why did you cut it all off?"

"Well, thanks for making my morning." Sarah fluffed her cropped do-it-yourself haircut. "It's easier this way."

"How about dinner tonight? Come on, Sarah. We're friends, right?" His eyebrows lifted in expectation.

Dinner with Chris or five-for-a-dollar ramen noodles at home? Accepting dinner wouldn't be selling out, would it? "Maybe. Call me later, okay?"

"Great. See you later, then." He turned to leave.

"I said, 'maybe', remember?" Sarah walked him to the door and flipped the sign from "Closed" to "Open". She rearranged the crystal in the front window to catch the light and dusted the brightly colored pottery, shifting a pot, turning a vase so its pattern was visible from the street. Once she was satisfied with the effect, she meandered through the shop, adjusting animal carvings and moving a display of stationery to a roll-top desk.

An hour later, Sarah refused to let the lack of customers bother her. Easter was approaching, then Mother's Day and people would flock to That Special Something in droves to find that perfect gift. Maybe not droves. She'd settle for a trickle right now.

The door chimed. Sarah assessed the well-dressed woman who had entered the shop. Probably in her sixties, with a large designer purse draped over one shoulder. A hat with ribbon trim and black leather gloves made her a bit old-fashioned and out of place for the tiny Oregon town. Sarah gave the woman her biggest smile and stepped out from behind the counter. "Good morning, ma'am. Welcome to That Special Something. Are you looking for anything in particular?"

"My niece is getting married. I thought I might find something out of the ordinary here." Her voice was clipped, with a touch of sophisticated arrogance that said she was used to getting her way.

"Unique gifts are my specialty." Sarah motioned to a display of crystal. "Perhaps she'd like these hand-painted wine goblets? Or some of these Egyptian perfume bottles?"

"Thank you. I'll browse for a while, if you don't mind."

"Take your time. I'm Sarah. Feel free to ask any questions." Fighting the urge to follow her customer around, Sarah retreated and let the woman roam the shop.

The way Chris had referred to David's death churned through her thoughts. That horrible pause. The same one everyone else used. But Sarah knew it had been an accident. David would never commit suicide. This afternoon, she'd get a loan from the bank and rehire the private investigator or find a better one. The investigator would get the police to reopen the case and they'd find out it wasn't suicide. Then she'd get the insurance money, which would pay off the loan and the shop would be safe from foreclosure. It all made perfect sense. And maybe it would take away some of the guilt.

Sarah dragged her thoughts to the present, straightened her shoulders and found her professional smile again. Her customer was studying some silver picture frames. Expensive ones. She thought about how hard it had been to get Anjolie to display her work in the shop, that her work was *too good* for a mere boutique. She telegraphed mental messages to her customer — *Please, show Anjolie she was wrong. Buy one. Buy six.*

The woman set the frame down and turned away.

Sarah wouldn't let her disappointment show. "Can I show you something else?"

The woman strolled back and fingered the frames again. "You know, I like this one." She picked up the most expensive one, the one with the lacy pattern of roses and leaves. "And I think I'll take the matching vase over there."

Not good to let a customer see you jumping up and down clapping your hands. Instead, Sarah called up her most professional tone. "Excellent choices, ma'am. Would you like them gift-wrapped?"

"No, thank you. But if you have boxes for them, I would appreciate it."

Sarah ducked beneath the counter for the boxes, calculating what the sale would mean to her bottom line. When she rose, she stared into a gun barrel.

Sarah's mouth went dry. Her knees wobbled and she grabbed the edge of the glass, transfixed by the gleaming metal.

"I'm sorry, my dear." The woman's voice seemed to come from nowhere. "I'm a bit short at the moment, but I do want these lovely things." She slid the picture frame into her purse.

"What?" The word came out as a hoarse croak.

"I believe you heard me." Keeping the gun trained on Sarah, the woman stepped around the counter. "Unlock the register...Sarah, is it? I could use a little spending money."

Time froze. Sarah glanced toward the street, but saw no one who could have heard her scream, if she'd even been able to get a sound past the tightness in her throat. There was a pair of shears in a drawer, but the woman was standing in front of it. Not that she'd have the nerve to stab someone holding a gun. The woman leaned over Sarah, her breath smelling of peppermint. Sarah felt the press of cold steel against her back.

"Now," the woman said. "Slowly."

"I will. Please. Don't hurt me." Barely able to get the key into the lock with her trembling fingers, Sarah did as the woman asked. At least there wasn't much in the drawer. Sarah watched the woman empty the register of all but a single twenty-dollar bill.

"You see, I'm not leaving you penniless." Without lowering the gun, the woman backed toward the door. "I don't want to appear greedy, but I think I'll take a few of these animal carvings, too. Give my compliments to the artist." Still training the gun on Sarah, she set the vase down on the display table and filled it with the small wooden creatures. "Have a nice day." She picked up the vase and backed out the door.

* * * * *

Sarah struggled to decipher the legalese of her insurance policy as she awaited the arrival of the police. She dreaded the thought of another claim. Getting everything straight after the electrical fire in January had been a nightmare. She had been reading the same paragraph over and over when a knock and a voice at the front door set her heart pounding.

"Ms. Tucker? It's Detective Randy Detweiler, Pine Hills Police. We spoke on the phone."

She unlocked the door to a tall, lanky man dressed in black denim pants and a gray sweater, gripping several bulky plastic bags. At five-foot-four, Sarah didn't consider herself exceptionally short, but she had to tilt her head to meet his eyes.

"Thank you for coming," she said.

"No problem. Normally, we'd send a uniform first, but you've described someone we call Gracious Gertie. I've worked her case."

He brushed past her, spread the bags on the counter, then flashed a leather case with a gold badge. "Gertie's a sore spot with me. Do these look familiar? I found them in the alley about half a block away."

Sarah froze at what appeared to be Gertie's head in a bag on the counter, until she realized it was a wig, still attached to the black hat. The suit coat, shoes and even the large designer bag filled the rest of the counter space. "What—?"

"It's her typical MO, although this is the first time she's left her costume behind. Usually, she hits places that don't get a lot of traffic, always disguised differently and she never takes much from any one place. She hit several shops on the other side of town about a year ago. Looks like she's back."

"Then you should be able to catch her, right?" She forced herself to slow down. "You don't understand. I need my things. You have all that stuff. Can't you find some clues or something?" Sarah heard her voice quaver. No way was she going to break down in front of this police officer. Hands clutched across her middle as if to still the churning inside, she turned and walked away.

"I know you must be upset, ma'am, but I have to be honest. She's been getting away with this in small towns all over Oregon for at least two years. Believe me, I'd love to be the one to bring her in, but I don't think you should get your hopes up about recovering your merchandise."

Sarah leaned against a display table and fought nausea, dizziness and then fury. She took a deep breath.

Finding Sarah

"Why don't you tell me as much as you remember," the detective said. His voice seemed to float from the distance.

"What?" She started to walk toward him and her legs gave way. A strong hand grasped her elbow.

"Are you all right? You've been held up at gunpoint. Sometimes it gets worse once you realize you're safe. Let's sit down. No need to rush into the paperwork."

"No, I'll be fine." She looked into the detective's face, saw an aquiline nose and scrutinizing brown eyes. A wayward lock of dark brown hair hung over his forehead, calling attention to a small scar above his left eyebrow. There was something vaguely familiar about him, but before she could bring a memory forward, the door chimed and she turned away.

A slender man sporting a stubble of beard, dressed in blue coveralls and baseball cap, stood in the doorway, taking a slow look around. He held a large metal case. Eyebrows raised, he looked at the detective. "You think we'll get anything?"

"I'm not sure," Detective Detweiler said. "You'll have to dry the clothes—I found them in a puddle."

"You get pictures?"

"Yes." Detective Detweiler turned to Sarah. "This is Connor from the lab. He'll dust for prints. Can you remember what she touched?"

"The silver over there." Sarah pointed to the table. "Those animal carvings and I think she was looking at the baskets. I know she was wearing gloves when she came in." She faltered. "I can't be positive she still had them on when she came to the register. All I remember is the gun." Speaking the word aloud brought back the fear.

"I'll need her prints for elimination," Connor said. He faced Sarah. "This won't take long."

As if it were happening to someone else, Sarah watched Conner ink and roll her fingers. He slipped a card into an envelope and handed her a paper towel dipped in some gooey cleanser. She held it, transfixed, until she felt a warm touch and realized Detective Detweiler was wiping the ink from her fingers. She snatched her hands away and scrubbed them herself.

"Ms. Tucker can give me all the details over coffee," Detweiler said to Connor. "We'll be at Sadie's down the block."

"Is that normal police procedure?" Sarah asked.

"It is when the victim of a crime is in obvious distress. Where are your keys?"

"In the office. On a hook by the door."

His long legs covered the distance in three strides and he returned with Sarah's coat as well. "Let's go." He draped the coat over Sarah's shoulders and held the door for her.

"The back door locks automatically," Sarah said to Connor. "You can go out that way when you finish."

The fresh air, damp with traces of rain, revived her and she navigated the short distance to the café with only an occasional hint of support from Detective Detweiler.

They found a booth in the back and the detective ordered coffee and muffins. "You want your usual decaf, Sarah?" the waitress asked.

"Please."

When the waitress left, Sarah eyed Detective Detweiler. "What? No doughnuts?"

"Don't let it get out. I hate 'em. Probably have to turn in my badge if anyone found out."

Sarah was surprised to feel a grin tug at the corner of her mouth.

The waitress appeared with coffee and a napkin-covered basket. Detective Detweiler lifted the napkin and pushed the basket toward Sarah. "Now, eat a muffin. We'll talk later."

She broke off a small piece of blueberry muffin. The jittery feeling in her stomach hadn't disappeared and she hesitated before putting it in her mouth.

"Please. Eat. You look like you're bordering on shock." He took her coffee cup and stirred in a liberal amount of sugar. "The sugar will help. Cream?"

She nodded and he poured. "I skipped breakfast, that's all."

"That and a gun in your face will do it every time."

Sarah swallowed a bit of the sweet muffin. Suddenly ravenous, she relished the rest of it. She looked up into those deep brown eyes again, glimpsing flecks of hazel this time. "Thank you. I guess I was hungrier than I thought."

"Eat another one and relax while I make some notes." He pulled out his notebook and started writing.

Sarah resisted only an instant before plucking a muffin from the basket. The detective seemed engrossed in his notes and she was grateful for his silence. Once she finished her coffee, she grasped the table's edge. "I guess we'd better do whatever we have to do, Detective Detweiler," she said.

"Please. Call me Randy. Detective Detweiler doesn't roll off the tongue."

"Then it's Sarah." She studied his face again. "I'm sorry, but you look familiar. Have we met?"

His expression turned somber. "Briefly, after your husband's…death. Are things all right?"

That pause again. Realization hit her like this morning's mud puddle. This was the man who'd told her to hire a private investigator. That there was nothing they could do in Pine Hills because it was out of their jurisdiction and the Polk County cops in charge had closed the case. Had he thought she was right? Or was he trying to get her out of the police department's hair when she'd demanded they keep investigating? The memories turned the muffins to lead in her stomach.

"I'm managing." At least she had been until half an hour ago. She blinked back tears. "Can we just get on with the stuff about the robbery?"

"Of course. I understand." He held his pen above his notebook. "How are sales? Any reason for Gertie to think your shop would be a lucrative hit?"

She shook her head. "We're small, but we were doing well enough. Tourism is flowing out this way from Salem and Portland and local artisans are being recognized. We've had some financial setbacks, but things seemed to be coming together." She couldn't tell him that the robbery probably meant she would have to sell the shop. Tears threatened again. She willed them away and stared at him.

"We?"

Sarah twisted her napkin. "I guess I still think of the shop as 'ours'—that David—my husband—is a part of it. Technically, his sister owns twenty percent, but she doesn't do anything except demand her cut every month."

"I'll need her name and address," he said. His pen clicked and hovered again.

"Diana Scofield. Lives in Portland, but I'll have to get the exact address for you." While she watched Randy make his notes, she wondered where Diana's next check, dismal as it would be, would come from. The only way to keep that woman out of her hair was to give her the money on time. She concentrated on the pen, as if its clicking was the only sound in the diner.

"Any trouble between the two of you?"

"I would have thought all of that came out during the investigation of my husband's death." She moved her hands to her lap where he couldn't see them tremble, wiping them on her napkin.

"I wasn't part of that investigation." He paused. "I know this is difficult, but if we get the preliminary stuff done, I can start looking for Gertie and your merchandise."

She nodded. "Diana and David were close. He was her father figure when their parents divorced. She worshipped him and I think she resented me for marrying him—stealing him away. She blames me for his death."

This time, the pen was silent. Randy leaned closer. "Why would she blame you?"

Sarah struggled to find the detachment she'd needed the past fifteen months. The ability to become a different Sarah when she had to talk about David. "We were trying to turn the store into more of a gallery than a cutesy gift shop and it was stretching the budget." She heard her voice go flat. Reciting words she'd repeated too many times before. "Diana wasn't good with money. David kept bailing her out and I thought it was time he let her suffer the consequences of her spending habits. We were arguing about it the day he died."

Sarah raised her eyes to meet Randy's. "David would never have killed himself because money was tight or we were having a few arguments. We were making a go of things, working them out."

"Does Diana think it was suicide?"

"I think she needs someone to blame for David's death and I'm the handiest scapegoat." She heard the bitterness and took a deep breath. "Please. This can't have anything to do with the little old witch who robbed me."

"I'm sorry, but we have to consider everything. We can come back to this if it seems to fit." Three more clicks of his pen. "Do you know what kind of gun she used? Revolver? Automatic?"

Sarah shuddered. "I don't know anything about guns. It looked...big."

"If you saw a picture, would you recognize it?"

"Maybe. I usually notice things, but—"

"It's all right. And not unusual when you're frightened. Let's move on. Who else has been in the store today? It'll help Connor eliminate more prints."

Sarah relaxed a little at the shift in the conversation. "Nobody was in the shop before Gertie, except me...and—"

"And who?"

Sarah paused a moment. "A friend. Chris. Christopher Westmoreland. He was there before Gertie came in. But there's no way he could be involved."

"You know him well?"

"Yes, as a matter of fact I do. I can't see him rubbing elbows with a thief. He's a bigwig at Consolidated Enterprises."

Randy made his notes. "Thank you. I'll talk to him. Next question. How much did Gertie take?"

"Two expensive silver pieces and a handful of small carved animals. And about two hundred in cash." She managed a wry grin. "She left me twenty dollars."

"Do you have any recollection of her being in the shop before today?"

"I don't think so. It's been quiet, unless she came in during the Christmas season. We were busier then."

"You have any other employees? Someone else who might remember her?"

"No. Just me." She tried not to think of working side-by-side with David, but her voice quavered.

As if he sensed he'd taken her to the edge of her emotional limits, Randy stood up. "Let's go."

Back in her shop, Sarah flinched when she saw the remnants of the black fingerprint powder all over the counter and Anjolie's silver. The bags of Gertie's belongings were gone, presumably taken by Connor. She dashed into the back room and returned with a spray bottle of cleanser and a roll of paper towels, wishing she could clean away the events of the previous hour by rubbing hard enough. She showed Randy an inventory photo of Anjolie's vase and samples of the animal carvings and she answered the rest of his questions.

She gave the counter one more swipe. "Look, it's almost twelve. I should reopen if you're done. Is there anything more you need?"

"I guess not. If she was wearing gloves the whole time and the wig, it's doubtful we'll get much here, but sometimes the lab folks can pull rabbits out of very tiny hats. I'll do some door-to-door and see if anyone else noticed Gertie. If I need anything else, I'll call."

"Thanks." She walked over and held the door for him. When he left, she reached for the "Open" sign, but couldn't face customers yet. She turned and leaned against the closed door, contemplating the shop. Their life. Hers and David's.

Sarah meandered through the space, seeking comfort from the merchandise. She remembered working with David—refinishing the old shelves and tables they used instead of conventional store fixtures, the arguments about whether to carry high-priced oil paintings, the joy when they discovered a new artisan at a craft show. As she had so many times, she pushed the memories away, but now they refused to relinquish their hold.

She had no idea how long she'd been daydreaming when the back doorbell summoned. She peered through the small glass window. Anjolie. What was she doing here? Sarah opened the door.

Anjolie pushed past Sarah, her waist-length raven hair swaying as she marched to the table where her silver sat on display. She set a large cardboard box down on the floor and began loading it with her picture frames. "Someone from Pandora's called and said I would do better over there."

The muffins congealed in Sarah's stomach. "Wait. Can't we talk about it?"

"There's not much to talk about." She put her hands on her hips and stared at the display. "You didn't mention you'd sold the vase and one of my frames," Anjolie said. She looked at Sarah with narrowed eyes. "I'll take my check now, please."

"They were stolen. This morning. The police were here. They think they know who took them and I'm sure they'll get them back soon." She lifted her chin and met Anjolie's gaze. "Can't you leave your work with me for a few months longer? I know things will pick up." She heard her voice rise and hated herself for it.

"Sorry. It's settled. I agreed to bring my work to Pandora's."

Too drained to think, much less argue, Sarah went to the storeroom for some tissue paper. Without speaking, the two women wrapped and packed Anjolie's silver.

"I'll give you a week," Anjolie said. "If the cops don't find my stuff, I'll expect a check."

Sarah watched Anjolie load the carton into her van. When the phone rang, Sarah let the heavy back door swing shut and hurried through the shop. At the sound of Mr. Chatsworth's condescending voice, her stomach sank. Her bank appointment. She looked at her watch. She was twenty minutes late. Her attempts to explain were cut short.

"I'm sorry Sarah, but there's no reason to reschedule. I've reviewed your loan application and it wouldn't be prudent for us to grant the loan at this time."

"I understand." The words barely made it past her constricted throat. "Thank you for your time." She waited until she heard him disconnect before she slammed the phone down. She would not be defeated. Not by some little old lady, not by a temperamental artist, not by a cheapskate banker. This shop was her life and by God, she would see it survive.

Sarah stormed into the storeroom and dragged out the boxes of Easter merchandise. She was too upset to open the shop and it seemed as good a time as any to begin her new displays.

Even the fingernail she broke when she ripped open a carton didn't bother her. She dug through Styrofoam packing material and pulled out hand-painted wooden tulips, their smooth surfaces soothing her nerves. She fetched some vases from another display and arranged wooden bouquets.

After an hour lost in the creative process, Sarah stepped back. The store reflected a vision of a springtime garden, replete with wooden bunnies hiding among caches of decorative eggs. She let that familiar glow of satisfaction wash over her as she surveyed the results of her labor, remembering how she and David had agonized over the carpet. It had to be neutral to set off the artwork, but beige or gray was so boring. They had finally settled on an amber brown and now it became freshly turned garden soil.

Outside, ominous rumblings of thunder sounded in the distance. Sarah clutched her arms around her waist, her thoughts returning to the rainy night the Highway Patrol officer had come to her door. In that instant, Sarah had known her life would never be the same. Her David, her soul mate, dead at twenty-six. He had finished her thoughts, known what she needed before she did.

She touched her sweater, feeling David's wedding band on the chain beneath it. Even a year after he'd died, she still felt incomplete without him.

He couldn't have killed himself. It was an accident, no matter what anybody said. In good weather, the mountain road was dangerous enough with its twists and turns and it had been stormy that day.

The pangs of guilt returned. If she'd been with him, would he still be alive? They'd never had secrets. Or had she missed something?

Accident or suicide, could she have had anything to do with his death? Had his mind been on their quarrel and not the road? Her eyes and throat burned. She might as well go home. She gathered the insurance papers, locked up and hurried toward the bus stop, hoping the bus would arrive before the rain.

Chapter Two

    Sarah sloshed her way to her four-plex apartment building, its faded pink paint looking even duller under the cloud-filled sky. What else could go wrong? True, she'd beaten the rain to the bus, but the skies had opened while she walked the last block home. She stepped up the boxwood-lined concrete stairs, pushed open the heavy wooden door and wiped her sodden shoes on the mat inside.

    Standing in the foyer, Sarah let her eyes adjust to the dim light. Broken strains of Beethoven's *Minuet in G* drifted from Mrs. Pentecost's apartment. Eight-year-old Lydia was having her piano lesson. Sarah trudged up the flight of carpeted stairs to her apartment.

    She exchanged her rain-soaked clothes for leggings and an old, faded sweatshirt and curled up on the couch to pore over the insurance papers. The value of the pieces stolen by that Gertie crook barely met the deductible. Not much point in filing another claim. Two claims in three months would wreak havoc with her premiums.

    As Sarah rubbed her neck, the blinking light of the answering machine caught her eye. She punched the message button and heard Chris' voice asking why she wasn't at work and reminding her about dinner. Would dinner be so bad? But as dejected as she felt right now, she'd probably give in to his offers of charity. There had to be another way, a way that didn't entail being in debt to anyone but the bank. Not that the bank wanted her in any more debt than she already was.

    Sarah hit the redial on Chris' message, got his machine and begged off dinner. Company was the last thing she wanted. Blue funks were best wallowed in alone. She'd barely hung up when the shrill ring of the phone made her jump. She picked it up and heard Randy Detweiler's voice.

Sarah's heart quickened. "Did you find her? Did you get my things back?"

"No, but I have some more questions. If it's all right, I'll come over in about an hour. I think it'll be easier to do this in person."

The blue funk evaporated into hope of solving the robbery. Sarah blew her hair dry and repaired her makeup. She pulled off her old sweatshirt and replaced it with her favorite kelly green sweater. She had scarcely finished putting away the weekend's clutter when the doorbell rang.

Randy stood in the doorway, holding a canvas briefcase, raincoat dripping, that one lock of hair hanging over his eyebrow. Wet, it was almost black. She motioned him inside.

He hung his coat on a hook by the front door, then crossed to the dining room table. "Is this a good place to talk?"

"Sure."

He pulled out a chair and sat down and Sarah took a seat across from him. Randy reached into his briefcase and pulled out a stack of photographs. "Do any of these look like the gun you saw?"

Sarah took the pictures and leafed through them, trying to be objective, trying to forget the way her mouth got dry just looking at them. She handed him two. "More like these, I think."

She searched Randy's face for a hint that he was pleased with her choices, but saw nothing. "I could be wrong, though."

"No, these are semi-automatics and that's what other witnesses said she used."

"Other witnesses? Did someone else see her?" Maybe this would be over. He put the photos back in his briefcase and she relaxed. Stupid. They were pictures, not real guns.

"No, he said. "I'm talking about last year's robberies. They're still open cases."

"That's right. You said she was here last year, but I must have totally missed it." She lowered her eyes to the table. "Of course, back then, there was a lot I was missing."

He was silent and she raised her gaze. His brown eyes locked on hers for a moment, then he looked back at his notebook, clicking his pen. "Gertie hasn't turned up anywhere else lately, so it's possible she's back in Pine Hills. We'll alert the other shopkeepers. Maybe I'll get her this time around."

She thought of all that black powder. "Did you get any fingerprints?"

"Some. We're running them, but Gertie's never left prints before, so we don't have anything to compare them to. If Christopher Westmoreland was in the shop, I'll need to get his for elimination as well."

She laughed. "I'd love to be there when you do. I can just picture his face when a cop comes to the door."

Randy raised an eyebrow. "You think he has something to hide?"

"Oh, no. He's always seemed—above us mere mortals, you know. Image is everything. Nothing ever goes wrong for him."

"Really. What can you tell me about him?"

"I can't believe he had anything to do with this. He's so…proper."

"I don't make any assumptions when I'm working a case. Gets in the way. But the more I know, the better I can see the big picture. Eliminating data is as important as finding it. Are you seeing Chris?"

She raised her eyebrows, but he sat, his expression neutral. "As in dating?"

"As in anything." The words were spoken casually, but there was a hint of anticipation in his tone. "I'm simply trying to get as much information as I can."

She dismissed the fleeting idea he'd asked for personal reasons. "Not really. Chris came around after my husband died, trying to get back together, but—well, I don't think of him that way. He pops in from time to time—coffee, the occasional dinner. He's a friend. Like I said, he showed up at the shop this morning."

"What did he want?"

"The usual—to help me. But I don't want his help. I get the feeling there would be too many strings attached and I'd rather flip burgers than be indebted to him. I like being in charge of my own life."

"Go on, please," Randy said. "About Chris."

Right. David was dead and now she was talking to a cop about Chris. She waited for the twisting in her belly to pass. "When Chris came back for Christmas break the first year, he seemed upset that I'd found someone else, but he got over it. Besides, it wasn't like he'd been faithful to me. Rumor had it he was pretty popular with the girls."

"Do you know anything about what Chris did while he was away at school?"

"No. Sorry."

He nodded. "All right. What else can you tell me?"

"Not much. He's just—Chris. After I got married, he was friendly enough—even pointed us to some local artists from time to time."

Randy's pen clicked again. "Do you remember which ones? Are they still with you?"

"Some." She met his gaze. "I know. You'll need their names. I'll get you a list." She went to her desk and turned on the computer. Once she'd printed the list for Randy, she circled the current artists and went back to the table. "I don't think this will be much help—there's not much they have in common, aside from being artists, of course."

He looked up, pen at the ready. "Was he in contact with Gertie while he was in the shop?"

"No, I don't think so. Let me think a minute." She tried to replay the exact chain of events. "Chris showed up and we were talking. But he left before Gertie got there. My shop is such a tiny operation. What could anyone gain by having it robbed?"

He gave his head a quick shake and the wayward lock of hair bounced. One corner of his mouth curled upward. "If we knew the answer to that one, we might solve a lot of crimes a lot faster." His smile widened and she couldn't help but notice how it warmed his entire face. Something inside her warmed, too and she blinked in surprise at her reaction.

"I guess you've seen a lot of this."

"Enough to know people will do crazy things for even crazier reasons. The first thing you learn is to leave all your assumptions at the door."

"Well, I still don't see how any of this is connected to your Gertie, but I'll help any way I can. The sooner you find my merchandise, the better. What else can I tell you?

"That should do it for now. Thanks." Randy closed his notebook and put everything back in his briefcase. "I'd appreciate it if you kept everything relating to the case confidential." He pulled out a business card and handed it to Sarah. "You call me if anything unusual happens. Any time."

After Randy left, she studied his card before putting it in her purse. He'd said to call any time. Of course he'd say that. Cops were always on duty, weren't they?

Unable to settle, Sarah ran a hot bubble bath. Her head pillowed on a rolled-up towel, she closed her eyes, the soft crackle of popping bubbles the only sound. As the hot water released the tension in her body, burning tears threatened. She was not going to cry. Crying wouldn't solve anything. She brought her right hand to the chain around her neck where David's thick gold band hung. On the anniversary of David's death, she'd gone to his gravesite and moved her own wedding band from her left hand to her right and vowed that the crying was over.

The chill of a bath gone cold made her realize she'd drifted off to sleep. She rinsed, then toweled off and bundled herself into David's old plaid flannel robe. This was the only piece of him she hadn't been able to part with when she'd cleaned out the closets. Even after so many washings, she swore she could still smell his essence when she put it on. Enveloped in the robe's softness, she felt the swirling tide of her emotions begin to ebb. There was nothing she could do and dwelling on her misery wouldn't help.

Without warning, the tears returned, streaming down her face. Tears of self-pity? Of grief? Guilt? Or maybe anger. Sarah didn't care—she threw herself onto the couch and succumbed to the sobs until she was exhausted. When the phone rang, she let the answering machine pick it up, too drained to move. Randy's voice pulled her from the couch. Could he have found her things already?

When he told her he needed yet more information, her heart sank. She couldn't deal with more questions tonight. "Is tomorrow all right? I've got a class at St. Michael's after work, but I'm usually home by eight-thirty."

"Eight-thirty. It's a date."

She hung up and stared at the phone. Date? No, that was only a figure of speech. They were trying to solve a crime.

Finding Sarah

Chapter Three
ঞ

First thing the next morning, Randy jogged up the three steps to Chris Westmoreland's massive front porch and rang the bell. He composed his face into his friendly but firm interview mode and waited, enjoying the warmth of the early morning sun. Sounds of padded footsteps followed by a growled, "Who's there?" came from behind the door.

When Randy identified himself, the door swung open. Chris stood before him, unshaven, wearing leather slippers and an expensive robe. No. A dressing gown, monogram on the pocket and all. "What can I do for you, Detective?"

Randy displayed his badge. "I have a couple of routine questions. I understand you were in That Special Something shortly before a robbery yesterday."

Chris nodded and motioned him inside. Randy took in the large, elegant and decidedly masculine space, with a fieldstone fireplace and dark wood wainscoting. A group of framed black-and-white landscapes adorned one wall, while three abstract watercolors dominated another.

"I heard about the robbery on the news. Poor Sarah. If I'd had any idea, I would never have left the shop. I still wonder if I could have prevented it." He perched on the edge of an oversized brown sofa and gestured toward a large leather easy chair. "Please sit. How can I help?"

Randy set his briefcase on the floor and lowered himself into the chair. "Do you remember seeing anyone before or after you stopped in at Ms. Tucker's? Older woman, well-dressed?"

Chris waited, as if he were replaying the morning. "No, I went straight from Sarah's to Salem. Sorry I can't be of more help."

"Actually, you can," Randy said. "I'd like your fingerprints. Strictly for elimination, of course. We found prints in the shop and it would help if we knew which ones were yours and which might belong to the robber."

Randy remembered what Sarah had said and studied Chris' reaction. She'd have been disappointed. Calm, collected, without a hint of indignation. He could usually read his suspects. Chris' cool green eyes had no trouble meeting his own, yet they didn't lock on the way liars' often did. Liars either stared you down or never met your gaze.

"Of course, Detective. Do I go to the police station?"

"No, I can do it now." He pulled the kit from his briefcase and rolled Chris' prints onto the ten card. Chris remained nonchalant, showing little interest in the process until Randy was done. Then he examined his fingers with some disgust.

Randy handed him a foil-wrapped cleansing towel. "This should take it off," he said.

While Chris worked on removing all traces of the ink, Randy packed everything back into his briefcase.

Chris escorted him to the door, still wiping his fingers. "Sarah's a nice woman," he said. "We go back a long way. Her husband's suicide—a real tragedy."

"Yes, I know." Randy pulled himself up to his full height and smiled at Chris. "It would be a real shame if anything else happened to her."

* * * * *

Randy parked his pickup under a light in the far corner of St. Michael's parking lot and flipped pages in his notebook. He asked himself why he hadn't waited and met Sarah at her apartment as planned. When he'd decided to give her a ride home, it seemed logical. But what had possessed him to get here over an hour early? And at a nursing home, yet. He gave himself an internal kick in the head and started reviewing his notes. Inside, memories of Gram would overwhelm him. He popped the plastic lid from his takeout coffee and sipped.

He let his mind float, searching for connections, but he needed more dots to connect. Eventually, the coffee made it clear he couldn't sit in the truck much longer. He put everything in his briefcase and quick-stepped across the parking lot to the building's entrance.

After a stop in the men's room, Randy ambled down the speckled linoleum hall to the recreation center where the silver-haired receptionist had told him he would find Sarah's class. At least the smell of antiseptic wasn't so strong here. Ten feet from the open door, he froze. After a deep breath, he found his wall of detachment. At the doorway, he had to stop again. Gram was gone. It'd been eight years, he reminded himself.

He could hear Sarah's voice and it centered him. He stood to one side, peering through the door. His mouth dropped open and he clamped it closed. Sarah roamed around a room of a dozen or so elderly men and women, some in wheelchairs, some sitting at tables, some standing. All were working with slabs of wet, gray clay. Dumbfounded, he studied her as she moved from one person to the next, offering encouragement, taking their gnarled hands and helping them shape the clay into whatever their mind's eye projected.

His automatic cop assessment—white female, late twenties, brown hair, blue eyes, five-four, one-fifteen—hardly did her justice.

Deep chestnut hair that shimmered in the light. Stone blue eyes that reflected every thought in her head. He snorted as he thought of the way that would go over in a briefing.

She must have heard him, because her head snapped toward the door. Wearing a plastic apron, covered to her elbows in clay, she straightened and raised her eyebrows. And smiled.

"Keep going everyone," she said. She crossed the room, hands raised in front of her like a surgeon after scrubbing. "Does this visit mean you've found something?"

He hated to erase the look of hope from her face. "Sorry, not yet. I thought—I don't know what I thought. I didn't realize this was the kind of class you meant. That you were the teacher. I guess I saw you sitting in some boring lecture and we'd sneak away and finish our business early. But you're busy. I can come back."

"I can't talk now, but I could use another pair of hands. As long as you're here, can you help?"

"I don't know anything about this." He started inching toward the door, trying not to look at the people in the room, trying to push away the memories they dredged up.

She lowered her voice to a conspiratorial whisper. "That's okay—neither do most of them. It's therapy more than art. Just offer encouragement."

"Hey, Sarah!" Randy followed the crackling voice to its source, an elderly woman whose hand trembled as she tried to shape a mound of clay into what Randy could only envision as a differently shaped mound of clay. "I need one of those stick things."

"Why don't you help Mrs. Rasmussen? She had a stroke a few months ago and she needs to use her right arm more. There's an apron by the sink and tongue depressors on the table—help her hold it and move it along the clay with her."

He could feel the color draining from his face. "I'm not sure I can be much help."

"Relax. It's not supposed to end up being a Maria Martinez. It's the doing that's important."

Forget Gram. Maintain. "Fine." He rebuilt his wall and went to help Mrs. Rasmussen.

Finding Sarah

At seven-thirty, staff escorted the residents from the room. Randy followed Sarah, helping as she collected tools, folded plastic sheets and wiped down tables.

"You look happy," he said. "How was work?"

Her eyes were blue Christmas lights. "I haven't had so many customers in weeks, even if most of them probably came in out of curiosity. They bought, which is good enough for me right now."

"And this? You obviously enjoy it."

"Maggie, my neighbor, got me started doing this about three years ago. Sometimes it's the high point of my week." She started covering the unfinished creations with plastic wrap. "Why don't you ask your questions while I finish cleaning?"

"I can help," Randy said.

"I'm fine, but I think I'd rather be doing something," she said. She turned her eyes to his and he thought some of the light had dimmed. Had he caused that?

Randy retrieved his briefcase, pulled out his notepad and pen. He took a seat at an empty table. "I understand." He clicked his pen open and printed the date and time on a clean page. "I want to know everything about your store."

"There's not much. After we graduated, David and I managed the shop. Back then, all the merchandise was mass-produced, everyday stuff. We did all right, but we wanted to add that special something—that's what we called the shop when we bought out the owner. It took a while but we convinced some of the local craftsmen and artisans to let us carry their work on consignment."

"You'd think they'd have jumped at the chance to have someone showcase their work."

Sarah collected scraps of clay and put them into a large plastic bucket. "About a year later, we found out they'd heard we weren't reliable. Rumors in the art community, but we proved them wrong." She added water to the bucket, covered it and looked at him. "Do you think that might mean something?"

"I told you, I like to find out as much as possible about a case. I'm looking for common denominators. Go on."

"We had the normal business snafus. Little things. Broken merchandise, shipment mix-ups. Things like that happen. I remember some exclusive hand-painted dinnerware that ended up at a rival shop in Cottonwood."

"What shop?"

"Pandora's. Wait a minute," she said. "Anjolie." She dried her hands and took a seat across from him.

"What are you talking about?" He could almost see the synapses firing as he waited for her to answer.

"I don't know how or if this fits," she said. "But Pandora's is one of our chief competitors. It opened right after we took over our shop. Some of our orders ended up there. And Anjolie—it was her silver that was stolen—showed up right after the robbery yesterday. She pulled the rest of her stuff. Said she got a better offer from Pandora's. I could understand if she wanted to move her things. We didn't have a contract." Her eyes widened. "Do you think Anjolie's lying about Pandora's? Do you think she had something to do with the robbery?"

"I need to pay Anjolie a visit and ask her. What's her full name?"

"Anjolie Du Bois."

"Do you have her address?"

"I'll get it for you."

"Was there any kind of pattern to the stuff that was lost or broken?" Randy asked. "Same kind of merchandise, same manufacturer, anything that would connect them?"

"I don't think so."

"Any other problems? Unhappy customers? Someone trying to buy you out?"

"Not really."

The way she hesitated told him there was more than she was saying. "Not really, but...?"

Sarah manipulated a leftover scrap of clay. "When we were trying to expand, David and I needed money. Diana's husband—he was her fiancé at the time—thought owning part of a gift shop would be a nice wedding present and his investment helped us out. Diana tried playing shopkeeper a couple of times, but between the commute from Portland and the hard work, she stopped caring. Now, it's strictly a financial relationship. As long as she gets her check every month, she's satisfied."

"You think she wants more?"

When Sarah locked her blue eyes on him, Randy knew he was dredging up memories she wanted to put away and every question he asked caused her pain. But, painful or not, doing his job was the only way to make things right. He shoved those thoughts deep down where they couldn't disturb his objectivity.

"Our will said that if anything happened to both of us, Diana would get the shop. She's saying that since he's gone, she deserves half."

"Why the sudden interest?"

"She didn't get a whole lot after moneybags Scofield divorced her. Just the house, a small allowance and her twenty percent of That Special Something. And twenty percent of not much doesn't even cover her nail appointments. God forbid she should have to get a real job. She keeps telling me to sell, or make it into a Hallmark franchise or something. As if she has a clue how that could happen."

Randy heard the bitterness. But he also heard the pride. "You don't want to do that, do you?"

Her eyes flashed bright blue. "Never. Things were bad after the accident. I held on. I can ride this out."

"I'm sure you will." He glanced at his notes. "Not much more. You talked about some waylaid shipments, mixed-up orders. Do you remember when the problems started? Before or after your husband's accident?"

Sarah's lips tightened and the muscles in her jaw clenched.

Damn. He'd hurt her again. Without thinking, he reached across the table to take her hand, catching himself just in time. He pushed a lock of hair out of his eyes. "Sorry if this is painful."

"No. David's gone. I have to get used to that. But sometimes… We were so happy… It's hard…"

She lifted her head. When their eyes met, his physical response had him shifting in his seat. He was working a case, for God's sake. "Go on."

"I'd say there were always glitches, but I didn't pay a lot of attention. David did the bookkeeping. Afterwards, I assumed I was messing up orders because I was such a wreck. But you have to understand, things like this happen all the time. It's part of the business."

Something more was in there and it was his job to find it. "What else?"

She paused, twisting the ring on her finger. "Not much—unless you count the fire."

"Fire?" He flipped to a clean notebook page. "Tell me about it."

"It happened in January. It wasn't very big. A short in the electrical system—faulty wiring, overloaded circuits. I didn't lose much merchandise, but I had to close for almost two weeks while they repaired the damage. Those two weeks cut into my Valentine's Day profits. And then, I had to fight with the insurance company. They didn't want to pay the claim."

"Did they?"

"Yes, but I had to have inspectors and adjusters come out three or four times. Seems like there was some discrepancy in the reports. A computer error, they said, once it was straightened out."

"Sounds like you've overcome some troubles."

"I'm sure it will be quiet again tomorrow. But I should be all right once Easter sales get going."

"I'm sure they will." He closed his notebook. "I think the worst is over. Can I do anything else to help? Please?"

Sarah filled a large plastic dishpan with hot water and started cleaning the sculpting tools. "I guess you can dry. There are towels in that drawer." She pointed with her chin. "Can I interrogate you now?"

He laughed. "Fire away."

"Tell me about yourself," she said. "Let me guess. You played basketball in school, right?"

He chortled and shook his head. "Debate team in high school. I was tall, but totally uncoordinated. Couldn't get a ball near the hoop if I was standing on a ladder. Crewed in college. No fancy footwork required. Just had to be able to count."

"Okay, so you're a six-foot-something cop who doesn't like doughnuts and you don't play basketball. Any other surprises?"

"Not really. And I'm six-six. Nowadays, that's barely tall enough for pro ball."

"Why did you become a cop?"

"It felt like the right job for me. Maybe it's because my mom always used to say, 'Why isn't there a cop around when you need one?' Then, when she was killed in a hit-and-run, it seemed like making another cop available was the thing to do. I found out I liked it and I'm good at my job."

"I'm sorry about your mom. Has she been gone long?"

"Since I was six. I was lucky. My grandparents lived nearby, so I always had family around, even when Dad couldn't be there for us. Until I went away to college, I spent more time at their place than at mine." He turned away, fussed with arranging all the tools into a straight line. "When my grandmother died, she left the house to me." If Sarah heard his voice shift, she said nothing.

"Brothers or sisters?"

"One older sister. Married, three kids, lives in Akron, Ohio."

"I'm an only. I always wanted a sister." Sarah gave the room a final inspection and retrieved her coat and purse from a closet. "That's it. Thanks for helping."

"My pleasure. Can I give you a ride home?"

When she hesitated, he pressed, telling himself it was his responsibility as a cop to take care of a citizen. "I insist. It's dark and getting cold."

His pulse jumped when she accepted.

They walked across the parking lot to his truck. Twice he resisted the urge to put his hand at her back to guide her, finally shoving them into his pockets. What would have been perfectly acceptable in an ordinary social circumstance was forbidden him as a cop with a victim. He glanced her way, noticing that she kept more than a discreet distance between them.

What was he thinking? He was a cop doing his job.

And why was he responding, anyway? Those blue eyes? The way she'd looked at him when he walked into her store, as if she knew he'd make everything right. Damn. He never got involved with his cases outside the scope of his job. By the time his mind drifted back to reality, they'd reached his truck.

"This is it," Randy said. Sarah gave Randy a quizzical look.

"What?" Randy asked. "Don't like my F-150?"

"Oh, no, it's fine. I guess I was expecting...you know...a police car."

"No, those are for the patrol officers. Took some doing, but I can use my Ford instead of the standard unmarked cars.

Got tired of driving with my knees on my chin." He unlocked the door and helped her up, letting himself enjoy the feel of her touch as she gripped his hand. When he took his seat, he glanced over at her. What animation she'd displayed when she was working with her class had disappeared. She stared straight ahead.

He let the cop take over. "I'd like to look at your business files. I think I might get a better feel for this if I looked at the paperwork."

"I guess so, if you think it would help." Her voice was flat.

"It might. Ninety-five percent of what I look at usually turns out to be nothing. It's finding which pieces make up the five percent of useful information that solves cases."

"You can come by the shop tomorrow and look at whatever you think's important. Or should we go back now?"

He saw the exhaustion overtaking her. "Tomorrow is fine." Randy gave up on his rusty attempts at small talk for the rest of the drive. He slowed in front of her building, searching for a nearby parking place. Before he could drive around back, to the building's parking area, Sarah broke the silence.

"This is fine. You can drop me off here." She'd already unfastened her seat belt.

"I'll walk you up," he said after stopping beside a fire hydrant. "I'll park around back."

"No, really. This is fine." She opened the door and jumped down. "Thanks for everything. See you tomorrow."

But before she closed the door, she gave him a smile that had more than his hopes up. "She is a victim — you are a cop" became his mantra as he drove home.

Chapter Four

Sarah picked up her mail and climbed the interior stairs of her building, thoughts of Randy churning through her mind. He wasn't like the gruff, impersonal cops who had investigated David's accident. His eyes—they said he cared. And the way he'd worked with her class—he'd seemed nervous at first, but once he got started, he fit right in. She thought of his huge strong hands with their long, slender fingers helping Mr. Foster's knobby ones. And the way he joked with Mrs. Evans until she stopped complaining about everything. Sarah had almost forgotten Randy was a cop while he was working with her.

But he was a cop. Maybe he'd look into David's accident report. She'd almost had the courage to ask him on the ride home. Almost. Maybe tomorrow.

Sarah unlocked her door, tossed the mail on the coffee table and powered on her computer. Tired as she was, she looked forward to entering the day's sales for the first time in weeks. A pop-up on the monitor told her she hadn't logged off properly the last time she'd used the computer.

"And it'll probably happen again, you nasty little machine," she said. "Don't you forget who owns you. I'm Sarah. David doesn't do this anymore. You do what I say, understand?" She clicked the window shut and moved on to her data entry.

Her totals looked reassuring until she opened her mail and saw the bills. Before David died, they'd never carried a balance on their credit cards and now she'd been cut off on her Visa. It would take more than today's profits to pay the monthly minimum, to say nothing about the interest that would be added. And the electric company said she couldn't be late again.

There was only one payment she might be able to put off. She marched to the phone before she could change her mind.

"Diana? It's Sarah." She heard the breathless way Diana answered, a man's mumbling in the background. Well, what else was new? With her sister-in-law preoccupied, Sarah should be able to slide the robbery in before Diana's little brain wrapped around it. Sarah smiled. "Am I interrupting? I'm afraid there's some bad news."

* * * * *

The next morning Sarah walked the three blocks from the bank back to her shop. Clouds began to roll in, high and white. Yet, even as she tightened her coat, the buildings along the way seemed brighter, the birds in the trees sang more cheerfully and the traffic seemed to be flowing smoothly, unpunctuated by honking. She rounded the corner toward her shop, noticing the fresh pink and white blossoms emerging from the flowering plum trees that lined the street. Diana hadn't seemed to mind delaying her check, which meant she was going to make it through the month.

When she arrived, Randy was leaning against the door of the shop, hands stuffed in his jacket pockets, one ankle crossed over the other. That one lock of hair still hung over his brow. Aviator sunglasses over his hawk-like nose obscured his eyes. She took in the angular planes of his face. Handsome in a rugged kind of way, she decided. He didn't seem quite as tall as he had yesterday.

She smiled. "You're quite the early bird. I don't open for another twenty minutes."

"I figured it'd be better to get here before you had to deal with customers."

"Thanks." Sarah unlocked the door and led Randy to her office. After hanging up her coat, she surreptitiously adjusted her sweater and gave her hair a quick finger comb. She went through the filing cabinet, pulled the folders from the insurance company and extended them to Randy. He'd removed his sunglasses and yes, his eyes most definitely had hazel flecks. "These are the insurance files," she said. "For the merchant files, we marked the problems in red, but they're not separated. I'm afraid you'd have to go through each file."

"That's what I do," Randy said. He flexed his fingers. "Contrary to popular belief, most detective work is paperwork."

Sarah gave him an intense stare. "This is about more than Gertie and the robbery, isn't it?"

"Let's say I've expanded my horizons."

"I can't imagine you'll find much, but suit yourself. I told you, things like that just happen. If someone wanted to put me out of business, why waste time with little mix-ups? There's got to be a more effective way to do it."

Randy stepped to the file cabinets and withdrew a stack of folders. Sarah put a pot of coffee on to brew.

"It's decaf, but help yourself. There's a restroom behind you. I've got to open up now."

Randy was already sitting at the desk, tapping his pen on its surface, engrossed in the files.

Customers trickled in throughout the morning. As Sarah expected, the novelty of the robbery had worn off, but business was steady. More spring merchandise would arrive any day now and she began to plan for her new displays, trying to ignore the man working in her office. The *cop* working in her office, she reminded herself. Last night had been police business, nothing more.

Shortly before noon, Randy emerged, hands on his lower back, stretching and twisting. He'd taken off his jacket and his turtleneck hugged his chest when he moved. Unsettled by her attraction, she moved her gaze higher and found his hazel-flecked eyes just as disconcerting.

"I guess that office wasn't designed for someone your size," Sarah said. "Did you discover anything interesting?"

"It's too early to say. I'd like to borrow some of these files and do some more checking. I've made a list of the ones I'd like."

"Fine. You'll let me know what you find out?"

"Of course. You still have my card, right?"

"I think so." She checked her wallet. "Yes, right here."

"Give it to me a minute." She handed it to him, almost dropping it as their fingers touched. He wrote something on the back. "That's my personal cell phone number. You call me if anything happens." He closed the short distance between them and set the card on the counter. "Day or night. Understand?"

"Should I be worried?" *Ask him. Ask him to look at David's accident.* But the words wouldn't come. Not yet.

"I don't think so, but I prefer to be cautious. I'm a cop. I see too much of the bad side of things. Keep my card handy—consider it an ounce of prevention. I'll check back with you tomorrow."

Sarah watched Randy walk away, his long stride easy and relaxed. Something told her with him on the case, her life would get back to normal. For a minute she debated forgetting about the accident. David was dead and she needed to move on. But she thought of the biddies who came in from time to time, buying the cheapest thing they could find as if they were on a charity mission and all the while looking at her like she was a black widow spider. They had no idea how much it hurt. She fingered her wedding band. *David, why? Was it me?*

* * * * *

By evening, the clouds had blown away and the crisp evening air revitalized her on the walk from the bus stop to her apartment. When she reached the top of the interior stairs, she saw Maggie juggling her purse and two grocery bags while trying to fit her key into the lock.

"Hi, Maggie. Let me help you," Sarah said. She took one of the shopping bags.

"Thanks, Sarah. I don't know why I never put the bags down first. By the way, did you get your heater fixed?"

"Heater? There's nothing wrong with my heater—at least I don't think so. I haven't had it on in a while. Why?"

"I saw someone coming out of your place yesterday. He said you'd called him to fix the heater. I meant to tell you, but things have been hectic and it must have slipped my mind. I assumed Mrs. Pentecost let him in."

Someone in her apartment? Not fixing her heater, Sarah was sure of that. Wearing sweatshirts was cheaper than heating bills. Mrs. Pentecost would have said something. She heard nothing beyond a pounding in her ears. Maggie's voice finally broke through.

"Sarah? Are you all right? You just went three shades lighter."

"No, Maggie, I'm not all right. There was a robbery at the store and now you tell me a stranger was in my apartment yesterday. I'm having trouble believing it's a coincidence."

"A robbery! Why didn't you tell me? Oh, dear. Are you all right? How much was stolen? Come in and call Mrs. Pentecost about the heater man and then tell me what happened."

Maggie got the door open and gestured Sarah in. "Put the bag on the kitchen counter. Mrs. P is speed dial three. I'm going to change out of these exercise clothes."

Sarah punched in the number. When Mrs. Pentecost confirmed that she hadn't called a repairman, Sarah's mouth turned dry. She fished in her purse for Randy's card, called and told him what had happened.

Sarah tried to relax. She took comfort in the way Maggie swooshed into the kitchen, now dressed in a flowing orange and pink caftan and started taking groceries out of the bags, pouring water into the teakettle, filling the cat's food dish and setting a plate of cookies on the living room coffee table. Sarah shook her head at the woman's energy. She knew Maggie was well into her sixties, but she could easily pass for someone in her mid-forties.

Sarah sat on the couch and watched Maggie carry a wooden tray holding a blue calico teapot and two mismatched cups and saucers. Maggie set the tray next to the cookies, poured two cups of tea and sat down in the easy chair. The chair's blue satin stripes clashed delightfully with the caftan's orange and pink swirls.

"Now, tell me about the robbery," Maggie said. "And what did Mrs. P say?"

Sarah took a deep breath and relayed the information as succinctly as she could before sipping her tea. "Mmm. This is good. What kind is it?"

"Jasmine Pearls. There's a new tearoom on Baxter Street. FeliciTea. Don't tell anyone, but the cookies are from there, too." She winked at Sarah.

"My lips are sealed. Randy said to wait here if it's all right with you."

"Oh, so it's Randy, is it? Tell me more." Maggie's eyes twinkled even bluer.

Sarah knew she was blushing. "He's the detective who's been trying to catch the old lady who robbed my store."

"And—?"

"What, 'and'?"

"He wouldn't be about six-foot-thirteen, now, would he? Brown eyes, brown hair hanging in his eyes? Nice ass."

"How did you...?" Of course. Maggie didn't miss much when she was home. Sarah leaned forward. "Maggie, did you get a good look at the heater man?"

"Pretty good, I'd say."

"That's great. You can describe him to Randy."

The doorbell rang. Sarah jumped up. "I'll get it."

Sarah smoothed her hair, forcing back the grin that seemed to insist on breaking through when she saw Randy through the peephole. She motioned Randy into the living room and made the introductions.

"Nice to meet you, Detective," Maggie said. "May I offer you some tea and cookies?" She pointed to her chair. "Please, sit down." Maggie was already up and on her way to the kitchen.

Randy took a seat in the blue striped chair Maggie had vacated. Sarah watched Randy look around the apartment, an expression of incredulity on his face. Eclectic was an understatement. There was a blue lava lamp below a psychedelic Peter Max poster in the entryway, a beanbag chair that doubled as an ottoman for a Victorian easy chair, a chrome and glass coffee table and a Shaker dining table with a Van Gogh sunflower print above the sideboard.

Randy called out toward the kitchen, "Ms. Cooper, Sarah tells me—"

"Call me Maggie." She returned to the living room with another cup and saucer, poured the tea and handed it to Randy. "Have a cookie, too." A mass of black fur streaked in from the kitchen and pounced onto Randy's lap.

"Othello!" Maggie said. "Shame on you. You know better than to bother a visitor." She reached over to pick up the offending feline.

"I don't mind. I have two cats myself." He scratched Othello behind the ears. The cat kneaded his paws into Randy's thighs and settled down, purring with contentment.

Randy took a cookie and set it on his saucer, then resumed scratching the cat. "Sarah says you saw someone leaving her apartment yesterday. Can you tell me what time, what he looked like, anything at all?" He reached into his shirt pocket and pulled out his small black notebook. Sarah smiled when he clicked his pen three times before he wrote something down. Othello looked up once he stopped getting the attention he expected, then retreated to the kitchen.

Maggie's expression became businesslike. All the frivolity left her voice. "It was about three-thirty yesterday afternoon. I stopped to ask him what he was doing in your apartment and he said he was fixing the heater."

"And you're sure he was leaving?" Randy asked.

Maggie thought a minute, searching the ceiling as if it would provide an answer. Sarah watched Randy's gaze follow Maggie's. She swallowed a giggle as Randy fought to maintain his composure when he noticed a poster of the Chippendale dancers staring down at him. His eyes snapped back and met Maggie's when she spoke again.

"He was standing in the doorway, holding the door behind him, facing into the hall. He stepped out and told me he had been fixing the heater, that he'd had an emergency call that morning. I didn't want to be late for my reading, so I went on downstairs. Yes, he was leaving, because he followed me down."

"Did you see which way he went when he left the building?" Randy asked.

"No." Maggie reached for a cookie. "I can't say that I noticed. I was hurrying, you see and I assumed he'd be stopping at Mrs. Pentecost's to say he was done, or give her a bill, or return the key."

Randy continued. "Can you tell me about the man? Height, age, physical characteristics?"

Maggie's voice was more subdued now. Her pride in being a good observer had been questioned and Sarah could tell she was doing her best to be as accurate as possible with her description. Maggie stood and tilted her head upward. She raised her hand a few inches above her head. "There," she said. "That's the way I had to stand to look him in the eyes."

Randy looked at Maggie. "So, I'm guessing about five-nine, five-ten."

Maggie sat back down. "That seems about right. His eyes were light brown, fair skin. He had on a baseball cap. Plain, navy blue. He was wearing jeans, brown leather boots and black gloves." Her eyes opened wide. "Wait. They were too thin to be work gloves. I should have noticed."

"You're doing fine. Keep going."

Maggie put her hands to her mouth and looked at Sarah. "Oh, sweetie, I'm so sorry. I can't believe I was that stupid. No tool box. I am such a fool. If I hadn't been in a hurry, I'd have wondered and at least checked with Mrs. P."

"People see what they expect to see," Randy said. "It's natural. Go on."

Maggie shook her head. "A black turtleneck and an olive green windbreaker. No company logo, no name, but a lot of the people Mrs. Pentecost calls are independent workers and don't wear uniforms."

Maggie's face blurred. Sarah put her hands to her cheeks—her fingertips were ice cold.

"Are you all right?" Maggie's warm hands clutched Sarah's. "You're white. Did you forget to eat again?"

"Things were busy."

Maggie poured more tea into Sarah's cup and added a liberal amount of honey. "Drink this. I'm sure just this once the tea gods will forgive me for adding honey to Jasmine Pearls. You need the sugar. And have another cookie."

Sarah sipped the hot, sweet beverage and listened while Maggie continued. "If you want, I could go look at mug shots." She sounded excited. "If you still do things like that, I mean. I have time and a pretty good memory—"

"Thanks for offering," Randy said. "I'll let you know." Sarah could tell he'd figured out that if he didn't jump in, Maggie would keep on talking.

"How are you feeling, Sarah?" he asked. "Maggie's right. You're pale."

The look of concern in his eyes brought a catch to Sarah's chest. "I'm fine, really." She set her cup on its saucer, glad it didn't clatter.

"I'd like to check out your place if you're up to it," Randy said.

Sarah took a deep breath and stood. The room hardly spun at all.

Chapter Five

At Sarah's door, Randy pulled on a pair of latex gloves, took out his penlight and squatted down to examine the antiquated lock. It wouldn't have presented a challenge to any third-rate crook. He rose from his crouch and held out his hand. "Key?"

The spark when Sarah's fingers touched his palm unnerved him. Dealing with a female victim was not a new scenario, but it had never been like this. He cleared his throat and inserted the key in the lock, then unsnapped his holster. He heard a sharp gasp and sensed Sarah pulling back.

"Just a precaution," he said. "Standard procedure."

Wide-eyed, she nodded. "I understand. You don't think he's here now, do you?"

"No, I'm almost positive he isn't." She stepped closer to him and he took a deep breath. He placed his hand on the grip of his pistol. The feel of the cold metal reminded him he had a job to do. "I'm going to take a quick look inside, just to be sure. Wait out here. I'll be right back."

She gave him a weak smile and stepped across the hall. "Yes, Detective."

Randy stepped inside and gazed around the orderly space for signs of disturbance. Everything looked exactly as it had the first time he'd been here. If anything, a little neater. The same silk flowers and candlestick lamp on the table by the door. To his left, the rust colored sofa and two patterned upholstered armchairs. Maybe a few more magazines on the coffee table. He took in the rest of the space. A side table held an answering machine. His eyes roamed across the polished dining table with its four chairs into the open kitchen. A small home office occupied what would otherwise have been a breakfast nook. No indications anything was amiss.

Beyond the kitchen, he found a small service porch, more a laundry and storage space than anything else. He unlocked a door to a flight of stairs that led down to the backyard, noticing a matching staircase from Maggie's apartment. Randy rattled the knob, swearing softly under his breath. Might as well not be a lock at all.

A quick check of the closet and bathroom showed no signs of an intruder. Telling himself it was cop nerves that had his pulse racing and his mouth dry, he went back to the hall where Sarah waited. She raised her eyebrows at his approach.

"Nobody's here," he said. Her eyes were fixed on his holster and he resnapped it. "All right, Sarah. You were here all last night, right?"

"Yes. I had no reason to think there was anything wrong."

"Did the man Maggie described sound like anyone you know?"

"No. I mean, I'm sure I've met dozens of people who fit that description, but I don't *know* them personally."

"All right. Let's try to go over everything you did. When we go inside, I want you to take your time, look around and see if there's anything that seems out of place or doesn't feel right."

"Just thinking that someone was in here gives me the creeps." He saw her shudder and took her elbow to support her.

She smiled up at him. "You can relax. I'm fine."

Randy removed his hand, far from relaxed. Sarah entered the apartment, stopping just inside the door and recapped her movements of the evening before. "Nothing seemed unusual except the computer message."

"What message?"

"I got an error message when I logged on about not shutting down properly. I didn't think that much about it—I've done that enough times."

"Would you remember what files you worked on?"

"Sure. The shop files and my email. I made some tea and went to bed."

"Anything seem out of place anywhere else?"

Sarah stood in her entryway and stared through her apartment and Randy knew she was trying to look beyond her familiar surroundings. "Nothing seems different," Sarah said.

"All right. What about the kitchen. Anything wrong there?"

Sarah crossed to the room and opened a few cabinets. "No, it looks fine. I cleaned up, which means I probably removed any evidence if he'd been in here."

"Okay, then what about the bedroom?" Randy followed her to the short hallway that separated the living area from her sleeping quarters.

Sarah checked the closet and looked in her dresser drawers. "I put my stuff away last night and got dressed this morning. Nothing seemed weird. I have to admit, I'm not the neatest when it comes to putting away my laundry, but I don't think anyone's taken anything."

"So you'd say your clothes are all where they belong?" He hesitated, but he had to ask. "Your underwear?"

She jerked her head around and stared at him. "Why are you so interested in my underwear?"

"I'm not, but sometimes—"

"Sometimes what?"

Randy couldn't answer right away.

"Oh, God." She yanked the top drawer open again. "You think he might have been someone who got his jollies from women's underwear."

Finding Sarah

"It's not uncommon. But in this case, no, I think he came here to get what he could from your computer and left everything else pretty much alone."

The expression on Sarah's face said she didn't believe him, but he kept his gaze steady and moved on with his questions. "When you logged on, aside from the error message, were your files intact? The same as they should have been?"

"I entered the day's receipts and everything seemed normal enough. I have backups of everything on disks."

"If you don't mind, I can look to see if I can tell when these were last opened."

"Go ahead."

Randy sat down in front of the computer and powered it on. "You used the computer last night. I'm sure your prints have obscured any that might have been left on the keyboard or mouse even if he took his gloves off. Besides, other than the fact that we're pretty sure someone was in here, nothing was taken or damaged." He turned and focused his eyes on her. "I can call the lab and they'll come by and make a big mess out of everything. Or, we can assume that whoever was here was only interested in your computer files."

"What's your recommendation? You're the pro here, after all."

"I have to be honest. Since nothing was taken and nobody was hurt, I'm afraid it might take quite a while to get someone out here. This kind of thing is low priority."

"I don't think I can face another round of fingerprint powder, especially if it's not likely to give us anything. Do you think I'm being stupid?"

"No, I think you're being realistic." When Randy reached for the mouse, she began to pace the living room. He noticed her rush to the back of the apartment, but kept his attention on her computer files until she came from the bedroom carrying an armload of flimsy garments.

59

"I'll be right back," she said. "I'm going to wash these things. Probably twice. I can't afford to replace them and there's no way I'm wearing them until they're clean."

"You know, he probably never touched them."

"Probably isn't good enough. Just the thought…ugh."

Randy watched Sarah try to open the porch door without dropping any of her bundle. He started to offer help, but didn't think she would want him dealing with her underwear, either. He focused on the computer screen, reminding himself that this was supposed to be a professional relationship. For God's sake, he'd met her two days ago.

All he knew was he couldn't let her down. His gut told him he was dealing with something deeper than a series of coincidences, even if he didn't have much evidence beyond a probable breaking and entering.

Fifteen minutes later, Sarah wasn't back. It shouldn't take that long to start a load of wash.

Randy pushed his chair back, crossed through the kitchen and stopped in the porch doorway. Sarah leaned against the washing machine, head down. Randy's heart tugged. First the robbery, then the break-in. She was hanging on by a thread.

He hesitated, then walked up behind her and let his fingers brush her shoulders. Sarah stiffened at his touch. She kept her head down, her soft trembling resonating through the woolen bulk of her sweater. He turned her around and gathered her against his body, inhaling faint traces of peach as she wept.

The washing machine clunked and she pulled away. "I am so sorry. I don't know what got into me. I'm not usually such a crybaby."

Randy tilted her chin up with his fingers and looked into her eyes. Sarah looked down, avoiding his gaze. "It's all right, Sarah. It's a normal reaction." He told himself that his automatic response to holding a woman in his arms was a normal reaction, too. And hoped she'd been too upset to notice.

"You must think I'm such a wuss."

He pulled her face back up, forcing her to meet his eyes. "No, I think you're someone who's had a run of trouble. And I'm here to make things right."

"Did you find anything in the computer?" Sarah asked, sniffling and wiping her hands on her skirt, a resolute expression on her face.

Randy returned to the business at hand. "Not much. I didn't see anything modified yesterday except your shop files. All we have is the suspicion that someone was in your apartment."

Sarah pushed past him and went toward her bedroom She returned with a shoebox. "These are the shop records from last week." Pulling a disk out of the box, she inserted it in the drive. Sarah opened several files, then turned back to Randy. "Everything looks the same, so, I guess he didn't change anything. What should I do?"

"Do you bank online? Do a lot of online shopping?"

"No, the bank is close to the shop, so I never bothered with that and I don't use the Internet much."

"Okay. Get a locksmith in here. That lock on your front door is barely adequate and the one on your back porch is worse. Change them and make sure you get good deadbolts. And see if the owners will put a security system on the foyer door. There's no excuse for such easy access to the building."

Sarah nodded.

"And, I'd like to make sure he didn't bug your phone."

Sarah's mouth dropped open. "What?"

"Just a precaution, but if nothing was taken, maybe something was left. If the landlady can let the techs in, you don't have to be here."

Her head slumped into her hands. "All right. Whatever."

"Look, it's getting late and you haven't had anything to eat. Again. Not a good habit. Let's get some food and I'll tell you what I found out."

Damn. He wanted to surround her and crush her to him, protect her from all the evil in the world. Instead, he looked at her with what he hoped was a professional expression. "What do you feel like eating? Italian? Thai? Barbecue?"

"I don't know. I'll let you pick." She made no move to get up from the chair.

Randy stepped beside her and pulled her up. His hands touched hers and that tightness in his chest came back. Her eyes, still moist with tears, held that same trust he'd seen when he first met her. He was a heartbeat away from breaking every rule in the book when doorbell chimes, followed by Maggie's voice, shattered the moment. Thank God. What was he thinking?

"Sarah? It's Maggie."

Sarah worked her hands from Randy's grasp. "I'm coming, Maggie. Just a second." She wiped her eyes before opening the door.

"Hello, sweetie. I know you didn't have lunch today and I figured the two of you would be busy looking for clues, so I nuked some of my lasagna." She bustled past Sarah into the kitchen and set the casserole on the stove. "If you wait two minutes, I've got some salad, too. And some brownies for dessert. Nothing like chocolate to get the brain in gear, I always say." She was almost out the door when she turned back and looked at Randy. "I brought enough for both of you, of course."

"How can I resist? It smells wonderful," he said. "Please join us. It looks like more than enough for three."

"Nonsense. I don't have anything more in the way of clues to offer. Besides, Othello and I are going to watch a movie on the tube tonight. *Tomasina*. He absolutely adores it." And she was out the door.

Finding Sarah

"She is something else," Randy said to Sarah.

"That she is. But she's a wonderful something else. After David died, I don't know what I would have done without her. She took care of so much. And she is a great cook. Why don't you set the table while I get some rolls?" She indicated a cabinet.

Maggie was back with the salad and brownies before Randy had finished laying out the silverware. After depositing the food with Sarah, Maggie went to the living room and returned with the bowl of silk flowers from Sarah's entry. She plopped the bowl down in the center of the dining table. "You make sure she eats," she said, giving him a stern look, then whisked away. Randy stared after her, shaking his head.

"So, let's eat," Sarah said. She sat down and Randy was glad to see she'd served herself a portion almost as generous as the one she gave him. The two ate their lasagna, their silence paying tribute to Maggie's cooking. When they finished, Sarah suggested coffee and dessert in the living room.

"I've only got decaf," she said.

"Decaf's fine." She began clearing plates. He pushed back his chair. "Let me help you."

"No, I'm fine. I know where everything belongs. Relax."

Randy remained at the table, leaning on his elbows, watching her work in the kitchen. Her movements reminded him of the way she'd worked with the seniors last night. She moved with a feline grace, rinsing dishes, measuring coffee, wrapping leftovers. Once again, he forced himself back to reality. He was on a case. She was a victim. He collected his thoughts and moved to the living room. Sarah followed with the platter of brownies.

"Now," she said. "Tell me what you found out today." The meal had wiped away her look of fatigue and despair. Her expression held a look of expectant optimism.

Randy settled himself into a corner of the couch. "I spoke with Anjolie and she is not a happy camper. A Mr. Brandt told her Pandora's would double her profits if she'd pull her things from your store. But when she brought her pieces to the shop, they denied everything."

Sarah's eyes popped wide open. "Now I'm totally confused. If Pandora's isn't trying to lure away my artists, then who is?"

"The call to Anjolie came *during* the robbery." Randy flipped through his notebook. "From a pay phone at a rest stop on Interstate Five. However, nobody at Pandora's has heard of Brandt. Have you? Unhappy customer?"

Sarah's brow wrinkled. "No, sorry." She raked her fingers through her hair. "This is too confusing. Let me get the coffee. Maybe that and another brownie will make things clearer. How do you take it?"

"Black is fine."

When Sarah brought the coffee, he took a mug and he swore her fingers lingered a second or two longer than necessary. A faint blush rose to Sarah's cheeks. She sat down facing him from the opposite end of the couch.

"What about Gertie's clothes? Can't you use them for DNA or something?"

Randy smiled. "It's not quite like television. Pine Hills doesn't have its own lab, but we could send samples to the state lab if we thought we had something. But they're busy with murder cases, so a robbery like this one could take a year to process. Plus, nobody has any DNA from Gertie to match it to, so it wouldn't do us any good. We checked her clothes, but nothing was remarkable enough for us to track down."

"What about the fingerprints?" She kicked off her shoes and tucked one leg under her.

Randy watched as she adjusted her skirt, averting his eyes once he realized he had looked somewhere he had no business even thinking about. He shifted on the couch and cleared his throat, holding his coffee mug in front of his lap, praying she wouldn't detect the effect she was having on him. "They belonged to Chris Westmoreland. I ran him through NCIC—that's the National Crime Information Center—and the DMV. No arrests. He's worked for Consolidated Enterprises for the past five years in Development, he drives an Eclipse and has had one speeding ticket."

"I told you, Mr. Good Citizen. Anything else?"

"I'm looking for Mr. Brandt, but without more to go on, it's tough."

Sarah nodded, her bright eyes peering over her coffee cup. "I'm sure you'll find more soon."

Randy tried to ignore the way his heart seemed to skip a few beats every time he looked at her. He went on.

"The company Chris works for has very far-reaching fingers. I'm going to have to see if any of them dip into anything that would tie to your shop. But even if there's a connection, there's nothing to indicate there's anything untoward going on. Consolidated has holdings in hundreds of small companies and the fact that some of them might be connected to your store could mean nothing."

"So, where do you go from here?"

"I keep looking. It's going to be another day of computer work, paperwork and phone calls." He set his mug down on the table.

"Can I help?"

"No, this is plain, old-fashioned, boring police work. Just my style."

"You're not plain, old-fashioned, or boring," Sarah said. "I think what you do is fascinating." She jumped up and took the coffee mugs to the sink, busying herself rinsing them and putting away the leftover brownies, but not before Randy saw that blush cross her face once more. Was she responding to him, too? Or embarrassed that the conversation had turned personal? He'd better get out of here before he did something he'd regret. He stood and reached for his coat.

"I need to get going," he said. "It's getting late and I have lots to do tomorrow. You going to be all right?"

"I'm fine now. And Maggie's right across the hall."

"You'll change the lock tomorrow, right?"

"Yes, I promise."

Randy stood at the door, looking back through the apartment. Sarah stayed in the kitchen. He swallowed and tried to keep his voice steady. "You have my cell phone number."

She flashed a quick smile. "I'll even add it to my speed dial and keep it next to my bed."

He knew the grin he gave her was anything but professional. She rewashed a glass, holding it to the light, studying it, rinsing it again.

"Lock the door behind me," he said.

"Yes, Detective." She walked toward the front door, stopping a few feet from him. "Now, if you'll excuse me, I have to get back to my laundry."

* * * * *

Randy smiled as he heard doors open and close upstairs. Maggie would be giving Sarah the third degree any minute now. He couldn't explain why she affected him the way she did. Maybe he'd been alone too long. Six years since he and Debra had called it quits. Not that they'd had anything serious to begin with. Being a cop didn't leave a lot of time for developing relationships and he'd never found anyone who understood what the job meant to him. A couple of flings, but no one had hit him the way Sarah had. Like a brick wall falling on him. God, just thinking of her made him hard. Stop. Letting people get close just got in the way.

He paid a call to Mrs. Pentecost. She'd been out that afternoon and hadn't seen anything and confirmed that she hadn't called anyone to fix a heater. He radioed Dispatch from his truck to report Sarah's address, a description of Chris Westmoreland and his Eclipse. Something about the man raised the hairs on the back of his neck and it wouldn't hurt to keep an eye out. "I don't expect anything, but if you see him, make sure I get a call."

Randy replaced the handset and drove across town to his house without realizing how he got there. Damn. He needed to focus. He grabbed Sarah's files, retrieved his mail and unlocked his door. Inside, he dropped everything onto the narrow table behind the couch, then hung up his jacket and secured his weapon. Starsky and Hutch wound themselves around his ankles, yowling that their dinner was late. "Sorry, guys. I got detained." He scratched both felines behind the ears and went to the back porch to refill their food and water dishes. They bounded across the house ahead of him and waited impatiently for him to finish. "Enjoy," he said. He left them to their meal and went back inside.

He crossed to the liquor cabinet and poured a generous two fingers of Jameson's. Tonight called for the good stuff, the twelve-year-old he saved for special occasions. He stared at the bottle, turning it in his hands. Almost full. That didn't say much for special occasions. He swirled the amber fluid, watching it trickle down the sides of the glass, then let that first sip linger on his tongue before swallowing. The fiery heat worked its way down his throat. With a sigh, Randy ran his fingers through his hair and sat down on the couch. He fingered the remote and stared at the television with unseeing eyes. The cats joined him while he made two trips—or maybe it was four—through the channels and finished half his drink.

Sarah. Hair that smelled of peaches. A splash of freckles across her nose and cheeks. Eyes the blue of the stone in his grandmother's brooch. The one he'd loved to run his fingers across as a child, feeling safe and secure whenever he touched its smooth, cool surface. Sodalite, she'd called it.

Enough. Do your job.

Randy groaned and extricated himself from the stack of cats on his lap. He retrieved Sarah's files, went to the kitchen table and set his glass down on the flecked yellow formica surface. He could hear his grandmother telling him to slow down, take things one step at a time, think things through. What had worked for his struggles with algebra should work here as well. The bright fluorescent lights in the kitchen brought things into sharper focus. He pulled a yellow legal tablet from a drawer and began making lists. Lists of the companies Sarah bought from. Lists of the companies Consolidated owned. Lists of shipments gone awry, of damaged merchandise. Next, he got out the highlighters. Eventually, he had rainbows of lists. Somewhere, there had to be connections, common denominators, but whatever they were, they hung just out of reach.

Finding Sarah

Chapter Six
෨

Sarah floated up from the depths of sleep to see faint patterns of light playing around the room. Her fingers fumbled for the clock at her bedside, encountering instead a cut crystal bowl of wax fruit. Maggie had insisted Sarah spend the night.

Fully alert now, Sarah wriggled her way out of the old waterbed. Once she had become accustomed to the faint gurgling every time she moved, she'd spent a restful night. She hoped to get back to her own apartment before Maggie woke, but instead found her neighbor humming tunelessly in the kitchen.

"Good morning, Sarah! I hope you slept well."

"Like a baby. Thanks again for putting up with me. Sorry to dash off, but I have to call a locksmith to change my locks and still get the shop open on time."

"Call the locksmith from here, sweetie. You can eat breakfast while you're waiting. Or you can ask Mrs. Pentecost to take care of it. After all, she is the manager and ought to do something besides making us listen to Lydia practice piano for hours on end."

"You like to listen to Lydia and you know it, Maggie."

Sarah stepped over to the workspace where Maggie had a small desk and wall-mounted phone. Why was she not surprised to find the Yellow Pages open to "Locksmiths"? And a red circle around one ad, no less. She suppressed a smile and dialed the number.

"Okay," Sarah said to Maggie after hanging up the phone. "They'll be here within an hour."

"That's the company we recommend at the Women's Center. You've got plenty of time to eat. Come. Sit."

Sarah knew better than to argue. Maggie set a plate of pancakes, scrambled eggs and sliced honeydew in front of her.

"Start on that while I get the juice and coffee."

Sarah nodded, her mouth already full of eggs. How long had it been since she'd taken the time to eat a real breakfast? She reached for the syrup container. Genuine maple syrup, too, not the imitation stuff. After pouring a liberal quantity over the pancakes, she smiled at Maggie.

Maggie beamed back at her. "You eat every bite of that."

"Yes, ma'am." Sarah applied herself to the task at hand.

Maggie flopped onto a chair and sipped her coffee. "Did you notice your new neighbors?" she asked.

"No. Where?"

"The building next door, where the Fredericks lived. I saw a couple of guys carrying some chairs and things up. I thought I'd give them a day before welcoming them to the neighborhood. If it's even a 'them'. I haven't seen much evidence of anyone."

"That place has been empty almost a year. It'll be nice to have someone living there. Any idea who might be moving in? Kids? Young? Old?"

"Not yet, but I'll find a reason to pop over. Maybe you can give a shout when you see some activity. Your kitchen window looks right into their dining room."

"I'll do that." Her plate empty, Sarah carried it to the sink. "Maggie, this was delicious. Sorry to dash, but I have to get dressed before the locksmith comes. Thanks again."

"Think nothing of it. I enjoy the company. I need to get ready myself. Thursday is my day at the hospital." She paused. "But I could come and work with you—I'll worry about you being alone."

"Don't, Maggie. Randy said this woman doesn't hit the same shop twice. I'll be fine." She leaned over and kissed Maggie on the cheek. "I'll stop by after work."

With only slight trepidation, Sarah entered her apartment. Everything looked the same as always, but she missed that warm feeling of welcome. Trying to ignore her uneasiness, she hurried to shower and dress. She had to wait until her hands stopped trembling before she could apply her makeup. The doorbell put a stop to her fussing and she hurried to the living room.

"Triple A Locks," came the voice from the other side of the door.

"Be right there." Sarah peeked out at the distorted image of a stocky man in green coveralls, three entwined As embroidered over the pocket, before opening the door. The man handed her a business card.

Sarah read his name off the card and pointed out the lock. "Thanks, Mr. Foster. I need something a little more burglarproof here and on the back door. We're pretty sure someone picked it the other day."

"I've got the deadbolts you asked for and spare keys. Shouldn't take long to switch them over."

Sarah left the man to his work and went to her kitchen window to see if there were any clues to who the new neighbors might be, but the blinds on their windows were closed.

The locksmith finished his work in efficient silence and handed Sarah four keys and an invoice. Her stomach sank. She'd have to revisit her budget. No, she would take it to Mrs. Pentecost. The building management should have to pay at least some of this charge. "Let me get my checkbook." She returned and recorded the amount in the register, afraid to do the math beyond knowing she could cover the check.

The locksmith latched his toolbox. "Nice neighborhood here. We don't get many calls in this area."

"Glad to know I'm the exception," Sarah said under her breath. She handed the man his payment. "Thanks."

"No problem. Call us any time. Remember, you need a key on both sides. It's a good idea to keep one either in the lock or close by when you're home in case you have to get out in a hurry."

Sarah took one of the keys and placed it in an empty candy jar on the entryway table. The locksmith whistled something that sounded like "Oh Susannah" as he packed his tools.

"One more thing," Sarah said. "Can you verify the lock was picked?"

"Not officially. But I'm sure the cops could. You can bring the whole mechanism to them."

"Thanks. I think I'll do that." Sarah loaded the old parts into a plastic bag.

She watched the locksmith leave, listening to the whistling fade down the hall. Feeling safe and secure as the key moved like a knife through butter in the new lock, she went downstairs to drop off a key and alert Mrs. Pentecost about someone coming to check the phone lines. The manager answered the door wearing a floral robe, a cup of coffee in her hand. Sounds of the morning news came from a television set somewhere in the apartment.

"It's not my responsibility to pay for the new lock," Sarah said. "It was a building security issue."

"I'll have to see what the management company says. If you can't prove there was someone in the apartment, I don't know if they'll pay."

"I've got the old lock. I'll talk to the detective about getting a police report and see what he says. And I'll bring you a copy of the locksmith's bill." Sarah stepped back. "Say hi to Lydia. Tell her she's getting very good."

"I'll do that." She gave Sarah a half-smile and closed the door.

A black pickup drove by as she walked toward the bus stop and Randy wormed into her thoughts. Her cheeks flamed as she remembered how she'd felt when he held her. He probably treated everyone like that, trying to comfort and help deal with traumas. She vowed to let him do his job.

* * * * *

Sarah opened the door to the shop and locked it behind her, glad to have an excuse to put thoughts of Randy aside while she dealt with her daily routines. The extra weight of the lock in her purse reminded her she needed a police report. Maybe she could call the station and leave a message. She wasn't ready to talk to him yet.

The doorbell buzzed at the back door. "Coming," she called. She hurried through the shop and peered through the window.

A disembodied voice came from behind an array of roses, lilies, gerbera daisies and something purple she couldn't identify. "Delivery for Sarah Tucker."

"I'm Sarah," she said. She took the flowers, revealing a stocky deliveryman. "Thank you."

"I'll need a signature, ma'am."

"Sure. Sorry." Sarah set the vase down on the nearest table and signed the clipboard.

"You have a nice day," he said and then hastened back to his van.

Sarah closed the back door behind him. She poked through the greenery until she found the plastic pick with its tiny envelope.

Forget him, the card said. *Let me help. Dinner tomorrow. CW.*

She dropped the card on the counter. Why had she thought they might have been from Randy? She pulled the gold chain from beneath her blouse and ran David's ring back and forth along its length. She needed Randy to find her stuff. Nothing more. She didn't need Chris either. If things kept up, she'd be out from under in three months. She was the expert scrimper. What was a few more months of ramen noodles?

Giving the ring one final squeeze, she tucked it back inside her top. She picked up the vase and carried it to the front window. By the time she finished rearranging things to showcase the flowers, several people gathered to admire the display. She flashed the browsers a smile, then went to unlock the door and turn the sign to "Open".

The flowers created a conversation piece all day and Sarah made a mental note to change her front window display more often and to put something unusual in there. Maybe she'd be back on top in two months.

Shortly before closing time, when the shop was empty, Sarah took the cash out of the register and went in the office to lock it up. She heard the door chime and left the safe ajar in case she had to make change. Happiness at yet another sale made a smile effortless as she went to the front.

She could feel the smile drop off her face. "Diana? What brings you to Pine Hills?" Her sister-in-law stood just inside the door, the hem and necklines of her red dress threatening to meet in the middle. The diamond pendant she wore drew the eye to breasts Sarah didn't remember being quite so…round.

"I wanted to give you this in person, Sarah. After all, we used to be family as well as business partners." She held out a large, blue envelope. "I talked to a lawyer last night after you called."

Sarah felt her face glow until she was afraid it matched Diana's dress. "Let's cut the legal lingo. Give me the abridged version."

"Well, what it says is that if you're so much as a day late with any of my checks, we're going to get the shop."

"You can't do that." At least Sarah didn't think so.

"Oh, he says I can. There's a bunch of stuff about liens and whatever. But look. I have a much simpler solution." Diana strolled across the shop to an easy chair Sarah had for customers to sit in while they browsed some of the books she carried.

When had Diana called a lawyer? Why did she think it was just her luck that Diana was probably sleeping with one? That it had probably been him with Diana when she'd called? Sarah ripped open the envelope. The letterhead said, "Lincoln and Gross, Esq., Attorneys at Law." She tried to skim the contents while she listened to Diana's saccharine voice. She recognized lien and foreclosure, but she'd have to study this — no, she'd have to get someone else to translate it. She looked into Diana's deep brown eyes. The only trait she shared with David. "What?"

"It's no secret I don't want to work here. And we both need money. Let's face it. This place is half a step from Chapter Eleven. I didn't exactly come out on top after my divorce. So." She leaned forward.

"Cut to the chase. I need to finish closing." Sarah flipped the door sign and went behind the counter to settle the credit card machine.

"So. We sell. Make it a Hallmark franchise. You get to be the manager and we split the profits."

Sarah felt like she'd gone over the first drop of a roller coaster. She waited for her stomach to catch up. "Hallmark? A card shop?" As if Diana had a clue how franchising worked.

"Oh, come on. They sell other stuff too." Diana pointed to some bears. "Stuffed animals, just like those."

"Those are handmade and one-of-a-kind," Sarah said. "Hallmark shops don't sell those."

"You know what I mean. Come on, Sarah. It'll solve both our problems. I already know someone who's interested. He thinks this is a great location."

"Well, you tell that someone to get uninterested. There's no way this is going to be a card shop. It was better than a card shop when we started it." She whirled into her office and counted to ten, then twenty, then wrote Diana a check. She put the checkbook into the safe and kicked the door shut. The pain in her toes was worth it. She found her sister-in-law wandering through the shop, fingering merchandise. Sarah shoved the check into Diana's hand. "There. You're paid in full. I'll see you next month."

"Why is it so hard for you to admit defeat and move forward?" Diana folded the check into thirds and slipped it into her purse. "David's gone. Why are you still hanging on?"

"I'd think you, of all people, would know about honoring someone's memory." The words came out sharp, clipped and thankfully, without a trace of crying.

Diana tugged on her skirt and sashayed to the door. "I'll see you in a month."

Sarah let her take five strides before calling out. "Diana? If you're meeting someone, you might want to change your pantyhose. You've got a big run in back." Sarah closed the door. She leaned against it, afraid if she tried to walk across the shop, she'd collapse. It took several minutes before her head cleared.

All right. She'd been juggling money for months now. She'd owe the artists from today's sales, but she paid them monthly. There was time to recoup what she'd given to Diana before she had to pay them. First thing in the morning, she'd have to make sure today's cash hit the bank to help cover Diana's check.

It had been a long time since Sarah had been able to draw a line between her household and shop budgets, although that had been one of David's hard and fast rules. With a silent apology, she ran the numbers through her head, starting with this morning's check to the locksmith. The building manager wasn't going to make her pay. First, she called the police station and asked to speak with Detective Detweiler. Almost relieved when the voice on the phone told her he was unavailable, she left a message that she needed a copy of the police report on the break-in. She hoped whoever gave him his messages didn't report the way her voice was shaking. She couldn't cry in front of him. Not again.

She hung up and stared at the phone for a long time before making the next call. She'd give herself one more day.

"Chris? It's Sarah. Thanks for the lovely flowers. Can we move dinner to Saturday?"

Chapter Seven

Sarah sat in her office, fighting off a rising feeling of anxiety as she rushed through balancing the sales and getting her deposit ready for tomorrow. She kept listening for the door, half expecting Diana to come back with a lawyer, or Gertie to come back with a gun. She'd been working alone for months and it hadn't bothered her until today. She chided herself for her nerves, but she didn't relax until she locked up and was on the bus.

On the ride, she wondered if she could squeeze out enough money to rehire Jennifer for a few hours a week. An art student and an excellent photographer, Jennifer had been great at Christmastime. Maybe she'd work strictly on commission if she let her sell her own work in the shop. There was always a way.

By the time she got off the bus, Sarah felt in charge again. She dropped a spare key off with Maggie, declining the invitation for dinner and a chat. When she unlocked her door, the new deadbolt released with a satisfying thunk. Sarah started a U2 CD and headed for the kitchen. The blinking answering machine could wait until after dinner.

Poking through the refrigerator, she decided a salad and a frittata would be perfect. She even set the table with a Battenberg lace placemat and treated herself to opening a bottle of wine—one of her last Christmas gifts, which she'd been saving for a special occasion. She poured a glass into one of her good crystal wineglasses. Almost as an afterthought, she lit a candle. She whisked eggs, added some onions and zucchini and sipped her wine while she sautéed the mixture. While it cooked, she assembled her salad.

Once she'd finished eating and had done the dishes, she refilled her wineglass and went to deal with the phone messages. Mrs. Pentecost said the management company would be willing to pay half the lock installation charges. Better than nothing, but she'd push for a full reimbursement once she got a report from Randy.

Sarah punched the delete key and played the next message.

"It's Randy. No problem with a report for your landlady and your phone's not bugged. Also, I have a couple of things I'd like to run by you. Call my cell phone."

Sarah took a sip of her wine. Eight-thirty. Not too late to return the call. Randy had sounded businesslike on the phone, nothing personal. Maybe he hadn't noticed that she'd gone a bit beyond detective-victim last night.

Stop. Pick up the phone and call.

Sarah took the handset to the couch. Three deep breaths later, she pressed the speed dial for Randy's cell. After four rings, she thought maybe he wasn't available. Before she could decide if she was glad he wasn't there, he picked up.

"Sorry. I was feeding the cats. I've been working on your case all day. Can I come by the shop, or you come by the station tomorrow? There are some things you might be interested in."

"If you stop in either before opening or after closing, that would be fine. I can't predict what kind of free time I'll have during business hours."

"After work, then. And I'll have a copy of that report for you. That lock was cheap and you should have a better one."

"I got a better one. Top of the line." She swallowed another mouthful of wine. "The management company will pay half, but I thought with a police report, I could get them to cover the whole cost." She wanted desperately to ask what he'd found out, but forced herself to keep quiet. "I guess I'll see you sometime tomorrow."

"Sounds good."

Almost as an afterthought, she went on. "I think you ought to dig into Diana Scofield. She came by the store today and tried to get me to sell. She says she's having her own money issues." Sarah thought if Diana sold some of her jewelry, those issues might go away. Or moved to a smaller house.

"I'll do that. But remember, try not to discuss the case with anyone. Chris, Diana, or anyone who you do business with."

"Why? I'm having dinner with Chris on Saturday. Are you afraid I can't keep my mouth shut?"

A pause. "No, it's more like you can't keep your face shut. You have a pretty transparent face and I'd prefer nobody knew I was digging."

All of a sudden, fatigue engulfed her. "I'll be careful. It's only dinner. I want to get my data entry done and go to bed."

"I'll see you tomorrow."

It wasn't until after she'd hung up that his words registered. She had a transparent face. God, that line last night about keeping the phone by her bed. She was definitely going to have to keep things impersonal tomorrow. He was doing his job. No more, no less.

And she was going to do hers. She picked up the phone and called Jennifer.

* * * * *

In her small office, Sarah rummaged through the packets of her "just add boiling water" collection while she waited for a kettle of water to boil. Corn chowder would be today's lunch, albeit a late one. The chimes over the door announced a customer and Sarah pushed away from her desk.

Chris strolled into the shop, beaming. "Hi, Sarah. The flowers look wonderful in the window." He roamed the shop, picking up one item after another before setting it down exactly where he'd found it. Sarah wondered why he never carried one to the counter and bought it. That was the kind of help she'd accept from him. Not his charity.

Chris spoke, still roaming. "It turns out I probably saw the old lady who robbed you Monday. Some overgrown cop came by Tuesday, questioning me. Fingerprinted me. At seven-thirty in the morning, for God's sake. Can you believe it?" He glanced back at Sarah for a moment.

"He was just doing his job." Maybe she wouldn't have to worry about her transparent face, if Randy had already questioned Chris.

"Well, I hope he catches her." Chris turned. "Where's Anjolie's silver? Did the thief take it all?"

Sarah gave him the abridged version of Anjolie's visit. The shriek of the kettle from the back room stopped her explanation. She lifted a finger and motioned behind her. "Sorry. Be right back," she said and turned toward the office, away from Chris.

"I've got to run, Sarah," she heard him say. "I'll pick you up tomorrow. Seven. Do you still have that black and white sweater? It'll be perfect."

"Fine," she called. She wasn't in the mood for an argument. "See you tomorrow." She ate her soup, trying to forget about tomorrow night, about Diana, about losing her shop. When Randy invaded her thoughts, she reminded herself it was only natural to be thinking about him. He held the key to solving the robbery and if what he said was true, maybe more.

* * * * *

Randy adjusted the visor against the afternoon glare and pulled on his sunglasses. Diana Scofield was his next and, thankfully, his last interview today. He'd gotten the same story from all the artists he'd talked to. Chris had never been a middleman. None of them admitted knowing him.

He found the address Sarah had given him in a neighborhood of well manicured lawns tucked behind privacy hedges or stone walls. He left his truck on the street and ambled up the long driveway to Diana's house. The wraparound porch with its carved stone columns made Chris' dwarf in comparison. Scofield made his fortune in a dot-com before the bust and must have known how to invest it, because he wasn't hurting for bucks. Owned an art gallery, two restaurants and a night club. He could handle the mortgage payments on this house without sneezing and that was his only leftover expense from his marriage to Diana.

Randy ran his handkerchief across his face, stuffed it back in his pocket and rang the bell. Ascending and descending tones chimed behind the double doors. He glanced up at the security camera and suppressed the urge to make a face. The door opened a few inches and a dark brown eye peered through the opening.

"Diana Scofield?"

"Yes. What can I do for you?"

"Detective Detweiler, Pine Hills police," he said. He displayed his badge and ID and the door shut to release the security chain and then opened, revealing a tall, leggy blonde exuding too much expensive perfume. She wore black leggings that left nothing to the imagination and a tightly fitted white t-shirt that didn't reach her navel.

"Police? Pine Hills?"

"I have a few questions, ma'am. Just routine. I shouldn't take up much of your time."

She stepped back, not disguising the once-over she was giving him. "Come in, Detective. We can sit down and be comfortable." She flipped her hair back from her face and pivoted, her three-inch heels clicking on the tile floor.

Randy shook his head as she walked ahead of him, knowing damn well that wiggle in her ass was for him. What the hell? He enjoyed the brief trip to a formal living room, where she sat on an uncomfortable-looking yellow sofa.

He gave her an easy smile and sat across from her in a matching upholstered chair that he hoped would take his weight.

"Can I get you something? Coffee? Tea? A drink? Oh, but you're on duty. Would it be all right if I fixed myself something?"

"I'm fine, but be my guest."

She leaned forward to rise from the couch, revealing her generous cleavage and crossed to a bar at the far side of the room. Randy enjoyed the view once more, both coming and going, before she returned with two glasses. She held a rocks glass and set a tall glass of a clear liquid on the coffee table between them. "Ice water," she said. "In case you get thirsty with all the questions." She settled herself onto the edge of the sofa and ran the tip of her tongue across red-painted lips. "Now, is this where you ask me where I was at the time of the robbery?"

Praying for strength, Randy thanked her and opened his notebook. "Why not? Where were you on Monday morning—let's say between nine and noon?"

She locked her gaze on his. "Monday? I had a session with my personal trainer from nine-thirty until eleven. I'm sure he'll remember. We had an excellent workout." She winked. "And I had lunch at the tennis club with friends. I'll be happy to provide names. Besides, it was a little old lady who robbed Sarah. Surely I don't fit that description, Detective."

Randy reached for the water, suddenly grateful she'd provided it. Once he was sure he could keep his face straight and his voice even, he answered. "No, I don't think you do, Mrs. Scofield."

"Oh, call me Diana. Everyone does."

"Yes, ma'am. I need to cover all the bases here. I imagine the robbery came as a shock. But nobody was hurt and the thief didn't get much."

"Yes, thank goodness for that. My loss—well it'll hardly be noticeable. I only own twenty percent, you know."

"Yes, your loss was negligible. I'm thinking maybe someone put that little old lady up to the robbery."

She crossed her hands over her ample chest. "You can't think I had anything to do with it." Diana picked up her drink and swirled it around. "You should look at Sarah. She could have set up the robbery herself. Like you said, she didn't lose much and it made for some good publicity, I'll bet."

Randy gave her a noncommittal nod. "Do you get along with Ms. Tucker?" He waited, pen poised, watching her eyes narrow for an instant before she brought them under control.

"She's my sister-in-law. Or was. I'm not really sure how all that works now, but it doesn't matter. I have my share and I tried to get Sarah to give me half—if she had, we'd be splitting the losses fifty-fifty now. But she's pigheaded about doing everything all by herself." She downed half of her drink, extending her cleavage as she placed the glass next to his.

"Do you know anything about business problems other than the robbery?"

"Like what?"

"Orders not showing up, broken merchandise, things like that."

Diana gave him a blank stare and fanned her fingers through the air. "Oh, I leave those details to Sarah. It's too much trouble to drive all the way to Pine Hills to check up on things. She sends me reports with my checks, but she doesn't cheat me."

"You seem very trusting."

"Hey, I see the auditor's reports. Before the divorce, my husband insisted on them and things don't seem much different. It's a struggling business and we'd both be better off if she'd wake up and get out."

"You think she should sell?"

More cleavage when she picked up her glass again. "Yeah. My checks are chicken feed. If she'd sell the stupid place, I'd get my lump sum and have a little nest egg. But she's going to have to go bankrupt before she'll quit."

Randy looked at his notes. "You know a man named Brandt?"

"Maybe. I know lots of people. What's his first name?"

"I don't have one."

Diana studied her nails, turning her palms away and spreading her fingers. "Could be Billy. Haven't seen him in months, though."

Randy enjoyed the quick hit of adrenaline. "Can you give me anything more?"

She shrugged. "Not much. Tall, blond, killer blue eyes. I met him skiing. He was an instructor at Timberline."

And probably did a lot of après ski tutoring, too. "You have an address or phone number?"

"No. He moved around a lot. But he came into town from time to time during the off-season. We had…drinks."

"Thanks." This might eliminate the twenty-seven Brandts he'd found in the Marion County databases and save a lot of legwork. "What about Consolidated? Do you know anyone who works there?"

She wrinkled her nose. "Not that I'm aware of. I don't usually discuss work with people. And most of them are from around here, not out in the sticks like Pine Hills. Unless you mean Frank, of course."

"Frank? You mean your ex-husband?"

"The one and only. He sits on the board of Consolidated." She snorted. "He sits. That's what they call it and that's about all he does for them, it seems."

Randy jotted a note. Somehow his search into Frank Scofield hadn't discovered that one. "Would he have any reason to want to put your sister-in-law out of business? Maybe see her as competition?"

"Not that little shop. Trust me, Sarah's idea of art is nothing like what Frank exhibits. Besides, if he wanted it, he'd find a way to walk in and take it over. He never was one for subterfuge. Does what he wants when he wants with whoever he wants."

Randy ignored the bitterness he heard in her tone. He figured Diana had probably given her husband his share of headaches.

"Where might I find him?" It looked like Diana wasn't going to be his last stop, after all.

She gave him a wicked grin. "Oh, are you going to talk to him, too? That'll be rich. It's Friday—he's probably at the gallery getting ready for their new show. Some avant-garde photography exhibit, I think."

He read off the names of companies from Sarah's problem files. "Any of these ring a bell?"

"Just one—Kavelli. They make excellent crystal. I've got a few pieces. Sarah sells it. I get a discount."

Randy felt the start of a headache at the base of his skull. He drained the water and handed Diana the empty glass. "Thanks for your help. I'll be in touch if I have any more questions."

"I'm glad to do whatever you need. Are you sure I can't do anything else for you?" She actually batted her eyelashes.

Chapter Eight

As he drove, Randy chewed the facts. Sarah had been robbed. Not by Chris. Not by Diana. Not by Frank Scofield, although after spending twenty minutes with the man, Randy sure as hell wished he could have dragged his royal pompousness down to the station for questioning. No, Sarah had been robbed by Gracious Gertie, either of her own accord or at someone's coercion.

Then, someone broke into Sarah's apartment but didn't take anything. He'd better find a lead to Gertie, or the chief would have his butt in a sling for wasting time on a non-case. Was Diana's Brandt the one he needed? What could a ski bum have to do with a Pine Hills gift shop? One step at a time, he reminded himself. Collect the data, then see how it fits.

Randy stepped on the accelerator, but the late afternoon traffic wasn't going to let him cover the distance back to Pine Hills fast enough to suit him. He tried to convince himself he needed Sarah to identify the silver he'd found at Pandora's but gave up. She could do that tomorrow. He just wanted to see her.

Something about Sarah was making this case personal and he dug for professional detachment. Shit. His mind had wandered again and he slammed on the brakes at the glow of red taillights ahead of him, narrowly avoiding rear-ending a Toyota. Five-thirty already. Had Sarah left? He hadn't confirmed their appointment.

He reached for his cell phone and punched in Sarah's work number. Three rings. Four.

"Pick up, Sarah. You've got to be there," he said, as if speaking the words aloud would make it happen. When the machine answered, Randy waited out the recorded message, his hand squeezing the phone until the beep gave him his cue.

"Sarah, it's Randy. I guess I missed you."

A click, then Sarah's voice. "I'm here."

His grip on the phone eased. "I'm glad I caught you."

"I'm doing busywork."

"I'm still about half an hour away. Do you want to wait there, or shall I come by your apartment later?"

There was silence on the other end of the phone. He'd probably scared her again. Professional distance, keep it impersonal. "If you want to wait until tomorrow, I understand," he added.

"No, tonight's fine. But I'd like to take care of my data entry before I get too tired. Maybe we could meet a bit later? After dinner? Unless something came up on your end and you need to postpone."

For someone with a transparent face, Sarah had an awfully opaque voice. Damn women anyway. "Tell you what. I'll come by your place around seven-thirty. If you prefer, we can go back to the station and talk there."

Sarah agreed and Randy held the phone in his hand for a while before disconnecting. Unless something had come up, she'd said. If she only knew what came up every time he thought of her. He exhaled and watched the road stretch out in front of him.

Randy picked up some takeout chicken, eating most of it in the truck. Once he got home, he showered, shaved and set food out for Starsky and Hutch. They gave him disapproving looks when he picked up his keys to go out again.

"Sorry, guys. Duty calls. You know what it's like living with a cop, don't you?" He gave them each one more quick scratch behind the ears and started for the door. In true feline fashion, they turned their attention back to their dinner.

Randy pulled into a slot in the parking lot behind the municipal building and took the stairs at a run. The light was on in Preston Laughlin's office and his door was open. Randy glanced in as he passed and the chief looked up from behind his desk.

"Detweiler. Glad I caught you. Come in for a minute."

"Sure, Chief. What's up?" Randy glanced at his watch, then looked at his superior. A slight man, but deceptively powerful, as Randy had discovered to his embarrassment during a hand-to-hand workout at the gym several years before. He'd sported bruises for a week. Laughlin always dressed as if a television crew might need his statement—pinstriped business suit, tie neatly knotted, its matching silk square peeking out from his breast pocket. Underneath the façade, however, was an experienced street cop.

"Sit." Laughlin took off his glasses and set them on his desk beside a picture of his wife and kids. "You're on the Gracious Gertie case, right?"

"Yes. As a matter of fact I've got an appointment with the victim in less than an hour. I stopped by to update my reports and pull a couple files."

"Looks like you'll be off the case soon. Woodford P.D.'s reported someone matching her description and MO in their area. Should give you time to get caught up."

Randy sat for a moment, sorting his thoughts before answering. He had court dates, a few interviews on other cases and the usual backlog of paperwork. Nothing urgent. "Look, Chief, I'd like to stick with this little longer. I might have a lead on the man who called Anjolie Du Bois. I'll be happy to cooperate with Woodford, of course."

"Something you haven't told me?" Laughlin's steel gray eyes bored right into Randy's, as if he could cut out the middleman and get the answer directly. Randy thought sometimes he could.

"Not exactly."

"Try me."

Although Laughlin had to answer to the bean counters at city hall, Randy knew him to be a fair man and if he thought some extra hours were justified, he'd permit it. Randy made sure he kept his gaze steady. "While I was investigating the robbery, I found what might be the possibility of business sabotage and there were Consolidated connections. Consolidated is big business around here and if they're doing something shady, we should know about it."

"Might be? Possibility?" Laughlin's eyebrows stretched for his hairline. "What kind of sabotage?"

"Ms. Tucker's shop. She's been having some financial trouble and I think there's more than run-of-the-mill snafus behind it."

"Has she filed any complaints? With Kovak on vacation, you're pulling double duty. You got time for this? Or are you letting things get personal?"

"No, sir. It's a gut feeling. I'll check on my own time if you don't think it's justified."

"How many open cases?"

Randy did the mental math. "Six, but most of them are in the 'wait for someone else' phase."

Laughlin picked up his pen and twirled it in his fingers. "I remember David Tucker. A shame about the accident. He was in Rotary with me. Tell you what. You take half a day to coordinate with Woodford." He pointed the pen at Randy, using it to punctuate his remarks. "You can continue your work on this Consolidated-Tucker investigation for a couple of days, but only after your other work is done. That includes the paperwork, too. Things have been quiet, but if anything new comes up, you drop this in a heartbeat, okay?"

"No problem. Half a heartbeat." Randy stood and started to leave Laughlin's office.

"Detweiler?"

"Sir?"

"You're a loner and that makes you a damn good cop. I've always trusted your gut. But I'm wondering if a different part of your anatomy's leading you around on this one."

* * * * *

Randy recited his cop-victim mantra all the way to Sarah's apartment. Nonetheless, he had to wipe his hands on his jeans before he knocked on her door. "It's Randy." The sound of the deadbolt being released brought a smile to his lips.

Sarah opened the door and motioned him inside. She wore an oversized blue sweater over faded jeans that hung on her slender body. Her feet were bare, revealing pale pink toenails and a silver toe ring. Sounds of Mozart drifted from the stereo system.

"So, you said you have some information," she said.

"I might have found some of your things."

"That's great!" Her smile brightened the room. "Which ones? Where? Did you catch Gertie, too? Tell me." Her eyes sparkled.

He dropped his files on the dining room table and took a seat. "Whoa. Slow down. I guess what we have is one of those 'good news, bad news' situations."

"What do you mean?" She sat down across from him. "I thought you said you found some of my things."

"I said *might* have found some. I went to Pandora's and saw a silver frame that looked like the picture you showed me and some animal carvings, too." He pulled the Polaroids out of one of his folders, dropping them on the table in front of her.

Sarah picked them up and studied each photograph. "It's hard to say. I don't have exclusivity with Dylan—he does the animal carvings and Anjolie pulled her silver from my place right after the robbery." She continued to go through the pictures.

"You've got several pictures of frames here," Sarah said. "Gertie only stole one from me. I thought you said Pandora's didn't want Anjolie's work."

"I talked with the manager. They accepted it, but gave her the same deal you did. I guess she was too embarrassed to bring her things back to you when she found out they hadn't made that great offer."

"Her stuff was stolen from my shop. I can understand why she wouldn't come back."

Sarah tapped the stack of photos on the table while she talked. "Each of Anjolie's pieces is slightly different. Did you compare the one you took from my files to these?"

"I tried, but I can't tell if it's the same frame, or another one just like it. I thought you might know what to look for." He pulled the picture of the stolen frame from Sarah's files.

She scrutinized the pictures, comparing the stolen frame to several in the stack. "I can't be positive. I had strictly 'one-of-a-kinds'. There are a few here that have a roses and leaves pattern. It's obvious that Anjolie brought a lot more work to Pandora's than we displayed."

That "we" brought Randy down in a hurry. David was still in the room with them. He fumbled with the files. "Can you identify the stolen frame?"

"Sorry. Not from a picture."

"I don't think it's too important at this point. I don't think Anjolie was involved in the robbery." He didn't mention that he thought Anjolie had been duped in order to hand Sarah yet another setback in her shop operations.

Sarah leaned across the table and extended the photos to Randy. David or no David, the scent of peaches in her hair and the featherlight touch of her fingers sent an electric shock all the way down to his toes. He squirmed in his chair, trying to ignore the ache in his loins. "Now for a summary of where things stand."

"Please." Her eyes looked right through him.

He cleared his throat before continuing. "Gertie has shown up in Woodford, so I'll be turning that part of the investigation over to them. I did find that Consolidated owns more than half of Pandora's and has had dealings with most of the companies that you've had problems with."

"So you think Consolidated is trying to put me out of business? That doesn't make any sense at all. I'm a tiny operation. And if they wanted my place, why didn't someone simply come right out and make me an offer? No, I don't buy that."

"Not Consolidated. But someone who's connected might be behind it." He rearranged the photos. "I talked to Diana today. Her husband's on Consolidated's Board of Directors."

"You think moneybags wants my shop?"

"No, but I think maybe Diana might have met Consolidated people—maybe at functions with her husband. Maybe there's some connection. I don't know. And she gave me a possible lead on Brandt." He massaged his temples. When he looked at Sarah, she was grinning.

"Headache? Diana can do that to you. Want some aspirin?"

"No, it's nothing."

She stared at him and her mouth gaped. "She hit on you, didn't she?"

Had Sarah read him that easily? "I think she was just doing what came naturally."

"Most of what she has didn't come naturally," Sarah mumbled. "I don't blame you for reacting."

"Believe it or not, I was doing my job and wasn't…reacting, the way you put it." Diana might be built like an adolescent's wet dream, but it was Sarah who had his blood surging south.

"Diana knows how to get what she wants. And now she wants the shop." Sarah pushed back from the table and wandered into the kitchen. She leaned against the counter, then walked back to the living room, picking up and setting down the pictures on her shelf.

Randy got up and stood behind her, jamming his hands into his pockets. He ached to hold her again, to offer comfort, to inhale her scent. But he couldn't help but notice that she lingered over a photo of herself with another man. Sarah's hair had been longer, pulled back in a casual ponytail, her face fuller. The man's hair, thick and curly, hung about his face in windblown disarray. Against a backdrop of pine trees, the two held hands and even from where Randy stood, there was no mistaking the love in their eyes. They stared at each other like nothing else in the universe existed.

David. Randy kept his voice steady. "What's wrong?"

She swiveled away and sat on the couch, head down, twisting tendrils of her hair. Randy lowered himself into one of the armchairs.

Sarah spoke softly, obviously trying to keep her voice from breaking. "She's trying to force me to buy out her twenty percent. I can't come up with that kind of money without selling the shop. Unless..."

"Unless what?"

"Unless—" The phone's ring cut through the soft background music. Sarah let it ring three times before picking up the handset. "Hello?"

Randy saw her expression change from pain to resignation. "Look, I can't talk now. See you tomorrow, okay." She clicked off the phone and set it down. "Sorry."

The room felt very crowded. "Chris?"

She nodded.

He got up to leave. "I still want you to be careful."

"I will." She stood, headed toward the door. "Can I ask you something?"

"Of course."

"Is this...normal? All the personal visits?" She turned away. "I'm sorry. I didn't mean that. You're doing your job. I'm tired."

"No, you asked a legitimate question." He took a step backward while he searched for the words. "I like to think that I devote this much time and energy to every case. But I don't think that would be the truth."

She closed the distance between them, stood on her tiptoes and reached up to put her hands on his cheeks. "Bend down a little," she whispered.

"Sarah, I shouldn't...I can't." His voice cracked. He needed to get out of here fast.

"I know. But I can."

Against every professional instinct, every bit of common sense, he bent down. Her lips touched his, their soft warmth sending that shock coursing through his body again, a hundredfold more electrifying than before. Then, before either had a chance to respond further, she pulled back. "Thanks," she said. "For everything."

What she had given him scarcely crossed the boundary of chaste, yet it was as erotic as any kiss he could remember. He wanted to pick her up and smother her with kisses—deep and soul-baring. Instead, he grabbed the files and backed out the door.

Chapter Nine

Sarah locked the door behind Randy, sighed and leaned against it, waiting for the pounding in her head to stop. What had she done? How long ago had she vowed to keep this impersonal? A day? Two? Good grief, she'd hung up after talking to Chris and turned around and kissed Randy.

The memories lingered, the scent of his aftershave, the softness of his freshly shaven cheeks, the warmth of his lips. That all-over tingling she hadn't felt in so long. Her panties were damp—a dull ache in her belly lingered. She knew it couldn't go further. But how hard it had been to pull away.

It wasn't until she was in the bathroom that she realized Randy hadn't been the sole cause of those feelings. She had been so caught up in the week's activities she hadn't bothered to look at a calendar. Of course, she'd get her period now. No wonder she'd been such a wreck.

When she pulled off her sweater, the chain with David's wedding band caught in the bulky knit. Still warm from its contact with her flesh, the touch of the smooth gold brought another set of memories flooding back. How could she betray David? She grasped the ring in her fist, squeezing until the pain of metal against flesh brought tears to her eyes.

Hugging herself, she stumbled into the bedroom and eased herself onto the edge of the bed. She stared at the phone on the nightstand for a long moment. Three times she picked up the receiver only to set it down again. Finally, she pressed the speed dial button.

"Hello," came the familiar voice from the other end.

Sarah tried to speak, but her voice couldn't squeeze through her constricted throat.

"Hello? Who is this?"

"It's Sarah," she managed to whisper. "I think I need some company."

"Oh, you sweet thing. Of course. Can you make it over here? I'll put on some tea and you can stay as long as you need to."

Sarah sniffed back the tears. "Yes. I'll be right over." She pulled on her old flannel nightgown and her heavy plaid winter robe, shoved her feet into heavy socks and slippers and shuffled across the hall. Maggie was at the door, waiting for her. Othello looked up from his basket, gave a quiet mew in greeting and tucked himself back into a ball of fur.

"You poor dear." Maggie clucked. "Come in. The tea will be ready in a jiff. Go sit on the couch."

"Oh, Maggie, I'm sorry to bother you. I couldn't be alone. I'm so confused. And miserable."

Maggie was at her side with a box of tissues. "Don't you worry about a thing."

Sarah looked up. Maggie's hair was wrapped in a towel and she, too wore a warm robe.

"Just finished my hair." She pulled off the towel. "What do you think?"

Sarah sat there, too stunned to speak. Maggie's hair was Lucille Ball red. "I...I think...it's—"

"A bit over the top, eh?"

"Maybe a little." The teakettle whistled.

"I'll give it a week, then I'll decide," Maggie said. "Everyone needs change, you know." She wrapped the towel back into a turban and went to the kitchen to get the tea.

She came back with two steaming mugs and handed one to Sarah. "You sip that slowly, dear. Chamomile with valerian. It'll help you relax."

Sarah took a tentative sip of the hot liquid. This was more than herb tea. She gave Maggie a questioning look.

"Okay, so I added a little brandy. You look like you need it." Maggie scooted closer and patted Sarah's knee. "Now, tell me everything."

Sarah closed her eyes for a moment and everything poured out. "It's Randy. And the robbery and the break-in and Diana and Chris and I kissed Randy and…I got my period and I feel awful and David—" The tears welled up in her eyes. She gulped. "How can I do that to David?"

Maggie pried the mug from Sarah's fingers and set it on the coffee table. She put her arms around her. "First, you cry. Let it out."

Sarah had cried so many tears this week, she didn't think there could be any left. Yet, under the protection of Maggie's touch, the softness of her robe, her lavender scent, they came. In torrents. Wet, messy, blubbering sobs. When they finally dried up, Sarah took in a long, shaky breath and gave Maggie a weak smile. "Guess I needed that."

"Cleanses the body. Straightens out your chemistry. Nothing to be ashamed of. Now, you said something about kissing Randy."

Leave it to Maggie to get to the heart of things. "It was a stupid thing to do. Now if it had been Chris, I'd understand. I've known him forever and we have a history."

"What does Chris have to do with any of this?"

"He's always offering to help. And I might have to take him up on it." Sarah decided to leave out the gory details of Diana's bomb. "But when he called tonight and Randy was there…I don't know. Chris leaves me feeling…well, nothing. He's a friend, but I think he wants more and I can't decide if I could ever go there with him."

"And Randy?" Maggie winged her eyebrows.

Sarah felt the heat rise in her cheeks. "Definitely not a nothing feeling. It's probably because if I accept help from Chris, I'm admitting defeat. Randy's just doing his job, so it's not the same kind of help. But why did I kiss him? Maggie, how can I think about another man? And why am I thinking about a man at all, especially now? One I hardly know."

"You're afraid you're betraying David?"

Sarah nodded.

"That's a normal feeling." Maggie patted Sarah's knee. "But, listen to me. David's gone. It's been well over a year. There shouldn't be any betrayal here. Let me tell you, there's a lot to be said for the cultures that enforce a strict mourning period. There's a nice line to cross, a way to say 'it's over'. By the time the dreariness is finished, the wearing black, not seeing people, they're ready for some light in their lives. I think Randy might be your light."

"You do?" Sarah asked. She worried a tissue in her hands.

"Yes. But you have to think so, too. You have to listen to your heart." She ran a finger down Sarah's cheek. "Tell me. How did that kiss make you feel?"

A warmth radiated through her. Sarah didn't think she could attribute all of it to the brandy. "It was one little kiss—like a friendly kiss on the cheek, but on his mouth. I kissed *him*, Maggie. He tried to do the right thing and say, 'no', but I insisted." She set the shredded tissue on the coffee table and picked up her mug, staring into its steamy depth.

"And did he like it?" She gave Sarah a mischievous grin.

"Maggie! It's not like we pressed up against each other, you know. He's six-six. He had to lean down to let me kiss him. Those parts...they were out of contact. But..."

"But?"

"Okay, so I might have noticed. But he was definitely trying to hide it, so I didn't think it would be right to bring it up."

"I'd say that's exactly what you did!"

"Oh, Maggie, you're terrible!" Sarah burst into an uncontrollable fit of giggling, soon joined by Maggie.

When Sarah could breathe again, she gasped. "I didn't mean it that way."

Maggie wiped tears from her eyes. "Freud might say differently. Now, finish your tea. Do you want anything to eat?"

"No, thanks. I feel so much better. Thanks. I'm sorry I've been so much trouble lately."

"Don't you worry about it. That's what friends are for. And you're more like family. You can call me any time. You know that."

"I do. Thanks for the tea. I think it's done its job."

Maggie embraced Sarah and walked her to the door.

Her spirits lifted by her visit to Maggie, her body relaxed by the doctored tea, Sarah went back across the hall to her apartment, swallowed two ibuprofen and crawled straight into bed.

* * * * *

Sarah pushed open her shop door. Saturday had dawned bright and brisk. Not fair. How dare the day look so cheerful when she felt so miserable. All she wanted was to lounge on her couch with a heating pad and a mug of hot tea. Thank goodness Saturdays meant short hours. She'd have time to lie down for a few hours before dinner with Chris.

Jennifer appeared moments later carrying a large cardboard storage box. "Good morning, Sarah."

"It's so good to see you." Sarah turned and extended her arms for a hug. Jennifer set the box down and squeezed Sarah. She pulled away and gave Sarah a scrutinizing look. "Are you all right? You look tired."

"I'm fine. Just cramps. The usual misery."

Jennifer nodded. "Bummer. Hey, if you want to take the day off, I think I can manage by myself. It's been a while, but it's like riding a bike."

"No, I'll be all right. With you out front, I can sit down in the back and catch up on all the stuff I keep putting off." She tipped her head toward the carton. "Your photos?"

"Yeah. You said it would be okay."

"And I meant it. You keep one hundred percent of any of those sales and a commission on all the rest of the merchandise you sell. I wish I could give you a salary on top of it."

"Hey, I understand. It's more than fair for two afternoons a week and every other Saturday. Just having my work on display here is a coup, believe me." Jennifer pulled off a knit cap and shook out a dark mass of shoulder-length waves.

Sarah couldn't help but think of them as tresses, flowing tresses. What she wouldn't give for hair like that. "Nothing much has changed. Why don't you look around and get familiar with the stock. We have a couple of new artists since you were here last. Francisco Flores—he does small watercolors of the Cascades—and Margo Winters. Her blown-glass sculptures are on the back wall."

Jennifer shrugged off her backpack, flung it behind the counter and zeroed in on the new work. "These are nice. Do you have bios? The customers like it when I can provide details about the artists."

"Yes, in the back. I'll get them for you." Sarah went to the storeroom, found the papers and brought them to Jennifer. "Here you go. And if you don't mind, I'm going to be in back catching up on paperwork." She gave Jennifer a smile and went back to the office.

Sarah started plowing through the pile of papers on her desk. She had no idea how long she'd been working, the sounds of typical shop business muted by their familiarity.

"Sarah? I think you need to come out here."

Something about the hesitant squeak in Jennifer's voice had Sarah's heart going double-time. She winced at the pain in her belly when she moved and clutched the corner of the desk for a moment. "What's wrong?"

"I was busy, but I was watching. Honest. You know I don't ignore the customers."

Sarah gripped Jennifer's shoulders. "Calm down, Jen. Tell me what happened."

"I was rearranging some things, to make room for some photos and...look." Jennifer picked up a three-hundred-dollar etched-crystal urn. One of the handles was snapped off.

There was a new pain in Sarah's belly. "How did it happen?"

"I don't know. But...that's not all." She brought Sarah to the Egyptian perfume bottles. Three were missing, Sarah saw at once. From the look in Jennifer's eyes, they hadn't been sold this morning. Jennifer pointed to a pile of brightly colored broken glass behind the case.

Her cramps forgotten, Sarah rushed through the shop, checking the merchandise. A gouge in the corner of an oil painting. Not a lot of damage. Just a few pieces. Expensive pieces.

She felt the room spin and Jennifer leading her back to her chair in the office. "Close the shop," Sarah whispered. "Now."

Jennifer hurried to obey and Sarah picked up the phone. Darn. She fumbled with her Rolodex looking for Randy's card. Why didn't she have him on speed dial here? She punched in his cell number, relieved when he answered on the second ring.

"Sit tight. I'm out of town, but I'm going to call the station right now and someone will be there." Sarah heard muffled sounds of Randy using the radio.

"Do you think someone broke in and did this last night?" he said when he came back on the line.

Sarah shook her head, unable to find her voice. She cleared her throat. "I'm not sure. When I got here, Jennifer took over. I didn't even look around. But the door was locked. I know that."

"Jennifer?"

"My part-timer. She started today."

She answered the unasked question. "No. No way. She's worked for me before. Absolutely no way did she do this. She's as much of a wreck as I am." Sarah looked up to see Jennifer in the doorway, shaking her head and looking contrite.

"Who was in the shop today? Chris? Diana? Anyone acting suspicious?" Randy said.

"I don't know. I was in back. Hang on." Sarah repeated Randy's questions to Jennifer.

"She says no. Mostly moms with kids, but I keep that kind of merchandise too high for little fingers. Jennifer knows what she's doing. She knows how to watch the merchandise." Adrenaline surged through her system, clearing her head. "Diana!"

"Was she in today?"

"Not today, but she was in yesterday and she was wandering around. I wouldn't put it past her to do something like this. I was in the back for a while getting her check."

"For now, please wait for the investigators."

"Does this mean more fingerprint powder?" Sarah asked.

"Afraid so. Someone should be there soon."

Sarah hung up and looked at Jennifer. "I guess you can go home now. We're closed until the police get here."

"I'm not leaving you."

Without bothering to move the files and papers, Sarah leaned forward and pillowed her head on her arms like a schoolchild at naptime, when her biggest challenge was getting Joshua Baker to trade his peanut butter sandwich for her tuna salad.

Jennifer came up behind her and kneaded the muscles in Sarah's neck. "I'll make some tea."

Sarah had barely started drinking her tea when the back doorbell buzzed. Jennifer told her to stay put and hurried out to answer it, returning a moment later with a young policewoman.

"Ms. Tucker? I'm Officer Colleen McDonald. I understand there was some trouble here." Tall and lean, with the red hair and freckles her name personified, Officer McDonald gave Sarah a friendly smile. "Detective Detweiler said this wasn't the first incident." She pulled out a small notebook and uncapped a pen. "Can you tell me everything you remember?"

By the time Sarah and Jennifer had answered all of Officer McDonald's questions, Connor had come and gone. An ache in her head threatened to overtake the one below Sarah's belly and she felt herself trembling. Officer McDonald snapped the cap back on her pen and slid the notebook into her pocket. "I'm under strict orders to give you a ride home, ma'am," she said.

Sarah looked at the mess. "No need. I'll clean up here and I can take the bus."

"I'll clean," Jennifer said. "You go home. Get some sleep."

"My car's out back," the policewoman said.

Sarah turned to Jennifer. "Thanks. You can leave the receipts in the safe. I'll come in early Monday and finish."

Sarah followed the officer to the patrol car parked in the alley. "Do I know you? You look familiar. Maybe from high school?"

"You might have known my older brother, Greg. He would have been a couple of years behind you. Me, I was a bit of a hellion. My folks sent me to St. Luke's to let the nuns straighten me out. Guess they did—look what I'm doing for a living." She stopped at a blue and white patrol car. "Here we are," she said. She unlocked the passenger door. "You can ride up front."

Sarah winced as she lowered herself into the seat.

The officer must have noticed. "Are you all right, ma'am?"

"I'm fine. Just killer cramps." Sarah rested her head against the glass of the car's window, letting her eyes half close. "It wasn't so bad when I was on the Pill. But since my husband died, I haven't taken them and the last few months, I've been miserable for about two days."

"Maybe you ought to start again. Make things easier on you."

"Mmmh. Maybe." If getting back on the pill would mean she didn't have to feel like this several days a month, that was a good enough reason to consider it. As for the other benefits, well, if it turned out they would come in handy, so be it. Good lord, where had that thought come from? Randy was a cop working on a case. Her hormones were really doing a number on her.

Sarah hoped she wasn't blushing. She turned her face toward the window and away from any possibility of carrying the conversation any further, making a point of studying the streets. When they passed Loomis Drugs, she said, "Take a left at the corner. You can drop me off in front."

"No way, ma'am. Strict instructions to make sure you're secured before I leave. I don't know how much you've dealt with Detective Detweiler, but I'm sure as heck not getting on his bad side."

The officer parked and was opening the passenger door before Sarah could unbuckle her seat belt. Sarah accepted the outstretched hand.

She dragged herself up the steps to the building and opened the foyer door. The flight of stairs loomed like Mount Hood. Gripping the handrail, she supported herself through the climb, barely aware of the police officer staying one step below her.

Inside her apartment at last, Sarah let her purse fall to the floor, followed by her coat, then collapsed on the couch with a groan. "Thanks, Officer," she said. "You can go. I'm fine."

"Detweiler told me to give you the VIP treatment and I'm on duty for another fifteen minutes. You're stuck with me until then." She crossed the room and began perusing Sarah's CD collection. "Nice variety. You like Simon and Garfunkel?"

"Brought up on it, I guess. My mom played them all the time when...when things were rough. And when my husband died, I found they worked for me, too."

The policewoman roamed the room, looked out the windows and Sarah felt a flutter of panic. "Are you my bodyguard? Are you afraid I'm in danger?"

The policewoman came back and settled in the armchair nearest Sarah. "We have no grounds to protect you like that, ma'am. No threats have been made, no personal harm has been done."

Sarah swung her legs over the side of the couch and pushed herself up to a sitting position. A flicker of motion from her kitchen window caught her eye. She'd have to let Maggie know the new neighbors were in. Some other time. Right now, she didn't care if she ever found out who had moved in. All she wanted was to crawl into a hole. A deep, dark hole.

"Thanks," Sarah said. "For everything. I'm fine."

"You get some rest." Officer McDonald left and Sarah locked the door behind her.

"Rest. Sounds good." Sarah went to her room. She undressed, pulled on an oversized t-shirt and snuggled under the comforter. With her emotions roiling like a witch's cauldron, some dead-to-the-world time would be a blessing. The phone rang. Probably Chris reminding her about dinner. She let the machine handle the call. A glance at the clock told her she could sleep for three hours and have plenty of time to get ready. Her eyes closed. That was the last thing she remembered until she was awakened by the doorbell and someone pounding on the door shouting her name.

Groggy, she staggered to the front door and peered through the peephole. Chris. Sarah fumbled with the deadbolt key and yanked the door open.

"God, I fell asleep," she said. "Come in before Maggie has a fit and calls the cops."

At that, Chris clamped his mouth shut. "Did you forget our date?" He glanced at his watch. "We have reservations at Martinelli's in half an hour. Get dressed quick and we can make it."

Sarah rubbed her temples and sank onto the couch. "I can't, Chris. I'm sorry."

"What do you mean, you can't? Why not?"

When she gazed up at him, his expression had softened. "Some of my merchandise was damaged. At the shop. I had to call the police. Again."

He sank onto the cushion beside her and put an arm around her shoulder. "That's terrible. I had no idea."

Sarah leaned into him. "I feel lousy, Chris. I want to go back to bed, okay?"

"I could call for delivery. Whatever you want."

"I don't think I could face it. Please. We can go out another night. I need to do some serious thinking about the shop."

"I've told you, all you have to do is ask. Anything."

She straightened. "I know. And I've told you I'm going to make it or break it on my own."

"You've become stubborn since..."

"Say it. Since David died. Committed suicide? I will never believe that, but he's dead. Gone. And I'm on my own and I'm going to manage, or it won't mean anything." She looked into his eyes. He wanted to help. He wanted more, she was positive, but she'd deal with that later. With a hollow feeling of defeat, she got the words out. "Maybe there is something."

He perked up. "Anything."

Sarah worked her way out from under his arm and found the letter Diana had given her. She brought it back to the couch and pored over it again. "Do you remember David's sister, Diana?"

"Can't say that I do, but I'm sure we've met. What does she have to do with this?"

"She owns twenty percent of the shop. She says if I'm a day late with her payments, she's going to demand her share. Do you have legal people at Consolidated who can look at this and tell me if she can do it?" She handed him the letter.

Chris barely glanced at it before folding it back into the envelope and sliding it into his sport coat pocket. "Monday, first thing."

"Thanks." She walked to the door and held it open. Sometimes you couldn't be subtle with Chris. "I'm going to go back to bed now. I'm sorry about missing dinner."

"I understand. I hope that cop catches whoever did this to you. But he seems more big than brains, if you ask me."

"Randy's a good cop. He'll catch her." Sarah saw Chris' back stiffen, his lips tighten.

"Get some rest, Sarah," he muttered. "I'll call."

"I will." Puzzled at his abrupt mood swing, Sarah watched him storm down the hall and disappear down the stairs. Too tired to consider it further, she locked the door and crawled back into bed.

Chapter Ten

Randy punched Sarah's number into his cell phone while he sat waiting for the light to change. Sarah's machine played out its message and when she didn't pick up after he announced himself, he called Colleen.

"Calm down, Detweiler. I saw her in and she was going to bed. You know how it is after the adrenaline leaves your system. The neighbor across the hall caught me as I was leaving. She'll keep an eye out."

Yes, Maggie would. He took a calming breath. Was this event connected to the robbery, or yet another of Sarah's business problems? Or were they all related? He checked his watch. None of the shops in the area would be open until Monday.

"Were there any other calls?" Randy asked. "Anyone else report anything?"

"Negative. But the damage was subtle. Ms. Tucker can't be sure when it happened. It's possible other merchants might still find some damage."

"I'm going to have to follow up with the owners." Randy hesitated. He had no right to ask Colleen to go beyond her patrol duties for him.

"Ask it, Detweiler. What do you need? Your partner's on vacation. Let me pitch in even if I'm not a detective. Yet."

Why not? "If you could get a list of phone numbers for me, I'd really appreciate it. No immediate rush, but if you could have it on my desk Monday morning—"

"No problem. You want me to make the initial phone calls?"

"No, thanks. You've done plenty. Thanks, Mac."

"I said no problem. And Detweiler?"

"What?"

"I like her. I can understand your…concern."

Randy heard the click of the disconnected phone. Damn. Was he that obvious, even over the phone? Could she read him that easily? Sarah wouldn't have said anything to her. Or would she? Crap, that woman thing again. Solving crimes was nothing compared to understanding women.

The light changed and he let his mind chew on the new developments as he drove. Maybe it was kids, out to see what they could get away with. He wished he could believe it.

Randy was convinced someone had talked Gertie into robbing Sarah. Why else would she have returned to a town she'd already hit? He turned to the positive. Woodford had Gracious Gertie, whose name had turned out to be Louise Franklin, in custody. For some reason, when he heard the news, not being the arresting officer didn't rankle the way he'd expected it to. He allowed himself a smile. Tomorrow, Sarah would ID the woman, he'd confront her and she'd talk. And maybe she could give him the connections he'd need to pull everything together.

Before going to the station, Randy made a quick trip around Sarah's block. Her apartment was dark. On impulse, he pulled in behind Sarah's building and went upstairs to Maggie's unit. He tapped on the door and had almost turned to leave when it opened. Cooking smells reminded him he hadn't eaten in a long time. He did a double-take at Maggie's new hair color.

"Hi, Randy. Come in. The *I Love Lucy* look threw you, right? Can I get you something to eat? I've got some leftover chicken I can reheat."

Randy checked the time. After seven. Tempting, but he had work to do. "No, I'm fine. I wanted to touch base before I went to the station." He looked around. "Where's Othello?"

"He was acting sluggish, wouldn't eat. I took him to the vet. They want to watch him until Monday."

"I hope he's all right. He's a nice cat."

"It's probably nothing. He was out in the yard a couple of times this week. Maybe he picked up something there. He's getting old. Nearly twelve."

"I wish him a speedy recovery."

"I'll tell him. I'm sure he'll appreciate it." She peered into his eyes. "Christopher Westmoreland came by a while ago, but he left. Alone." She smiled.

"Sarah said they were going to dinner."

"I'm certain she cancelled after the to-do at the shop. Sure I can't get you something?"

"No, I'm fine. But I want Sarah to go to Woodford tomorrow and identify Gracious Gertie—the woman who robbed her." He'd never be able to think of her as Louise Franklin.

Maggie shot him a huge grin. "They caught her? Fantastic. I'll bet you're thrilled."

Randy smiled down at Maggie. "I am. I need to get back and pull all my paperwork together." He planted a quick kiss on Maggie's forehead.

"The color grows on you," he said. "I think I'm starting to like it."

Maggie glowed and shut the door behind him.

Randy stopped at Sarah's door. He placed both palms on its smooth surface. "Sleep well," he whispered before going downstairs to his truck.

At the station, Randy sat at his desk, waded through his emails, filled out his paperwork and read the reports Colleen filed. He scribbled a note for Connor to put as much of a rush as he could on the prints from today's call, for all the good it would do. All his suspects had been in the shop, with plenty of opportunity to leave prints all over the place. But, there was always the possibility they'd get a hit on someone new.

What he needed was time to let his brain digest today's new wrinkle. Randy stuffed the files into his briefcase, stood and stretched, his fingertips grazing the ceiling.

* * * * *

A pizza box and six-pack balanced under one arm, Randy propped the screen door open with his foot as he worked the key into the lock of the front door. Inside, he set the pizza on the counter, popped the top off a beer and called for Starsky and Hutch.

"Hey, guys. I'm home! Sorry I'm late. Again. Ready for dinner?" He went out to the porch to fill their food and water dishes and clean their litter box. When he had finished and still saw neither cat, he pushed the door to the backyard and whistled. Although he knew they could roam the neighborhood if they wanted to, they rarely went far. He left the porch door propped open and went back to his pizza.

The NCAA basketball season was reaching its peak and Randy spent the rest of the night caught up in a double-header. At the final buzzer, he realized it was nearly midnight. When he checked the porch, everything was exactly as he'd left it.

Randy put on his jacket, took a flashlight and whistled again, trying to ignore the gnawing feeling in his stomach. As he probed shrubbery around the perimeter of the yard, he continued to whistle softly between his teeth. The breeze made the foliage rustle—the clouds and moon played off one another, casting shadows that moved through the yard, but the cats were nowhere to be found. As he started up the porch stairs, a faint mewing sound caught his ear.

"Starsky? Hutch? That you, boys?" He lowered himself to a crouch and shone his light under the porch. Starsky lay across Hutch's body, blinking his eyes as the light beamed across him. Randy stuck his fingers through the wooden lattice that framed the bottom of the porch and jerked away the section nearest the stairs with a resounding crack. On elbows and knees, he crawled toward them. Shit. They were limp, barely breathing. "It's okay. I've got you," he whispered.

Randy bundled both cats against his chest, flew up the stairs and snagged his wallet and keys. In the truck, he placed the cats on the passenger seat, wriggled out of his jacket and wrapped it around them. Hell and damnation, he didn't care about regulations, he pulled out his flashers and turned on the siren as he sped to the veterinary clinic, giving silent thanks that Pine Hills and the neighboring communities had enough animal lovers to support twenty-four hour emergency vet service.

Randy screeched the truck to a stop at the clinic's door and carried the cats toward the clinic. "Stay with me, guys. We're there."

A young Asian woman in a blue lab coat had the door open and was rushing to meet him.

"I heard the siren. What's the matter?" She reached for the cats, but Randy maintained his hold until they were inside.

Randy set his pets on the examining table. "I found them a little while ago, under the porch."

The vet had her stethoscope in her ears and was moving it slowly across Starsky's inert body. She looked in his eyes, pried open his mouth and ran her hands down his black and white body, then repeated the exam for Hutch. Randy shifted from foot to foot as he waited for the doctor to speak.

"They're very weak. I can't tell what's wrong based on a quick exam, but I'm leaning toward poison. We have another cat here with the same symptoms."

"Othello," Randy gasped.

"Yes. Does he live in your neighborhood as well?"

"No, but there might be a connection. Will they be all right?"

"I can't promise anything. I'm going to try the same treatment we're using on Othello. He seems to be responding, but he was in much better shape when he was brought in."

"Damn. I should have looked for them sooner. It's not like them to skip dinner. I thought they were busy in the yard and then I got involved in the game—" He was aware of a hand on his elbow. He looked down to find the doctor gone and a young woman leading him to the waiting area.

"Dr. Lee has taken your cats for treatment. Are you a regular patient here?"

Randy nodded. "Detweiler. Starsky and Hutch. We usually see Dr. Stetter."

"Why don't you sit here for a few minutes? I'll pull your files." She stopped in front of one of the hard plastic chairs.

"I need some air," Randy said. "Be right back."

Outside, Randy leaned against the rear of his truck and took several deep breaths, the fresh air washing the antiseptic smell of the clinic from his nostrils. He was upset, but more than that, he was angry. His palms burned and he realized he had clenched his fists so tightly that he'd nearly drawn blood. Had it only been Starsky and Hutch, Randy might have written the incident off as an isolated case of sadistic mischief. But not with Othello being targeted as well. This was no longer a coincidence. Sarah was the only connection between him and Maggie. This had become personal.

Randy walked slowly around the parking lot, collecting his thoughts. Once he'd calmed enough to speak to the vet's assistant he went back inside, but she wasn't at her station. Randy leaned on the counter until she returned a few moments later.

"Dr. Lee said you should go home and she'll call you as soon as she knows anything."

"Thank you." Randy said. "Let me give you my cell phone number." He wrote the number on the back of one of his cards and handed it to her.

Randy left the clinic and got into his truck. Not until he had trouble getting the keys into the ignition did he realize his hands were shaking. He gave the steering wheel some emphatic thwacks with his fists and tried again. The key slid into the ignition this time and he drove home in a fog, too angry to think.

As he started to hang his jacket on its hook by the door, its cat smells and stains overwhelmed him and he let it fall to the floor. He went straight to the liquor cabinet. He swigged his whiskey from the bottle as he paced through his house before settling on the couch.

* * * * *

Sunlight forced its way past closed eyelids. Randy squinted against the daylight, saw the open whiskey bottle on the floor by his side. His fingers fumbled for the bottle and he lifted it to the table. Half empty. That explained the pounding in his head. He swung his legs over the edge of the couch and pushed himself to a half sitting position. God, who'd turned his living room into a merry-go-round? He staggered to the kitchen and forced himself to brew a pot of coffee.

A drink of water came up as fast as it went down, but he felt a little better. He hadn't been like this since his grandmother died. He knew better than to drink to excess, especially in anger.

Careful not to move his throbbing head, he picked up the phone. Dr. Lee wasn't in. The tech told him Starsky and Hutch showed no signs of improvement, but they were holding their own. The news did nothing for his headache. He headed for the shower.

Randy started the water as hot as he could stand it, then gradually brought the temperature down until he shivered under a frigid waterfall. He dried off, put on khakis and a long-sleeved polo shirt and went back to the kitchen for a cup of coffee. Carrying it to the couch, he sat down, reached for the remote and tolerated about ten minutes of Sunday morning evangelists before shutting off the noise.

Sarah. He'd better wait before he called her. He had thought about suggesting a picnic lunch before the drive to Woodford, but his stomach flipped cartwheels at the thought.

With a grunt, he pushed himself up and into the kitchen. He found a box of saltines in the cabinet and fought with the waxed wrapper, finally ripping it apart with his teeth. He nibbled on the corner of one of the salty squares. Not bad. He chewed his way through half a dozen and his stomach settled a bit.

He decided to try a piece of toast when the phone rang. He plopped a slice of bread into the toaster and pressed the handle before picking up. Sarah's voice, sounding excited, made up for the knives it shot through his skull.

"Maggie said you caught Gertie!"

Randy hooked the handset onto his shoulder and retrieved his toast. "Not me, but the Woodford police have her in custody. I want you to come to Woodford with me to identify her."

There was a brief silence. "When?"

Randy glanced at the kitchen clock. Eleven. He was definitely not ready to take a two-hour drive through the mountains. "How about I pick you up around one? Will that work?"

Another silence.

"Sarah," Randy said. "Are you okay with this? She'll never know you're there."

"I can do it. That's not it. But...is something wrong? You sound tired."

"No. Shaking off a hangover."

"Oh." Another pause.

He couldn't bear the disappointment in her voice. "My cats got into some poison and I had to rush them to the vet. I drank too much when I got back. Stupid and I'm paying for it."

"That's awful. I hope they're all right. You know, Maggie took Othello to the vet yesterday, too." Another silence, longer this time. The hairs on his neck rose. He said nothing.

"You think they're connected." Sarah's voice was tremulous.

"I don't think it's a coincidence. Would Chris do something like this? Or Diana?" He waited out a long silence.

"I can't imagine either of them doing something that awful. I don't think either of them has pets, but they wouldn't...they couldn't..." Another dead interval. "I am so sorry. If someone hurt you and Maggie because of me, I'll—"

More silence.

"Sarah, leave this one to me. I'll see you at one, okay?"

He heard her sigh. "Okay. One."

Randy threw the cold piece of toast in the trash and ate some more saltines. They sat like a leaden mass in his stomach.

Chapter Eleven

Randy rose from his knees in his bathroom and rinsed his mouth. What a waste of his good Irish. Next time, he'd stick to the cheap stuff. The sound of a car driving off, followed by the beep of the motion detector on his front porch, halted his course of self-pity.

Wiping his mouth with the back of his hand, he eased the curtain beside the front door aside just as the doorbell rang. He yanked the door open.

"Sarah! What the—? How did you get my address?"

She smiled up at him. "Aren't you going to invite me in?" Without waiting for an answer, she pushed past him, hung her coat on the rack, glanced around and marched into the kitchen.

Randy's frantic visual search of the house revealed no underwear strewn on the furniture. Too late to dispose of the empty beer cans on the kitchen table. He made a quick trip down the hall and shut the bedroom doors. He returned to find Sarah opening and closing cabinets. The beer cans had disappeared.

"Maybe if you'll tell me what you're looking for, I can help," he said.

"No matter. I found it." She had commandeered his chef's knife and was filling a saucepan with water. A small plastic bag lay on the counter.

He'd expended enough energy. The room had started its carousel imitation again. He sank onto a kitchen chair and watched her open the bag, pull out a gnarled brown root and slice thin discs from its length.

She dropped a few slices into the water and turned the flame on under the pot. A spicy scent filled the room, reminiscent of Christmas gingerbread men. He struggled against the memory—he, Gram and his sister rolling, cutting and decorating. So long ago.

"It needs to steep for about ten minutes. Ginger tea," she said. "Old family hangover recipe. Mom and I used to make if for my dad—kind of a Sunday morning ritual." One corner of her mouth turned up.

Randy swallowed and willed his stomach to stop churning. "Must have been tough."

"That was years ago. He and Mom split up. She's happily remarried. We don't hear from Dad." She pulled a chair out from the table to face him and laid a hand on his knee. Her eyes, looking so much like the stone in his grandmother's brooch, haunted him. He bowed his head. He felt her move behind him, felt her soft hands massaging his neck.

"I'm sorry about your cats," she whispered, still kneading knots from his neck and shoulders. "Have you had them a long time?"

Oh, God. Anger, fury, rage. Those feelings he understood. Those he could deal with. But now anguish pushed itself to the surface and his eye burned. That was the last straw. Even when his grandmother had died, he'd kept everything locked inside. He jerked away, ignoring the spinning of the room, stumbled to the living room and threw himself onto the couch where he turned on ESPN as loud as he could stand it. Sarah stayed in the kitchen.

He sensed her approach, but kept his head down, raising only his eyes. She held a steaming mug in her hand. "Sip it slowly. It should help."

When he didn't move, she said, "I'm not going anywhere. Drink." Her tone brooked no nonsense.

Randy reached for the mug and took a sip of the spicy liquid. A hint of honey underscored the ginger. He raised his eyebrows and looked at her. It was surprisingly good and he managed a weak smile.

Sarah perched on the arm of the couch. "I'm not moving until it's finished."

He took another sip. Whether it was due to her presence or the tea, the knots in his stomach loosened, the churning eased.

"You going to tell me how you found me?" Randy asked.

"Maybe I'm not such a bad detective myself."

He looked at her over his mug, waiting.

"I called the station, asked for Colleen. Anyway, we worked a deal and she drove me over."

"A deal. What kind of a deal? What have you two been doing?" He hoped the heat rising in his face was from the tea.

"Nothing. Don't be mad at her. I told her I'd take a cab, but she insisted on driving me."

"She never should have given you my address."

"Technically she didn't. She just drove me over. And if it makes you feel better, we were talking, so I wasn't paying attention to where we were going. Plus, I have no sense of direction. I get lost in elevators, so I don't think I could find my way back here." She nodded at his mug. He drank some more.

"Please don't blame her," she went on. "I can be pretty insistent. And," she continued, her voice lowered, "she told me the cats were your grandmother's. Starsky and Hutch?"

"Yeah. My grandmother got them as kittens. She died before they were a year old. I've had them ever since."

The phone rang and Randy went to the kitchen. The room had stopped spinning and the up and down motion was a fraction of what it had been. Dr. Lee's voice on the phone sent the adrenaline surging. He clutched the edge of the table.

"I wish I had better news," she said. "Your cats survived the night, but they're still extremely weak. Othello is improving, but I'm still trying to identify the poison. Once I

Finding Sarah

know what it is, I can begin more specific treatment. I can't make any promises."

Randy nodded. "Thanks for calling." He hung up the phone. Sarah stood behind him, her hand on his back.

"They're alive," he said. "But that's about all."

Sarah crossed in front of him, took both of his hands in hers and squeezed them. "They'll make it."

Her compassion stretched his control to the limit. Unable to get words past the lump in his throat, he walked back into the kitchen and poured the remaining ginger tea into his mug.

Sarah followed. "Think you can eat something? I saw the crackers. Smart move."

"I can't say that they're still with me," he admitted. "I tried some toast, but couldn't face it. I'm feeling better now."

"Sit down and I'll make you some."

Randy finished three slices of toast, then called the Woodford police department. Gertie-Louise still wasn't talking. They had three reliable eyewitnesses to tie her to the robberies in Woodford and another one in Maple Grove. Sarah would make her the prime suspect for the Pine Hills crimes as well and he could close those cases. And something told him he'd find another link to Consolidated.

He watched as Sarah wandered into the kitchen, found an apple, took two bites and set it down. She read a section of the paper, got up for a drink of water, then went back to the couch.

"What's the matter?" Randy asked. "Nervous?"

"That's not it. It's…I can't believe anyone would do this. Or why. Poison cats? Hurt innocent animals just to get at me? Every time I think of it, I get angry all over again." She tugged on her hair. "It's got to be some sort of strange coincidence."

"To a cop, coincidences send up red flags." He went to the sink and rinsed his mug, then grabbed a pen and his legal tablet and sat in a chair opposite Sarah. "We should talk."

She eyed the tablet and her posture stiffened. "About what? I thought all I had to do was identify Gertie for you."

Randy tried to ignore the new roiling in his stomach. "I think the robbery is only part of it. I think a lot of your shop problems might not have been everyday business snafus."

Her lips tightened. "Diana, right? She tried to make it so I'd sell the shop, but when the little things didn't work, she went all legal."

"I don't know—"

"No, listen." Sarah's eyes went stormy blue. "Diana wanted more money. Twenty percent of a mass market shop would be more reliable than what she was getting from me. But I wouldn't sell. If she bankrupted me, she'd be stuck with nothing. The only answer was for her to convince me that I couldn't make a go of things on my own. Little things. Chip away until I gave up. Don't you get it?" She stopped to take a breath. "You're not writing anything. You're not even clicking your pen."

"What?" Randy looked at the pen in his hand.

"You click your pen when you're thinking. You assume because you're the cop, you're right and how could I know anything?"

His head throbbed. "No, that's not it. Let's forget the earlier snafus for now. The fact that she's gone to a lawyer put her lower on my list. Why would she damage your merchandise once she's decided to force you to sell? It would make the shop less valuable, not more."

Randy could see the scenario playing out in Sarah's head. It was a good thing she wasn't a crook—she telegraphed every thought. She ducked her head and rubbed her temples before meeting his gaze.

"The way you put it sounds logical, I guess. But she's still on your list, right? You ran her through the computers like you did Chris, didn't you?"

He nodded. "Everyone's on my list. I'm just trying to put them in order."

She narrowed her eyes. "Am I on your list?"

There was nothing teasing in her tone and his stomach lurched. Because he knew she'd accept only the truth, he gave it to her. "Not anymore."

"You investigated me? I was the one who got robbed, remember."

"Standard procedure."

"When you came to St. Michael's that night. Was all that standard procedure, too?"

He fisted his hands in his hair. Studied the floor. Then met her eyes in an even stare. "I showed up early because I wanted to see you. Not a suspect. Not a victim. You."

She was quiet for a long moment, but her eyes never left his. "I'm sorry. Maybe I'm more nervous than I thought. You have a job to do."

"Yes, I do and I'm sorry when it hurts you." He set the tablet on the coffee table and leaned forward. He kept his voice neutral, did his best to muster a comforting smile. "I'd like to know more about David's accident. Did you hire one of the PIs I suggested?"

She nodded and her eyes went from stormy to blank. "Dobrovsky. But according to him and the Highway Patrol, it was suicide."

"I was at a convention in Florida when the accident happened. Tell me about it."

He could see her searching to center herself. When she spoke, her voice was dull and flat. "First they thought it was an accident, but they found the note."

"He wrote a note?"

"No. It was a card."

"Maybe you should start at the beginning."

She inhaled, then exhaled a slow, shaky breath. "David had an appointment with an artist—to sign a contract for exclusive handling of his work. Before he left, we had another argument about giving money to Diana." She adjusted the skirt of her long denim jumper. "When the cops found the card, they started thinking suicide." She snorted, almost a laugh. "It was a Hallmark card—one of those generic 'I'm sorry' ones. He was apologizing for the argument, not saying that he was going to kill himself. But nobody listened."

"That wouldn't have been enough for a suicide ruling."

"They found an insurance policy he'd taken out a few months before. I tried to explain that his best friend had died suddenly and he realized anything could happen. Ironic, isn't it? He was trying to protect me and instead, I'm up to my eyeballs in debt." Her voice grew quiet. "And we were talking about starting a family." Tears brimmed, but she wiped them away. Anger filled her voice now. "And then they found antidepressants in his blood."

Randy wiped his palms on his jeans. "Was he—"

"Say it. Depressed? A mental case?" Sarah stood up. "I don't know, dammit. He never said a word to me, never complained and I never saw him take pills. But they added everything up and said it was suicide. The report was full of mumbo jumbo about something jamming the accelerator, skid marks or no skid marks, tire tracks or no tire tracks."

Her voice had faded and he went to her. "Come here." He gathered her into his arms. She relaxed into him for a minute, then pushed away.

"I don't know what's worse. Knowing or not knowing. The private investigator said he couldn't find enough to dispute the official findings and that it would be a waste of my money to go further. And since I didn't have any more money, it seemed like calling it off was the best plan. But—even if it wasn't the insurance money, everyone looks at you funny. Sometimes I just get angry. At David, at everyone."

"Survivor's guilt," Randy said. "You wonder if you'd done something different, maybe he wouldn't have died. But there was nothing you could have done."

She turned her eyes up to meet his. "You know." Not a question.

He nodded. "I was on the road, on a case, when my grandmother had a stroke. Technically, it was my day off and she'd wanted us to go to dinner, but I'd begged off. Work first, even though there was nothing that couldn't have waited a day or two. A neighbor found her. I didn't get back in time. I'll always wonder if things would have been different if I'd been home. I could have had her to the hospital sooner." Or if he hadn't been engrossed in a damn basketball game and checked on his cats… He cleared his throat against the constricting heat, raised his hand, palm out, to cut off Sarah's response.

"It's about time to hit the road. Bathroom's in there if you want." He motioned to the guest bath and went in search of a clean jacket.

* * * * *

They drove in silence. About fifteen minutes down the road, Sarah reached for the radio buttons. "Do you mind?"

"Be my guest."

Sarah pressed each button in turn, listening for a moment before pressing the next.

"I thought it was guys and TV remotes. What are you doing? Radio surfing?" Randy asked.

She giggled. The sound sent quivers through his body.

"No, just trying to get more of a feel for who you are, I think you can tell a lot about a person by their taste in music."

"Do I pass?"

"I expected country and the classical surprised me, but four of them are the same ones that were in my car. When I had a car. And they're on my stereo at home, too."

Randy didn't miss the "my" instead of "our". Had David's memory faded a little more? "Why don't you pick one and we can listen?"

Sarah settled on a soft jazz station, leaned back in her seat and closed her eyes.

They were almost to the worst stretch of mountain road and he turned his concentration to his driving.

When they arrived at the Woodford police station, Randy chatted with Lou Hodges, the officer in charge of the case. "So, she still won't talk?" Randy asked.

"Clams have nothing on her," Hodges said. "If you'll follow me, we've got the lineup ready."

Sarah chewed on her lower lip. She looked pale, but perhaps it was due to the station's poor lighting. Randy put a hand on her shoulder. "You okay?"

"Fine."

Hodges held the door for her. "You understand the procedure, right? We've got five women in there. They can't see you. They'll step forward one at a time and say, 'Unlock the register. I could use some spending money.' Then you tell us which one is the lady who held you up."

Randy watched as Sarah nodded, her eyes wide. She sat on a folding metal chair behind a narrow table, peering through a glass window. He positioned himself against the wall where he could watch Sarah and the lineup. Hodges clicked a switch and the room was plunged into darkness. The room on the other side of the window was awash in light. The door behind the glass opened and a line of gray-haired women paraded in. Randy waited for his eyes to adjust to the dim light and studied Sarah, trying to see what she was thinking.

She examined each woman in turn. He could feel her straining to compare their voices with the woman who had frightened her barely a week ago.

"Do you recognize her, ma'am?" Hodges asked.

"No," Sarah said. Her voice quavered. "She's not there."

* * * * *

Randy helped Sarah into the truck. After swallowing a huge helping of pride, he'd admitted his screwup to Hodges and got a booking photo of Gertie—Louise—to do what he should have done in the first place—confirm her identity with her previous Pine Hills victims, not rely solely on Sarah. Hodges had positive confirmation that the woman in custody had pulled the Woodford robberies. Randy tossed the folder behind the seat and took his place behind the wheel.

"It wasn't her," Sarah said. "The height was wrong, the body type was wrong and the voices were all wrong. I have an eye for detail."

"I believe you, Sarah. It was my mistake."

"But if it's not her, who robbed me? What do we do now?"

"We go home." He rechecked his cell phone display, although he knew he hadn't missed any calls.

"They'll be all right," Sarah said. "The vet would have called if anything had happened."

"I'm that obvious?"

"I know those cats mean a lot to you. And it's all my fault. Someone is mad at me and he's taking it out on you and Maggie. I'm so sorry."

"Don't you dare think that. This is not your fault."

Sarah gave him a weak smile. "Tell me about your grandmother. She must have been nice."

He couldn't. Randy saw his grandmother, the day she'd brought home the kittens. He'd been staying with her over winter break and she'd let him name them, although she preferred Patches and Midnight.

"Look, Sarah. I know you mean well, but I don't feel like talking. Please drop it."

"I understand," she whispered. She turned those blue eyes on him and he felt like a jerk, but he couldn't deal with it. She'd cut too close. His cats…Gram…he refused to think about them anymore.

The weather had turned blustery and Randy fought the crosswinds and driving rain as they made their way over the winding road through the mountain. Randy concentrated on seeing the road between passes of the windshield wipers. He stared at the road ahead and tires on asphalt were the only sounds for the rest of the drive.

* * * * *

Once they'd reached the other side of the mountain, the weather cleared. They were driving through the Pine Hills business district when Sarah said, "Stop at Thriftway, please."

"What for? Are you all right?"

"I'm fine. Just stop."

Randy pulled into the lot behind Thriftway.

"I'll be right back." She grabbed her purse and darted into the store.

Randy drummed his fingers on the steering wheel. This had been one hell of a day. What was she doing in the store? He heard the door open and Sarah climbed in, two bunches of flowers in her hands. She placed them behind the seat and said, "Drive."

"I don't suppose you'll tell me where we're going?"

"Drive. Left out of the parking lot. Right on First."

Randy did as he was told. The look of earnest determination on her face left him little choice.

"Right at the light," she said when they reached the outskirts of town. "Pull into the parking lot."

"There's nothing here but the cemetery. Why did—"

"Because I have some unfinished business. And I think you might, too." She waited for him to stop the truck, then turned to him. "She's here, isn't she? Your grandmother. Colleen told me on the drive to your place."

"Yes, but—"

"When was the last time you were here?" She gave him that blue-eyed stare that pulled the answer out of him, pain and all.

"For the funeral."

Her expression said she'd known. She handed him a bouquet and took his other hand in hers. "You have to do this. It's hard, but it's important. Trust me."

They strolled along the path. It took Randy a few false turns, but he found his grandmother's grave and knelt to place the flowers in the receptacle by the headstone. He felt Sarah's hand on his shoulder.

"I'll leave you alone. I'll be across the path by that big oak tree. But you have to say goodbye. Talk to her." Sarah gave his shoulder a squeeze and walked away.

Looking to make sure there was no one else around, Randy took a deep breath and eight years of suppression slammed through his defenses.

Chapter Twelve

☙

Sarah slowed as she approached David's grave. She had been here so often after his accident, but it had been three months since her last visit. The visit where she had vowed to stop grieving. As if saying something like that could make it so.

She ached for Randy. He had never completed his grief. It was devastating not being able to say goodbye to loved ones, to have them taken without warning. She turned and saw him, still kneeling at the graveside, shoulders shaking, as he dealt with the feelings he'd kept inside all these years.

She walked the rest of the distance to David's grave with confidence. She knelt, placing the flowers one at a time into the container as she spoke.

"Hi, Sweetheart. It's been a while, hasn't it? I still miss you." She brushed away some leaves. "I think of you every day. I know you're not here because…because you wanted to leave me. Us. I can't prove it and I don't think anyone can. I guess you're the only one who really knows."

After she made final adjustments to the flowers, she traced the letters on his headstone with a forefinger. "I met someone. I like him. You'd like him, too." Her voice cracked, but she forced herself to speak aloud. "I know you don't want me to be alone the rest of my life. No one can ever replace you. You'll always be a part of me. But there's room for so much more. I know you'll understand." She remained still for several minutes, hardly aware of the drizzle, feeling a warmth course through her body despite the chill in the air. She wiped a tear from her cheek. David understood.

Sarah rose from her knees at a light touch on her back. She turned to Randy and gave him a damp-eyed smile. His eyes were red, his cheeks were wet, but he looked at peace.

"You all right now?" she asked.

"Yes." His voice was hoarse.

"You never cried for her before, did you? You never said goodbye. You have to grieve, you know, or you never heal."

He nodded.

"I had a few things to clear up myself," she said. "I think David understands."

"Understands what?"

"This," she said and she pulled him under the shelter of the oak tree and kissed him. A gentle kiss, one that spoke of friendship, of understanding, of sharing. His moist lips pressed against hers. She tasted the salt of their intermingled tears, felt the sweet tenderness of his lips and then, without warning, her tongue sought his. Not a chaste kiss, but one deep with passion. He returned the kiss and she pressed her hips against him. He reached down and cupped her bottom in his hands, lifting her tight against him, giving her clear evidence of his arousal and they lost themselves in the depths of their hunger.

When the rain began in earnest, they pulled apart and Randy placed one gentle kiss on her cheek before he grasped her by the hand and they raced back to the truck.

When Randy pulled to a stop in front of Sarah's building, he reached over and stroked her cheek. "This can't go further, you know. Not while I'm working on your case." He took her hand and pressed her fingers to his lips. "I'll work round the clock to close it."

"I understand. But please call if you find out anything." She saw the underlying pain in his eyes. "Or if you need to talk."

She closed the door to the truck, then ducked her head and hurried inside. Once she was in her apartment, Sarah crossed to the window and pulled the curtain aside. Randy's truck was still there. She raised her hand. He flashed his headlights and she watched the black pickup crawl away.

While she fixed her dinner, Sarah saw the lights go off in the apartment across the way. She reached for the phone to let Maggie know. No. She brought her plate to the table. Tomorrow would be soon enough.

* * * * *

Randy drove to the station, his emotions in turmoil. He sat behind the wheel in the parking lot until he gathered the composure to go inside. Sarah had yanked the bandage off an old wound, releasing all the festering guilt. He'd heal cleanly this time, thanks to her gentle touch, but the incision was still sore.

Memories of her kiss made him all the more determined to solve the case. He made a quick stop in the men's room to rinse any evidence of tears from his face and went straight to his desk, giving only cursory nods to the few officers he passed on the way. Behind a closed door, he checked his voice mail, thumbing through his pink message slips while he waited for his computer to power on. Nothing from Dr. Lee, but Maggie's name leapt off one of them.

He seized his phone and punched in her number.

"I'm sorry to bother you on a Sunday, but I knew you were working," Maggie said. "I thought I'd check with you before I said anything to Sarah, in case it's nothing. She's had enough scares lately."

A chill ran through him. "What, Maggie?"

"I went to the building next door to welcome the newcomers with some brownies. A man came to the door, probably in his forties, kind of fat. There was no furniture in the living room, just a card table in the kitchen covered in pizza boxes and burger bags."

"And…" He forced himself not to snap at her. Let her talk. She was obviously trying to make up for the mistake with the heater man.

"And, I saw these two easy chairs parked right in the dining room area. Kind of strange for a dining room, wouldn't you say?"

"Maggie, I'm sure there's a point here someplace. So far, you've got a fast food-eating man whose furniture hasn't been delivered who decided to put a chair in the dining area of an empty apartment. Maybe he likes the view."

"That's exactly what I'm trying to say!"

"What are you talking about?"

"The view. That dining room looks right into Sarah's kitchen window. And I can't be sure, because the guy was doing his best to get me out of there before I could see anything, but I think there were some binoculars and maybe some other fancy techno stuff on a little table by the chairs. Anyway, it didn't look kosher and I thought you might be able to find out who rented the place. We don't need peeping Toms in the neighborhood."

The thought of someone watching Sarah made his skin crawl. "Hang on a second, Maggie. Let me think." How much would someone know if they'd been watching her apartment? Techno stuff, Maggie said. Listening equipment? Could he hear what went on in Sarah's place? Shit. He wanted her out of there. Now. "Would the man have a view of Sarah's front door?"

"No, it's off to the side."

"Okay, here's what I want you to do. Go across the hall and get Sarah to your place. Call me when she's over there. Sarah has my cell number."

He paced his office while he waited for the call. Today was Sunday. When did Maggie say he'd moved in? Was it only one man? Damn. No matter what Sarah said, he couldn't see Diana as a major player here. But this whole case looked like someone was playing puppetmaster. Diana didn't seem to have the brains. But the more he thought about it, the more he wondered. She knew how to use her...charms...to get what she wanted.

Slow down. He was a cop and it was time he started acting like one. He had a whole bunch of nothing, but it all surrounded Sarah. He took his legal tablet and had half-filled a page with disjointed notes when Sarah called.

"All right. I'm at Maggie's. Now, will you tell me what's going on?" Any fear in her voice was hidden beneath the indignation.

Randy forced himself to keep his tone neutral. "I'm sorry. Your new neighbor might be spying on you."

"That's ridiculous! Watching me? If he is, why don't you arrest him?"

"It's not that easy. Watching someone isn't against the law. I'd like you to stay with Maggie for a little while. I'm going to do some database searches and see if I can trace the rental."

"I'm not running away because some pervert might be looking in my windows."

"It seems too much of a coincidence that a peeping Tom would move in now, on top of the fire, the robbery and the break-in. I'd like to see if I can figure out who this guy is." He clicked his way through layers of links until he reached the database he needed.

"How long should I stay out of my apartment? I'm getting pretty angry that someone can force me out of my own home."

"Will you give me an hour? That should give me enough time to do some research."

Nothing but silence.

"One hour, Sarah." When she didn't respond, he hung up.

Randy turned to his computer. While he worked his way through databases, directories, reverse directories and property tax lists, he made a quick call to Dr. Lee. She'd left for the day, but according to the receptionist, Starsky and Hutch were hanging in. Othello was improving and they might have identified the poison.

Randy permitted himself a moment of relief, then returned to his monitor. After another half hour, he rubbed his eyes and leaned back in his chair. Ownership of the building was buried under layers of holding companies, but ultimately, it was yet another of Consolidated's tentacles. Consolidated was showing up all too often for his taste. He added Diana's husband to his list.

His stomach growled and Randy glanced at his watch. Seven-thirty. Pleased that he was hungry, he rummaged through his desk for any leftover snacks while he punched Maggie's number into the phone.

Ripping the wrapper from a Snickers bar, Randy heard Maggie's voice come on the line.

"Have you found out anything?" she asked.

"Yes and no," he said around a mouthful of candy. "There are lots of players, but the building is owned by one of Consolidated's holding companies." He took a deep breath. "The vet said Othello's doing better. Do you know what happened?"

"Dr. Lee started to explain, but I don't remember. Sounded like he might have chewed on a cigar or something. Frankly, I was so glad he was all right, I wasn't paying attention. How are your cats?"

"Hanging in." That was all he would allow himself. "Would you ask Sarah to sit tight for a little longer? I'm going to go pay a visit to her curious neighbor."

* * * * *

Randy bounded up the steps and pounded on the apartment door. He took a deep breath, telling himself to act like a cop, not an irate boyfriend. The door opened to a man matching the description Maggie had given him, a beer bottle in one hand. His bloodshot eyes squinted at Randy's badge. The apartment reeked of cigarette smoke, pizza and stale beer.

"Is there a problem, Detective?"

"I hope not, Mr.—"

"Mazzaro. Tony Mazzaro."

"Mr. Mazzaro, are you new to the building?"

"Oh, I don't live here. I've just been waiting for the power hookups and some furniture."

"They do that stuff at eight at night?"

Mazzaro's eyes roamed before they returned to Randy. But his gaze fixed on Randy's chest, not his eyes. Beads of sweat started to pop out along his receding hairline. "Technically, I'm not supposed to be here nights. Only, the missus and I have been having some trouble. This beat a hotel."

"Who hired you?"

"I work for Temps Unlimited. I think Consolidated hired them."

Even from the doorway, Randy could see the binoculars, headphones and a parabolic sound reflector. Fancy techno stuff indeed. Thank you, Maggie.

"You want to explain that?" Randy said, pointing to the dining room. "I've got some concerned neighbors across the way."

The man slumped. "Come in," he said. Randy followed him to one of the two chairs in the room. "I didn't want to do it. But he knew about me and Dolores."

"Let's back up," Randy said. "Who's 'he'?"

"Some guy. Said if I'd keep an eye on the comings and goings in the apartment over there—" he pointed to Sarah's kitchen window "—that he wouldn't tell my wife about the affair I had with Dolores." He gave Randy a pitiful look. "A divorce would kill me."

Yeah, he'd probably have to get a real job. "Who called you?"

"Someone called Adams, I think." He thought a moment. "Yeah. Andrew, maybe. Mostly it was Mister Adams."

"Can you describe him?"

"I've never seen him. It was all done by phone. Said he worked for Consolidated and would get me this assignment and the money was good for sitting around. Then he mailed me pictures of me with Dolores. I had to do what he asked."

"You have the pictures? The envelope?"

"Are you kidding? I burned them."

"What about his phone number?"

"You're not going to arrest me, are you?"

Randy shook his head. "Give me the number. And who gave you the equipment?"

"It was delivered last week. All new, in factory boxes."

"You have the boxes?"

"No, they went out with the trash. But look, you can have all the stuff. I'm out of here tomorrow anyway—the lights and gas are already in and the furniture's coming." He was scribbling something on a scrap of paper and when he finished his eyes finally met Randy's. "You won't tell him I squealed, will you? This is the number I called. I left messages. He called me with instructions and I haven't heard from him since." He handed Randy the paper.

"What sorts of things were you reporting to Mr. Adams?"

Mazzaro ran his fingers around the neck of his t-shirt. "I was supposed to listen to phone calls, see who came and went." He looked up at Randy. "Oh, no, no I never—I didn't—I mean, she's not my type. And she never did anything. Came home, sat at the computer or watched television. I couldn't see into her bedroom. I wouldn't."

"I'll pretend I believe you, Mr. Mazzaro and you're going to go back to your temp agency and ask them for a new assignment."

"Yes, sir. I'm done here tomorrow, anyway." He scuttled to the kitchen and brought a large plastic bag to Randy.

Randy packed the gear into the bag and carried it to his truck, leaving Tony Mazzaro to his misery. On his way back to Maggie's, he punched the phone number Mazzaro had given him into his cell. One ring and a mechanical voice told him to leave his name and number. He didn't.

When Maggie opened the door, Sarah jumped from her perch on the couch. "What did you find out? Can I go home yet?"

Randy got the same rush that he did every time she spoke. Or smiled. Or entered his thoughts. He gave Sarah and Maggie the Tony Mazzaro sob story. "Do you know anyone named Adams?" he said. "Andrew, or Andy?"

Sarah wrinkled her brow. "No, not that I can think of. He's not one of my artists. It's possible he was a customer, but definitely not a regular."

"I'll look into it. You can go home, but I still want you to be careful. For all I know, there will be someone taking this guy's place."

"Stop it," Sarah said. "You're acting like I've got a mad stalker who's going to jump out of the bushes and grab me."

"Why didn't you arrest that peeper?" Maggie asked.

"He hasn't broken the law," Randy said. Much as he wanted to throttle Mazzaro for watching Sarah, his hands were tied.

"What about a restraining order?" Maggie went on. "Has he done anything that would let Sarah get one of those?"

"No, there are no grounds for a restraining order." Randy fumed inwardly. Hell, he didn't even have legal grounds to look for this Adams person. He'd have to bend the rules a little.

Sarah spoke next. "No matter who's behind all this, he's trying to hurt people I'm close to, not me. Face it—the only really hurtful thing he's done has been the cats. Maybe you should be the one looking over your shoulder all the time."

He smiled at the way her eyes flashed bright blue when she was angry. Wanted to wrap her in his arms. Forced himself to be the cop instead. "All right. You win. Sticking to your normal routine is probably the best way to go for now."

"Thank you very much, Detective." She looked at him, then at Maggie. "And if the two of you don't mind, I have a normal routine to return to. Good night." She pushed past him and flounced out the door.

Chapter Thirteen

Randy looked at the clock again. Six forty-five a.m. After a fitful night, filled with erotic dreams quashed by visions of tortured cats, he had given up on sleep at five. He emptied the remains of the cats' food and water dishes into plastic containers, scouted the house and yard for their toys, putting them into a plastic bag. He stopped short when he saw an unfamiliar stuffed mouse. He was sure he knew every feline plaything. It went into its own bag. He wondered if he should send them out to the police lab for testing, or if the vet might be able to run tests at her clinic.

Seven-thirty. He picked up the phone and called the vet. She was with a patient, but she'd call him back when she was free, her assistant said. Randy stuffed all the cats' things into a large paper bag and placed it behind his seat in the truck before driving to work.

He grabbed a cup of coffee in the break room, took a sip and grimaced. All these years and he still couldn't get used to the sludge at the station. He brought his cup to his desk and turned on the computer.

"Hey, Detweiler. How's it going? You gonna shoot me?"

Randy looked up to see Colleen standing in his doorway. "Fine, Mac. And no, I'm not going to shoot you. You did all right."

Colleen looked around, then came in and shut the door. She leaned over the desk. "Be straight with me, Randy. Are you okay?" Her deep green eyes demanded the truth.

Randy looked down at his desk. "I'm dealing with it."

"She's good for you, you know. Let her in."

He paused for a moment, then looked up and stared back into those eyes. "I have." Never mind that this case might end up pushing her away.

"Good. Here are the phone numbers you asked for. Shop and emergency home contacts."

Randy took the list, scanned it and glanced at his watch. He set it by the phone. "Thanks. I owe you."

She punched his shoulder and moved to the door. "Now. Anything else you need—help with the case, escort duty, whatever—just call. I've got to go."

"Be safe," he said. Already dreading the false alarms from those who would call him if a single book was out of place, or a blouse had fallen off a hanger, Randy started calling merchants. He'd barely finished the last call when the phone rang.

"It's Dr. Lee, returning your call. I've identified the poison."

Randy ripped off a clean sheet of paper and clicked his pen open. "What was it?"

"Are you familiar with ciguatera?"

"No. What is it?"

"It's a kind of seafood poisoning."

"How do you spell it?" Randy wrote down Dr. Lee's reply. "Okay. Go on."

"It's caused by a dinoflagellate—"

"Whoa. Slow down. English, please," Randy interrupted.

"Sorry. A microorganism. This one produces a poison, ciguatoxin and all three cats tested positive. The toxin is common in large reef fish, like barracuda and some groupers. One of the early ways that fishermen tested for tainted fish was by feeding it to cats."

"That's terrible."

"I admit, it's not a particularly pleasant thought, but that was the only way they could tell if their catch was safe. "

"So you think someone fed tropical barracuda to my cats?"

"Probably not. There's a synthetic toxin. While I was in vet school, I worked in a local lab that manufactures test kits. They used a synthetic in the process."

"How local?"

"It's in Portland. Med-Tekke Industries. I can give you their number."

"Thanks." Randy wrote down the number she dictated. He'd call them later.

Dr. Lee went on. "Othello is recovering quickly, but apparently your cats ingested a much higher dose. It wouldn't take much—the synthetic is highly concentrated. I can't lie to you, Detective, their condition is critical. But the fact that they're still fighting is a good sign."

Randy's throat tightened. "I see," he managed. A sip of coffee helped. "Dr. Lee, if I brought you the cats' toys, their food and water, would you be able to test for this poison?"

"I should."

"I'm on my way." Randy snatched his jacket and dashed to his truck.

On the drive, the churning in his gut was back, but this was the feeling he got when he was following a lead. At the vet's office, Randy approached the receptionist. "I was speaking to Dr. Lee about testing for poisons."

"She's expecting you. Why don't you have a seat?"

Dr. Lee appeared moments later. "You can come back now, Mr. Detweiler." She held the door for him.

Randy gathered his paraphernalia and followed the doctor to her office, her rubber soles squeaking softly on the tile floor. She motioned Randy to a chair and took a seat behind her desk.

Finding Sarah

Randy got right to business, laying his packages on her desk. "I brought their food, water and all their toys." He pointed at the mouse in the plastic bag. "I don't recognize this one. I'd suggest you start there. Please keep everything in case we need it as evidence."

"I'll get to it tonight. I'll call as soon as I know anything." She stood and looked at him, a solemn expression in her deep brown eyes. "Would you like to see your cats?"

"Please." Fighting the feeling that he'd be saying goodbye, he followed her down the hall.

She stopped in front of a large door with a glass window. "They're semi-comatose, so don't be alarmed if they don't respond." When she pushed the door open, he followed her into a narrow room with a bank of stainless steel cages along the far wall. The antiseptic smell was stronger here and the sweat trickled down his neck.

Dr. Lee unfastened the front of the first cage. Starsky lay there, an IV dripping into his front leg, the neon green bandage in stark contrast to his black fur. "Can I touch him?" Randy asked.

"Of course," Dr. Lee said. "I have to get back to my appointments, but Heather's here to answer any questions."

"Thank you. For everything." Randy reached into the cage and stroked Starsky with an index finger. "Hi, guy. They're taking good care of you." His voice caught and he swallowed hard. "You rest and get well, okay?" He did the same for Hutch and stood in front of their cages for several minutes, watching their small chests rise and fall with each breath. Before he left, he glanced at Heather. She gave him a sympathetic smile. He couldn't muster one in return.

Randy walked out to the parking lot and looked at his watch. Nine-twenty-three. This was going to be a long day.

* * * * *

Randy sat in his truck for a full ten minutes before went inside. Head lowered, he hurried to his office and shut the door. Thank goodness Kovak was still on vacation—he had the place to himself.

Work. He needed to work. He looked at the pile of papers on his desk. One thing at a time. Prioritize.

Timberline Lodge confirmed Billy Brandt worked for them, but he'd been giving lessons at the time of the phone call. Scratch him from the list. A call to the receptionist at Consolidated told him they had three employees named Adams, two male, one female, none named Andrew and that the phone number Mazzaro had given him wasn't one of theirs. He'd started looking through phone directories and reverse directories when the chief called.

"In my office."

Randy went to Laughlin's office, tapping on the doorjamb before walking in.

Laughlin looked up from his files. "Fill me in on your Gertie case. Woodford has her, right?"

"Yes and no. They have her for the Woodford and Cottonwood robberies. She's not the person who held up Sarah Tucker's store."

"What about the robberies in town last year? Did she do those?"

"I'm still working on that." Randy studied his fingernails. "I blew it, Chief. I brought Sarah Tucker to Woodford for a lineup. I was sure she'd ID the woman and that I could use that ID to connect her to Consolidated. I didn't check with the other victims first. But I'm doing that today. I need to pull some comparables from our photo files for an ID."

"Not like you, Detweiler."

Randy looked up. "I jumped to a conclusion and left out some steps. Won't happen again."

"You're damn right it won't happen again. You know better than to get involved. I want reports on all your open cases before I go home. And I'm planning to go home early today."

So much for following up on Adams. "Yes, sir. On my way." Randy got up to leave.

"Detweiler."

Randy turned back. "Sir?"

"You don't look so good. Are you all right?"

He hesitated. "Someone poisoned my cats. I was up most of the night."

A few of the lines in Laughlin's face dissolved. "You know who?"

"No, but I'll bet a week's pay there's a connection. One of Ms. Tucker's neighbors—her cat was at the vet with the same symptoms."

"Look into it." He paused. "Oh and I just remembered something else I have to get done before I go home. End of the day for those reports will be fine."

"Right." Randy walked double time back to his desk and pulled the files on the other three Gracious Gertie cases. He took the photo of Gertie and brought it to the clerk. "I need you to find me four other women of similar height and build. Hair color doesn't matter—she wore wigs. Full body and head shots. Bring them to me ASAP." Nothing like a chewing out from the Chief to help you focus.

* * * * *

Sarah hung up the phone and put away her bank statement, satisfied that she was in control. For the first time since the robbery, she felt like Sarah. Randy hadn't called with an update on her case. Maybe she'd pissed him off last night, but she was tired of letting everyone else tell her how to live her life.

It was almost five when he called. She could hear the exhaustion in his voice. "I'm still wading through paperwork, but my eyes are crossing, I'm starving and...I miss you."

All testiness floated away like a carnival balloon. Give him a break. The man had finally dealt with his grandmother's death, his cats were barely alive and he was doing his job. "I miss you, too. I should be free by five-thirty. Want to meet at Sadie's then?"

"I had something else in mind. I thought we'd go to Martinelli's."

"Martinelli's?" Quiet, private, on the outskirts of town, someplace where his shaky hold on his emotions wouldn't be in plain view. She warmed at the idea that she wouldn't have to avoid Randy entirely while her case was still open. After all, he'd laid those ground rules, so he ought to know what was acceptable.

But Martinelli's was where she and David had shared special dinners, including one shortly before he'd died. And it was one of Chris' favorite hangouts as well. The thought of the two of them bumping into each other was not something she wanted to deal with. She searched her mind for an alternative. "I'm not in the mood for Italian," she countered. "What about Rob's?" It was even more remote and likely to be nearly empty early on a Monday.

"That'll work, too."

"I'll be waiting." As she went through her closing procedures, Randy's grief wouldn't leave her alone. She knew all too well that leaping back into work masked the symptoms, it didn't cure.

At the tap on the front door, Sarah peeked through the window and felt a smile spread across her face. There was no mistaking Randy's silhouette and she unlocked the door. Her grin faded as she saw the slumped shoulders, the dark circles under his eyes. She ached for him.

Finding Sarah

He gave her a smile, one that shone over his exhaustion. "You ready?"

She nodded. "Are you sure you're up to this? You look a little...tired."

"You mean I look like hell, but yes, I'm up to this. And you look lovely, by the way."

"Thanks." Randy's touch as he helped with her coat sent goose bumps down to her toes. She shivered.

"You cold?"

"No. Quite the contrary." She smiled up at him and they walked down the block to his truck. "Nice clear evening," Sarah said, trying to find something neutral to talk about. "Look at the stars peeking through."

"Should be even better when we get to Rob's." Randy's truck lights flashed as he used the remote to unlock the door. He pulled it open for her and extended his hand. "Watch your step."

When he climbed behind the wheel, Sarah studied him in the overhead light of the truck's cab. His eyes were bloodshot and the muscles in his jaw moved as he clenched and unclenched his teeth. Then the light went off and he was in shadows.

"Randy, we don't have to do this."

"Drop it, okay. You deal with things your way, I'll deal with them my way. Besides, don't you want to know what I found out?"

"Of course, but we don't need to go to Rob's for that."

"Look, I'm tired. And hungry. You're not the only one who gets too busy for meals. Rob's isn't that far. We'll be there in twenty minutes."

Sarah conceded and twisted in her seat so she faced Randy. "Tell me what you detected, then."

"Good news first. Mazzaro's story checked out. Consolidated owns the building and plans to use the apartment to house new employees until they find somewhere to live, since they haven't been able to rent the place in over a year. You shouldn't have any more people looking in your window."

"I'm glad."

"But if the guy who broke into your apartment was part of the Mazzaro scheme, it looks like all he got was your computer files."

Might as well tell him now. "Umm...maybe not."

His head whipped toward her. "What do you mean?"

"I got my bank statement today and noticed that there was a fee for online banking, which I don't use. I figured it was a mistake and called the bank to get the charge removed. They said I'd activated it last Tuesday."

The day of the break-in. "Why didn't you call me?"

"You had enough to deal with. Besides, I'm not in the habit of calling the police to help me with my finances, thank you very much. I've managed just fine on my own."

His jaw was working again. "I shouldn't have missed it." She saw his knuckles whiten on the steering wheel.

"You're like everyone else, caught up in the internet. I'm not. I have a bare-bones dial-up I use for email, maybe ten minutes a day. You know, some people still use things like checks and paper bank statements. Easy enough for anyone to open my desk drawers and see my records. Since I didn't have an online account, he didn't need to hack in. He just created one using my information. But, it's over, it's done, it's fixed. No harm, no foul and can we move on?"

"This is part of an ongoing investigation. I'm supposed to be kept informed."

"I'm informing you now. I know the bank tellers and they said they'd make sure nobody could access my accounts. And tomorrow I'll go change them. The bank will do a full investigation. See. I took care of it. All by myself."

"Sarah, I have a job to do."

"And I have mine and banking is part of it. It's done." She turned to watch the trees speed by the side of the road.

*****

They walked across Rob's unpaved parking lot, Sarah half skipping to keep up with Randy's long stride. As they climbed the wooden steps to the entryway, Sarah felt Randy's hand on the small of her back. When he held the door for her, she realized that she hadn't been this comfortable, this much a part of someone else's life, in over a year. It felt good. Before Randy opened the door to the restaurant, Sarah stopped him. "I'm sorry I snapped at you."

"We're both strung a little tight. I'm sorry, too."

Comfortably ensconced in a booth, Sarah leaned forward. "Did the vet ever get back to you about the poison?"

"She knows what it was, so she's treating the cats. I brought her all their paraphernalia and she's going to check for poison tonight." He squeezed the bridge of his nose before looking back at her. "I saw them. Hooked up to IVs. Helpless. They didn't know I was there." His voice cracked.

"They'll make it."

A bored-looking waiter hovered by the table. "Getcha something to drink?"

"A glass of white wine for me," Sarah said. She looked up at Randy, who was staring at the table.

"Club soda," he said without raising his eyes.

"Gotcha. Be right back," the waiter said. He plopped two menus on the table and shuffled away.

Randy buried himself behind his menu and Sarah studied hers without speaking.

Once they had their drinks and ordered their meals, Sarah moved the candle aside and grasped Randy's hands, wondering if her tiny hands could offer the comfort she felt when his enveloped hers. His long, tapered fingers, with hints of calloused roughness, seemed more like the hands of an artist than a cop.

She gave a squeeze. "Now. Why don't you give me the bad news about Gertie? Make it official."

"I think you guessed it. All three of the other shopkeepers picked her out of the stack of photos without a moment's hesitation. Gracious Gertie is in custody in Woodford. I have no idea who robbed you."

Although she had expected it, a wave of dismay sluiced over her like a waterfall. "What now?"

Randy took a gulp of his club soda. "I keep working."

The waiter returned and placed salads and a basket of hot sourdough bread in front of them. Sarah lifted the basket, savoring the tangy aroma of the bread. "For now, let's forget work and enjoy the meal." She offered the basket to Randy. He pulled out a piece and slathered it with butter, holding it poised in front of his mouth, waiting for her.

"Eat. Don't wait for me. I'm enjoying my wine," she said.

Randy started his salad, accompanied by the crunch of the crusty bread.

When the waiter brought their entrees, Sarah watched as Randy attacked his chicken. The man must have been starving. Even small talk seemed too much of an effort for him. He ate with undisguised relish, his enjoyment sensual. Sarah worked on her salmon and left him to his meal.

After declining dessert, Sarah looked at Randy. Some of the strain had left his face, but the exhaustion was still there. "We'd better be going," she said. "You could use some sleep."

Randy set down his coffee cup and motioned for the check. He wiped his mouth with his napkin. "You're right." Randy pulled out his wallet, left some bills on the table and stood up. "Shall we go?"

"You know," Sarah said. "I've been alone in that apartment for over fifteen months now. I think being scared and angry last night was a lot easier than all those nights of feeling abandoned and alone."

Randy squeezed her shoulder. "You should feel safe and warm at home, not scared, angry, abandoned or alone."

Sarah allowed some of her weight to rest against Randy and a few more butterflies were laid to rest. They stepped outside and lingered on the restaurant porch for a moment. She looked up at the sky. "All that's missing is a full moon."

Randy laid a hand on her shoulder. "That's about a week and a half away. Maybe we can come back."

"I'll put it on my calendar."

Sarah took his arm and started down the steps. The restaurant had never filled and Randy's truck was off by itself in the parking lot. They stood beside his truck and he opened her door. Before she climbed in, she looked up at him. "I need a favor. A big one."

"Just ask, Sarah."

"Can you look at David's accident? I mean, you're a cop and you must have access to stuff regular people, even a private investigator, wouldn't. I know it wasn't suicide."

Her heart sank when he stiffened and pulled away. His lips formed a straight line and his eyebrows came together. She blinked back her embarrassment. "I understand if you don't want to."

"It's just—are you sure you really want to know? Could you deal with it if it was suicide?"

"I've dealt with it every day since he died. The not knowing is worse. I'll live with the truth."

Randy took her hands in his. "I'll see. There's only so much digging I can do. It's not a Pine Hills case, it's closed and real life cops can't work like they do on television. Our hours are accounted for. And some of the databases require my name and a case number and they're audited randomly. It's supposed to make sure we don't start poking around for personal reasons. I've kind of pushed the envelope already looking for stuff that's not tied to your robbery."

She felt a flush rise to her face. "I'm sorry. I didn't know. I don't want you to get into trouble."

He pulled her toward him and she buried her face in his chest. The scent of his spicy aftershave and the beating of his heart calmed her.

"I'll see what I can do on my own time. Things aren't too busy now, but I don't want you to get your hopes up."

"Thanks."

"We should be going."

"Right." She reached for the grab bar. His hand at her elbow made her feel safe. He closed the door and she watched him walk around the truck. His eyes never left hers, even though she doubted he could see her in the dark cab. The light came on when he opened his door and she couldn't keep a smile from rising to her lips as he eased himself behind the wheel.

Randy put the key in the ignition but made no move to start the truck. Instead, he leaned over and kissed her. Sarah returned the kiss, butterflies replaced by an entirely different sort of fluttering. She felt his tongue probing, heard his breathing accelerate. She enjoyed one long, coffee-flavored moment before she forced herself to pull away.

"Please. Let's go. We both know this isn't right."

Chapter Fourteen

When he awoke the next morning, Randy found himself in bed, fully clothed, with no recollection of how he got there. The last thing he remembered was driving back from Sarah's and collapsing on the couch. A long, hot shower and a steamy cup of black coffee returned the soul to his body and he was able to think clearly.

Sarah had been right to break things off last night. She was using her brain and he was using something a lot lower down. Yet there was something about the way she invaded his thoughts when he least expected it. This must be what Gram had meant all those times she'd said, "You'll know it when it's right. You can't explain it, but you'll know it."

Randy popped two waffles into the toaster, ate them while he waited for two more to finish heating to eat on the road, and left for work. He had a good feeling about the day.

He twirled his Rolodex and found the number for Matt Dobrovsky.

"Long time no hear, Detweiler. What's up?" Dobrovsky's gravelly voice spoke of too many cigars and too much Johnny Walker, but the retired cop knew what he was doing.

"You remember the Tucker case? Suicide about fifteen months ago?"

"Yeah. Too bad. She was a basket case, but the pieces seemed to fit—nothing I could refute."

"Talk to me. O'Farrell's at six?"

"You buying?"

"Of course."

"I'll be there."

That good feeling evaporated when Laughlin caught him in the break room before Randy had finished pouring his coffee. "My office."

Randy followed him down the hall and took a seat. Laughlin settled in behind his desk.

"How's your little investigation coming?" Laughlin asked. "Anything more concrete?"

"Still trying to find out who Brandt and Adams might be."

"It'll have to wait. We had five break-ins last night and Kovak can't handle all of them. He's got the reports. He'll fill you in."

Randy's stomach sank, but he knew he'd been lucky to have as much time for Sarah's case as he'd had. "Yes, Chief. I'm on it."

He found his younger colleague at his desk in their shared workspace, file folders strewn over its surface. "Welcome back, partner. How was San Diego?"

"A lot warmer than here. Looks like I got back from vacation just in time." He gathered the folders and handed them to Randy.

Randy took the files to his desk, perching on its edge. "Didn't I tell you about fair skin and sunscreen? You look like a boiled lobster. And your nose is peeling."

"Who thinks about sunscreen when you go to a theme park? It's not like I was at the beach."

Randy waggled the folders. "You think these are all related?"

"Doesn't look like it. What's your load like?" Kovak pulled the folders from Randy's hand.

"Lots of phone and paperwork and no court for a change. They caught Gertie in Woodford, by the way."

"That's great, but too bad it wasn't your collar."

"Turns out one of the Gertie robberies was a copycat. I'm back to square one with that one, but I have a couple of leads."

"Tell you what," Kovak said, separating the folders. "I'll take these three. They seem totally unrelated and they're all over town. He handed Randy two folders. "These burglaries are close by and seem to be the work of kids. Sherman and Zimmer. Malicious mischief, I'd guess. You could be back by noon."

"I owe you one. No, I owe you two." Randy sat at his desk for a few minutes, reviewing the files. Entry made via broken windows in the back of two houses a few blocks apart. Kitchens were trashed, only small things stolen. The owners were still trying to verify what was missing. He gave his phone a reluctant glance before getting into his truck. He'd start at the Zimmer's.

* * * * *

It was almost four o'clock when Randy staggered back into his office. He pulled back his chair and sank into it, leaning his elbows on his desk and pressing the heels of his hands against his eyelids.

His head throbbed and he'd missed lunch again. Like he'd thought, none of the other merchants had found any damage he could relate to Sarah's. But four had insisted he come see them in person, just in case. And then there was what he'd coined his Kitchen Caper case.

"Just getting back?" came Kovak's voice from the next desk.

Randy glared at him. "If you're finished with those other three cases, I don't want to hear it. I no longer owe you anything. What a mess."

"Hey, how was I supposed to know? I've got someone in custody for the smash and grab at the hardware store. The real estate office turned out to be someone trying to get even with her ex for selling the house below market value and I'm following up a pretty good lead with the insurance company."

Randy wadded up a piece of paper and threw it at his smirking partner. "Shut up. The parents were useless, so I spent the afternoon at the high school. God, you need permission from the tooth fairy to talk to those kids. And rude. Shit, I'd have been grounded for a month if I'd talked to an adult that way." He massaged his temples, trying to rub away the pounding.

Randy shook three aspirin out of the bottle he kept in his desk and headed for the break room, stopping on the way at the water fountain to swallow the pills. He poured a cup of muddy coffee, stuck some coins into the vending machine and extracted a bag of peanuts. He wasn't going to be good for much until the aspirin kicked in, but he was determined to make time for Sarah's case before he went home.

Randy scanned his messages and stared at the one from Dr. Lee. With clammy hands, he punched in her number, his pulse racing as he waited to be connected.

"I'm sorry I missed your call," Randy said. "Did you find the poison?"

"You were right about the mouse toy. It was stuffed with catnip and the stuffing was saturated with the toxin. It wouldn't take much, I'm afraid."

He envisioned Starsky and Hutch in catnip-induced rapture. Took a shaky breath. "They love their catnip. Thank you, Doctor. I appreciate the trouble you went to."

"No trouble at all. And I'll certainly call you if I see any more cases."

"Thanks, but I don't expect you will." Randy paused before asking his question. "How are Starsky and Hutch?"

"No change, but that's not a bad thing at this point. The next couple of days should tell."

Randy thanked her and hung up the phone to find Kovak had stopped his typing and was staring at him.

"Couldn't help but overhear. Starsky and Hutch? Someone poisoned them? That sucks."

"They're hanging on," Randy said.

"Damn, I'm sorry. Anything I can do?"

"Thanks, but I'm on it. Checked with neighbors. Nobody saw anything unusual. But I'm going to get the bastard, don't worry about that."

"If you want me to cover any of your caseload, or help put this guy away, just ask."

"Thanks. I've got things under control for the moment." Randy reached for the pink slips again, looking to see if Med-Tekke might have returned his call as well. Nothing. He glanced at his watch. Four-thirty. He could still reach someone. He was about to place the call when a buzzing in the back of his mind reached the surface.

"Kovak? The break-in at the insurance company. Which one?"

"Oregon Trust. Why?"

"Just wondering. What happened?"

"Someone came in through a bathroom window, vandalized the copy machine, spray-painted the walls, trashed most of the computers, ransacked files. Big mess."

"And you said you have leads?"

"One or two. Couple of big claims were denied recently. I'm looking to see if someone's getting even. Hey, at least these guys ought to have insurance, right?" He laughed. "And besides, all their records are backed up at the main office in Portland, so it's not like anyone is going to be without proof of insurance or anything." Kovak walked to the door and picked up his sport coat. "I'm out of here for tonight. See you tomorrow. And let me know if you want me to cover those other break-ins."

The buzzing got louder. Oregon Trust. Sarah's insurance company. But it was probably the insurance company of half the businesses in town. Another coincidence? Maybe he'd offer to trade cases with Kovak. He thought again. Better to let Kovak investigate. If there was a connection to Sarah's troubles, Kovak would be the visible one.

He picked up the phone and called Mr. Yamaguchi at Med-Tekke.

"Yes, Detective. I'm sorry I haven't been able to get back to you. What exactly do you want to know?"

"You manufacture test kits for ciguatera, right?"

"That's right. One of only a few companies that do, I might add."

"That's very good, I'm sure. But, tell me. In order to make the test kits, don't you need a source of the toxin?"

"Yes and that's one of the things that we're proud of. We've been able to synthesize a chemical that is virtually identical to ciguatoxin."

"You manufacture this in your plant?"

"We do. May I ask why you are inquiring? Is there a problem?"

"I'm not sure. What kind of security measures do you have in place? Could someone walk out with some of the toxin?" Randy waited out the silence on the other end of the line.

"I see. So you believe someone has taken our product and used it improperly. You understand that ciguatera is a bothersome illness, but is not usually fatal and is treatable."

For humans, Randy thought, as Mr. Yamaguchi went on. Not cats.

"Our research is designed to make sure that any fish reaching the market are safe to eat. And, I assure you, we exceed every government security standard."

"Mr. Yamaguchi, I do understand. However, we've had a case where some cats have been poisoned and the poison has been identified as ciguatoxin. As you've said, there aren't a lot of the right kind of fish on the Oregon coast. I'm looking for a possible source and your lab came up."

"I find it hard to believe that any of our employees would remove any toxin from the lab. They know the importance of our integrity."

"But could they?"

"Detective, I'm sure someone in your position knows that an enterprising person is capable of doing almost anything."

"Anybody named Brandt work for you? Or Adams?"

"Give me a moment."

Randy waited and a few minutes later, Mr. Yamaguchi reported that no employees by those names worked for Med-Tekke. Why wasn't he surprised? "I'd like a roster of any employees with access to the toxin, please. Names, addresses, phone numbers." If those didn't pan out, he'd start working his way down the ranks.

"Of course. I can fax it to you."

"Thank you." Randy dictated the number. "One more question, Mr. Yamaguchi. Is Med-Tekke privately owned?"

"Oh, no. We're a subsidiary of Consolidated Enterprises."

"Thank you. You've been very helpful. I'll be in touch if I need anything more." His headache showed no signs of abating. Randy rubbed his temples again. Maybe some fresh air would help. He walked out to the back parking lot and leaned against his truck. In an almost unconscious motion, he pulled out his cell phone and called Sarah. His spirits lifted when he heard her voice.

"You have some news? Anything to do with my case? Oh God, not your cats."

"No, they're hanging on. And I think I know where the poison came from. Now I have to figure out who took it."

"That's a start, isn't it."

"Yes. A start. But I caught another case and I'm going to be working late again."

"Another robbery?"

"A burglary, to be technical, since nobody was home. Some kids, probably. Minor theft—mostly they trashed the kitchens."

After a brief silence, Sarah spoke again. "Are you busy Friday night?"

"No. But that comes with the standard issue cop disclaimer, 'unless something comes up'. Why?"

"Maggie has two tickets to a community theater production in Cottonwood, but she can't make it. Would you like to go? Or, does going to a play violate that open case thing you have?"

Guilt appeared and dissolved like cotton candy. Damn, he wanted to be with her. "No. Sounds great." Anything with Sarah sounded great. And by Friday, he might have found the copycat Gertie. "What time?"

"The play starts at seven-thirty."

"Tell you what. I'll pick you up at five-thirty. We can drive to Cottonwood, have dinner and still be in plenty of time."

Randy looked up to see a uniformed officer motioning to him from the back door. "Gotta run. See you Friday." He stuffed the phone in his pocket and jogged back.

"What's up?" he asked the officer.

"Someone was here to see you about those kitchen break-ins. Menendez, she said. She wouldn't stay, but she said to give you this." He handed Randy a neatly folded piece of paper.

"A kid?"

"No, older woman. Hispanic."

Finding Sarah

Randy thought about his visit to the Shermans and the Zimmers. The Shermans had a Hispanic maid. She'd been cleaning up the mess in the kitchen when he'd come by and didn't seem too happy about it. He unfolded the paper and saw three Greek letters on it. A fraternity?

Randy dashed to the front of the building and recognized the maid getting on a bus. He looked at the paper again. Delta Theta Delta. Maybe he could clean this one up quickly after all.

* * * * *

Randy sat in the corner booth and watched Matt Dobrovsky work his bulk between the high-top tables of O'Farrell's. The bear-like man stopped to clap a shoulder or shake a hand as he passed old colleagues. He picked up a bowl of peanuts. By the time he made his way to the back of the room, the waitress had delivered their drinks.

Randy stood. "Good to see you, Dobs. Thanks for coming."

Dobrovsky shook Randy's outstretched hand and eased into the booth. Bushy white eyebrows lifted as he sniffed the drink that waited for him. "You must need something big to spring for a single malt."

Randy raised his beer glass. "It's been too long. You're looking good."

Dobrovsky's eyes, a shade or two darker than the whiskey he drank, disappeared when he laughed, which he did with gusto. "I'm looking older. But, yeah, I don't miss the stress. He ran his palm over his silver buzz cut. Too bad all the gray I earned on the job didn't go away, too." Dobrovsky chomped on a cigar in between sips of his whiskey while they exchanged the usual pleasantries.

"You gonna light that thing?" Randy asked. He worked on his beer and munched on peanuts.

The old man took the stogie from his mouth and guffawed.

"Doctor says I can't smoke these, but he didn't say nothing about chewing 'em. Can't think right without one." He set the cigar down in the ashtray. "Let's cut to the chase. You didn't call me here to just to buy me a drink, Detweiler. What do you need?"

"I need your gut on that suicide."

Dobrovsky grinned and patted his rotund belly. "Got a lot more gut since I quit the force."

"Tell me what you know."

"Honest gut reaction—I'd say it was fifty-fifty. But Polk said suicide, the insurance agreed and I didn't have anything concrete. That poor girl could have spent every dime she had and it still might not have given her the answer she wanted. Is she all right?"

Randy took a sip of his beer. "She's living with guilt. You know the drill—that suspicion that she might have had something to do with it."

"Not to mention she's out the insurance money."

Randy shook his head. "I don't think that's her main concern."

Those whiskey eyes squinted across the table in the subdued lighting of the bar. "She was a sweet kid. I'm thinking you think so, too."

"Remind me not to play poker with you."

"Remind me to invite you to the next game." Dobs plopped a folder onto the table. "These are my notes. Ms. Tucker has a copy. You could have asked her. She's a lot prettier than I am."

"I don't want her to know I'm meeting you—or that I might ask you to take another look, if you think it's warranted. She doesn't like charity."

"I don't know. The car had stopped at a pull-out. It had been raining pretty hard. Maybe the guy wanted to wait until it let up. Visibility would have been almost nil. It honestly looked

Finding Sarah

like he'd stopped while he got up the guts to go over. Taped something heavy to the accelerator, released the brake and let it fly. ME's report was consistent with that sudden stop at the bottom of a hill. Or, in this case, the trunk of a tree."

Randy cringed at the matter-of-fact way Dobs referred to the death, but knew it was a common enough defense mechanism. Kept things impersonal. "Did they find pills?"

"No bottle, but if it'd been loose in the vehicle, it could have flown and disappeared."

"He have a prescription for them?"

"Nothing local, but you know damn well you can buy that crap on the internet."

"Sounds like you did your usual good job."

Dobrovsky shrugged. "But—I did wonder if there wasn't something hinky with the trooper. Darnell."

"Hinky?"

"He was in a hurry to sew it up. I mean, I was as ready as the next guy to turn in the badge after I did my time, but he might have missed something."

"You think he did?" Randy turned the beer glass in his hands.

"Kid, the only reason they got anything at all was because the car hung on a tree for a couple of hours. Rain, mud and whoosh." Dobrovsky's hand swept up and then downward. "The car was history. Rocks, trees, ravines—there were bits and pieces everywhere. No telling what came from the car and what came from people dumping trash over the side of the road. Nobody could do anything in that storm and the suicide evidence was enough for Darnell."

Randy leaned forward. "Would it have been enough for you?"

"Sitting here, I'd say no. In a rainstorm, a week from retirement, I don't know what I'd have done. I know they checked out possible homicide. I might have worked that angle a little more. But the man-hours it would have taken to ferret out what belonged to the accident and what didn't and all the CSI expenses — I can't say I blame them. I came in way after the fact. Monday morning quarterbacks don't win football games."

"What do you know about Darnell?"

"Good officer by reputation. I heard he came into some money right about the time he retired. Rumor has it he's on some tropical beach drinking fancy concoctions with umbrellas in them ogling half-naked broads. Lucky man."

Dobrovsky finished his drink and clapped the glass onto the table. "Thanks for the drink, kid."

"Can I get you another?" Randy asked.

"Nah — I've got to get back to Carla." He gave Randy a broad grin. "Retirement's done some good things on the home front."

"Hey, thanks for the time."

"No problem. Call if you need anything else." Dobs squeezed out of the booth and headed for the door, stopping to chat with more old friends at the bar on his way.

Randy sat and finished his beer, trying to digest the information Dobs had given him. Something roiled his gut like a bad clam in a bowl of chowder.

Chapter Fifteen

Sarah hurried to put away the last of the St. Michael's clay sculptures, remembering how Randy had come in and helped her last week. Chris would be waiting in the parking lot. The sooner she got this dinner over with, the better she'd feel. Normally, she'd have had a free dinner in the cafeteria—a perk of her volunteering, if you could call their food a perk. Still, the price was right. Only Chris' refusal to tell her what the legal department had said about Diana's letter until she had dinner with him had convinced her to accept his invitation.

She let her memory drift back to last night in Rob's parking lot. To the pleasure of Randy's kiss. But she'd sworn to herself that they should slow down, that she and Randy were rushing into things. Both of them were dealing with emotional issues. Were they just reaching out for comfort, or did they have true feelings for each other? Distance, she'd told herself. And then she turned right around and invited Randy on a date. But that wasn't until Friday and here she was, having dinner with Chris.

She finger combed her hair, slipped into her coat and took a deep breath. Please, let him tell her that Diana didn't have a leg to stand on.

The Eclipse's lights flashed across the parking lot and she trotted over. Chris had the passenger door open for her. Other than a package of Big Red gum on the dash, his car was immaculate. When she'd had a car, it was more like a purse on wheels. She picked up the gum and tossed it into a well of the console.

"Help yourself," Chris said. "Can't seem to give it up, but it beats smoking."

"No, thanks." She adjusted the seat belt, holding her purse in her lap and staring straight ahead. "Where are we going?"

"Won't change your mind about Martinelli's? It's not that late."

"No, I told you. I'm tired and I wanted something close…and casual." No dark rooms illuminated with candles. Something bright, businesslike. This was a business dinner. Nothing more.

"Then it's the Wagon Wheel. They can manage a halfway decent steak." Chris flipped on his blinker and turned the corner. Sarah wasn't surprised that he found a parking place right in front of the restaurant, or that he could parallel park and end up exactly the same distance between the cars in front and behind him.

Once they were seated, Chris ordered a bottle of wine and some potato skins. Sarah flashed back to their dating days. Had he ever let her order for herself? But then, she had to admit, all they ate was burgers or pizza. She buried herself in the menu, determined to choose something different. "I'm going to have the shrimp kabobs."

"At a steakhouse? Besides, I ordered a Cabernet. Let me order the rib eye for you. You'll love it."

"I feel like shrimp tonight." She closed her menu and set it at the edge of the table.

The wine came, Chris proclaimed it satisfactory and the waiter poured two glasses. Sarah took a deep sip, letting the tannins sit on her tongue for a moment before swallowing.

"It should breathe for a few minutes," Chris said. "And I wanted to propose a toast. I think I've found the solution to your problems."

Sarah's mood brightened. She hadn't dared hope that Diana couldn't demand her share of the shop. But maybe Chris' connections had found a loophole. "Really? Tell me." She raised her glass.

Finding Sarah

Chris tapped his against it and took a sip of his wine. "I want to help you. You don't want my charity. I've finally figured that out." He smiled and reached in his breast pocket. "But if we're a team, it's a partnership, not charity."

"What do you mean? Partnership?" She took a huge gulp of her wine.

Chris pulled out the blue envelope Sarah had given him. "I ran this by our legal department and they said she can pretty much do what it says."

"Pretty much? That means they found some loophole, right?"

"Not exactly a loophole. But if you'll check your contract, they said there's almost always a grace period of half the payment cycle. So you'd have some extra time."

His green eyes sparkled. "But what if I buy her out? She gets her money, she's off your back and I'm a business partner."

Sarah's heart stopped. She felt her mouth opening and closing. Afraid she looked like a dying fish, she clamped her lips together. Grateful for the waiter's arrival with their food, Sarah gave Chris a nod. Business partners. Even an eighty-twenty split was too much. He'd want more. More from her, she knew it. "That's very generous, Chris, but—"

"You don't have to say anything right now, Sarah. But think about it. I'm sure once you look at the options, it'll make perfect sense. We're good together. We always have been. Let me help."

"I'll think about it. I've paid her for this month, so I'm fine for now." She worked a shrimp off the skewer. Somewhere, she unearthed the strength to look him in the eyes. "But it would be business. Nothing more and I'd run the shop. If I'm going to consider it at all, you'd have to agree to be a silent partner."

"As a mouse, Sarah." He reached across the table and squeezed her hand.

Sarah heard Chris' voice, saw that the food on her plate had diminished, but she had no recollection of the conversation or the taste of the meal. She looked at the empty wine bottle.

She pushed her plate away. "I'm stuffed." The boulder in her belly had displaced any room for food.

"No dessert? They have a great chocolate mousse pie."

"No, thanks."

"I'll order one and we can share." He motioned to the waiter.

Well, if nothing else, Chris couldn't read her face the way Randy could. If he could, he'd never have that eager puppy-dog look. Puppy dog. She thought of the cats. Could this man have deliberately poisoned cats? Why did Randy think Chris would rob her or poison house pets? It made no sense.

The pie arrived and the waiter set an extra fork in front of Sarah. She toyed with it while Chris ate, refusing his urges to taste. "Do you have any pets?" she asked.

He wiped his mouth and looked at her, a puzzled expression on his face. "No, I'm on the road a lot. Irregular hours. Why?"

"I don't know. I was thinking about getting a kitten." She studied his face for some kind of reaction, but saw nothing.

He forked up another piece of pie chewed and swallowed. "I guess I think of myself as a dog person, but if you wanted a cat, I'd be fine with it." He reached across the table and took her hand. "I'd do anything for you. For us."

Oh, God. Had he thought she was talking about them, as in a couple? He most certainly couldn't read her face, or he'd see the dismay. "There's no *us*. Not the kind of *us* I think you mean." She felt his hands tighten around hers. "I value our friendship, but I don't want you to think it can be more than that. Even if I take your offer, it will be strictly business and I need time to think about it."

She pulled her hand away and excused herself. "I'll just be a minute. I'll meet you at the door." She stood, definitely feeling the effects of the wine. She had no idea how much of the bottle she'd drunk—either the waiter or Chris had kept her glass full. Feeling lightheaded, she wove her way through the restaurant to the ladies' room.

As she washed her hands, Sarah stared at her reflection. Too pale. Worry and lack of sleep were etched on her face. She knew she could never live with Chris owning a single bit of her shop. What had she done? What if Diana accepted his offer? All she could think about was Chris, slowly inching his way into the running of the shop. Choosing her merchandise the way he chose her dinners, or the clothes he wanted her to wear. Although, in all fairness, he had found some decent artists.

And then memories of her conversation with Randy hit her like a two-by-four across the skull. Survivor's guilt, he'd called it. Of course. Chris had recommended the artist David saw the day he died. Chris felt guilty. That was why he'd become so persistent after David died. She'd make him see there was no need to blame himself. That she could hang on without him. She freshened her lipstick and went to find Chris.

She listened to him chatter as they drove home, trying to tune him out and collect her thoughts. Just tell him. But the words wouldn't come. He parked the Eclipse in the alley behind her house. She opened her door before he had a chance to. As she swung her legs around and got to her feet, she wobbled a little and felt his arm at her waist.

"A little too much wine, Sarah? Let me help you."

"I'm fine," she said. But she gripped the handrail as she made her way up the stairs. At her door, she turned to face Chris, forcing herself to speak. "Thanks for everything." She formed her words carefully, hearing them from a distance. "You don't have to feel bad, you know. It wasn't your fault."

"What are you talking about?"

"David. You feel guilty, that's all. It's called survivor's guilt. Randy explained it." Oops. She wasn't going to talk about Randy in front of Chris. Too late. "Just because you gave him the name of that artist, it wasn't your fault. I don't blame you. So you don't have any obligation to help me."

She squinted to see if Chris reacted, but his face was blurry. "You're out of it, Sarah. Get some sleep and we'll talk later." He kissed her forehead and squeezed her hands before leaving her at the door.

She rubbed her fingers, staring at her hands. The man had quite a grip. She sighed. He'd been right about one thing. She'd had more than her share of that bottle of wine. It only took two tries, but she unlocked the door, remembering to lock it behind her.

Her head swam, but it wasn't just the wine. David, Randy and Chris whirled through her brain like horses on a carousel. She floated to the stereo and put a CD into the player. "Building a Mystery" filled the room. Knowing sleep wouldn't come easily, she powered on her computer. As she had done so many times after David had died, Sarah sat playing Mahjong solitaire. With enough complexity to require her full attention, the game had filled the lonely days and nights. She hadn't played in months and she began refamiliarizing herself with the intricate tile markings.

* * * * *

Mahjong's magic hadn't faded. Sarah rubbed her eyes and looked at the clock. Ten-thirty. She remembered the other benefit of the computer game—staring at the screen numbed her brain and made her tired enough to sleep. She got ready for bed and crawled under the covers. The phone on the nightstand beckoned and she fell prey to its lure. Without turning on the light, she punched the button for Randy's home number, her heart thumping.

She heard his voice, the television in the background. She almost hung up.

"Hello?" she heard again.

"Hi. It's me. Are you busy?"

"Not that busy." The television noises disappeared.

She stifled a yawn. "Anything on my Gertie?"

"Sorry, not yet. She's a phantom. And you sound tired."

Sarah turned onto her side and snuggled deeper under the covers. She felt her body sinking into the mattress, her eyes closing. "Had wine with dinner." No need to tell him she'd had dinner with Chris. She didn't want to think about Chris now.

"Where are you? It sounds like a bad connection."

"In bed. Under the covers."

Sarah heard a deep intake of breath. "God, Sarah, don't do this to me. I've spent the last two days trying not to think of you like that." Randy's voice had become hoarse. "You are making things very hard."

Sarah giggled. "Hard, as in difficult?"

"That, too." He groaned.

Now she felt things start to stir. Time to change the subject. "Can you tell me about the kitchen case?" She heard Randy take a breath, pause and when he spoke again, she heard the professional cop.

"The Sherman's maid ratted on the daughter and I found evidence at a frat house at Willamette University. The Sherman girl was pissed at her parents for not letting her date the older guy and thought that having someone trash the place, take a few things, would be a good way to get at them. She told her boyfriend that her parents would be out and suggested the Zimmer's house, too, as a cover-up."

"That's rotten."

"Yes, but it's in the hands of the court system now and I'm back on your case. Kovak's got a case involving Oregon Trust and I'm going to see if there's any connection to yours."

"Mmm hmm." His words barely registered.

"You didn't hear any of that last part did you?"

"Of course I heard it. But I think you'll have to tell me again another time, when it makes sense."

"Good night, Sarah. Sleep well."

"Mmmh." She pressed the button to end the call and slipped the phone under her pillow.

Chapter Sixteen

ಜಾ

Friday morning, Randy dragged himself to his desk and stared at the paperwork that had accumulated. Damn, the stuff must multiply when the lights went off. He pressed the power button on his computer and headed for the break room for a caffeine fix.

Only the fact that some idiot had scheduled his three court cases over the whole damn day was keeping him in the office. More database searches. More phone calls. Maybe make a dent in the pile of reports to review and file. Ignoring the headache that had settled at the base of his skull two days ago, he went back to work. A little of that headache disappeared when he saw the notation, "Sarah" on his schedule. Dinner and a play.

Randy didn't realize Kovak was in the room until he spoke. "You've got an hour before you're due in court. Come with me?"

"I'm busy."

"You've been busy for the last three days. Your cats?"

Randy rubbed his eyes. "Hanging in."

"No more leads?"

Randy shook his head. He saw Kovak standing in the doorway holding his coat.

"Okay, I said come with me."

"I can get in some more searches before court," Randy said.

"Yeah and you can collapse from exhaustion, too. Let's get out of here. Consider it an early lunch. I'm buying."

Randy recognized the irritation in Kovak's tone. He massaged the back of his neck and pushed away from his desk. He followed Kovak outside, squinting when the sun hit his face. The cool breeze erased some of the fatigue. "Where are we going?"

"Follow me." Kovak led the way until they were at the entrance to Pioneer Park, stopping to buy two hot dogs and sodas from a cart. He handed one of each to Randy and slowed his pace, ambling down the dirt path until he came to a picnic table near the playground. "Sit."

Randy lowered himself to the wooden bench and set his hot dog on the table behind him. He sipped his cola and watched moms push little ones on the swings and mediate sandbox arguments. Kovak sat beside him.

"Deep breath, big guy," Kovak said. "Smell the flowers."

Randy cracked a grin. "More like pine trees, but I get the idea."

"Now, you gonna tell me what's going on? How much sleep you had in the last few days?"

"What's it to you?"

"What's it to me? Only that we're partners and if we get a call, you're the one who's going to be covering my ass and right now, that's not a comfortable proposition."

Not having an answer, Randy turned and picked up his hot dog. "Shit, you had to get the works? I'm not eating chili and sauerkraut before court, you idiot." Or before his date with Sarah.

"Hey, don't toss them." Kovak extended his half-eaten dog.

Randy scraped the toppings onto Kovak's bun, resisting the temptation to slip and let them fall into Kovak's lap. He took a bite of the denuded hot dog, feeling the snap as his teeth bit though the skin. The juices hit his tongue and he was suddenly ravenous. He decided to worry about the garlic later and devoured the rest.

"Now, talk to me," Kovak said. "I've never seen you like this. If I didn't know you better, I'd say it was a woman."

A pink and blue plastic ball bounced against Randy's legs and he bent to pick it up. A blonde toddler of indeterminate gender stood about three feet away, hands outstretched. "Here you go," Randy said. He rolled the ball along the ground and watched its owner grin at him before picking it up.

"What do you say?" came a feminine voice from across the playground. The toddler stopped, turned and said something close enough to "thank you".

"You're welcome," Randy said.

"You know, that's almost the first civil word out of your mouth since I got back," Kovak said.

"Three words. Or does the contraction count as one?"

"I didn't drag you out here to discuss the finer points of grammar. I've covered half your cases for two days while you've been gallivanting all over the state about a robbery that didn't amount to much more than a few hundred dollars. Then I figured it was your cats. I know...well, I know what they are."

Randy shrugged.

"Shit," said Kovak. "It *is* a woman. Someone finally got through that brick wall of yours."

Kovak broke the long silence. "What's going on? There's nothing in the case files that would keep you this busy. And shit, don't tell me I've been covering for you so you can spend time with her."

Indignation flashed like a summer storm. Randy glared at Kovak, snatched up his trash and slam-dunked it in the nearest trash can. "Thanks for lunch. A veritable feast. Now, I need to find some mints before court."

He felt Kovak's hand on his shoulder. He twisted away, but the hand came back, to his forearm this time, gripping like a falcon. Randy yanked free, clenched his fists.

Kovak's eyes blazed, but he lifted his hands in surrender. "What the hell has gotten into you? I was out of line with that crack, but—shit. If something's going down, I'm here." His voice was gruff but Randy heard the concern.

"You're partly right," Randy said. "All those extra hours have been for her. Not seeing her, though. Trying to find out if someone's trying to put her out of business. Maybe do her a favor and see if her husband's suicide was really suicide. Get her the insurance money. Ease her mind a little."

"But?"

"But it's like you said. The robbery's open, but it was a negligible amount. There might have been some vandalism afterwards and someone was watching her apartment. Most of the investigating is outside the box, though."

"Chief's getting pissed, you know. I can cover only so far."

"Yeah, well I appreciate what you've done. Really. I've got a bunch of names with no bodies. Some hooks to Consolidated, but there are too many layers. I'm tugging at threads, but they're not unraveling the right parts of the cloth."

"I don't know if it'll help or make things worse, but those two insurance files you asked about? Oregon Trust finally got everything put back in order and five files were missing. Your two among them."

"Thanks. Another thread that might lead nowhere. I'll follow up."

Kovak tilted his head back and drained the last of his soda. "Monday." He tossed his soda can toward the trash can, giving a fist-pump when it landed inside.

"What?"

"Take your weekend. I'm on call and if something hits, I'll get Fletcher to back me. Get some rest." He tilted his head to meet Randy's gaze. "I mean it. I'll call if something pops with your cats, or the robbery. Big guy, you need to regroup. Maybe see your woman?"

When Kovak smiled, Randy knew he'd have to work on his poker face. Sarah's transparency must be contagious.

* * * * *

When Sarah slid into the empty rear seat of the bus after work, her anticipation of the night ahead changed to apprehension.

Stop it. She was going to dinner and a play. Community theater, nothing fancy. Why was she thinking about the afterward part?

What was she doing? She barely knew Randy. Never mind that he turned her to jelly every time she thought of him—she'd known him less than two weeks. She hadn't slept with a man in over a year. Of course she'd be aroused. Could that be all it was?

Her mind flew through all the other possibilities. He couldn't want her just for sex. Surely he could get any woman he wanted. How many other women had he already had? What did she actually know about him? She didn't even know how old he was. Somehow, they'd hardly spoken about anything but the case.

But he felt so...so... right. When he held her, she melted right into his body. She told herself she couldn't sleep with him, not yet, not tonight. She swore she wouldn't do anything to encourage him, but she knew if he made the slightest move, she'd be all over him like someone lost in the desert stumbling on an oasis.

Protection? No way was she going to buy condoms. And even if she did, what would she do when...if...the moment arrived. Tell him it was all right if he didn't have anything, because she just happened to have a six-pack in her purse? She sucked in a deep breath. She knew she was fine, because she'd been celibate since David died and he'd been her first and only lover. But Randy. How could she ask him that? But how could she not?

Her face had to be beet red by now. She looked out the window and realized she'd almost missed her stop. She jumped up and pulled the cord and stood at the back exit of the bus, positive that anyone who looked at her would be able to tell exactly what she'd been thinking. Darn her transparent face.

Now she wanted to call Randy and call the whole thing off. Maybe he'd have to work late on a case or something. The walk from the bus stop gave her some time to calm down. She would enjoy the evening. She would be calm and proper and they'd watch the play and then they'd both go home. And if he tried to kiss her good night, she'd say she never kissed on the first date. Right. She kissed before the first date. She'd even made the first move. Scratch that plan.

Sarah got back to her apartment and shut the door with a bang. Her heart dropped to her stomach as she looked at the beat-up table and two chairs that now graced her dining area. No regrets, she'd told herself last night when the eager newlyweds had come by to pick up her old set. The memories of meals shared with David were just that. Memories. She didn't need a table to retrieve them.

According to Diana, Chris hadn't called her yet and the money from the sale of her dining room furniture had bought her a promise from Diana not to listen to him for at least another month. And there was enough of a cushion to make sure the utility bills would be paid on time.

She stepped around the table, letting her fingers explore all the scratches and gouges in its dull beige laminate surface. With a sigh, she found a tablecloth in the linen closet and spread it over the table. Memories were one thing. Constant reminders of her failures were something else. A pair of candlesticks, a vase with some silk flowers and…and it was a cheap table with a couple of candlesticks and some silk flowers. Nothing more, nothing less.

She sighed. Randy wouldn't be here for two hours. She shouldn't have let Jennifer talk her into leaving early to get ready. Time would have sped by at the shop with Jennifer and customers to talk to. What was she going to do for the next two hours to keep from going crazy? She turned on her computer and started running the bath water.

Sarah soaked in a peach-scented bubble bath until her fingers and toes turned to prunes. She tried a curling iron on her hair, pronounced it intolerable, shampooed it and began again. Some gel, some fluffing, some hairspray and she was finally satisfied. Next week, for sure, she'd get a professional trim.

She stood in her closet agonizing over what to wear. She settled on a blue print skirt and a pale blue silk blouse. Nothing fancy, something she'd worn to work many times. What shoes? She pulled out her highest heels and slipped them on. Three steps to check the mirror and she almost twisted her ankle. She'd need stilts to bring her height anywhere close to Randy, so what was the point? Being able to look at his collarbone instead of his sternum wasn't much of an improvement. She kicked the shoes back into the closet and put on a pair of black pumps with a much lower heel.

Sarah stared at the pile of clothes strewn about her bedroom and burst out laughing. She took one final look in the mirror. Almost as an afterthought, she unbuttoned the top button on her blouse. A casual look, not revealing. She'd play Mahjong until Randy showed up.

Sarah lost count of how many times she got up and peeked out the living room window for a glimpse of the black F-150. At five-fifteen she saw it drive past the building. She put on her coat, picked up her purse and checked her hair and makeup in the mirror again. She strained her ears for sounds of footsteps approaching her door.

The knock on the door came at last. Sarah squinted through the peephole and her heart raced even faster. She knew she had a stupid grin on her face, but there was no hiding it. She pulled the door open.

Randy stood there, in charcoal slacks, a black and white tweed sweater over a gray shirt—and a tie. Had he worn a tie for her? The smile stayed on her face all the way down to his truck.

It wasn't long before they'd left Pine Hills behind. Traffic was light and Sarah enjoyed watching the sky turn pink with the approaching sunset.

"I'm glad we're doing this," Randy said. "It's nice to get away from work. Thanks for inviting me."

"We'll both have to thank Maggie."

"You never said what we're going to see tonight."

"*The Mousetrap*. Agatha Christie. It's a mystery. Right up your alley."

"I'm sure it'll be wonderful."

"How are Starsky and Hutch?" When he didn't answer immediately, she studied him more closely and saw shadows under his eyes. She hadn't talked to him since Tuesday night. Had something happened to them? She wished she could suck back the words, not remind him.

"No change. But at least they're not getting worse." His voice was flat, but controlled.

Sarah felt a weight lift from her shoulders. "I'm so glad. Othello's home, but he's really weak. How old are you?" Where had that come from?

He looked at her, eyebrows lifted. "Thirty-four. Why?"

"No reason. It occurred to me that I don't know a whole lot about you. We haven't talked about much other than your detective work. Maybe we can forget it for tonight."

"You're probably right. All right, but turnabout is fair play. How old are you?"

"Twenty-eight. At least for another few months." She nibbled on her lower lip. "Have you ever been married?"

"No."

"Ever come close?"

"No again." Randy reached over and let his hand rest on Sarah's thigh. "The closest I came was a two-year on-again, off-again relationship that's been over for at least six years. She realized I cared more about my police work than going to fancy parties to meet all the right people and I realized I couldn't live for fancy parties."

He took his hand away to shift gears after a red light changed to green. Sarah noticed that his hand didn't come back. She'd spent all afternoon asking herself these questions and now they were all pouring out. He must think she was giving him the third degree. And all about his love life. Darn!

"What do you want for dinner?" she asked, desperate to change the subject. "Italian, maybe, since we didn't have that Monday?"

"Sounds good to me."

When Randy said nothing for several miles, Sarah pleaded with him. "It's your turn. Ask me something. Anything."

"What kind of shampoo do you use?"

"What? What kind of a question is that?"

"You said ask you anything. So, answer."

"Thriftway's Peach Blossom. But I meant something more personal. I was rude asking you all those questions. I thought you'd like to get back at me."

"That was a personal question. The scent of your hair is unbearably erotic."

She looked at Randy. His expression was dead earnest. "I'm blushing, aren't I?"

"And it's very becoming."

She covered her face with her hands. "I think I'll sit here and look out the window and keep my mouth shut until we get to the restaurant."

Chapter Seventeen

Randy and Sarah excused themselves across the row of seats of the small theater until they reached theirs in the center. Dinner conversation had been comfortable and she thought Randy had forgiven her for the questions she'd thrown at him in the truck. She still cringed to think of them.

The lights dimmed and she glanced at Randy. These seats weren't designed for someone his height. He had slouched down as a courtesy to the people behind him and his knees were practically under his chin. She patted his leg. He smiled and whispered, "I'm used to it."

Strains of *Three Blind Mice* sounded from the stage and the curtain rose to darkness and a woman's scream. Sarah reached for Randy's hand and settled back to enjoy the play.

Halfway through the first scene, "Mrs. Boyle" entered and recited her first line, "This is Monkswell Manor, I presume."

Something about that voice made Sarah sit bolt upright in her seat. She leaned forward waiting to hear more, imagining the woman dressed in a sophisticated suit rather than the trappings of a sensible dowager. She felt Randy prying her hand from his. She must have hurt him, she'd been squeezing so hard. She leaned toward him and he lowered his head so she could whisper in his ear. "That's her. That's my Gertie. 'Mrs. Boyle.' I'd know that voice anywhere."

A not-so-polite throat clearing came from the row behind them. Randy squeezed her hand gently and nodded, putting his finger to his lips. Sarah could barely contain herself for the rest of the first scene. During the brief pause between scenes, she saw Randy studying the playbill.

"I don't want to disrupt the play," he whispered. "I've got her name and I'm sure we can find her."

"I hope you don't mind me giving it away, but I know the play. She's going to get killed at the end of the first act and won't be back until curtain calls. Do you think she'll stay?"

"She's got no reason to think you're here. The playbill says the cast comes out to the lobby to chat with the audience after the play. If you give me a positive ID, I can arrest her tonight."

The curtains opened and Sarah had to restrain herself from leaping up and pulling Gertie—Mrs. Boyle—Eleanor Wainwright off the stage.

During intermission, Randy called the Cottonwood police. Sarah fidgeted in her seat now that it looked like they'd caught Gertie. Her Gertie.

The rest of the play was a blur. As soon as the house lights came up, Randy and Sarah moved toward the lobby, where two uniformed police officers were already waiting. Randy identified himself and spoke to them. They nodded and one walked down a side corridor.

"What did you say? Where's he going?" Sarah asked.

"He's going to let the manager know what's going on, but we're going to be cool and not do anything until after this meet-and-greet business is over. Assuming she's the right person, Cottonwood will keep her in custody and we can question her at their station."

"She's the right person. I know it."

"I'm sure you're right, but I want you to look again out here where the light is better and you can see her up close. She was in costume up there and in stage makeup."

"It's her. It's her," Sarah insisted. Randy put his hand on her shoulder and gave her a gentle squeeze.

By now, members of the audience were milling around the lobby waiting to see the cast. Gertie arrived first. Randy held Sarah back.

"Take it easy," he said. "Slow and careful."

Sarah took a deep breath and studied the actress who had played Mrs. Boyle. There was no doubt in her mind that the woman was Gertie and she told Randy so.

"Wait with the officers by the door," Randy said and approached the woman.

Sarah joined the uniformed men and gave them a polite nod. The drone of conversation in the lobby made it impossible to hear what Randy was saying. She watched the woman's eyes widen when Randy pulled out his badge. The woman shook her head. She seemed more confused than afraid.

Randy brought the woman back to where Sarah waited. "Eleanor has agreed to explain what she did," he said.

"Come on back to the green room," Eleanor said. "I'm sure we can clear up this little misunderstanding."

The woman's voice had lost the arrogant sophistication Sarah had noticed in the shop. Now that she wasn't playing a role, a Midwestern twang took over. Sarah followed the officers down the corridor.

Inside the green room, which was actually a pleasant shade of peach, Eleanor fidgeted on the edge of a brown vinyl armchair. "I can't believe this is happening. I was assured everything was taken care of. Like I told you out there, I'm sure if you check back with your superiors, you'll find this is all a big misunderstanding. He told me everything was cleared."

"He? This guy have a name?" Randy asked. He pulled out his notebook and pen.

Sarah watched as Randy leaned forward just enough to get into Eleanor's personal space. His size alone was intimidating. Those extra few inches of encroachment would have made anyone uncomfortable. She saw him at work now, doing his job. A quick thrill of excitement ran through her and she almost forgot that she had been the victim of this so-called misunderstanding.

"Of course he had a name," Eleanor said. "I don't remember it offhand, because I dealt with him by phone. I remember better when I see someone."

Sarah heard Randy's pen start to click and he leaned in a little closer. "Go on," he said.

Eleanor sat up straight, her hands in her lap. "He told me he needed someone to do a small job in Pine Hills. A practical joke. There was good money in it for me for a morning's work."

"Tell me exactly what the job was," Randy said.

Eleanor fussed with her skirt, tugging it over her knees. She studied her fingers as she spoke. "He said he'd been trying to talk his fiancée into a burglar alarm for her shop, because she spent all day alone in there and he worried. He told me he'd send me everything I needed—clothes, wig, even a prop gun and if I did a good job, he might recommend me to a big-time producer. I got the costume and a down payment in cash. He said he'd have it cleared with the police."

Sarah couldn't contain herself any longer. What kind of a person would believe such a story? "Didn't it seem funny? A total stranger asking you to rob someone at gunpoint? What did you do with my things? My money?" She heard the edge of hysteria in her voice, felt one of the officers touch her shoulder.

"Let the detective do his job, ma'am," he said.

Heat rose in her face and she sank down in her chair.

"Oh, you mean the frame and all?" Eleanor asked. "I left them in the alley with the clothes like he said. The money was in the purse." She peered at Sarah. "You didn't get it back?"

Sarah shook her head.

"Ms. Wainwright, I think you're right about a misunderstanding," Randy said. "There's no such thing as police permission to enact a robbery. Whoever hired you is not Ms. Tucker's fiancée and she never got her property back. You were set up to carry out an actual robbery, for whatever reason this man had.

"Simply because you thought it was a joke doesn't mean it isn't still a crime." Randy's voice was even, but Sarah saw the way he set his jaw and held his eyes focused on Eleanor's. He sat there and waited. Neither officer moved. Sarah could hear her own heart pounding in her ears. Eleanor remained silent.

Randy broke the silence. "Holding someone up at gunpoint, even with a fake gun, is still a felony. You will be arrested. What happens after that depends on how much you cooperate and whether Ms. Tucker decides if she wants to testify against you." He turned to the two officers. "You want to read Ms. Wainwright her rights, gentlemen?"

The two officers stood. One began reciting her right to remain silent and the other removed the handcuffs from his belt and took two steps toward Eleanor.

She jumped to her feet. "Hey, just a darn minute. You're serious about this, aren't you?" Her face paled as her hands were restrained behind her back. She looked at Sarah again. "What if I pay you back the money I took, plus whatever those trinkets were worth? Would that be okay? Forget the whole thing?"

Sarah's head spun. She wanted her money, but this woman couldn't be allowed to walk away like nothing had happened. She stared at Randy in confusion.

Randy held off the officer with a raised hand and spoke to Eleanor. "I'm sure that making restitution will help your case. What will help even more is for you to tell us who you were working for. Perhaps you'd like to go to the station and call a lawyer? I'm sure one would be there before they finish booking you."

"To hell with a lawyer. What do you want to know?" Eleanor asked.

Randy gave Sarah a quick smile that sent a shiver down her spine.

Randy turned back to Eleanor. "How about the truth this time?" he said.

"Everything I told you was the truth," she whimpered.

"Then why don't you tell us the rest of the truth?" Randy said. "You expect us to believe that you never thought you did anything wrong?"

"I had to do it. You don't understand." She stepped back toward the chair and Randy helped her sit down.

"Why don't you try? I can be an understanding kind of guy."

"It's my father," Eleanor began. Her voice was low. "He's eighty-three years old and has Alzheimer's. He's the only family I have. But it was too hard to take care of him. I tried. Took him into my home. But he'd wander off and he didn't even know who I was anymore. I had to find someplace that would take care of him. But not one of those horrible homes that smells like piss, where they sit around in bathrobes all day, drugged and drooling. He was in good health otherwise and could be sharp as a tack sometimes."

"I understand," Randy said. "It must have been rough."

"I found this fantastic place. Assisted living, they called it. Kind of like a big college dorm for senior citizens. Round-the-clock care, with lots of activities and things to keep their minds active. But it cost a fortune. I'm working three jobs to pay his expenses."

"I can see how the extra money might have been tempting," Randy said, "but that doesn't erase the fact that you committed a crime."

"It wasn't the money," Eleanor cried. "I turned him down when it was just for money. But then he said he'd get my father kicked out of the facility if I didn't cooperate. I couldn't move him. That place was perfect, the only place around. He was blackmailing me."

Finding Sarah

Sarah saw Randy sit up straighter, flip a page in his notebook. His pen clicked a rapid staccato. She observed a gleam of excitement in his eyes.

"Go on," he said. "How could he do this?"

"Woodland Meadows—that's where Dad is—is owned partly by Consolidated. This guy, whoever he is, said he had connections there. About two months ago, I got a letter from the Meadows saying there had been some problems with the account and I was behind in my payments. I managed to straighten it out, but then this guy calls me back and says that that was only the beginning—that things would get to the point where I couldn't straighten them out if I didn't cooperate. So after a while, I agreed." She looked at Sarah again, an expression of abject apology on her face. "I didn't know it would be this bad for you. I thought that someone who could manipulate the administration at Woodland Meadows could pull some strings with the police."

Sarah looked at Eleanor's pathetic face. The woman was an actress. But not that good. Sarah believed her. Randy's face revealed nothing. She couldn't tell if he believed Eleanor or not. She waited to see what Randy would do next.

"That's helpful," he said to Eleanor. He fixed his gaze on hers. "What's your father's name?"

"Ralph. Ralph Wainwright."

Randy wrote in his notebook. "Thanks. And would you have managed to remember the name of the person who set you up for this?"

Eleanor's face was grim. "You better believe I remember." She stared at Randy. "Can you make sure nothing happens to my father?"

"We can get in touch with the people at Woodland Meadows and make sure that anything involving your father is double-checked through you first. I don't see a problem with that."

"Then if I go down, he goes down," Eleanor said, her eyes narrowed. "His name is Brady. Mitchell Brady. I never saw him—everything was done by phone. That much was true."

"Do you have the phone number you called?" Randy asked.

"I can get it for you."

Randy stood and helped Eleanor to her feet. "I'm still going to have to send you with these officers, but the fact that you've been helpful should make a difference when you come up before the judge."

Eleanor dropped her head and allowed the two officers to escort her from the room.

* * * * *

Randy parked behind Sarah's building and helped her out of the truck's cab.

"This isn't exactly how I expected the evening to go," she said, "but you caught her. And now you can find that Brady guy and maybe everything will be back to normal." She gave him a puzzled look. "You don't seem happy."

"Sorry. It's been a long couple of days. And I probably have an hour of paperwork left. She has to be transferred to Pine Hills."

"Can it wait until tomorrow? Come up for some coffee or something?"

The rush of the arrest had left, more quickly than usual, since he still didn't have the person he needed—the man who'd hired, or coerced her into the robbery. He wished he had Sarah's optimism. But after days of trying to make connections, he was ready to admit that he could close the case, but would have the wrong person behind bars. And that Laughlin wasn't going to cut him any more slack on this one. He didn't realize he'd accepted her invitation until they were standing in front of her door.

She opened the door for him. He took a seat on the couch, his gaze halting at the dining room table. The checkered tablecloth didn't disguise the fact it wasn't the table he'd sat at a few days ago. He started to comment when Sarah turned and shook her head.

"Nobody's getting my shop," she said. "If I have to sell every darn piece of furniture I own, I'll do it." Her voice was tight and he thought he ached more than she did herself.

She went into the kitchen. "I think we need some hot chocolate. Comfort food. Sorry it's only instant packets, though." She filled a teakettle and set it on the stove. On her way back to the living room she stopped at the stereo. "Bridge Over Troubled Water" began playing.

"Cocoa and Simon and Garfunkel. Mom's cure-all for the blues."

"Do I look that bad? Are you taking care of me?"

She smiled. "Tell me about what happens next."

"They'll bring Eleanor to Pine Hills. She'll appear before a judge where he'll explain the charges. My guess is he'll release her on bail, assuming he believes her story."

"Do you?"

He nodded. Sarah was quiet for a moment. "I get it. You caught Gertie—Eleanor—but you still haven't figured out why she did it. The mysterious Mr. Brady is still out there."

"Good detective work, Ms. Tucker."

She came back to the living room and sank to the couch. Now she looked like he felt.

"And," she continued, "whoever he is, catching this woman doesn't mean he'll go away."

The kettle whistled. Sarah made no move to get up. Randy went into the kitchen and pulled it from the stove. Sarah had laid out mugs and two cocoa packets. He mixed the drinks and brought them back to the living room. "*If you need a friend,*" he intoned. "I always liked that song. Sad, but comforting, too." He set the mugs on the coffee table and shut off the lamp.

He sat down next to Sarah and when she didn't draw away, he pulled her against him. She leaned into his chest. He put his arm around her shoulder and they sat in the dark while their cocoa grew cold.

Finding Sarah

Chapter Eighteen

ಐ

Sarah rushed into the kitchen, dragging her collapsible shopping cart behind her. What had she been thinking when she invited Randy to dinner? Last night had been a disaster in the get-to-know-you-when-you're-not-a-cop department and she was determined to give it a chance. They'd promised no shop talk. But she hadn't cooked for anyone in ages.

Everything had taken twice as long as it should have—she had a dawdling customer and she'd missed a bus, then there was a huge line at the checkout at Thriftway. At least it wasn't raining.

Sarah started unloading the bags, arranging the ingredients on the counter. She'd worried about the menu since she talked to Randy yesterday. Today had been Jennifer's Saturday off and being alone in the shop didn't leave her a lot of time to cook, only a lot of time to worry about it. She'd pored over her recipes trying to find something affordable, quick and elegant without being pretentious.

What did Randy like to eat? Why couldn't she have asked him that instead of how many girlfriends he'd had? She finally decided on rigatoni. What the heck, she made a darn good spaghetti sauce and rigatoni didn't have that embarrassing dangle factor. Garlic bread? Why not? Salad and vanilla ice cream for dessert. With chocolate sauce. Thick, gooey chocolate sauce.

She changed into jeans and a T-shirt and began her preparations. There was no way she would be finished before Randy got here. Too bad. He could watch, or he could help. She was not opening a jar of spaghetti sauce. This was a family recipe and she wouldn't rush it.

While the onions sautéed, she cleaned the greens for the salad and put them in her salad spinner, getting rewarded with a nice cold shower when she took the top off before it stopped. She had to calm down. Relax. Get the sauce simmering, change her clothes. She'd done this dozens of times.

She crushed a clove of garlic into the onions and let them sauté for a minute before tipping them into a large saucepan. She chopped the tomatoes, added some tomato sauce, a hint of Worcestershire, some fresh basil and oregano, a generous glug of red wine and gave it a good stir. A quick taste, a little more salt, some red pepper flakes and she was satisfied.

She adjusted the burner and went to set the table. Loud plopping noises sent her racing to the stove to pull the Vesuvius-like liquid from the burner and lower the flame, but not before she was covered with splotches of hot, red sauce.

She heard a knock on the door, followed by Randy's voice. She wiped her face and managed to blind herself with the onion residue left on her fingers. Eyes streaming, she worked her way to the front door, tripping over the folding metal shopping cart she'd left in the middle of the living room.

"Darn!" She extricated herself from the wire cart and hobbled to the door. She opened it and bent to rub her throbbing shin.

"Sarah! Are you all right? What happened?" He kicked the door shut behind him, put his arm at her waist and half carried her to the couch. "Sit down. Let me look at you."

"I'm fine. Bumped into the cart," she said when he sat beside her, his hands on her shoulders, staring at her.

A blush spread over his face. "I'm sorry. I heard a crash and you shouted and you were doubled over and I saw you'd been crying. For a second I thought you were covered in blood, too."

"Onions," Sarah said. "And spaghetti sauce." She looked down at her shirt. She did look like she'd been wounded in battle. She tried not to laugh. "It's nice to know you care."

Finding Sarah

Randy dropped down onto the floor and retrieved the bag with the wine bottle he'd dropped in his haste to rescue her. He ducked his head. "Sorry."

He looked so sheepish, Sarah couldn't contain herself any longer and the laughter burst out. Randy's laughter joined hers and they both gasped for breath.

Sarah sat up, wiping her eyes on her sleeve. "If you could have seen the look on your face," she said. "Every woman needs a white knight to save her from erupting tomato sauce. I'm glad you're mine."

"Any time, my lady." He reached to her face and wiped her cheek with a thumb. "It's good to see you laugh."

"You, too." She took his hand and kissed his thumb. His face grew serious and he leaned forward and reached behind her neck with his other hand. Sarah continued nibbling his thumb, flicking her tongue over it, watching Randy's eyes half close, feeling his breathing escalate. Randy pulled his hand from Sarah's mouth and put his lips over hers. She kissed him, gently at first, but with more passion as he sought her tongue and pushed her back down on the couch. Heat rose within her. She reached for his hand again and placed it on her breast. She felt his fingers on her nipples as they strained against the lace of her bra. She pressed tighter against his hand and the heat flowed from her breast to her groin.

He rose from the floor and Sarah shifted herself as far back onto the couch as she could, turning her body to face his. His kisses never stopped as he lay next to her. She rubbed her body against his, feeling her breasts against his torso, her hips against his erection. His kisses moved from her lips to neck, to ears and back to her lips.

God, how she wanted him. She gasped for breath. They shouldn't be doing this. Not here. Not yet.

"Wait. Stop," she panted. She heard Randy's groan, but he released her and lifted himself on one elbow.

"What's the matter? Am I hurting you?"

"God, no. It's...it's... I don't know." She reached up and traced the line of his jaw. "There are things to consider."

Randy took her hands and nibbled her fingertips. "I understand. I have protection."

"Let me up for a minute, please." She tried to read Randy's face, but his wasn't transparent like hers. She knew he was frustrated, but he didn't look angry. He swung himself around and helped her to a sitting position.

"I'm sorry," he said. "I thought you wanted this as much as I did."

"I'm sure I do. More, maybe." She closed her eyes for a moment, then continued. "I never slept with anyone but David," she whispered. "And we waited until we were married. This. With you. It's scaring me. I want you so badly, but then I think about how fast it is and I panic. I don't know your favorite food, or your favorite color, or what movies you like."

"I won't lie and tell you this is easy," he said. "I want you so much it hurts. But it has to be right. For both of us. If you want to wait, I'll wait. I told you that and I meant it. If we're right for each other, we'll be right for each other for a while longer. And, to answer your questions—lamb chops. Blue, stone blue. And I've seen *Blazing Saddles* twelve times."

"Thanks," she whispered, turning to face him.

"But we're not going to take up where we left off, are we?"

"Not until after dinner. All those tomatoes shouldn't have sacrificed their lives in vain. And maybe we should try a proper bed instead of this couch which is easily three sizes too small for you."

Randy stroked her cheek, but not before she'd seen him glance around the room, his gaze stumbling on the photos of herself with David. He rested his chin on her head. "I've thought about that. I'm not sure I want to have my first experience with you in a bed you shared with David. I think his ghost might get in the way."

She'd made her peace with David, but Randy's remark touched her. She gazed into those brown eyes flecked with hazel. "Let's have dinner here. I've got ice cream for dessert. Do you think it would survive a trip to your place without melting?"

He smiled. "Most definitely."

"Okay. You can open the wine while I get into some dry clothes. Corkscrew's in the second drawer, left side." She tousled his hair and kissed his cheek and scampered to the bedroom.

Eating took precedence over dinner conversation. The anticipation was almost tangible. Randy helped clear the table and wash the dishes. Their fingers touched, their bodies rubbed against each other as they maneuvered in the small kitchen.

"I'll be right back," she said. "Why don't you get the Styrofoam cooler from the cabinet on the back porch. And the fudge sauce is on the counter." Smiling in anticipation, she went to her room, plucked some clean underwear from the drawer and jammed them into her purse along with a toothbrush.

Suddenly, she sobered. She reached behind her head and eased the chain from around her neck. Holding the ring in front of her, she gave it one loving kiss and put it in her jewelry box. "No more ghosts," she whispered. "I love you, David, but it's time to move on."

* * * * *

On the ride to Randy's house, Sarah found an oldies rock station. Trying to keep a conversation alive when she knew they both had only one thing on their minds was impossible. She began swaying to the beat and soon they were both belting the chorus to "Sweet Caroline".

"My mom loves Neil Diamond," Sarah said.

A few more songs and they were at Randy's house. He opened the door for her and turned on a lamp by the couch. "You want dessert now?"

"Right after the ice cream."

Randy chuckled. "I'll serve. How about we eat on the couch?"

Sarah settled on the couch and toed off her sneakers and socks while she adjusted the three-way bulb in the lamp to the lowest setting. Candles would be better, but she hadn't thought to bring any.

Randy appeared with two sundaes. "What are you thinking?"

"Nothing."

"That was not a 'nothing' look, that was a 'something's missing' look."

"I thought candles would be nice. But they're not important. The moonlight is enough."

Randy set the ice cream down and disappeared down the hall, returning in a moment with a green foil gift box. He arranged half a dozen pillar candles on the coffee table and lit them. The scent of vanilla filled the air. Sarah turned off the lamp and picked up her bowl. An ice cream purist, she turned the spoon over as she put it into her mouth so that the initial sensation on her tongue was the creamy richness of the ice cream. She grinned as Randy followed her example, eyebrows raised.

"This way, you don't get the metallic taste of the spoon," she explained. The scent of the candles intensified the vanilla flavor of the ice cream.

Randy nodded in agreement, matching her bite for bite.

Sarah scraped the remains of the sundae from her bowl. She licked the spoon, enjoying the chocolate's creamy sweetness. She glanced at Randy, sitting beside her on the couch in the flickering light. She saw a flush rise to his face as he set his bowl on the coffee table. Lowering her spoon, she glued her eyes to his and let her tongue dance circles around her half open mouth while she savored both the chocolate sauce and the thought of his mouth against hers. The look in his eyes made her forget the chocolate and her breath quickened.

Randy dipped his fingertip into the chocolate residue in her bowl and brought it to her lips. Her tongue swirled around his finger. Randy pulled his hand away and covered her lips with his own. She pressed deeper into the kiss, her tongue feeling the chill in his mouth turn hot. Somewhere in the distance, she felt him remove the bowl and spoon from her fingers, heard the soft thud as he placed them on the coffee table, but the kiss took on a life of its own, transcending awareness of anything else.

He pulled her on top of him so that she straddled his lap. She leaned her head into his chest, listened to the pounding of his heart, the rapid rhythm of his breathing. His hands sent shivers down her back as he reached under her sweater and unfastened her bra. Murmurs of pleasure intertwined as one voice. She wanted his hands to envelop every inch of her. Shifting herself closer into his body, she began rocking gently, her mind oblivious to all but the fluttering sensations building deep within her.

She ran her fingers through his hair, touched the velvety softness behind his ears, rubbed her hands up and down his back, began working his shirt free of his pants. His hands moved to the front of her chest, kneading her breasts, rolling her nipples under his thumb. Sparks shot through her at his touch. She reached to unbuckle his belt, to touch him, to share the pleasure.

"Sarah," he gasped. "Wait." He put his hands over hers.

She let go of his belt, unable to speak. He couldn't have changed his mind. Not now. Randy put his hands at her waist and shifted her down toward his knees.

"You're making me... I'm so... I'm not sure I can... Oh, God, Sarah, I don't want to spoil it for you. It shouldn't be this quick."

She slid off his lap and ran her fingers across his lips. His breathing was rapid and shallow. She extinguished the candles and extended her hand. "We said we were going to do this in a proper bed. Will you take me there?"

Randy got up from the couch. Sarah found herself lifted off her feet. Putting her arm around his neck, she kissed him again. She nestled her head into his chest and he nuzzled her hair. His strength sent a feeling of peace through her as he carried her to the bedroom. There was a dip as his elbow hit the light switch and a lamp on a night table across the room came on.

He lowered her to the bed and knelt at her feet. She waited as he unbuttoned the top three buttons of his shirt and pulled it over his head. His bare chest sent another quiver through her body and she longed to run her fingers through the mat of silken hair. When she reached forward, he grasped her hands. "I haven't...been with a woman in a long time," he whispered. "And I've wanted you so much. Give me a minute."

"Do we need the light?" Sarah asked.

"I want to look at you. All of you."

The tenderness reflected in his eyes obliterated any self-consciousness. She removed her sweater and let it fall to the floor along with her bra. "It's been a long time for me, too."

Sarah watched as Randy stood at the foot of the bed for a long moment, his eyes moving up and down her body. "I want to look at you, but I prefer the moonlight," she said. She pulled back the covers and went to the bedside table and switched off the lamp. Eyes locked on his, her hands moved to the button of her jeans.

"Wait," he said. "Come here. Let me."

Sarah stepped around the bed and stood poised before him. Her knees quaked. "I'm yours." She stared into his eyes, those brown-flecked-with-hazel eyes that melted her insides. His trembling fingers released the button and zipper of her jeans, slid them down past her hips.

His delicate touch sent another thrill though her. He lowered himself to his knees once again. She tried to control her ragged breathing as Randy planted kiss after kiss on her body. Any more and she would have to sit down. She tried to reach for him, but he refused her touch.

"Not yet," he said. His kisses continued down her legs as he slipped her jeans to her ankles. Every nerve ending fired pleasure to her brain. He lowered her panties an inch at a time, still kissing in their wake and his strong fingers played along the back of her legs. She clung to his shoulders to keep from collapsing with delight.

His kisses moved back up her body. She tried to catch her breath while he shifted from his knees to a sitting position on the edge of the bed. His hands were hot velvet at her waist as he positioned her between his knees. Lightning coursed from her breasts to her loins while his tongue played over her nipples. And then his fingers stroked between her legs and she forced herself away from his touch.

"Please, Randy. I want all of you." He met her eyes and lowered her to the bed beside him.

Trying to catch her breath, she watched Randy reach for his belt buckle. The sound of his zipper sent a magical thrill through her. He rose and finished undressing, flashed her a smile as he took a strip of condoms from his nightstand drawer. He ripped one packet from the strip and dropped them beside the lamp. She took a moment to absorb the sheer beauty of his form. His sculpted torso outshone the live models in her college art classes. The way his muscles flexed as he moved had her pulse thundering. She moved to the center of the bed and he lay down beside her. He stroked her cheeks, her neck, her shoulders. Every touch made her moan with pleasure.

She pulled him to her, guiding his head back to her breasts. The gentle suction of his kisses launched new surges of excitement directly to her center. Her pelvis arched toward him. She twisted his hair in her fingers, pressed his head harder into her chest as she lost herself in the growing heat of his touch. His hands played up and down her body, traced her contours, sent shudders in their tracks. Kisses followed, the warmth of his breath and the gentle tickling as his hair brushed her skin brought goosebumps of delight. His fingers probed, brought her to the edge and she ached to be one with him.

"Please. Now," she panted, pulling him to her.

He rolled away and her heart skipped for a moment and by the time she realized he was putting on the condom, he was back, poised above her. She guided him into her, slowly, as long-unused muscles adjusted to his entry and they gasped in unison.

"Oh, God," he said. "You feel so good."

She rocked gently beneath him and lost herself in the pleasure of feeling complete. Her hips, unbidden, arched higher, moved faster, as she sought release.

"No, you don't," Randy said, half withdrawing. "Not yet."

She dug her nails into his buttocks, but he waited. Counted to ten.

"Largo," he whispered. "Slowly." Rhythmic strokes dizzied her with pleasure.

"Adagio. Andante." As his passion grew, so did his tempo, until Sarah begged for fulfillment.

He pulled back once more. "Pausa. Rest." Fifteen counts before he began again. This time, the tempo quickened much faster and she could stand it no longer.

"Oh God, Randy," she cried. "I can't wait. Now. Now!"

Finding Sarah

And she felt her entire being focus on that one tiny part of her. The universe collapsed to encircle them. Suddenly, there was no Sarah, no Randy, just a glorious sensation that throbbed through her very being. She felt Randy give one final thrust, heard him call her name and a wild crescendo filled her.

When she could think again, she found him propped above her. She took a shaky breath. There was enough light from the not-yet-full moon to see his face, eyes barely open, a smile on his lips. He kissed her.

"I'm sorry. I wanted that to last a little longer," he said between kisses. "A lot longer."

"No apology needed."

He rolled beside her. She curled on her side and pulled his arm around her, tucking his hand under her chin. Snuggled back into his body, she felt herself descending toward sleep.

"Why the music terms?" she mumbled.

"Leftovers from my music lesson days. Trying to keep things slow. For all the good it did."

"You did fine. Any slower and I might have died." She sighed. "Music lessons. Remind me to ask you about that when my brain starts functioning again."

Chapter Nineteen

Randy drifted through half-sleep, aware of a feathery touch through his hair. Sarah.

He opened his eyes. The moon had moved along its nightly course, leaving the room in darkness except for a faint glow from a distant street light shining through the bathroom window. Just enough to reflect a glow in her eyes.

"Are you awake?" she whispered.

He managed something between a grunt and a groan. God, he wanted to lie here, semi-conscious and enjoy having a soft, warm body next to him. He pulled her to his chest.

With her head resting in the curve of his collarbone, Sarah moved her hand to his neck, shoulders and down to his chest, tracing the outlines of his musculature. "Can I touch you now? I love the feel of you."

Fully awake now, he reached over to embrace her, but she pressed him back, stroking his biceps.

"No," she said. "You lie there. No moving. It's my turn." She ran her fingers behind his ears. Her lips caressed his throat. The scent of her peach shampoo, the delicate tickle of her hair as her lips moved down his chest, the soft sounds she made as she kissed and he was more than ready.

"You're driving me crazy." He moved to flip her, but she grabbed his hands.

"I said it was my turn."

Her fingers ran down his chest, past his navel, to his thighs, behind his knees like so many butterflies. She hadn't touched his erection, but he throbbed with desire. She moved back to his throat, this time nibbling, scraping, tasting her way down his body. His body responded as if it had been months, not an hour, since he'd shared himself with her.

"Sarah. Oh, God."

"Quiet." She covered his mouth with hers, as if to enforce her command. He relented.

She stopped long enough to find a condom and tear open the foil. "I've never actually done this before."

"Let me help," he whispered and guided her hand as together, they rolled it over his erection.

"Okay, but you're mine now. Hands off." Her magic fingers went back to work, driving him to a frenzy. She straddled him. Found his cock. Wriggled against him, taking him in, drawing back, then allowing him another inch, until he was buried inside her. Her breasts hung above him, round and soft, and the memory of the taste of them, the feel of them beneath his fingertips had him twisting the sheets at his side.

"All right?" She started to move, riding him, rocking, clamping around him until he balanced on that razor edge of control. He looked at her, poised above him, back arched, head thrown back and a smile of utter pleasure on her lips. Sweet God, she was going to send him over. He reached for her, seeking the spot that would carry her with him.

She took his hands. "No," she said. She shifted, leaned forward and gazed into his eyes and in that instant he understood. Right now, she was in charge, not at the mercy of everything life had thrown at her. "For you. No holding back. Let go."

He'd give her that power—as if he had a choice. She moved again and he felt the pressure gather and his mind disconnect. And that marvelous moment of total release.

* * * * *

Shortly after dawn, Sarah awoke and found Randy leaning on one elbow watching her. She turned and smiled at him. "Hi," she said. She felt like she'd been waking up next to him forever.

"Hi, yourself. You want some breakfast? I can cook, you know."

"No argument there." She turned on her side and placed her palm against his chest, tracing lazy circles with her forefinger. Her hand roamed lower, fingertips barely making contact with his flesh. His eyelids lowered and his chest expanded as he drew in a breath. She paused at his navel before continuing down his torso, only half surprised to find him aroused. "But maybe breakfast can wait a little while. It would be a shame to waste this, wouldn't it?" She moved her hand to the small of his back and pressed herself tight against him.

This time, there was no urgency. Their bodies found the rhythm of that eternal dance, touching, exploring, learning. Fulfillment came gradually, building in ever increasing swells until together, they rode the crest and slid down into sweet oblivion.

Some time later, Randy spoke. "It's almost eleven. I think we're talking about brunch now. I can make French toast. I might have some bacon, too."

"Mmm. Yes. I think I could eat now. Can I clean up first?"

"Sure. Clean towels under the sink. Help yourself to anything you need." He kissed the top of her head and put on some sweats before leaving the room.

Sarah gave a longing look at the biggest bathtub she'd ever seen before stepping into the stall shower. Room for two, even if Randy was one of them. Maybe later. She washed quickly, borrowing some of Randy's shampoo. He'd have to forego the peach scent today. In the bedroom, she opened a dresser drawer and found a long-sleeved gray jersey with a large blue number seventeen on the front. Good, because she didn't think her jeans would be too comfortable this morning. A little tenderness was a small price to pay for the joy and peace Randy had given her. The shirt hung past her knees and she rolled the sleeves up enough to give her the use of her hands. She rubbed her hair with a towel and went out to the kitchen.

The aroma of bacon frying tantalized her nostrils and she realized she was ravenous. "Smells fantastic," she said and crept up behind Randy who was removing the strips from the pan to a paper towel-lined plate. She put her arm around his waist.

"Careful. This spatters."

"You make an excellent shield."

He turned and looked at her, gave a grin of approval. "That shirt doesn't look half as good on me," he said.

"I'm glad you don't mind. I wanted something comfortable." She helped herself to a strip of bacon from the plate. She saw the kitchen table set for two, with a heaping platter of French toast in its center. "Looks like you cook in the kitchen, too."

His laugh, natural and full of joy, was almost as rewarding as their lovemaking had been. It was obvious he was relaxed. Comfortable. At peace.

Randy brought the bacon over to the table and pulled a chair out for her. "Sit. Eat."

"You sound like Maggie." Sarah giggled.

"Ah, but would Maggie do this?" he asked and lifted her up to his waist and kissed her.

Sarah wrapped her legs around him and returned the kiss. He smelled like bacon and coffee, with some sex, sweat and a little of her own scent mixed in. "All right. Put me down. I'm hungry."

* * * * *

"Do you play?"

Randy took his eyes off the basketball game long enough to see the sparkle in Sarah's eyes as she gazed up at him. Her head in his lap was starting to affect him again and he shifted her to a sitting position beside him. "Play what? Basketball?" He took a slice of pizza from the box on the coffee table.

"Piano. I saw one in the other room."

"Now and then." He avoided looking at her, pretending to concentrate on his pizza and the game. Sarah had a way of digging up things he'd thought were well buried.

"That's what you meant by music lessons, right? Are you any good? Would you play for me?"

Damn, he couldn't resist her enthusiasm. He glanced at the score. No way Duke could blow their lead. He stood up and extended his hand. Sarah took it in both of hers, sliding her fingers over his.

"I thought your hands looked artistic. I can see them on a piano."

He helped Sarah to her feet. "Let me wash the pizza off my hands and I'll play for you." Randy led her to the spare bedroom, pointing to the chair by the window. "Make yourself comfortable."

He watched Sarah ease herself into Gram's chair and images he'd buried shimmered around her. "Be right back." In the bathroom, he took a deep breath. It was time to deal with it. When Sarah was around, all thoughts of Gram were pleasant memories, not painful ones. He dried his hands and went back to Sarah.

He opened the cover of the keyboard and sat down, felt the cool ivory beneath his fingertips and let the familiar wave of calm wash over him. He played a few arpeggios to warm up. It was time. He stood and opened the seat of the piano bench, found the yellowed sheet music for Beethoven's *Pathetique* and set it lovingly on the stand.

It had been more than eight years since he'd been able to bear even thinking about playing this, Gram's favorite. He remembered how she would sit beside him, insisting he go over and over the difficult passages until he thought he would never, ever want to hear the piece again. And then, one day, it was no longer notes, but music and the beauty brought tears to Gram's eyes and to his. When he would play it, she would come and sit in her chair, her eyes closed, to listen.

Randy looked first at Sarah, then at the page, put his fingers to the keys and let the music resonate through his soul.

When he finished, Sarah came and sat beside him. "What was that? It was wonderful."

He blinked hard before he spoke. "Beethoven. *Pathetique.* Gram's favorite."

"Do you only play classical music?"

"Nope. Gram laid the foundation with the classics, but she loved all music. I worked my way through college playing in hotel lobbies, lounges and piano bars. The tips were good if you could play the requests, so I kept on top of things. Once I got into the police academy, I stopped adding to my repertoire, but I have a good ear. If I know the tune, I can fake it."

"How did your Gram manage to get a kid to study classical music? I'd have thought you would have wanted to play the popular stuff you heard on the radio."

"Cartoons."

"What?"

"We'd watch television on Saturday mornings and after lunch, Gram would play the melodies from the cartoons. There's a lot of Mozart in Looney Tunes, you know. And Wagner."

"I never thought of it that way."

"It worked. I thought I was playing cartoon music. By the time I figured it out, I was hooked."

Sarah named songs, lyrics and composers—Randy met every challenge, enjoying the music as he hadn't in so long. Maybe the audience made all the difference.

"I can't believe you can play this stuff off the top of your head," Sarah said.

"After a while, the notes are in the muscles. The brain hears the melody and the fingers follow along. It's turning the notes to music that takes practice—'letting your soul through', as Gram used to say."

"I'm glad you're talking about her."

He kissed the top of Sarah's head. "I am too."

* * * * *

They stood outside the door to Sarah's apartment, fingers entwined. "I'd invite you in," Sarah said, "but I'm afraid we both might be late for work tomorrow."

"Can't have that. Now that we caught your Gertie, I've got a little more elbow room to dig. I'll be busy, but maybe we can get together after work?"

"I'd like that." She stood on tiptoe, tilted her head up in invitation.

Randy gave her a kiss that reached her toes. "Good night. Be careful."

"You, too." She locked the door behind him, the taste of his kiss lingering on her lips.

Wonderful as the day had been, it was Sunday night and she had things to do. As she navigated the back stairs with her trash, the night chill stiffened her nipples against the fabric of her shirt and she thought of Randy's touch. Smiling, she walked to the alley and set the bag down while she wrestled with the heavy lid of the dumpster.

A shadowy form appeared from behind it. Her heart raced. The lid fell with a loud clang as Sarah turned to run. She hadn't gone three steps before an arm wrapped around her chest.

"I said I'd take care of you. You didn't listen, so we'll have to do it this way."

Finding Sarah

She squirmed away from his grasp, but he was too strong. A cloth covered her mouth. When she took a breath to scream, she inhaled a sickly sweet smell and then blackness engulfed her.

Chapter Twenty

Randy strolled down the hall to his office Monday morning, relaxed, refreshed and feeling good about the day. He'd just hung up his jacket when Kovak walked in, the inevitable latte from the corner cart in hand.

Kovak's gaze moved over Randy, lingering on his face. He sat down at his desk and mumbled something that sounded all too close to, "I told you so."

"You say something?" Randy asked. He made a point of rooting through the notes and messages on his desk.

"Me?" Kovak grinned. "No. But you look well rested. I take it you took my advice? Enjoyed your weekend?"

"I did. After I brought in the woman who held up Sarah Tucker's shop."

"Way to go."

"Only partly. She was someone's puppet. I'm still looking for whoever's behind this."

"She give you anything?"

"Not much. Another Consolidated link. We found her in Cottonwood, so they'll bring her over this morning. I'll check their reports, see if she talked. Spending the weekend in lockup can loosen tongues."

Kovak picked up some papers from his desk, stuffed them into his briefcase. "I'm off. Snitch has a lead on the Oregon Trust break-in for me. Catch you later."

Randy grunted. He punched the codes for his voice mail into the phone, half hoping to hear Sarah's voice. Instead, he heard the nasal twang of the Cottonwood officer he'd worked

Finding Sarah

with Friday night. They'd gotten the phone number Eleanor had called. Randy thumbed through his notes, found the number from Tony Mazzaro. Not surprised when they were identical, he called Victoria at the phone company.

"Hi, Victoria. How's my favorite lady?"

"Fine, Doll Boy. Anything going on, or is this a love call?"

Randy smiled in spite of himself. "I need a favor." Victoria was seventy-two years old and refused to retire. When so many of her contemporaries had shied away from learning the new computerized systems, Victoria had no such qualms. There was nothing she couldn't ferret out of the phone company's database and Randy knew she had a lot more tricks up her sleeve.

"Ask away."

Randy gave her the number. "Can you tell me who this belongs to?"

"You got a court order?"

"Not yet. Any chance you can poke around and if things pan out, I'll get one?"

"Randy, my dear. You wound me. Are you losing faith? Or have you found someone else? You haven't been by to visit in ages."

Randy grinned this time. "Victoria, you know there will never be anyone but you. And you're right. I don't get to Woodford nearly enough. Next time I'm in town, I'll stop by. That's a promise."

"That's more like it. You want to hold? This should be quick."

He could hear Victoria sucking on one of the butterscotch candies that were a fixture in the jar on her desk. He made a mental note to get her some more.

Less than three minutes later, Victoria confirmed it was a Consolidated phone number.

"You're sure? Consolidated denied it."

"I'll pretend I didn't hear that. It's Consolidated. You need more, I'm going to have to get paper, you know."

"I'll be in touch." He hesitated only a moment. "But if you happen to have some time and want to pull the Local Usage Details on that number for me...let's say, six months?"

"Someday someone's going to take exception to the fact that you seem to get your LUDs almost before the ink's dry on the paperwork." She cackled. "I'll see, Doll Boy."

* * * * *

Sarah floated to a state of half wakefulness. She could feel the softness of her pillow, smell the freshly laundered sheets. Sunlight filtered through her closed lids. She turned away from the source of the light, trying to put her nightmare behind her. It had certainly seemed real enough. Her head felt two sizes too big, she needed to pee and there was an underlying feeling of nausea. She yawned and cracked her eyelids open.

As soon as she did, any remnants of sleep were eradicated by the surge of adrenaline. This was not her bedroom. This was not any bedroom she'd ever been in. She was lying in a king-sized oak bed, still wearing the jersey she'd borrowed from Randy. Her memory returned and she choked back a scream for help. Chris. He'd stolen her away last night. He'd drugged her—that's why she was so groggy. She heard herself hyperventilating and struggled to slow her breathing.

Her panic intensified the urgent need for a bathroom. Sarah crept out of bed, fighting the dizziness and tiptoed across the wood floor, trying the closed door at her right. Locked. She discovered an open doorway in the opposite corner, hidden behind a lattice screen. Thankful that the room revealed the necessary fixtures, she sighed as she relieved herself. She tried to be quiet, but there was no way to pee silently.

She fought to breathe normally and studied the bathroom, searching for a way out. A tiny ventilation window near the ceiling was useless. Laid out neatly on the counter was a

Finding Sarah

toothbrush still in its wrapper, a tube of toothpaste, a bar of soap, a washcloth and a pile of fluffy yellow towels. She peeked behind a yellow-flowered shower curtain into a tub-shower combination with bottles of expensive shampoo, conditioner and bubble bath.

Her mouth was dry and tasted like old socks. With shaking fingers, she unwrapped the toothbrush and ran just enough water to dampen it, taking a moment to run it across her teeth. She moistened a washcloth and rubbed it across her face and the back of her neck. She leaned against the sink, trembling from the exertion.

Mounting anger gave some of her strength back. How could she have been so stupid? So naïve? But Chris had been so passive in high school, so polite and proper. Hell, it had been almost two years before he'd French kissed her and even then, she'd had to convince him he wasn't out of line.

Using the walls for support, she tiptoed back to the bedroom and continued her exploration. Security bars covered the lone window in the room with a combination padlock securing the bars. This was a prison. She heard the blood rushing through her ears, felt the dizziness return. She sat on the bed and tried to stop shaking.

A photo album lay on a nightstand shelf at the side of the bed. She picked it up and ran her quivering hands over its textured surface. She began flipping through it, fighting off a feeling of horror. It was full of pictures of her. Photos taken when she and Chris were in high school. Some more recent ones, of her at the bus stop, walking downtown, outside her shop.

The click of a lock being released sent her heart rate skyrocketing. She hurried to replace the book, pulled the covers over herself and tried to feign sleep, striving to keep her breathing slow and even. Randy would find her and everything would be fine. She had to stay calm and give Randy time. Time. Let Chris think she was still asleep.

"I know you're awake, my Sleeping Beauty," Chris said. "I heard you moving around in here. Sorry about the locked door, but I'm not sure you can be trusted yet."

The touch of a hand to her hair made her recoil. She gave up pretending and opened her eyes.

Chris wore black denims and a plaid shirt over a black turtleneck. The beaming smile on his face made her seethe. She wanted to strike out at him, to scratch his eyes out. To kick him where it would do the most good. She inched up to a sitting position, leaning against the headboard as the room spun. Kicking him would have to wait.

"That's better, my love." Chris settled himself on the edge of the bed. "You've been asleep quite some time."

"How long? What time is it? What day is it, for that matter? Where are we?"

"My, aren't you full of questions? It doesn't matter where we are, as long as we're finally together. But, since you ask, it's Monday, around noon. I love you. I only used the ether because you didn't understand you needed to be with me, too. Now, everything will be perfect." His fawning expression disgusted her and the lifelessness in his eyes made her flesh crawl.

"You love me? You kidnap me, drug me, hurt my friends? That's not love, Chris. That's nuts." She had to stop and catch her breath, to wait for the room to stop spinning like a tilt-a-whirl.

"We're not talking about that now. That's behind us. Now, we can be happy." He stroked her cheek and she jerked her head away, sending another wave of dizziness through her.

She gasped. "Don't touch me."

"I'm sure you're feeling the aftereffects of the ether. I'm sorry I gave you so much, but I needed to take care of everything and get some sleep myself. I'll run you a nice bubble bath so you can wash away all the remnants of your past." He stood and crossed behind the screen.

Her mind raced. Could Chris possibly believe he could kidnap her and she'd agree to be part of his life? He had to be crazy. Once she heard the water running in the tub, she slid out of bed and half-crawled to the bedroom door. Before she reached the knob, strong fingers gripped her shoulders.

"I don't think you should be going anywhere," Chris said. "It's time for your bath."

He placed his hand on her elbow to lead her to the bathroom and she twisted away. "I said, 'Don't touch me,'" she repeated before her vision darkened into nothingness.

* * * * *

Security cleared Randy through the gate at Consolidated and directed him to a visitor parking area. The six-story brick building sat on a landscaped rise, surrounded by Garry oaks and Douglas firs.

Randy got out of his truck and wound his way up the tree-lined path past the granite "Consolidated Enterprises" sign to the main entrance. The immense wooden doors opened into a spacious marble-floored lobby that extended up two stories. Randy approached the curved wooden reception desk at the back of the lobby. A middle-aged woman looked up at him and smiled.

"May I help you?"

Randy displayed his badge. "I'd like to speak to someone in your Telecommunications Department regarding your telephone system."

"Is there a problem?"

"No, I just need to track down a phone. I thought it would be easiest to do it in person."

She consulted her computer. "I'll get someone for you."

While the woman made her call, Randy wandered over to an enormous fireplace and stared into the fire's dancing colors, calmed by its hypnotic spell. He heard his name being spoken and turned to greet a dark-haired man wearing faded jeans and an Oregon State sweatshirt.

"Detective Detweiler? I'm Gary Peterson, IT Services. How can I help you?"

"I've got what's supposed to be a Consolidated phone number, but your receptionist says it's not one of yours. It's come up on the periphery of a couple of cases and we'd like to be able to rule it out."

"Follow me." Gary turned and walked down a long carpeted hallway. He pushed open the door to a large office, although there was hardly any working room left beyond the banks of computers, files and bookshelves crammed with what looked like technical manuals. He swept a pile of folders off a chair and motioned Randy to sit down. Gary sat at a computer terminal and clicked the mouse a few times. "What was the number?"

Randy handed him a slip of paper with the number on it.

"All rightie, let's see what we've got." As Gary clicked his way through several screens. Randy noticed an employee directory on top of a stack of folders on the floor. He leaned over and picked it up.

"Mind if I take this directory?" he asked.

"I don't have a problem with it. They go out of date faster than we print 'em."

"Here we are," Gary said. "I think I've found the problem. That number belonged to someone who's no longer with the company and it's not been reassigned."

"Do you leave the lines active when someone leaves?" Randy asked.

"No, we shut 'em down."

"Would you mind checking?"

Gary moved to a different bank of computers and clicked some more. Randy thumbed through the directory, disappointed that it gave only work information. Still, better

Finding Sarah

than nothing. His scanning for his aliases was interrupted when Gary spoke.

"You're right. That line was never deactivated. Didn't show up because nobody's using it to make calls. Our reports only track outgoing calls."

"Would you show me where this phone line is?" Randy asked. He tucked the directory into his briefcase.

"Don't see why not. It's a boardroom on the fifth floor."

The elevator ride was swift and silent and Gary led Randy to a door halfway down the hall, swiped a card through a sensor and pushed the door open.

"Do all the offices have electronic locks?" Randy asked.

"Anything above the fourth floor. The suits work up here. The ones with the letters for titles." He grinned and held the door open.

Randy entered the room. Carpeted in taupe or mauve or whatever you called those non-colors, the office held a massive oak conference table surrounded by twelve chairs. A bank of cabinets and empty shelves adorned one wall, with a counter and more cabinets below. Randy saw a phone on wall. He looked at Gary.

"No, that phone number is active and it's not the one you gave me. That's a house phone so they can call and complain that it's too hot or too cold in here, or they're out of grub during one of their meetings."

"There's an empty jack," Randy said. "Could someone plug a phone in there and use it?"

Gary lifted one shoulder. "Suppose so, assuming they could bypass the lock. Of course any suit's key would work here and the maintenance crew has masters and so does Security. Dozens of people could get in if they wanted to."

Randy began opening the cabinets. He found an old city telephone directory, a lot of dust and three ballpoint pens.

When he opened the last cabinet door, his heart jumped. "What about this?" he asked, pointing to an answering machine.

Gary stepped over. "What the—" He reached for the machine.

Randy grasped Gary's arm. "Please. Don't touch anything." He pulled on a pair of latex gloves and moved the answering machine, revealing another set of electrical outlets and telephone jacks.

"Wait a minute," Gary said. "Now I remember. Five or six years ago, before I came on board, this office was used for a big research project. They hired a dozen temps to handle the data entry. It was rewired to handle the extra equipment and then when the job was done, they redesigned the space as a boardroom. I totally forgot about the extra outlets."

"I'd like to take this machine back to Pine Hills," Randy said.

"I don't think I'm authorized to let you do that. Let me make a quick call."

While Gary paced the hall talking into his cell phone, Randy fought the temptation to push the "play" button on the machine. This would be done by the book, one page at a time. Hell, one paragraph at a time. No way would this case get tossed because of some sloppy work on his part. They'd record the messages and Connor would run the machine through the fuming closet to raise any latents. Much as he wanted to do it here, now, himself, he knew fingerprint powder would wreak havoc with the machine.

Gary approached him. "Do you have a warrant?"

"No, but I can get one." Randy waited as Gary returned to his call.

"Okay, the boss says no problem." Gary said.

Randy exhaled, almost audibly. "Thank you. After I have this fingerprinted, I'll return it. I should be back this afternoon.

Would you have another answering machine to plug in here while this one's gone?"

"No, we use voice mail. But why not let me plug in a phone that rings directly to voice mail?"

More options to weigh. An incoming caller wouldn't pay attention to a different message. But what if his suspect came by to pick up his messages? "Is there any way to ensure that nobody gets in here until I get back?"

Gary smiled. "I can create a little electronic problem with the lock so nobody can get in."

That should cover everything but the guy calling the machine to retrieve messages remotely. All he could do now was hope that didn't happen.

"Thanks. I appreciate that. I would imagine that whoever is behind this does his work after hours, but I'd rather be careful. And, please, don't let word of my visit get out."

"Not a problem," Gary said. "I'll speak to security at the front desk as well."

Randy picked up the machine. "Thanks. I'll be back as soon as I can." This time, the elevator seemed to move in slow motion. Randy tapped his foot as he waited for the doors to open in the lobby.

* * * * *

Back at the station, Randy dropped the answering machine off with Connor and got busy running Mr. Yamaguchi's list of Med-Tekke employees though NCIC looking for anyone with a criminal record.

Aware that someone had entered the office, Randy looked up, expecting Connor. Instead, Kovak dropped a paper sack on Randy's desk.

"I brought you a sub," he said. "Meatball."

Randy mumbled a quick thank-you and reached into the bag, still reading the screen. His eyes burned and the aroma of the sandwich persuaded him to take a break.

"Get anything from Consolidated?" Kovak said.

Randy nodded, swallowing a mouthful of meatballs and bread. "Answering machine. Connor's got it."

"And Connor's done," came a voice from the hall. Connor came in with the answering machine. He set the machine on Randy's desk.

"And?" Randy said.

"Sorry—no prints. Wiped clean."

"Fuck," Randy said. "What about messages?"

"Only one."

"Dammit, Connor. Just play the damn thing for me."

Then a beep and the incoming message—"Mr. Steiglitz? This is Rose. I have done what you asked. The package is on its way. I expect payment in full tomorrow, in cash and the negatives, as we agreed."

"Any help?" Connor asked. "You're the detectives, but that doesn't sound like much to me."

"Sounds like you've got someone expecting payment for a job. Nothing too incriminating there," Kovak said. "The negatives might mean blackmail, though. You know this Steiglitz guy?"

"No." Randy pushed his sandwich aside and added Steiglitz to his growing list of names. "Play it again," he said.

Connor pressed a button and the message repeated. Randy concentrated. The woman's voice had a hint of an Asian accent. He reached for the Med-Tekke list. Scanning the pages, he found the name he was looking for. Rose Tanaka. Better than nothing. He picked up the phone and called Mr. Yamaguchi. The man wasn't in, but when he identified himself as a cop, a secretary told him Rose Tanaka had only worked for

Med-Tekke for six months and she hadn't reported for work in several days.

"She did it," Randy said. "Steiglitz, or someone using the name paid her to steal the toxin. She did the job, took the money and ran."

"No proof," Kovak said.

"I'll get some. Meanwhile, I'm going to take this machine back to Consolidated." He was halfway out the door when Connor's voice stopped him.

"Don't you want the remote code?"

He swiveled. "You mean so I can call in myself?"

"Well, duh. Yeah."

Shit. He was really losing his focus. "Yes, of course. Thanks. I owe you."

"You gonna eat that sandwich?" Connor asked.

"Help yourself."

Chapter Twenty-One

☙

The darkness lifted and Sarah's memory returned. Braving a peek through barely opened eyes, she found herself alone in the bedroom. She lay still, trying to make sure Chris thought she was asleep. At least twice she was aware of the door opening and closing. The third time it opened, it didn't close again and she heard faint footsteps and then the quiet sounds of breathing from the end of the bed. She counted to one hundred and her visitor remained. Chris wasn't leaving this time. She might as well find out as much as she could about where she was and what he planned to do to her. She turned over and raised her eyelids.

"Hello again," Chris said with a smile. "I think I know what's the matter. Wait right here." He darted out of the room, locking the door behind him.

The man was totally out of touch with reality, but she was too weak to do anything about it now. She sank into the pillows and closed her eyes again.

Chris returned, carrying a tray and set it on the nightstand. "I thought you might be hungry. It's been awhile since you've eaten."

Sarah contemplated the tray with its bowl of cereal and Styrofoam cup of milk along with some toast and jam. The Chris she remembered wouldn't hurt her. But then, he wouldn't have kidnapped her, either. He was bringing her breakfast, not coming at her with a knife. Knife. She checked the tray again. Only a plastic spoon.

"Eat something. Please," Chris said. "I remember how you would get if you skipped meals."

"Why should I trust you? You kidnapped me. You drugged me. You poisoned cats." Her stomach tightened as she spoke the words.

"I told you before, we're not talking about that now, Sarah. Please eat."

Her stomach rumbled. She would have to play along until she got her bearings.

"I swear, there's nothing in the food," he said.

As reluctant as she was to comply with any of Chris' fantasies, she knew he was right about eating. She'd already passed out once. If she was going to figure a way out of here, she'd need all of her faculties intact.

"Why am I here?" she asked. "And where's here, anyway?" Every instinct told her to run like hell, but something told her to keep him talking, keep things normal, keep her tone nonchalant. Drugs in the food or not, she decided to take her chances and eat something.

Chris took a seat on a padded trunk under the window. He crossed one leg over the other knee, revealing lightweight hiking boots on his feet. "We're at my uncle's summer cabin. He won't be using it for a while. And you'll see why we're here soon enough. Now eat."

Sarah reached for the toast, spooned some jam onto a slice and began nibbling at it, trying not to gag. The first bites were cardboard, but as the sugary jam worked its way into her bloodstream, she managed to choke down the rest. Watching Chris all the while, she took the bowl of cereal and poured some of the milk over the flakes. He sat there, a pleased expression on his face. Almost devotion. She suppressed a shiver and handed him the cup. "Here. You drink the rest."

"Of course," he said and gulped the milk, wiping his mouth with the back of his hand when he finished. "I told you, I only drugged you to get you here. We're together now and I'll never hurt you."

Sarah took a spoonful of her cereal. Trying her hardest to stay calm, she spoke to Chris between bites, studying his expression for any reaction. "You didn't answer my question. Where exactly is this cabin?" She struggled to remember anything. Had she walked into the house, or had she been carried? Was it day or night when they arrived? They could be anywhere. Would Randy be able to find her? She had no recollection of anything other than waking up briefly in the back of a car. A big car. More like an SUV.

He smiled and sat on the edge of the bed, just beyond her reach. "I can't tell you that yet. But, I can tell you there's not another cabin around for more than a mile in any direction and we're at least five miles from the main highway. My uncle liked his solitude."

"What about my clothes? I can't exactly wear this all the time." She tugged at her jersey.

"The dresser is full of clothes for you to wear. You finish eating. I'll run you another bath. And before you try to get out again, the front door's locked." Chris stood and went into the bathroom.

She heard the water running in the tub and Chris came back into the bedroom. He began rummaging through the dresser. "I'll lay your clothes out. You can come out to the front room when you're done. It's warmer."

"I'm not doing anything of the sort."

She pushed the covers away and swung her legs over the bed. The dizziness had passed. She stood. Chris turned and took her arm. "I think your bath is ready."

Sarah pulled away. "I don't want to take a bath." Heartened by her returning strength, she struggled against his tightening grip and swung her free palm at his face. He clasped her wrist before the blow landed. His eyes narrowed—his lips pressed into a straight line.

"It will be different with us, Sarah. Not like the bad girls. We won't have any hitting. We'll have true love."

She tried to kick out, but Chris dodged.

"I said we wouldn't have hitting," he growled. He twirled her and pressed her back into the wall, arms above her head, holding both her wrists. "I don't like it when there has to be hitting."

"Stop, Chris. You're hurting me!" He didn't seem to hear — his eyes were slits.

He pressed his body against hers and she felt his rising erection, his pelvis thrusting. She tried to bring her knee up to his groin, but he jerked his hips out of reach, took half a step backward. Keeping her wrists pinned to the wall with one hand, he brought the other up as if to strike her. "Don't make me hit," he said, each word a small explosion.

"Chris! Wait. Please. You're right. No hitting." She went limp against the wall and he released his hold. She dropped to her knees, covering her head with her hands. When Chris said nothing, Sarah peeked up at him. Her brain spun, trying to make sense of what he was saying. "Tell me what you want. I'm not a bad girl. You know that."

He gazed down at her. She watched his face relax and a blank smile return.

"Not with David," he said. "It was a mistake to marry him instead of me, but you were married. It's that overgrown cop. You spent the night with him. You need to cleanse yourself. Otherwise you'll be like those others and I might have to hit you. Please don't make me."

He guided her into the bathroom. "You need a bath," he said again. "You need to be cleansed. Take your bath, get dressed and come out to the living room where I have a fire."

"I'm not taking a bath with you in here."

"Of course not. I'll be waiting in the living room." Chris' voice returned to its matter-of-fact tone, as if he'd asked her what she wanted for dinner.

"I want your solemn promise you won't come back in here until I'm done."

"I promise. You'll have all the privacy you want until afterwards."

"After what?" A chill ran down her spine.

"Why, after we're married, silly."

She gaped at him. He left the room, the click of the lock piling despair on top of the chill.

* * * * *

Randy sat at his desk and stared at the fax from Victoria. No outgoing calls from that number. So, Mr. Consolidated hadn't plugged his own phone into the jack. No real surprise. Seven numbers had called in. Tony Mazzaro and Rose Tanaka were there. Likewise Sarah's Gertie. Three pay phones and one nameless number from Oregon Trust. He jotted down the number and grabbed his windbreaker. Enough driving for one day. The exercise would do him good.

The wind had picked up. He zipped his jacket and hastened his pace on the four-block walk to Oregon Trust. The receptionist checked the phone number Randy gave her and informed him that Bob was the man he needed, but he wasn't due back from lunch for another twenty minutes. Randy turned down her offer of coffee and was halfway through a *National Geographic* article about walruses when she informed him that Bob was back.

Bob, thin and bony with a receding hairline, sat at his desk in a cubicle at the rear of the room, almost identical to every other cubicle Randy had ever visited. Only the pictures on the desks varied. Randy touched a framed photo of a beaming adolescent wearing Pine Hills High School graduation attire. "Your daughter?" Randy asked.

"Yes. She's a freshman at Rutgers now. What can I do for you, Officer?"

"It's Detective and you can tell me why you called this number last January." Randy dropped a slip of paper in front of the man.

Bob looked at the paper. "Who was I supposed to have called?"

"Let's say it's someone at Consolidated. Maybe about an electrical fire at a gift boutique? That Special Something? Does that ring a bell?"

Bob's smile faded. He rooted through his Rolodex and compared the number on the slip to a card in his files. He slumped down in his chair. "Are you going to tell my boss? They promised me that nothing would happen. I did everything exactly like they asked."

"Who's 'they'?"

"He, actually. Name's Mr. Meierbridge or something like that." Bob stood up, shrugged and sat down again. "He said that if I'd slow down the payments on an insurance claim, he'd pull some strings at Rutgers and my daughter would be admitted on a scholarship. All I had to do was say the paperwork needed more information, or there was a computer glitch. Heck, those things happen all the time anyway."

Randy leaned in, taking satisfaction from the way Bob inched away. "I assume you investigated the possibility of arson?"

"Of course—it's an old building. She overloaded the system with a coffeepot, hotplate and a space heater in the back office. Fire department agreed—I can show you the reports."

Bob's story matched what he'd seen in Sarah's files. "I believe you. Have you ever met Mr. Meierbridge?"

"No. Everything was done by phone. Consolidated is a big client. I need this job and he said if I didn't cooperate, he'd pull the account."

"I'm going to need that in writing," Randy said.

Bob picked up the picture of his daughter. "I'm not sure..."

"We could do it at the station." Randy started to rise. "Or I could report it to the Insurance Commission."

"No, no need for that, Detective." Bob sat up straight and put his fingers to his keyboard. "I can type it up now if you'd like."

"Why don't you do that. I'll sit right here while you work." Randy pushed his chair back so he could extend his legs in front of him, sat down and crossed his arms across his chest.

Fifteen minutes later, Bob had produced a signed statement, which he placed in an Oregon Trust envelope and handed to Randy. "I hope this will be enough."

"One more thing."

Bob peered at him. "Yes?"

"I need the file for the Tucker car accident—happened a year ago. Suicide."

"I'll get it." He stood and Randy saw his eyes widen and his mouth drop. "Tucker. We're talking about the same woman here, aren't we? I don't handle life insurance, so I never connected the two cases." He crossed behind Randy. "I'll be right back."

Bob returned, a sickly expression on his face. "We don't seem to have a hard copy of the file. Must have gotten lost in the mix-up after the break-in."

"Or deliberately stolen," Randy said.

"Hey, you can't think I had anything to do with that."

"What I think is immaterial. Can I get a printout of the computer version?"

Bob stepped around his desk and got busy with his computer. He scanned the pages as they came off the printer.

"Anything strike you as unusual?" Randy asked.

"No—police did their report. Our investigator agreed. But you know as well as I do that the police report takes precedence over our investigation no matter which way it turns out." He handed the pages to Randy.

"She got the value of the car, plus a five grand death benefit from the car insurance policy. But we couldn't pay off on the life insurance—not on a suicide with a policy under two years old."

"I understand," Randy said. "I'll be in touch if I need more. And if Mr. Meierbridge calls you again, I want to know about it." He handed Bob his business card.

Randy half jogged back to the station. Maybe he had enough to get a warrant for phone records for all the numbers that had called the machine. Somewhere, there had to be one number that had called all of them back. And give him his first concrete lead to Mr. Consolidated.

Chapter Twenty-Two

༄

Fighting to control the surge of fear, Sarah tried to think. What had Chris meant about bad girls? He had been calm enough until she tried to fight him. And when she did, he became aroused. Could it be the fighting that excited him? He was talking about sex. He had needed the struggle for sex. Oh God. The realization pierced her like a sword. Her breakfast threatened to come back up. She forced herself to breathe deep, even breaths. Leaning against the wall, panting, trying to send her fear somewhere deep inside where she could function around it, she knew she would have to remain submissive, no matter what.

She examined the clothes Chris had laid on the bed. A long plaid wool skirt and a black turtleneck. Hers? No, they were too new. Black lace bra and panties. She picked up the bra and checked the tag. Her size. Everything was her size. Her mouth grew dry. Maybe that man had looked at more than her computer and bank statements.

Sarah took a quick bath, straining to hear signs that Chris was coming back into the room. She dressed as he requested. Play along. Keep him calm. She sat on the bed and waited, trying to be rational. True to his word, Chris was leaving her alone. Her head was clear. She studied the room, looking for a means of escape, or something to use as a weapon. No lamps in the room—the only light source was a ceiling fixture. The lock on the door appeared to be a standard interior door lock, but reversed so the locking mechanism was on the outside. That meant that when Chris was in the room, the door would be unlocked. She filed that piece of information away. Until she knew what was on the other side, she would play Chris' game. She sucked in a breath and tapped on the locked door.

"Chris? Can I come out, please? It's cold in here." She backed away and sat on the bed, twisting her hands in her lap. Within seconds, she heard approaching footsteps and two knocks on the door.

"Are you dressed, my darling?" Chris opened the door and peeked in.

"Yes, but my feet are freezing. Where are my shoes and socks?"

"I'm sorry about that. I have a fire going. You can warm your feet there."

A fire. Visions of sturdy pokers and tongs brought a glimmer of hope. She followed Chris into a large living area. The furniture was old but sturdy. A wood framed sofa looked out onto a deep wooden front porch and two plaid chairs sat at right angles to a fireplace on the adjoining wall. A small padded footstool nestled between the chairs. Security bars on all the windows.

"What's your choice?" Chris asked. "The couch will give you a view of the sunset, but it's warmer by the fireplace."

Sarah pushed one of the chairs closer to the fire and adjusted the footstool so that it was almost in the hearth. She sat in the chair and raised her feet, letting the heat from the fire begin to overcome some of the iciness. No fireplace tools. Not even a basket of logs. Tears rose again.

"You're so quiet," Chris said. "I do love your voice. I would call your answering machine to hear it."

Sarah felt like she'd fallen off a cliff. She'd had to be so darned stubborn, insisting Chris was harmless. How blind could she have been? Randy must think she was an idiot. "What do you want, Chris? Why am I here?" She kept her voice low so he couldn't hear it quaver.

"You. That's all I've ever wanted. You were supposed to wait for me."

"You mean after graduation? But you went away and I thought you had all those other girls."

"Those were bad girls, Sarah. Not like you. They didn't count. You and I had something different. You said you wanted to wait until you got married. And then you married someone else. That wasn't right."

"Chris, I don't know what to say. We were kids. It was high school. We changed."

"I never changed. After my father died, I knew you were my destiny. Soon, we'll be married and everything will be the way it should be. I have everything we need."

Sarah shivered despite the fire. "There's some daylight left—why don't you show me around outside? Give me my shoes and a coat I can use."

"Oh not yet. I think you need some more time to adjust to your new life. If I gave you your shoes back, I'm afraid you might try to run away."

He was darn right about that. Surely she'd be able to find some other cabin, one with a telephone. Five miles to the highway, if she knew which way to run. She needed to get an idea of where she was.

Sarah heard the start of irritation in his voice. She hurried to change the subject. "Can I get a glass of water? I'm thirsty. Must still be dehydrated."

"I'll get you some water. Today, you rest. Later, you'll be able to cook to your heart's content. Oh, Sarah, won't it be wonderful? I have a week's vacation left and we can be alone together here and when we go back, I'll go to work and you'll be there every night when I get home. We'll have a drink while you cook dinner and it'll be just the two of us."

Sarah choked back the gorge rising in her throat. A week. Chris planned to keep her here for a week. How could she put

Finding Sarah

him off for a week? Randy would have to find her before then. Before Chris thought they were married. Before he moved into her bed. She spun her head around, searching for a second bedroom. She looked at the couch. Not a sleeper, but Chris would fit. He'd have to.

"Do I get the grand tour of the cabin at least?" she asked. She stood up and strolled across the room, heading toward what seemed to be the kitchen. Chris took her hand and she couldn't control the shudder.

"Are you still cold?" he asked. "Why don't you go back by the fire? I'll bring you water and a blanket."

"No, I'm fine. I'd like to see where we'll be living for the next week." She continued around the corner of the room and through a doorway. The kitchen was about half the size of the living room, much of its area consumed by a large wooden table.

Chris released her hand as she opened cabinets. She found dishes and plastic microwave cookware and some cereal and bread. She pulled a Styrofoam cup from the shelf and crossed to the refrigerator. Inside were a container of milk, one of juice, as well as a dozen eggs, cheese and some lunch meats. She saw fresh fruits and vegetables in a crisper drawer. The door held an array of condiments, all in plastic squeeze bottles.

"Are we going to be living on cereal and bologna sandwiches?"

"Oh no. We have a wide selection." He pulled open the door to the freezer compartment. "You name it, I'm sure we have it."

Sarah looked at the stacks of frozen foods. Everything from Chinese to Indian. "Nice," she muttered, seeing the microwave on the counter. She went to the sink and filled the cup with water.

Chris had planned this all too carefully. She opened a drawer. All the eating utensils were flimsy plastic. She opened another. Not a knife to be found. Cereal, sandwiches and nuke food. Nothing needing any preparation. She pulled open more cabinets and drawers. Not even a frying pan. Shouldn't mountain cabins have heavy cast-iron frying pans?

Chris had been planning this for a long time. She was split in two. One Sarah was terrified, wanting to fight her way out of the cabin. The other understood that safety would come from waiting, from remaining calm until the right moment presented itself. She forced the calm Sarah to the forefront. She would be whoever Chris wanted her to be.

The sip of water chilled her all the way down. She poured the remainder down the sink and set the cup on the counter. The window over the kitchen sink sported the same security bars as the rest of the house. She forced a smile and extended her hand. "Show me the rest."

"There's not much to show. One more bedroom and a small bathroom." He pointed to two doors at the far end of the living room.

"Your bedroom, right?"

"Not for long. I thought we'd get married tonight."

"Tonight!" Her blood turned to ice in her veins. "I don't think two people can be married all by themselves. Maybe we can wait until we get back to Pine Hills and do it right. You know, the way good girls do it. Family, someone to give me away."

"We can have a big party when we're back. Maybe even a second ceremony. But I have everything we need." He went to a cabinet in the living room and opened it. Inside was a small television-VCR unit. He held up a video tape. "It's all on here. Come with me." Beaming, he dragged her back to her bedroom.

He flung open the lid to the trunk and removed a large parcel of tissue and laid it on the bed. He peeled back the crinkling paper and reverently lifted a white satin and lace gown in his arms.

She swallowed. He thought he could bring her out here, dress her up and marry her. Never mind that it wouldn't be legal. If he thought it was, he'd try to consummate the marriage. Sarah fought the rising nausea.

"Your wedding dress," he whispered. He held it out for her inspection. "Isn't it lovely? It belonged to my aunt. I'm sure it will fit you. You'll be the most beautiful bride on the planet." He moved toward her, arms extended.

* * * * *

Randy was halfway down the hall to his office when Laughlin's bark stopped him in his tracks. Shit. Had he missed a court appearance? Forgotten to file a report? His mind whirled through the possibilities as he turned and paced back to Laughlin's office.

"Sir?" he said from the doorway.

Laughlin jerked his head in a command to enter. "Shut the door."

Randy did as he asked and stood at attention across the desk from his chief. Laughlin lowered the papers he's been reading and took off his glasses. "Sit."

Randy edged around the chair and eased his body down. "Is there a problem?"

"You tell me, Detweiler." He picked up the papers and shook them. "You been harassing Frank Scofield?"

"No, sir. I called on him once."

"Mind telling me why you needed to see someone who lives in Portland and has connections up the yin yang—connections to *my* boss and upward?"

"I was looking for Consolidated connections to a case."

"Still that Tucker thing?"

Randy swallowed. "Yes, sir. His ex-wife is a part owner of That Special Something. Add that to the fact that he sits on the

Board of Consolidated, it seemed logical to question him. But I never harassed him."

"What about his ex-wife? She said you weren't a hundred percent professional when you interrogated her."

"Interrogated?" He balled his fists and jammed them into his pockets. "I questioned her. Like I would anyone. Have you ever met her?"

Laughlin shook his head.

"Sir, if there was any unprofessional conduct during that interview, it was hers. Shit, she practically shoved her tits in my face." He snapped to his feet, every muscle tensed. "I'm sorry you think I would behave in the manner they described."

"Sit down. You know the rules. I get a complaint, I have to investigate. For now, let's say I've investigated." Laughlin leaned back in his chair and Randy unclenched his jaw. He lowered himself back into the chair.

"Anything more, sir? I have a new lead on the Tucker case."

"Case? What case?" There was a new irritation in Laughlin's voice. "You caught the woman."

"But not who put her up to it. I've got a link between the robbery, an insurance claim that wasn't handled properly, a peeping Tom and in all probability, whoever poisoned Mrs. Cooper's and my cats."

"Tell me more."

Randy explained his latest findings, his stomach sinking as he watched Laughlin's brow furrow and his lips tighten. He could see the man's jaw twitch.

"It's got to be someone with a Consolidated connection," Randy continued. "I thought if I could get a warrant for the phone records for all these people my unknown has coerced, I'd find him."

"Aside from the cats, you got anyone who's actually broken a law here? Someone filing a complaint?"

"Not exactly."

"Well, I need exactly while you're on duty. Don't think I don't know Kovak's been covering your ass. Everyone's willing to cut you some slack because…"

Of my cats, Randy thought. *They think I'm losing it because someone came after my pets.* Not that it would be any better if they knew it was because of a woman he'd just met. "I'm fine, sir. I might have let my personal life get too close, but it's under control. And the cats are going to be fine, too."

"You've got a lot of vacation time. You want to use a few days and regroup?"

"No, sir."

"Then get to work. Have Kovak bring you up to speed on what he's been doing and let's play by the book."

"A page at a time."

"Right now, you'd better start thinking about a word at a time. I don't need any more complaints, warranted or otherwise." Laughlin pulled on his glasses and picked up the papers from his desk.

Randy trudged down the hall to his office. So much for calling Victoria without a warrant and so much for getting the damn thing.

Chapter Twenty-Three

๖๑

Before Chris could reach her, Sarah clapped her hand over her mouth and bolted for the bathroom. She heaved until there was nothing left in her stomach and sat back to catch her breath.

"Are you all right, my darling?" Chris called from behind the screen.

Another paroxysm overwhelmed her and she succumbed to the dry heaves until her stomach burned. "Leave me alone," she managed to cry between spasms of retching. She blew her nose and wiped her face before peeking around the screen into the bedroom. Chris stood there, a look of genuine alarm on his face.

"Are you all right?"

"No, I'm not. I think it's the aftereffects of the ether. I'm going to have to go to bed, Chris. I'm sorry to delay the wedding, but I'm sick." She hoped she managed to sound disappointed.

"Oh, you poor thing. Of course. I can wait a little while. I'll check on you in a bit."

"Please. Go. Leave me alone." She rushed back into the bathroom and ran the water in the sink, made some choking noises and flushed the toilet. She listened until she heard the door close before brushing her teeth to get rid of the bitter taste of bile and returned to the bedroom. Chris had rewrapped the dress and laid it on top of the trunk. Sarah curled up on the bed. Tears spilled down her cheeks and she made no effort to control them.

Finding Sarah

Once her tears ceased, she sat up. Chris was sick. No question. She could probably put him off tonight and maybe she could figure a way out of here.

Shoes. She needed shoes. She'd peeked out the windows and the trail, as far as she could tell, was not something she could navigate barefoot. Rocks, sticks, leaves. She thought she'd seen some snow patches, too—they must be up fairly high. They hadn't had snow in Pine Hills in over a month.

She went to the trunk, moved the dress to the bed and lifted the lid. He wouldn't expect her to be married barefoot would he? There would be shoes. She pulled out more tissue wrapped packets and at the bottom of the chest found a pair of white satin pumps with sturdy two-inch heels. Darn. Stilettos would have made a good weapon. She tried one on. It was at least two sizes too large, but she could stuff the toes with tissue. The height of the heels would be a problem, but at least she wouldn't have to risk shredding the soles of her feet on the trails in the woods. She heard Chris coming down the hall. She replaced everything and lay down on the bed.

Chris tapped on the door. "Sarah? Are you asleep?" The door opened. "I brought you some soup." He crossed to the bed and touched her shoulder. "You're not asleep, are you?"

"Not anymore. What do you want? I told you to leave me alone. I'm sick."

"I want you to feel better." He set a steaming Styrofoam cup on the nightstand. "Chicken broth. You can sip it."

"Thanks. Maybe in a little while."

"I hope so. Please don't make me angry. Those bad girls made me angry and sometimes they got hurt. I don't like it that way. I've been waiting for you, so we can do it the right way. You went off with that cop, so I can't wait any longer." He grasped her arm, this time hard enough to make her wince.

She yanked it back, trying to pull loose from his grasp. "Stop, Chris. You're hurting me."

She heard his breathing rasp as he slowly relinquished the grip on her arm. His eyes had taken on a feral gleam. "You put on the dress and come out. I've waited long enough. I said I don't want to hurt you." He squeezed her arm harder and there was a look of arousal on his face. She lowered her eyes and saw the evidence of his growing erection.

"Tell me about the bad girls, so I don't make any mistakes. Please. I don't want to be a bad girl."

"They weren't important, Sarah. Not like you. They were just girls, but they liked too many men. It didn't work with them, so I had to hit them and they hit back, but you're not a bad girl, so we shouldn't have to hit. Sometimes I forget."

She choked back her panic. "You won't forget with me, Chris, will you? That I'm not a bad girl? That we don't need to hit?"

"I'll try to remember."

"I'll try not to make you angry," she said. "Tell me what you want me to do."

"Finish your soup and get dressed."

"Oh, but I can't do that. You know it's bad luck to see the bride on her wedding day. I'll stay in here tonight and we can have the wedding tomorrow. Besides, my stomach is still queasy."

"No, I think not. We'll get married tonight. I've waited so long." His tongue darted in and out of his mouth, licking his lips. Sarah couldn't help but think of a snake.

"All right," she said, the smile frozen on her face. She prayed he couldn't read her face the way Randy could. "But it will take awhile. I don't have my maid of honor and bridesmaids here to help, you know. And I want to look beautiful for you."

"I'll go change and I'll be waiting. Call out when you're ready." He left the room and locked the door behind him.

She shoved everything she knew about Chris from her mind. This was a different person, someone walking a fine line between fantasy and reality. Sarah unwrapped the dress and removed the rest of the contents of the trunk. She gathered everything and took it into the bathroom. Thank goodness the lingerie was new. Nevertheless, she couldn't repress a shudder of disgust while putting on the bra and panties.

She slipped the dress over her head. Its cool satin caught on the fear-induced sweat that coated her body. The row of tiny buttons up the back fought her trembling fingers, but she managed to fasten them. She stared at her reflection in the mirror. A simple, elegant dress. High-necked, with long, lace sleeves. She remembered trying on her wedding dress and knowing that in it, she was truly beautiful. Chris' aunt had probably felt the same way. How sad that now the dress was going to be used for such ugliness. A tear slithered down her cheek.

She attached the train to the hooks at her waist and set the headpiece and veil into her hair. She hadn't washed it and it felt matted and grimy. What was she thinking? Put a wedding dress on a woman and she automatically wants to look her best? She balled up her fists and put them to her mouth against a rising wave of hysterical laughter.

Even with tissue stuffed into the shoes, she could barely keep them on her feet when she walked. How would she manage to run in them? She'd manage. She had to. With any luck, she'd be rescued before she had to go too far.

"Randy. Where are you?" she whispered. He was a good detective. He'd find her. She jerked at the sound of a tap on the door.

"Sarah? How are you doing?"

"Almost done." How long would he wait?

"I think you've had plenty of time. Everything is set."

She heard the impatience in his voice. That answered her question. "One more minute," she called. "I need to be perfect."

She peered into the trunk one last time. In the corner was one more tissue-wrapped package. She opened it and discovered a small bible bound in pale blue leather. Old, new, borrowed, blue, flashed through her mind. Chris had covered everything. She pulled the veil over her face and crossed to the bedroom door. After a shaky breath, she rapped on its wooden surface. "All right, Chris," she said in a tremulous voice. "I'm ready."

* * * * *

"Thanks to Mr. Flinn's confession, we might get out on time for a change," Kovak said. "I love it when they see the error of their ways."

Randy smiled. "Yeah, but catching them with three wallets, five watches and an eyewitness identification doesn't hurt."

"That's true enough. But I like to think it's my charming powers of persuasion that got Mr. Flinn to admit he'd been burglarizing that neighborhood." Kovak looked at his watch. "Look, the guy's been booked and as lead on the case, the paperwork is mine to file. Go. Find your woman."

It *was* officially end of shift. Randy raised his eyebrows. "You sure? I still owe you for last week."

"I'm sure I'll collect."

"Thanks, but call me if you need me."

"What part of 'go' don't you understand?"

Randy was out the door and in his truck in under a minute. He should be able to catch Sarah at the store before she went home. He punched her number on his cell phone and waited out the recording. It wasn't quite five-thirty. She should be doing paperwork. "Hi, it's me. You there?"

Finding Sarah

When she didn't pick up, he drove a little faster. He parked in the alley and rang the back doorbell. No answer. She must have had a slow day, not much paperwork. He got back in his truck and drove to her apartment, trying not to grin like an idiot as he knocked on her door. The grin faded as the minutes ticked away and she didn't answer. Okay, she could be on the bus. In the john. Taking a shower. On the phone. He called her apartment and could hear the phone ringing through the door, then her machine.

He told himself to calm down, to quit worrying and walked across the hall. Maggie answered his knock, Othello cuddled in her arms.

"Have you seen Sarah?" he asked.

"Not today, no. I was on a Big Sister retreat all weekend — didn't get home 'til late and was volunteering at the Women's Center all day. Why?"

"I don't know. It's not like we had plans. I stopped by the shop and she wasn't there and she's not here. Probably still on her way. Stopped at the store or something. Sorry to bother you."

"Wait here." Maggie passed Othello to Randy.

"Feeling better, guy?" The cat snuggled against his chest and purred. Dr. Lee had predicted Starsky and Hutch would be released in a day or two, but Randy enjoyed the moment with the warm ball of fur.

"Okay, I've got her key. Let's check."

"Maggie, I think that might be a little presumptuous."

She cocked her head and looked at him. "Well, maybe I thought I heard something and as a good neighbor, I should check it out. And since you're here and you're a cop, if maybe I did hear something, maybe you should come with me."

"Can't fault that logic." He swapped the cat for the key and they walked across the hall.

Randy unlocked the door. Maggie called out to Sarah, but there was no response. They stepped inside. Everything was neat. No signs of anything amiss. And then Randy saw the folded bundle of clothing on the couch next to Sarah's purse. The clothes she'd been carrying when he dropped her off last night. A steel band formed in his gut.

"Wait here," he said to Maggie. "And please don't touch anything."

"Oh my God. You think something's happened to her?"

"Is it like her to leave without her purse?"

Maggie shook her head.

"Okay, I'm going to check things out. I think you should go back to your apartment. There's nothing you can do here. And Sarah might try to call you." He cut off her attempts to argue.

"All right, but I'm going to call around to her friends."

"That's a good idea. Let me know if you hear anything."

She left, rubbing the cat to her cheek.

Randy walked through the apartment. Sarah's bed was neatly made, her closet orderly. Saturday night's dinner dishes were in the rack by the sink. The kitchen wastebasket sat in the middle of the floor, empty. Was she taking out the trash? He'd feel like an idiot if she came marching up the back stairs. But a happy idiot.

He went to the back porch and tried the back door. Unlocked. He called her name. Nothing. He dashed down the wooden stairs and stopped on the bottom landing. Stepping carefully, he crossed the yard and circled the dumpster, eyes scouring the ground for anything unusual, as if finding trash next to a dumpster might be unusual. He pried the lid open and peered inside. One lone plastic bag of trash sat in the middle of the container.

Back inside Sarah's apartment, Randy forced himself to slow down and think. He was a detective, for God's sake. This was his job and he usually did it very well. The answering machine light blinked. He pressed the play button. A mechanical voice told him there were seven unplayed messages.

Three beeps. One automated message about a foolproof investment opportunity. One from Sarah's mother asking why she hadn't called. That had been at seven—Sarah had still been with him. Another beep. Then Sarah's mother again. He listened to her voice. It could almost have been Sarah's.

"It's Mom. If you're not home yet, I hope you're having fun, whatever you're doing. Don't bother to call back. I'm going to bed. Talk to you next weekend. Love you."

He picked up her green sweater from the couch. He turned it in his hands, absorbing her scent. He folded it carefully and sat down to check her purse. She would have taken it if she'd left on her own. He spilled the contents onto the cushion beside him and suppressed a pang of guilt as he peeked into her private life. Her keys, wallet, a cosmetic case—all there. The steel band tightened another two notches. Wherever Sarah was, it was not someplace she had planned to go and she'd left in a big hurry.

Chapter Twenty-Four

ಐ

Sarah wiped her hands on the handkerchief she'd found in the trunk. The pounding of her heart almost overshadowed the sound of footsteps coming toward the door. She took deep breaths, trying to ignore the ringing in her ears. Stay calm. Don't get him angry. Thank goodness the veil would hide her face.

The door opened and Chris stood before her, decked out in a black tuxedo with tails, silver cravat, cummerbund and pocket square. Strains of Wagner's wedding processional issued from the living room. Chris handed her a bouquet of white silk roses. Her knees threatened to give way and Chris took her arm and led her from the room.

"You look exquisite," Chris whispered in her ear as he stopped in front of the television. Through the haze of the tulle, she could make out some sort of clergyman beginning to recite the ceremony from the screen. He looked vaguely familiar. She stood at Chris' side, dumbfounded as she watched a television wedding ceremony, complete with attendants and guests. Only when the clergyman used Chris' name did she begin to pay attention. Chris had taped some wedding and doctored it so that their names were being inserted into the ceremony. She looked again. Good Lord, a TV show wedding, not even a real ceremony. She didn't know whether to laugh or cry.

Now it was her turn to say, "I do." Unable to speak at first, she felt Chris squeeze her hands and she managed to croak the words. He beamed at her and reached into his pocket. He held her left hand in his and placed a gold band on her fourth finger. The ring burned like fire against her chilled hands. "You may kiss the bride," seemed to reverberate through the room. Chris lifted her veil and she closed her eyes in dread. His lips pressed against hers. She would bite his tongue if he went any further, but his kiss was a chaste one. The music changed to Mendelssohn's recessional and Chris led her to the kitchen where a platter of cheese and microwaved hors d'oeuvres awaited. A silver ice bucket and a bottle of champagne sat next to a tray of cookies.

He dropped her hand long enough to open the champagne and pour two glasses into plastic flutes. "To the new Mrs. Christopher Westmoreland," he said, raising his glass and handing her the second. He touched her flute with his and Sarah stifled a snicker at the dull click of the plastic glasses.

"Drink, my bride," he said.

She touched the glass to her lips and placed it on the table.

"Let's go sit in the living room and join the party," Chris said. He filled a large plate with an assortment of offerings from the table and handed Sarah back her glass. "Don't forget your champagne. It's a special occasion, after all."

With a sigh, she carried her champagne to the living room. Chris had stoked the fire while she was dressing and he gestured to one of the chairs. The television set displayed a ballroom filled with elegantly clad guests dancing to the music of a small orchestra. Chris set the platter on the hearth and lifted a cookie to her lips. "I'm sorry we couldn't have a real wedding cake, but it wouldn't have survived the trip. This will have to do."

So much for stabbing him with a cake cutter. She nibbled a bit of the cookie.

"Don't be so dainty," he said "Eat the whole thing. Then you feed me one."

Sarah chewed the cookie, although sawdust would have been easier to swallow. She took a sip of champagne to force it down. Tempted as she was to smash a cookie into Chris' face, she held one up to his mouth. He grasped her hands and guided the morsel into his mouth, licking her fingers in the process. She almost gagged.

Get him talking. Keep him occupied, out of the bedroom. "Why don't you get the champagne?" she asked. "Like you said, it's a special occasion."

"Good idea. You wait right here, my love."

She forced a smile. As soon as he left the room, she threw the remains of her drink into the fireplace. The fire hissed, then glowed. She tilted the empty glass to her lips, lowering it when Chris returned with the bottle. He smiled and filled her glass with the bubbly spirit.

"You, too," she said. "But finish yours first. No fair if I'm ahead of you." She watched as he quaffed the remainder of his glass and refilled it.

He took his seat across from her, sipping his champagne and gazing into her eyes. She met his for a moment. God, where to go next? Chris thought they were at their wedding reception. What would he expect the new bride to do? Eat? Dance? Both turned her stomach. The thought of the bedroom was worse. She tried more small talk. "You did a nice job with the wedding," she said. "How long have you been planning it?"

"The wedding? Not that long. But marrying you? I've known for years we were meant to be together. I decided it was time to do something."

"So you decided we'd get married here, in secret? And you kidnapped me to bring me here?" Sarah scrutinized Chris' expression, searching for any clue that he was getting upset. So far, he seemed content to be chatting away at their wedding reception. She held the platter out and he took some cheese.

"I've already told you I was sorry to have to do it that way. But I was running out of patience. I had to keep you from becoming a bad girl with that overgrown cop."

She heard the irritation returning to his voice, saw him clenching his fists. She smiled and stood, moving toward the television set, where the guests were still dancing. She began waltzing herself around the room, trying to see out the windows. The moonlight gave only glimpses of shadows and trees beyond the front porch, dimmed by the light inside the cabin. They'd come in a car. Where was it now? She glanced back at Chris, who was watching her with undisguised admiration as he sipped his champagne.

"You're beautiful," he said and stood up to join her dance.

An icy chill ran down her spine. Thank God, the music changed to an upbeat rock and roll tune. She could handle dancing as long as they didn't have to touch. She watched his moves, seeing no evidence that the champagne had affected him yet. Disheartened, she vowed to try harder. When the song finished, she whirled back to the hearth and poured another glass of champagne for Chris. "Here. I'll bet you're thirsty after all that."

He accepted the glass.

"Drink," she said.

"You, too."

"Sure. But would you mind bringing me one of those strawberries from the table? I love a strawberry in my champagne. A big one, please." As soon as he turned, she splashed the remainder of her glass into the fire.

Chris returned with the fruit and a huge grin. "Here you go, my sweet." He plopped it into her empty glass with a flourish.

"Drink. Once the cork is out, it goes flat." She topped off her glass. "I think I might be ahead of you again."

Chris drained his glass and accepted her refill. "You wouldn't be trying to get me drunk, now, would you? It's our wedding night, after all."

* * * * *

Randy sped back to Sarah's shop. Was she inside, unconscious? The front door was locked, the "Closed" sign in the door of the dark interior space. He forced himself to calm down, to regroup. After three calming breaths, he knocked on neighboring shop doors until he found someone working late at the Golden Needle. Someone who hadn't seen Sarah all day. Someone who had noticed That Special Something had been closed at noon when she'd gone to Sadie's for lunch.

"You didn't call anyone?" Randy asked the clerk.

"Who should I have called? Sarah worked alone. If she was sick, the shop would have been closed. It's not usual, but it's happened."

"You're right. Thank you, Miss…"

"Douglas. Dolly Douglas."

Randy remembered to write her name and comments in his notebook before he ran for his truck. When Randy got back to the station, he went straight to Laughlin's office. He rapped once on the doorjamb and barged in. "I need a subpoena for all incoming calls to this telephone for the past two months," he said and extended a piece of paper with Sarah's name and phone number to the chief.

"Reason?" Laughlin asked.

"Missing person."

Laughlin looked up and opened his mouth as if to question the request, but something in Randy's face must have telegraphed his despair. He nodded, picked up the telephone and punched in some numbers. "Preston Laughlin for Judge DeMaster, please. Yes, I'll hold." He turned toward Randy. "Go. Call the phone company. I'll make sure everything will stand up in court."

Laughlin began talking to the judge. Randy mouthed a thank-you and went to his desk to call Victoria. He had explained what he needed when Laughlin appeared in the doorway.

"My office. Now."

Randy thanked Victoria and followed the chief to his office. He knew he was in for it and he didn't care. He thought about all his cases where a loved one was involved. He'd always thought he'd been understanding. He hadn't been close. How had they stood it? Not knowing, wondering what someone was going through, if they were hurt, or—

"Out with it. What's going on?" Laughlin's concerned expression belied the gruffness of his tone.

Randy slumped down in his chair. "Sarah Tucker's been missing since last night. I found out about it a little while ago and went to her place."

"Signs of violence?"

"No, but—"

"Not even twenty-four hours." Laughlin said.

"I know that she wouldn't have left of her own free will."

"Didn't we have the talk about not getting your personal life involved in your cases?"

"Yes, sir." The steel band tightened again. "And because of that, I followed the rules and didn't dig when my gut told me there was something going on that didn't fit within the boundaries of a legitimate case." His heard his voice getting louder, but didn't bother to lower it, or to disguise the anger. "And now whether it's personal or not, someone is missing and fuck the rules, I'm going to find her."

"*We're* going to find her. I have permission for the subpoena—you start the paperwork, but put Kovak's name on it. Get your phone numbers, get whatever you can out of the computer and turn it over to Kovak. It's his case now."

"But—"

"Randy." Laughlin's tone was even. "Kovak is the lead. I don't want you doing something that will destroy the case or cost you your job. You can back him up, but from your desk."

"Yes, sir." Randy returned to his office. After kicking the desk a few times, he felt no better. He dug the heels of his hands into his temples. Sarah would be fine. They'd find her and she would be fine. She could take care of herself. Kovak came in with two cups of coffee. He put one on Randy's desk.

"Chief says you have a case for me."

Randy handed Kovak the subpoena form. "Chief's got the judge's approval. Needs a signature and I'll fax it over to the phone company. They're already working."

"I'll get right on it, but what's the case?"

"Sarah Tucker. She hasn't been seen or heard from since last night."

"Shit. All right. Let's get going. What do you have?"

Randy stood up and stormed to the window. "Nothing. A whole lot of nothing."

"Hey, take it easy. We'll find her. One step at a time. Chief was right. You're way too close. Start at the beginning. When's the last time someone saw her?"

"I saw her last night. Dropped her off at her place at eight-thirty. According to her answering machine, her mom called at nine-fifteen, but Sarah didn't answer, so I think she's been gone since then."

"You checked with friends? Neighbors?"

"Dammit, I checked what I could. I don't know that much about her friends, but her neighbor assures me that she wouldn't have left her purse behind if she was going somewhere of her own free will."

"Okay, okay. Relax. You said you had reason to believe someone was trying to sabotage her business."

"Yeah, but all I have is a bunch of names that don't seem to exist." Randy pulled out the sheet of paper where he'd written them down and handed it to Kovak. "None of these show up anywhere."

Kovak raised an eyebrow. "Any of your suspects into photography?"

"What?"

"Big guy, these names are all famous photographers, except you spelled Muybridge wrong."

"Shit, give me that list." Randy snatched the paper from Kovak's hand. "You sure?"

"Yeah, Janie took two years of photography at night school. I helped her study."

Randy felt the adrenaline surge. "Frank Scofield. Owns an art gallery. Big photography exhibit going on. Sits on the board of Consolidated. It connects." He jumped for his windbreaker. "I'm going to his place."

"Shit, Randy. Chief took you off the case."

"So, I'm not on the case. You are and you can go get the judge's signature, wait for the phone records and I'll bet some number registered to Frank Scofield will show up. Meanwhile, I'm going to find him and have a little chat."

"I thought Laughlin said to stay put. You don't want to compromise the case."

"Ringing someone's doorbell isn't compromising anything." He took a deep breath, trying to ease the tightness in his chest. Dammit, he was not going to be too late again.

"If she's there and I don't do something…" Randy took his badge case and slapped it on his desk. Placed his service weapon beside it. He gave Kovak an even stare. "I'm going."

Kovak opened his mouth, then closed it.

Chapter Twenty-Five

Her wedding night. Maybe she should get flat-out drunk. Would Chris do anything if she passed out? She'd have to figure out a way to stall. She smiled. "Get you drunk? Of course not. Like you said, it's a celebration."

"It's getting late, don't you think? The guests are all leaving."

Aware of a sudden silence, she twisted to see the television displaying the closing credits. Chris went over to the set. He pressed the rewind button on the tape and stood there while it whirred. "I can't tell you how happy I am this finally worked out. David was never right for you. And then, after you married him, you were never supposed to make a go of it in that store."

She blinked. What a fool she'd been, an ostrich with her head in the sand, thinking Diana was the one behind everything.

Chris went on talking, sounding proud of his accomplishments. "I knew if you lost money, you'd get tired of David and come back to me. It wasn't hard. People do what I want. They could mix up shipments for me, or tell people not to let you sell their stuff. But no matter what problems you had, you and your store kept coming back."

"You? You were trying to put us out of business from the time we opened?"

"The store was holding you and David together. If the store was gone, you'd come back to me. But it didn't work."

Sarah's mouth felt like sandpaper. She reached for her glass before remembering she was avoiding the alcohol. Chris was talking again, still watching the VCR counter wind down.

"I never wanted you to be hurt. You were supposed to need me and let me take care of you. The fire didn't work and I remembered that hold-up woman. I thought if I frightened you a little, you might sell the store, so I hired someone to rob you. But then your nosy neighbor and that cop started poking around. I needed to make them leave me alone, too."

"Diana? Did you — did you make her — ?"

"She was a lucky coincidence, but I don't think I'd really have bought her out. Now that we're married, we'll just sell the place. You'll have plenty to keep you busy at home." He twisted to face her. "But I'm not sure I'll let you get that kitten you want — I'm not much of an animal lover."

His satanic grin turned her stomach. "You really did poison the cats."

Without thinking, Sarah flew across the room and swung the champagne bottle as hard as she could at Chris' head. A look of incredulity crossed his face as the bottle approached. His arm came up to block it, but not quite fast enough. She heard a dull thwack and the impact of the blow surged through her wrist up her arm. His eyelids flickered and he slumped to the wooden floor.

The pulsing blood in her ears blocked all but the sounds of her own rasping breaths. Her brain refused to function. Some instinct took over and she reached down and dragged him into the bedroom. She patted his pockets, found a slim wallet, but no keys. Was he moving? Her panic mounted. There was nothing in this room to hit him with. She had to get out, get away from him. She raced out the door and locked it behind her. How long would he be unconscious?

She stumbled to the second bedroom. On the dresser were Chris' keys. One of them had to open the front door. She fumbled with each in turn until she found the one that released the lock.

"Sarah. What're you doing?"

She gasped and turned to the bedroom. The door was still shut. Chris' speech was slow, groggy-sounding, but he wasn't out cold. On television, people who got hit on the head stayed unconscious until the other guy got away. Crap. She heard shuffling sounds from behind the door. Hiking up her gown, she raced across the porch and down the steps. She had to get away from here. Away from Chris. Behind the cabin, the SUV faced a stand of trees. Clicking the entry remote, she saw the interior lights flash. She pulled open the driver's door and climbed in. Trembling fingers managed to insert the key into the ignition. She turned the key, but nothing happened. Double crap. Maybe the battery was dead. After three more tries, she looked down and saw a third pedal. A clutch. A stick shift. She had no clue how to drive a manual transmission, especially not backward. Did she hear pounding and shouting? She was breathing so loudly she couldn't be sure.

* * * * *

On his way out, Randy stopped by the first aid cabinet and grabbed a bottle of Tums from the shelf. With fumbling fingers, he worked his way through the safety seals as he hastened out to his truck. Why had he dismissed Scofield so quickly? He ran through motives as he drove. Would Scofield hurt Sarah just to get back at Diana? Her share of That Special Something was out of Frank's hands. Didn't make a lot of sense, since the man seemed to have more money than God, but greed had to rank in the top three motives for wrongdoing.

How did the cats play in? Revenge for what Frank had considered public humiliation when Randy had questioned him in his gallery in front of employees? Filing a complaint wasn't enough? But why Othello? Or did Frank have something specifically against Sarah? Had Diana whined that Sarah was turning her brother against her?

The questions twisted through Randy's mind like a summer tornado. He finally realized his cell phone was ringing and looked at the display. Kovak. Randy opened the connection. "What do you have?" he snapped.

"Hello to you, too."

Randy eased his pickup onto the shoulder and activated his flashers. Took a deep breath. "Talk to me."

"The phone records you didn't want to wait for—over the last two months, there were over fifty calls from Christopher Westmoreland, all during the day, all under a minute. I went to the judge and convinced him to let me take a look at his place."

"What did you find?"

"The guy's an amateur photographer. His den is a gallery of prints by the photographers on your alias list. Books, too."

A vat of acid spilled into Randy's stomach. Chris, not Scofield? "You have anything more? Now I've got two suspects hooked to photography." But Randy knew he'd moved without thinking. Kovak's evidence made more sense.

"Have you talked to Frank Scofield yet?"

"I'm about fifteen minutes away."

"I think you need to come back here, big guy. I'm willing to bet Scofield's not your man."

"Give me more."

"This Sarah Tucker. She brunette? Blue eyes? Freckles across her nose?"

Randy's stomach clenched. "Oh, God. Is...is she...did you find—?"

"No, no. Not like that. He's got a darkroom with a hidden room. I thought you could confirm that the woman in his pictures—and he has a *lot* of pictures—is the one you're missing."

Randy activated his siren and hung a U-turn across the median. "I'm on my way. Send a uniform with a picture to Maggie Cooper for ID. Get on the phone to a judge and get a warrant for every damn thing you can think of and start working the house as a crime scene."

"I'm going to assume that lack of sleep and stress has made you forget I've had a couple years of experience, big guy. It's covered. I'll call if I need you."

"You call me with every damn thing you find." And he did everything he could to convince himself that this time it would be different. Not like with Gram.

* * * * *

Randy screeched to a halt in front of Chris' house. Kovak's unit was there, as well as Connor's van. He raced up the steps. "Kovak!" Where are you? Why couldn't you tell me what you found on the phone?"

"Bedroom, to your left. Give us a minute. We're almost done."

"Where's this darkroom hideaway you talked about?"

"Through the den, door's at the rear of his office."

Randy marched through the office, into the darkroom and pushed aside a blackout curtain. Covered with cork, the walls displayed a gallery of photos of Sarah. Color, black-and-white, large, small, new, old. On top of the chest Randy saw a silver frame which he'd bet was the one Eleanor stole. Sarah's face smiled from the photograph.

"It's her, right?" Kovak said from behind him.

Randy nodded. "Bag that picture," he told Kovak. "The frame was stolen."

"Got it," Kovak said.

"I need you in the bedroom. But I need you to be a cop."

"Show me." He followed Kovak out of the room and down a hallway beyond the living room. "What? What's wrong?"

"How well do you know Sarah Tucker?" Kovak asked.

Randy spun Kovak around by the shoulder so his face was inches from his partner. "Why? You found something. Dammit, tell me."

Connor came out of the bedroom, carrying an evidence bag. "I'll check the panties for semen," he said.

"What are you talking about? Let me see that!" Randy reached for the bag. Connor held fast.

"It's nothing," he said. "Stained black lace panties. Looks like Mr. Westmoreland got his rocks off using women's underwear."

Randy didn't miss the glare Kovak shot Connor. "Why don't you take everything back to the lab," Kovak said.

Once Connor had left the room, Kovak looked Randy in the eyes. "Did the two of them have anything going on?" Kovak's voice was gentle and Randy stepped back.

"Sarah and Chris? No way. She dated him in high school, she said. Friends now. She said he wanted to give her money, but she refused it. Why?"

Kovak nodded toward the closet. "Try to be a cop. What would you think if this was anyone else?"

Randy pushed him aside and strode into the huge walk-in closet, the scent of cedar assaulting his nostrils. The right side of the closet contained uniformly spaced men's suits, dress shirts, slacks and sport coats, but the left held a section of skirts and dresses. Garments that looked like ones he'd seen Sarah wear. He yanked open a drawer, freezing at the display of women's lingerie. The steel belt in his gut tightened two more notches. He clenched his teeth.

"It's not like that," Randy said. "Look." He slammed the drawer shut, turned and yanked a skirt off the rod. "Most of the clothes in here are brand-new. Price tags still on them. She wasn't living here. I know it. You saw the rest of the house. Nothing female. He's going to bring her back. I was just at her place. Her stuff is all there."

"Okay, so if he's planning to come back with her, he's not going to hurt her, right? You said he wasn't violent."

"That's what Sarah keeps saying." Randy turned around. "Let me look around a little more." Trying to find some level of detachment, he opened a bathroom drawer. An unwrapped toothbrush and a new lady's razor turned his stomach. He peered into cabinets, checked the tub and shower. Two shampoo bottles sat side by side on a niche in the shower wall. One was half empty. He picked up the second. Full. He opened the bottle and took a sniff. Peach. His hand shook as he recapped the bottle and set it back where he'd found it.

Chris had planned to bring Sarah here. But when? Was the kidnapping always part of his scheme, or had he started improvising? He was breathing was too fast. Too loud.

He felt like he'd been kicked in the gut. Stepping back, he leaned against the bathroom wall, waited for the room to stop spinning. The next thing he knew, he was sitting on the edge of the tub, Kovak's hand pressing down on his head, keeping it between his knees.

Mortified, Randy didn't budge.

"Jesus, Randy, are you all right?"

Randy lifted his head. "Yeah. Shit, I'm sorry."

"Go back to the station. Start working the desk end. You know your job. Pull it together and do it. Or go home, get some sleep and come back when you've got your head back on your shoulders."

Finding Sarah

Chapter Twenty-Six
ಏ

Sarah gave a quick search of the glove box and found Chris' cell phone. Her heart soared as she pressed the buttons to turn it on and plummeted as she discovered there was no signal. The car was empty, save the blanket she remembered being covered with on the drive out. She seized it. The night was cold and she had raced out without thinking, without taking anything warmer to wear. She definitely heard her name being shouted. Was it from inside the cabin, or had Chris escaped?

Should she lock herself in the car? She tried weighing the options, but lucid thought had deserted her for panic. To reach the road, she'd have to go right past Chris. She heard the sound of a slamming door from the cabin and raced blindly along a path into the woods.

Propelled by fear, she clutched the phone, wrapped the blanket around her and ran as quickly as the darkness and terrain permitted along the wooded trail. All she had to do was hide until daylight. Keep away from Chris until she could see where she was. Maybe reach a place where the cell phone would work. Once she could make her way to a road, she would find a way to get help. She plunged on.

Tree branches whipped at her face. Roots snagged her wedding slippers. Clouds passed in front of the moon, obscuring her light source. She ignored them all and kept running. She had no idea how long she'd been running, or how much ground she'd covered when a sharp pain in her side became impossible to ignore.

Doubled over, sucking in huge gasps of air, she tried to get her bearings. The forest whirled around her, animated by her fear, exhaustion and emptiness. For all she knew, she'd been running in circles. Trails had converged, branched off. What had she been thinking when she ran off like that? She got turned around in the mall, for God's sake. The wind blew cold, chilling her now that she was no longer moving. A strange sound, almost like someone crying, came from above. She held her breath and listened. Tree limbs rubbing together. She exhaled. Something rustled in the undergrowth. She had never considered what else lived out here. What other dangers lurked behind these trees? She began to shiver.

Stop. Think. She looked down. In this white dress, she'd be an easy target for Chris. She left the open trail in favor of a narrower footpath through the trees, searching for denser cover. Stay hidden from Chris until she could see. She heard the satin fabric of the dress tear, felt the lace sleeves fall away in shreds. Her shoes kept slipping off and she twisted her knee. She limped forward, shivering with cold and fear. Somewhere, the blanket had been lost, probably snagged by a protruding branch. The car keys were gone. Here, where trees sheltered the ground from the daytime sunshine, snow covered large patches of the trail. A coat. She would have had time to grab a coat. But fear had taken over and her brain had ceased to function when she'd realized Chris was nuts. As she wrapped her arms around herself, her new wedding band glowed with reflected moonlight. She twisted it off her finger and hurled it as far as she could into the trees.

The shivering grew worse and her teeth began to chatter. She needed to keep moving, or find shelter. She plodded on, one arm in front of her face to fend off branches, one hand lifting her dress so she could walk, favoring her sore knee.

Eventually, she couldn't pick out any semblance of a trail, even when the moon gave forth its maximum light. She could go no farther in this direction. Leaning against a pine tree, she took a shaky breath. The scrapes on her arms and face were beginning to sting and she didn't want to think about the crawling sensations on her limbs. Could she hide here until daylight? How long would it be? Why wasn't Randy here? He was so big, so strong. He'd carry her out of the forest, he'd kiss her and the pain would all go away. She sniffed back tears.

Stop it. There was no point believing in fairy tales. Would Randy even realize she was missing yet? If she was going to get out, she'd have to do it herself. Shivering uncontrollably, she began picking her way through the trees. She stumbled, then got up and pushed forward again. It couldn't be the champagne—she'd hardly had any. She tripped again. Stupid tree roots. She didn't feel the crawling things on her legs anymore. Come to think of it, she barely felt her legs at all. Or her hands. She looked at her hands. There was something missing. She struggled through the cotton batting in her skull. The phone. She had had a phone. So tired. She needed to sit down and rest. Just for a while. She found a large fallen tree among some undergrowth and huddled behind it, trying to still the chattering of her teeth. With any luck, the tree would provide enough cover so Chris couldn't see her. The moon hung lower in the sky now. Morning would come. She'd wait here for a minute or two.

* * * * *

It was after eight by the time Randy got back to the station. He grabbed a cup of coffee, some crackers and settled in. Tried to regroup. One step at a time. When he was halfway to Dispatch to put a lookout order out on Chris' Eclipse, he realized how badly he'd lost it. Punched Kovak's number into his cell phone.

"Did you check the garage? Is the Eclipse there? If not, I'll put out a BOLO."

"No Eclipse," Kovak said. "A green Lexus."

"Plates?"

Kovak read off the number. "I'm going to knock on doors after I finish here. Are you all right?"

"Yeah. Sorry."

"Would you quit apologizing? I've requested Westmoreland's phone records. They'll fax them over. Some day they'll computerize them for us like the big city folks do. Hope your eyes can take it."

While Kovak talked, Randy called up the DMV database. The Lexus was registered to Metro Rentals in Woodford. Why the hell would Chris have a rental car in his garage?

"Thanks. And the car in the garage is a rental. I'll follow up. Keep me posted."

Randy popped another Tums and dialed the number for Metro.

The receptionist left him listening to Hank Williams for five minutes before the manager picked up. Yes, Mr. Westmoreland had rented a car. Always happy to cooperate with the police. A green Lexus. He'd rented it on Wednesday, no return date specified. Said his car was in the shop. Metro had an agreement with the Mitsubishi dealership. Of course he'd be happy to give Randy the number.

The Mitsubishi dealership was closed. Opened at seven the next morning. Randy called Woodford PD and asked them to dig up the service manager. He put out the BOLO on the Eclipse anyway. Sweat trickled down his neck and his shirt stuck to his back. He yanked off his tie and rolled up his sleeves.

Who else would know where Chris might be? Randy reached for the phone again. The night security guard at Consolidated checked the logs. No, Mr. Westmoreland hadn't been in today, but he was noted as being on vacation until the following Monday. No emergency contact numbers, no itinerary, but maybe his secretary would know, if Randy wanted to call back in the morning.

Randy grabbed his Consolidated directory. Found a secretary for Development. Clicked through phone directory databases and found her home number. No, she didn't have a way to reach Mr. Westmoreland. He was adamant about his privacy. If he checked in, she'd be sure to tell him Detective Detweiler wanted to speak with him.

Shit. Like the man would call him back. The pencil Randy had been clenching snapped.

He started calling the airlines and bus depot. Cab companies. His ear throbbed. His head pounded. His stomach churned.

Three cups of coffee and twice that many trips to the men's room later, Randy found that Chris Westmoreland's cell phone had indeed called Oregon Trust, Tony Mazzaro, Rose Tanaka and Eleanor Wainwright. Any gratification at having all this evidence was negated by the earthquake in his gut. He leaned his elbows on his desk and lowered his head into his hands.

For now, Chris was a dead end. Try it from the other direction. God, he'd have to call Sarah's mother.

Chapter Twenty-Seven

Sarah's head jerked up. She must have drifted off. In the distance, carried on the wind, she heard her name being called. Her heart fluttered. Randy had found her after all. She tried to get up, but her legs were missing. No, they had to be there. Concentrate. She pulled herself up to her hands and knees and listened again. Not Randy. Chris. Her heart plunged to her bowels. She braved one quick peek and saw a beam of light moving back and forth through the trees. She crouched into as tiny a ball as she could. Her name seemed to come from all directions as Chris called out for her. How could he possibly think she'd come when he called?

The wind picked up and she could no longer hear anything but the rustling of the trees and the eerie creaking of tree branches. Maybe Chris had moved on. She wondered why she was out in the cold. She should go someplace warm. Rest. Clear her brain. She sank back down, pulled her knees tighter into her chest and lowered her head onto her arms. Hot tears began to flow, their salt intensifying the stinging of her scrapes.

Something was pulling on her arm, dragging her to her feet.

"There you are, darling. Come with me."

Nothing made sense. She squinted into the darkness. She knew that voice. Chris. No, she didn't want to go with Chris. She tried to pull away, but her legs wouldn't obey. "Leggome," she said. She felt something placed over her shoulders. "No!" She was supposed to escape. How could she escape if he kept pulling on her?

"I've got you. Don't fight me. It's hypothermia. You're not thinking straight."

Finding Sarah

She let herself be tugged along. There was something wrong, but she couldn't put her finger on it. She needed to hide, to stay away from Chris. Randy would find her. That was it. She needed Randy. Chris was bad. She flung off the jacket that had appeared on her shoulders.

"Sarah. Don't. Leave the jacket on." He was trying to get her arms into the sleeves.

She struck out at him, flailing at his face, beating at his chest. "No. No."

"I'm sorry, my darling." Something covered her mouth and then the too familiar smell and then, nothing.

* * * * *

Randy paced his office, trying to gather the objectivity he'd need to talk to Sarah's mother. He punched the numbers into the telephone. A woman's voice answered. Almost Sarah's voice. Randy had to clear his throat before he could speak. "I'm sorry to bother you, ma'am. My name is Randy Detweiler. I'm a detective with the Pine Hills Police Department."

"Pine Hills? Sarah. Oh my God, has something happened to Sarah?"

"Ma'am, this isn't easy to say, but she's missing and might be with a Christopher Westmoreland."

"Missing? For how long? What happened? Oh my God. Frank!" He heard her call, away from the mouthpiece, "Sarah's missing."

Randy leaned back and rubbed his eyes. This part of his job was difficult enough when he was dealing with strangers. What he had to do now was ten times harder. "She was fine last night," he said, his voice still rough with emotion. "She didn't show up for work today. We've been trying to locate her."

"And you think Chris has something to do with it?"

"I can't say for sure, but he seems to be our best lead." Telling Sarah's mother about the photos and clothing wasn't necessary.

"I missed her call yesterday. She always calls on Sunday." Her voice shook. "How do you know she was fine last night?"

"I saw her at eight-thirty."

There was a moment of silence. Her voice came back, quieter and more controlled. "What can I do to help, Detective?"

"I need to know everything I can about Christopher Westmoreland. Anything you can tell me could prove to be helpful." He heard a man's voice in the distance before she spoke again.

"How do I know you're really with the Pine Hills police?" Now there was a hint of skepticism in her voice.

"Other than my word, you don't. But why don't you call the department and ask to speak with me? You can get the number from information."

"I hope you don't think me rude, but I'm going to do that." The line went dead.

Randy's anxiety had turned to a genuine pain in his belly. He sat with one hand poised over the telephone. She had to call back. It was her daughter. An eternity later, although by his watch it was less than a minute, the phone jangled.

"All right, Detective," Sarah's mother said. "I can be there tomorrow. Do I hire a detective, or someone with bloodhounds, or what?" Her voice was matter-of-fact, but he heard the urgency behind it. Still, she was doing a lot better than he was. He tried to take strength from that.

"I don't know that there's anything you can do here. We're doing everything we can. Speaking from experience, it's easier if you stay busy. You might do better following your normal routine."

"I'm not sure I can do that. She's my only child, you know. What are you doing to find her? I need to be doing something."

"What do you know about Christopher Westmoreland?" Randy found his voice had evened out now that he was back in familiar waters, gathering evidence.

"Chris? He and Sarah dated through high school. He was polite enough, from a wealthy family, but…unctuous. Like that character on *Leave it to Beaver*. The one who was always pretending to be so worldly."

"Eddie Haskell," Randy said.

"Yes. That's the one. But Sarah said Chris was always a perfect gentleman and I believed her. We'd had our mother-daughter talks and she assured me he had never pressed for anything more physical than a goodnight kiss. As a mother, I was delighted."

Randy's chest loosened. Maybe Chris wouldn't hurt her. Sarah had insisted he wasn't violent. "Do you have any idea of where he might have taken her? Did you know his family?"

"I'm sorry, no. It was so many years ago and I must admit I was preoccupied with my own problems. My marriage was reaching a turning point at that time. Frankly, I never thought that Sarah would continue the relationship after graduation, so I didn't go out of my way to meet his parents."

"I understand," Randy said. "Thank you for your help."

"I'm afraid it wasn't much. Are you sure you don't want me to come there? How can I stay here doing nothing?"

Randy heard the edge creeping back into her voice. "At this time, I don't think you can do anything from here," he said. "Sarah's been missing less than a day. We're doing everything we can to find her and as soon as we know anything, I promise to call you."

"Let me give you a cell phone number. I teach at the university and they don't like to interrupt classes for telephone calls, but I'll keep my cell charged and turned on." Randy heard her take a deep breath. "May I ask one more question?"

"Of course."

"You said she was with you last night. Was it in regard to this investigation you were doing? Excuse me if I'm out of line, but I'm getting the feeling you're not a detached police officer."

Randy closed his eyes. "No, you're not out of line. Sarah and I haven't known each other long, but the truth is, I'm quite attached to your daughter."

"So am I, Detective. So am I."

"I swear we're going to find her."

"I believe you. Please. Call any time. I doubt that I'll be doing much sleeping."

"Neither will I," Randy said quietly. "Goodbye."

Randy sat at his desk, staring at the telephone. He snapped to attention when Kovak came into the office and dumped a stack of folders on his desk. "You get anything from the neighbors?"

"Only that Westmoreland keeps to himself. Oh and that he uses a cleaning service. We can call them in the morning. If he's gone, maybe they can confirm it."

Randy nodded. Hadn't dared expect more.

"What have you found?"

Before he finished relaying his meager findings, the phone rang. Woodford PD confirmed the Eclipse was in the shop in Woodford. "Guess we can cancel the BOLO on the Eclipse. It's in the shop. Since Wednesday."

Kovak placed his hands on Randy's desk and leaned down until his eyes were level with his partner's. "We're going to find him. But you've got to be clear-headed. I'm lead on this one—you run everything by me before you go off half-cocked."

Randy massaged his temples. "Yes, sir."

"I mean it, big guy. You shouldn't even be working this case. You're too close. But I know if it was Janie, I'd be doing exactly what you're doing. So, let's get to work. I'll take the financials, you look at that photo album and see if anything rings a bell."

Chapter Twenty-Eight

Sarah drifted, floated, whirled through the air. Did she have wings? Was she an angel? Maybe she could fly. She tried to spread her wings, but they were trapped. The sky was too thick, like molasses. She needed to get free so she could fly and soar above the forest.

Warm air blew on her neck, tickled her ear. "Don't struggle, my darling. We're almost there. You're too cold. Moving around is bad. Hold still." She smelled something familiar. Not the sweet, sick smell anymore. If only she could remember.

"There you go. I'll take care of you. Nothing can hurt you."

She spun down, down, down until she was back on Earth. Cold. So cold. It was warm somewhere. Nearby, there was warmth. Warmth, touching and the smell of sandalwood and cinnamon. She sank into a dark, soft void. Let the warmth envelop her.

A clicking noise woke her and Sarah realized it was her teeth chattering. A hand lifted her head. Something warm was at her lips.

"Drink this, my darling. Just a sip. You need to get warm."

Warm. Yes. She let the liquid flow into her mouth. Warm and salty. Chicken broth. She raised her hands to the cup, felt warm fingers over hers.

"Don't move too much. Can't let the cold blood get to your heart. Lie still."

She finished the broth, then watched from afar as someone cut her white angel gown off. Her eyes closed. "You found me."

"That's right. Sleep. I'll be right next to you. I'll keep you warm."

* * * * *

Randy worked his way through the album's plastic-covered pages. All black-and-white. Chris' first projects? Lots of trees, a lake. A blurred picture of what might have been a deer. Some out of focus birds. People standing at attention under trees, sitting with forced smiles at a picnic table. Nothing that resembled the quality work Randy had seen when he'd called on Chris. Maybe his first attempts at photography? A photographic primer. As Randy moved through the pages, even his untrained eye could see the growth.

"Need some help?" Randy rubbed his eyes. Colleen hovered in the doorway.

"Some detective I am," Randy said. "I can't solve a simple robbery and I manage to lose the victim at the same time."

"Stop that." She crossed to the front of his desk. "Kovak says you think Westmoreland took her. Tell me what you've got."

"A terrible case of heartburn and an overwhelming urge to scream."

"What else?" Colleen asked.

"Not much. According to everything public, he's a model citizen."

"You want me to check with my brother? He might have known the guy in high school."

"Please. Anything's better than what I have now."

"I'll let you know."

Randy turned back to the album. Halfway through, the pictures were grouped by subject, not date. Pictures were crisper, the people looked more natural. He must have gotten some better equipment—the shots of wildlife were more frequent and no longer were the subjects hidden. Shots of a simple mountain cabin taken under varied lighting conditions, in all kinds of weather. Uncle Wes' cabin at the lake, according to the heading of that section. Well, assuming it was a lake in Oregon, that narrowed it down to what? A couple thousand possibilities?

Captions gave dates, not much more. An occasional flower or bird identified. "The lake after it rained." No help. He turned to the last page. The same cabin, a young boy posed in front of a woman and two men. According to the label, it had been taken on Chris' sixteenth birthday. "Me, Mom, Dad and Uncle Wes."

So, who the hell was Uncle Wes? Randy rubbed gritty eyes and stared at the picture. Was there some kind of a placard on the cabin? He grabbed the album and took it to the lab. Connor would have a magnifying glass in there somewhere.

He found a glass in a drawer and went back through all the cabin shots trying to read the sign. Definitely a six and a three, but there was a porch post that blocked a clear look at the writing. Then a K and an E and Rd. Something Road. Six-three-something-something road. Maybe Lake Road. Or Something Lake Road?

He took the album back to his desk, feeling for the first time since he'd found Sarah's purse in her apartment, that he might find her. He popped another Tums and started calling up databases of property tax rolls, glancing at Kovak's now empty desk. Having something resembling a lead quashed any curiosity about what Kovak was doing. He trusted his partner's skills.

An eternity later, Randy had been through twelve counties and found nothing but the property Chris owned in Pine Hills. Raking his fingers through his hair, he tried to rebuild the wall of detachment that made him a good cop, able

Finding Sarah

to help others get through times of stress. He took deep breaths, closed his eyes and envisioned his fortress rising, brick by brick. But now, every brick had Sarah's face etched in it. He sighed and looked at his watch. Again. Maybe he should get solitaire installed on his computer. He'd be about as useful playing games, for all he could get out of the damn machine. He dug the heels of his hands into his eyes until he saw a rainbow of lights, then tried to refocus. Four a.m. He started another search and watched the hourglass on the monitor. A quick break, just to rest his eyes, he thought.

He opened his eyes to the beginnings of daylight and the smell of coffee. Colleen stood in front of him. She held out the cup.

"You look like you need this more than I do. I just heard from my brother."

Randy flew awake. "What did he say?"

Colleen looked at him and Randy braced himself. "Not a whole lot. The football team had a seniors party every year and he remembered Chris inviting everyone to a mountain cabin, but since Greg wasn't a senior, he doesn't remember where it might have been."

"But in Oregon, right? They wouldn't go too far for a weekend retreat."

"That makes sense." She took the coffee cup from his quaking hands and took a sip, set it down on the desk. Randy glanced at the computer monitor for the time. Almost six. "You're in early," he said.

"Hey, I figured you wanted to know what I'd found out. Greg's on the Appalachian Trail with a bunch of Boy Scouts. It took a while to catch him in a place where he got cell reception."

"I owe you."

"What can I do? I'm not on for an hour."

Randy showed her the album. "Can you tell where this might be? I've just got a couple of numbers and a street name that has Lake Road in it."

Colleen flipped through the pages. "Dunno. Mountains. A lake. Looks like half of Oregon."

"Don't suppose you could at least narrow it down to which half?"

"Morning, campers." Randy looked up at the sound of his partner's voice. Kovak strode into the room and dropped a file folder on Randy's desk. "The financials gave me diddly, so I had the newspaper check the archives." He gave Randy an even stare. "I knew there was nothing more I could do and that you'd call if the album gave you a lead. I went home and caught some shuteye. You can't do the job on caffeine and adrenaline."

Randy ignored Kovak's words and reached for the folder. Glad his hands had stopped shaking, he leafed through some articles until he came to one with a photograph. From the obituary section. Taken at the funeral. Three people. Chris, for certain. Another man and a woman.

Randy laid the paper on his desk, staring at the words. They danced around the page and he leaned on his elbows, palms to temples, as if holding his head steady would stop the motion.

The widow, Elizabeth Westmoreland, plans to return to her native Colorado Springs with her brother, Wesley Christopher.

Uncle Wesley. In Colorado Springs. Randy jerked up and grabbed the computer mouse, found the search engine he needed. He picked up the phone.

"It's not even six a.m.," Colleen said.

"The beauty of being a cop," Kovak replied. "We've got it all over the telemarketers when it comes to disruptive phone calls." Colleen retreated to the far wall.

Randy waited out the rings. Three. Four. Five. A voice, thick with sleep, answered.

Finding Sarah

"Is this Wesley Christopher?" Randy asked and identified himself.

"Pine Hills?" A moment of silence, as if he were processing the information through a sleep-filled brain. "Chris? Is he all right?"

"That's what we're trying to ascertain, sir. We've been trying to locate him."

"Isn't he at the cabin? He told me he'd be there all week."

Randy clenched the phone. He felt Kovak leaning over him and pressed the speaker button. Colleen took a step toward the desk.

"I guess he didn't mention it. His office was unaware that's where he'd be. Can you confirm the address for us, please?" He held his breath, hoping the man was still groggy enough with sleep not to press for proof of who he was. At least Sarah's mom didn't give information to strangers on the phone. "Yeah, it's six thirty-nine Falcon Lake Road. Over in Deschutes County. Chris has had the run of the place since I moved back to Colorado. My car, too. He called me Saturday—or was it Sunday? Anyway, he said he was taking someone special there. I was happy he'd found someone. You sure nothing's wrong?"

Ice ran through Randy's veins. What would Chris be doing to Sarah? He regrouped. "No—I guess he forgot to cancel his paper." Randy felt Kovak nudge his shoulder and he shrugged. "The neighbors were worried."

"Well, I'm sure he's fine." He glanced up and saw Colleen mouth the word car. Shit, he was off. "What kind of car, if you don't mind? License?"

"It's a 2000 Blazer, dark green. Colorado plates."

"And the license?"

"Give me a minute," the man said. "It's not exactly on the tip of my tongue at this hour."

Randy clenched his jaw and waited out the silence. After what seemed hours, the voice came back.

"747 GPY."

"Thanks." He repeated the information.

Colleen was out the door and Randy knew she'd be putting the lookout order out for the Blazer. "Thanks, Mr. Christopher. Sorry to bother you so early."

"No problem. I'll remind my nephew to leave better contact information next time he goes on vacation."

Kovak spoke first. "I'll have the Deschutes sheriffs roll and see if I can get a warrant for Westmoreland."

"I'm going," Randy said. "I don't need a fucking warrant. Give me a map and I'll drag that bastard back here by his dick."

"Which seems to be what you're thinking with," Kovak said. "Mac, don't let him leave yet. Cuff him to the chair if you have to, but let me talk to Deschutes first."

Chapter Twenty-Nine

Warm hands stroked Sarah's forehead, lips touched her temples. She relaxed into the soothing touches, turned her body to stretch against his, absorbed his heat. In the darkness, his hands moved over her back, gentle caresses that sent warmth through her insides.

The lips moved down to her neck, stopping to nibble at an earlobe before planting kisses at her throat. The hands moved lower, caressed her buttocks, then stroked her thighs.

Her limbs felt heavy, her head fuzzy. For a moment, she sensed something was wrong, but she couldn't maintain a grasp on a conscious thought. She allowed herself to drift, to enjoy the sensations coursing through her.

Pleasure built and she floated through layers of sensation. Those hands rolled her onto her back, pried her legs apart. A throbbing in her knee brought her closer to the surface. Memories came back. Her heart began to pound and she rose from the depths of her dream.

Chris, not Randy, was lying beside her. His hands, not Randy's were all over her. Panic cleared the last clouds from her brain and she pulled away.

"Ah, so you're awake, my darling. I'm so glad. Your wedding night should be something memorable. For both of us."

She felt his penis, limp on her thigh. Good Lord, had he already taken her? While she was unconscious? She struggled to get away. His fingers clamped down on her wrists.

"No, Sarah. No fighting. You're not a bad girl, remember."

Bad girls. Don't fight him. Sarah closed her eyes and went limp.

* * * * *

"Go," Randy said to Colleen. "I'm not going anywhere and you don't want to be late for morning briefing."

"Are you sure? You don't look so good."

"Mac, leave me alone." Embarrassed by the way his voice broke, he swallowed hard. "Please."

She gave him a look filled with compassion and backed out the door.

Another bucket of acid dumped into his stomach and he pulled two more Tums from the bottle. He'd blown this case from the beginning. He'd be surprised if Laughlin didn't have him helping kids cross the street, or checking parking meters. Jackhammers pounded in his head and his stomach twisted. He stumbled out to the men's room and leaned on the sink, fighting the nausea. Holding his wrists under a flow of cold water, he felt some of the turmoil leave his system. The wild-eyed stranger in the mirror frightened him. He splashed huge handfuls of water onto his face.

He was useless in this condition. Furious with himself, he dug deeper, searching for the strength to disassociate himself, the way Kovak had, the way he always had been able to before Sarah. He pushed the damp hair out of his face and went in search of Kovak.

He found him in Communications, phone to his ear, nodding and taking notes. Randy fisted his hands in his pockets. Finally, Kovak hung up and turned around. "Let's go to the office," he said.

Randy held his tongue until they'd gone inside and Kovak closed the door. "What did you find out?"

"Deschutes is familiar with Falcon Lake. It's off the main road a good five miles, lots of cabins, mostly vacation or summer use. Dirt roads, very rustic. Only a couple of year-round residents."

"Do they know if Chris is there? Have they seen Sarah?"

Kovak sat down at his computer and pulled up a map. "Slow down. Here's Bend." He pointed to a spot a few inches away. "Here's Falcon Lake. There's a sheriff's station at Terrebone about ten miles away as the crow flies, but on these roads, it'll be at least half an hour before anyone can get there." He raised his eyes to Randy's. "And, because of the terrain, there's very little communication in there. They hit dead zones all the time. But they're rolling and they'll let us know as soon as they get there. I faxed them her picture."

"I need to be there. I want that bastard."

"Yes, you do, but you need to wait thirty minutes."

"I—"

"Listen and think. Do the math. It's going to take you three hours minimum to get there. And what if she's not there? You raced off after Scofield and what did that get you? What's more important? Making the collar yourself or getting the job done?"

Chagrined, Randy ran the timetables through his head. "I'd bet my life she's there."

Kovak put a hand on Randy's shoulder. "Hey. I'm with you on this one. But if you don't mind some friendly advice, why don't you grab a shower, clean up a little. Sarah would run for cover if she saw you like this—and, big guy, she'd smell you coming at fifty yards. I'll go sweet-talk the judge into signing the papers. By the time everything's ready, we should know something."

Randy stood under the hot spray in the locker room shower, wishing he could scrub away his anxiety the way he washed off the sweat. Half an hour before he could find out anything. Still, almost three hours sooner than if he went himself.

He dried off and pulled on the change of clothes he kept in his locker. Shaving presented a challenge. Waves of self-recrimination at not finding the property sooner sent tremors of fury through him. He braced himself against the sink, forcing his hands to follow the contours of his face without shaking. Swearing when his aftershave seeped into a nick, he was grateful that he hadn't done more damage.

Kovak wasn't back with the warrant yet. Randy wandered down to Dispatch. Maybe the planets were aligned just right, or there was some fluke in the atmosphere and he'd be able to receive the Deschutes radio frequency. Right. Like he still believed in Santa Claus and the Easter bunny. He asked the operator to switch frequencies. Static. He hadn't expected otherwise. He got the phone number for Deschutes Dispatch and trudged to his office.

He tested his voice to make sure he could keep it steady and called Deschutes. "I understand you've got communication holes, but I'd appreciate being in the loop whenever possible. This one's personal."

"I'll do whatever I can. I'll let the deputies know we need frequent updates."

"Thanks." He closed his eyes and rubbed his temples. When he looked up, Laughlin had entered his office, a white paper bag in his hands. The chief set the bag on Randy's desk, gave him a look of understanding that spoke volumes and left.

Randy opened the bag to find two bagels with fixings and a large orange juice. God, was he so pathetic that the chief was bringing him food? He pried the top off the juice and took a long swig. He pulled out a bagel, smeared it with some of the cream cheese and bit off a small piece. It went down easily enough and he devoured the rest almost without thinking.

The phone rang. Randy stared at it, afraid to answer. What if the worst had happened? Beads of sweat trickled down his back. He picked up the receiver. "Detweiler."

"I've got an update for you." The voice was the calm, detached voice of an experienced dispatcher. "The deputies found your suspect, Mr. Westmoreland at the property."

"What about Sarah—Ms. Tucker? Was she there?"

"Detective, normally I wouldn't have called with such sparse information, but you said it was personal. All I have is that they found your suspect. No woman."

A knife stabbed through Randy's chest. "Are you sure?"

"Detective, I'm not there. However, the deputies found female attire in the cabin, as well as a photo album containing pictures that match the one you faxed. They believe she was there. Some bruising on the suspect indicates some kind of a struggle. In addition, there was a torn wedding dress on the bedroom floor."

"Wedding dress?" The words were a hoarse croak.

"The suspect claims he's on his honeymoon and his wife is out for a walk."

"That's a damn lie. He kidnapped her."

"Detective, I'm relaying the information I have."

Randy was beyond being calmed by the dispatcher's soothing tones. "Dammit, what are they doing?"

"Please hold and I'll see if I can get more for you."

Kovak came in, waving the warrant. "What do you have?"

"Deschutes Dispatch. He's there—" The dispatcher came back on the line and Randy raised a finger. Kovak stepped around the desk and pressed the speaker button.

The dispatcher continued. "Detective, we've lost the signal, but they are taking the suspect into custody. The deputies are going to do a search for the woman and they've requested scent dogs. I'll have more details once they get onto the highway."

Randy gave the dispatcher his cell phone number. "I'm on my way." He opened his desk drawer and extracted his badge and weapon. "I'm going to find her. And then I'm going to deal with Chris."

"Work the logistics, big guy. We'll send a uniform to Bend. You're in no condition to drive for three hours and then go tromping through the woods. Give me your keys."

"I've pulled all-nighters before. I can drive."

"Not with me in the truck, you can't. You may be willing to gamble with your own life, but I'm not letting you risk mine. You can play with the radio."

Randy acknowledged his partner's logic and handed him his keys. Fifteen minutes onto the highway, Randy knew he probably owed Kovak his life. Nerves or not, he'd dropped off twice already. He glanced at Kovak, who seemed to be making a point of not looking at him.

"If you're waiting for me to say, 'I told you so,' you'll have a long wait," Kovak said, his eyes never leaving the road. "But I think you'll be more comfortable if you recline that seat."

Chapter Thirty

൭

Aside from her racing heart, Sarah remained motionless. Chris continued his seduction efforts, although she couldn't detect any arousal. Was she safe, or just safe until he recharged?

"We're married now, Sarah. There's nothing wrong with what we're doing. Touch me."

When she ignored him, his ministrations grew rougher. Fingers that had stroked became hands that gripped. She clenched her teeth, determined to remain submissive. Chris' mouth smashed over hers, pressed her lips against her teeth, until she tasted blood. She squeezed her eyes shut, tried to slow her breathing.

"Kiss me." His voice was gruff, menacing. His tongue probed and she jerked her head away. Fists grabbed her hair, pulled her face back toward his. "Kiss me."

"Never."

He gave a guttural laugh. "Ah, that's better. A little action. What else do you need? This?" He mashed her breast with his hand, then grabbed her nipple and pinched.

"You're hurting me, Chris. I'm not a bad girl, remember? You don't need to hurt me." To her horror, she felt him growing erect against her thigh. She stopped struggling.

"Of course not. You're my wife." He released her breast. "Wives help." He took her hand in his, moved it to his barely erect penis and began stimulating himself, guiding her hand. "We're both tired and you were so cold. It won't always be like this. It can't always be like this."

She heard his voice start to break and gambled with her reply. "Like what? Like, you can't perform? Like you're not a man, Chris?" Felt him soften. "We're not really married, are we, Chris? You haven't done your marital duty yet, have you?"

"Don't you dare say that. We are married. You're my wife and you've got your own marital duties to perform." He was crying softly, lying on top of her, his head buried between her breasts.

Sarah stroked his hair. "Let me go. You know this isn't right."

He tensed and Sarah feared she'd made a terrible mistake. His eyes were feral now and he gripped her arms, pinning them to her sides. "Maybe it's just going to take a while. I want you to need me, but I'm willing to wait." His knees pressed her legs apart and he yanked one arm, then the other, above her head. "Meanwhile, I want you. Now."

His breath, hot and sour on her face, turned her stomach. She felt him rubbing against her belly. His grip shifted so he had both her wrists in one hand and his other slapped her cheek. Tears sprang to her eyes. Unable to restrain herself any longer, she struggled to free her hands. Chris merely tightened his hold and slapped her again.

Abandoning any hope that being submissive was going to keep Chris from hurting her, whether or not he raped her, Sarah fought back. Gouged, scraped. Twisted, squirmed, did everything she could to free her legs so she could do some damage. Screamed. Begged. Cried. He drew strength from her thrashing. His fingers were everywhere, squeezing. Became fists, pounding. Drawing from some reserve she wasn't aware she had, Sarah wrenched free enough to drive a knee into his crotch.

She heard the air explode from his lungs, the scream and then he doubled over. Leaping from the bed, she darted away, wrapped the sheet around her. His hands reached for her legs.

Sarah locked the bedroom door and searched for something to restrain him. Rope? Tape? Anything? There wasn't time. It was daylight now and she should be able to find the road and get help.

She rushed to Chris' room, grabbed a pair of his jeans and a sweatshirt and tugged them on over her sweat-slicked body. Shoes this time, she told herself. And a jacket. She found her sneakers in his closet. She jammed her feet into them, wanting to get away, as far away as she could, before Chris recovered enough to chase after her. He should be immobilized for a while, shouldn't he? In too much pain to move?

No, that's what got her into trouble last time. Running without thinking. The ether bottle sat on top of the dresser. She opened a drawer, found a t-shirt and saturated it with the liquid, turning her head to avoid inhaling the fumes.

She crept to the bedroom, put her ear to the door. A soft moan. She twisted the doorknob as quietly as she could and peered into the room. Chris lay on the floor, curled in a ball, his back to her, breathing in short gasps. Holding the cloth in front of her, she tiptoed to his inert form, watching for any movement. Nothing. Then a groan and her heart jumped to her throat. The instinct to flee surged through her and she fought it long enough to take two huge paces to Chris and slap the ether-soaked shirt over his face. He twitched and then went limp. She pulled his belt from the jeans and used it to bind his hands.

She relocked the bedroom door behind her, then raced through the living room, out the front door toward what she hoped was the main road. Find another cabin. This time, she could see where she was going.

Chris' jeans rode down her hips. Hiking them up with one hand, she stumbled along the path, the relief of escape purging the adrenaline from her system. And as the adrenaline left, the throbbing in her knee returned. Fatigue and pain slowed her pace to a limping jog, then a hobbling walk.

Sunlight filtered through the trees and the scent of pine permeated the air. The forest was less frightening by daylight, but she was no closer to her goal than she had been last night. Was it only one night? Time had no meaning. She could have been walking for fifteen minutes or an hour and she had yet to see evidence of civilization.

Was that a cabin ahead? She ignored her knee and pushed on, dizzy with relief when she reached the small wooden structure. Her voice trembled, a hoarse croak. "Hello. Is someone there?" She struggled up the two wooden steps to the small entry and pounded on the door. "Help me, please." Only then did she notice the padlock and the layer of dirt and grime. Nobody had been here in a long time.

Deflated, she sank to the rough wood planks.

* * * * *

Randy was aware of someone calling his name. "I'm awake." Sunlight streamed into the window and he rubbed his eyes. "Where are we?" He fished his sunglasses from his shirt pocket and put them on.

"Just hitting the Terrebone station. Westmoreland is in Bend. Hamilton's starting the extradition paperwork. He'll wait for me and we'll escort the prisoner back."

Randy grunted, still trying to clear the cobwebs from his brain and the cotton from his mouth. "Kick Westmoreland for me, will you?"

Kovak laughed. "I've talked to the deputies while you were out. Apparently your Sarah did a pretty good job of that. Westmoreland'll be walking funny for a while."

For the first time in what seemed like forever, Randy managed a laugh. "And she won't lose her job for it, either." He sobered. "Have they found her?"

"Sorry." They pulled into a small parking area in front of a single-story brick and wood building. Before Randy could get out of the truck, a deputy came out to meet them.

"Kovak and Detweiler. Pine Hills, right? I'm Al Bennett. Which one of you gets the ride back to Bend?"

"That would be me," Kovak said. "At your convenience. Our guy isn't going anywhere."

"Now is good," Bennett said. "I've got an appointment there in about an hour." He turned to Randy. "They're still looking. An extra man can't hurt—there's a lot of terrain to cover in there."

"Tell me where and I'm gone," Randy said.

"Let me get you a map."

Kovak handed Randy the truck keys. "If you want, I can stick around here—help you search for a while."

"No need for both of us to piss off Laughlin. You do your job."

Kovak slapped Randy's shoulder. "You take care, big guy. She'll be all right."

Bennett came back with the map and showed Randy where the search team had set up. "It's close enough to the main road so we can stay in contact. This area has no cell signals and the radios only work half the time. Waples is in charge."

"Thanks." Randy grabbed the map and got in his truck. He readjusted the seat and peeled out of the parking lot.

Twenty minutes later, he found a van and a cruiser half a mile off the main road. He jumped out of the truck. "I'm looking for Deputy Waples."

"You found her." A young blonde, her hair ponytailed through a brown DCSO baseball cap strode out to meet him. "Melinda Waples."

Randy shook her extended hand. A warm, firm grip. Up close, Randy reassessed her age as mid-forties. "What can I do?"

She pulled out a map with a series of circles, some with Xs drawn through them. "These are the cabins in the area. We're doing a door-to-door, but most of them are empty. This time of year, it's mostly weekenders if anyone uses them at all. We started at Westmoreland's and are working outward."

"You've eliminated the X's?"

"Right."

"How many deputies do you have working?'

The deputy gave him a wry smile. "Counting me—three. You make four." She must have noticed Randy's look of skepticism. "Budget. We're spread pretty thin through this area—not a large population, so not a lot of personnel."

"Where do you want me to start?"

She pointed to a cluster of circles. "Take these three—they're fairly close together."

"Can I drive in?"

"Partway. But there are dozens of hiking and walking trails where your truck is useless. You'll have to hoof a lot of it if you want to cover all the possibilities." She drew an X on the map. "Park your truck here. She could be unconscious a few feet off the path and you'd walk right past her. But that's why we have Ginger."

"Ginger?"

"Best scent hound in three counties. She got here about half an hour ago."

"I'm on my way, then." Randy checked the map and went back to his truck.

"Wait," Waples trotted up to the truck and handed him a radio. "We're on five. As long as you're not too far away from the rest of the crew, you should be able to keep in touch."

"Thanks." Randy followed the road through the trees. The terrain forced his truck to a crawl and he rolled down the window, shouting Sarah's name, straining to hear a response. His radio crackled and he heard Ginger's handler reporting.

"She's found some fabric that looks like it came from the same dress we gave her. It should have a purer scent—the other one was handled by too many people. I'm going to bring her back to the cabin and we'll head out in the other direction."

Randy keyed his radio. "Detective Randy Detweiler, Pine Hills PD on scene. Waples has me checking points twelve through fourteen."

"Deputy Birmingham here." The voice was mellow, confident. "There are about six trails between those three cabins, Detective. Stick to the main approach drives to each cabin and the dog will pick up the side tracks."

"Roger." Randy drove his truck until he was in sight of the first cabin. He walked the remaining distance, scanning into the trees on either side. Nothing caught his eye, but Waples had been right. Someone on the ground would be nearly impossible to spot. He hurried up to the cabin and knocked on the door.

An elderly man, somewhere between sixty and a hundred and three, opened it and squinted out at him. "Yeah?"

Shit. He'd left his picture of Sarah in the truck. Not that this guy could see much, judging from the thick glasses he wore. "We're looking for a young woman who was at Wesley Christopher's cabin. Have you seen her?"

Apparently his hearing wasn't much better than his eyesight. "Christopher moved away years ago. Haven't seen him. Nope."

"What about a young woman? Five-four, brunette? Blue eyes?"

"Ain't seen nobody. 'Septin' if you count fish. Seen lots of those."

"Thanks, anyway." Randy pivoted and jogged back to his truck. Halfway there, he heard something between a howl and a bark coming from the radio. "Ginger's headed toward you, Detweiler. She's danged excited about it, too."

"I've just checked twelve. Negative. On my way toward thirteen." Randy set off at a full run. Over the radio, the howling got louder, the barks closer together. Glimpses of a brown-red blur moving through the trees beyond had Randy digging for more speed. He turned up the trail, saw the bloodhound poised, quivering and barking about ten feet from the cabin. On the small entry to the cabin was what looked like a pile of discarded clothing. Randy rushed forward and saw the clothes were filled with Sarah. Stifling a sob, he crouched down. Touched her neck. Strong pulse. Relief swamped him.

"Sarah. Sarah, it's me. Randy. You're all right. We've got you." He stroked her hair, saw a bloodied lip and a bruise forming on her cheek. "Wake up, honey. Are you hurt?"

Sounds of heavy breathing behind him made Randy jerk around. Ginger, looking as pleased with herself as it was possible for a bloodhound to look, accepted praise from her handler, a fit man wearing jeans and a plaid wool shirt. "She okay?" he asked.

"I think so. But I want to take her to the hospital."

"You think it's safe to move her?"

As if she heard, Sarah groaned. Opened her eyes. A look of panic crossed her face.

"You're safe," Randy whispered. "Lie still a minute." He ran his hands down her arms and legs, checking for any obvious injuries. When he reached her left knee, she winced and pulled away. "I'm sorry. I don't want to hurt you."

He pulled out his radio and let the team know they'd found Sarah, that he'd take her to the hospital in Bend.

"Guess we're done here," the dog handler said. "C'mon girl."

"Wait. I didn't thank you properly. I don't even know your name."

"Biggs. Darren Biggs. But it's Ginger who does the work. I just run along behind her." He gave Randy an easy smile and Ginger a friendly pat.

Randy fished his wallet out of his pocket, removed a ten dollar bill.

"Hey, I don't take tips. Just helping out."

"It's not for you. Buy Ginger a steak. A big one."

Biggs grinned, whistled for his dog and walked up the path. Randy turned back to Sarah. Her eyes were closed again, but her breathing was deep and steady. He sat down beside her and stroked her hair. When she flinched at his touch, he clenched his teeth until his jaws ached.

Chapter Thirty-One

∽

Sarah listened to the nurse, the doctor and a counselor, she thought they'd said. She suffered their indignities as they poked, prodded and plucked, tuning out everything. All she wanted to do now was get home. Back to her apartment, her shop, her life.

"The deputy needs your statement, Ms. Tucker," the counselor said. "I'll be right here. Would you like the gentleman who brought you in here with us? He's quite concerned."

"No. Not him. Not yet."

A woman wearing a brown sheriff's uniform came in carrying a notepad. Sarah heard her own voice answering the questions, but it was as if someone else was speaking and she wasn't really paying attention to the conversation. Finally, the woman gave her a nod and a smile and left the room. Seconds later, Randy came in.

"Hey. They said you'll be fine."

She nodded, adjusting the drawstring of the scrubs they'd given her.

"You want to go home now? If you're not up for the trip, there's a motel across the street."

She could hear the strain in his voice. Why couldn't she look at him? Braving a peek at his face, she took in the red-rimmed eyes, the shadows under them. His hair hung in tangles, as if he'd been pulling on it. For the last two days, all she'd wanted was for Randy to find her and now he was here and her stomach hurt more than her twisted knee. She shook her head. "Home."

The doctor, a young man with tired eyes, spoke. "I'm going to write you some prescriptions—there's a pharmacy off the main lobby. Anti-inflammatories for the knee. Two a day for two weeks and if it's not better after that, see your own doctor. Ice it today, then heat tomorrow. The pain meds are if you need them. You'll probably wake up stiff and sore." He stepped between her and Randy and waited until she met his gaze. "Your physical injuries are minor. It might take longer to get over the mental trauma. See a counselor, or a support group. Talk to someone. And I'm giving you some Valium, too. There might be some nightmares."

"I'm fine." She lifted her chin. "Can I go?"

"I'll call for a wheelchair. Regulations."

Randy spoke up. "I can fill the prescriptions while you're waiting." He shook the doctor's hand. "Thanks."

The doctor said something to Randy too quiet for Sarah to hear. She saw Randy nod, heard him say, "I will," and then the doctor left the room.

Probably telling him to take care of her. What did they think she was? Some wimp? she could take care of herself. Or she would, once she got home.

"I'll meet you out front. I'll get your meds and pull the truck around. We'll be home for dinner."

"I'll pay you back."

"Sarah, I—" He stopped, then extended his cell phone. "Why don't you call your mother? She's worried about you."

Sarah dropped the phone into her lap and watched him trudge out the door, shoulders slumped as if he carried an insurmountable weight. Her eyes burned and she swiped at the tears that escaped.

* * * * *

"We're home, Sarah." She waited, keeping her eyes closed until she remembered where she was. In Randy's truck. He was already at the passenger door, arm outstretched to help her out. Her knee had stiffened on the drive and she leaned into Randy as they walked toward the building. After ten slow paces, he simply scooped her up. Maggie was waiting at the top of the stairs.

"Sarah, you poor dear. How are you? I saw you coming. Here, let me unlock your door. " Maggie fluttered down the hall and held the door open. Sarah closed her eyes.

"I'm all right, Maggie. It's just a twisted knee. I don't even need crutches. Randy's playing white knight." She felt him stiffen at her words. He lowered her to the couch.

Emotions overwhelmed her and she had to fight for composure. Maggie was already in the kitchen making tea and Randy looked—well, she didn't know exactly what he looked like because she was afraid to look at him too closely. Every time she did, she got knots in her stomach and felt like she needed to hit something. She closed her eyes and tried to retreat into a safe place.

She opened them, aware Randy was speaking. "I turned off the ringer on your phone and set the answering machine to pick up calls on the first ring," Randy said. "The police beat reporter will find Chris' arrest report and let the dogs out. As a matter of fact, it's probably smart to avoid the press altogether. Tell them you're not allowed to discuss the case so that it won't influence the trial. Be firm."

A weight settled on her shoulders. "I didn't think of that. Thanks. I don't think I could face a reporter."

"Don't open your door either, unless you know who it is. They can be persistent."

"Right," she murmured. No, it wasn't right. But she could handle a reporter or two. She straightened her shoulders. She was home and she was safe. "I'm sorry, but I can't discuss it," she practiced under her breath. She looked at Randy again. "I'm fine now. You can go home."

"You shouldn't be alone tonight," Randy said. "I'll sleep on the couch."

Maggie came in from the kitchen, wiping her hands on a towel. "No. I'll stay."

"Be quiet, both of you. It's my apartment. I think I have a say in the matter. I've got some scrapes, some bruises and a tender knee. I don't need a nurse, a babysitter, or a white knight. I'd appreciate it if you'd just leave me alone. Let me go back to being Sarah." She couldn't tell them of all the images that had flooded through her on the drive from Bend. There was still a curtain in her brain, but it was transforming from thick velvet to filmy gauze.

She heard her voice crack and hobbled to the bedroom and if slamming the door was childish, so be it. It felt good.

* * * * *

Randy sank into one of the chairs and lowered his head in his hands. He took three deep breaths, counted to ten and looked up at Maggie. He heard the sounds of a tub filling. "I guess she told us."

"What happened to her?"

"I don't really know. We found her at Falcon Lake, out past Bend. Chris drugged her, she managed to get away and we found her. Chris is in jail."

"I think there's more."

"I know there is. But I don't know what it is. She's shut me out. Won't talk, won't look at me. I'm going to go get a copy of the police report and see if she told the deputy what went on."

"She'll have to face it, you know. But the mind will only accept so much and then it blocks the memories."

Randy stared into Maggie's eyes. "That's what scares me. That whatever happened to her was bad enough for her to withdraw like this."

The kettle whistled and Maggie went to the kitchen. She spoke as she worked. "I'm going to bunk on her couch tonight, whether she likes it or not. No matter what happened, she's going to have to work through it. The Women's Center has counselors, support sessions, referrals to doctors. I'll get her there." She came back with two cups of tea. "Let it steep a while. My guess is you could use a change from coffee."

He smiled. "Yeah. Thanks." He balanced the cup on his leg. "Give her time, give her space. That's the training we get and that's what the doctor said. I'll give her as long as it takes."

"But it's tough when you love someone, isn't it?"

Randy barely caught the teacup before it splashed to the floor.

Maggie gave him a gentle smile. "Don't tell me you didn't know you're in love with her."

Randy put the teacup on the coffee table and rubbed his hands across his face. "I think I knew it the moment I walked into her shop. But I've never admitted it. Not so simply."

"It is simple, really. And I'm sure she loves you, too. She just needs to get over this little setback."

He managed a grin. "Little setback? You heard her. She wants nothing to do with me."

"Right now, I don't think she wants anything to do with anyone with a penis." She glared at his startled reaction. "Oh, like you've never heard the word before."

"No, I mean, yes, of course, but—"

"But nice little old ladies aren't supposed to say it? What should I say? Dick? Cock? I know. Y chromosome. Is that proper enough for someone like me?"

"Maggie, if things don't work out with Sarah, are you available?"

"You go on." Her blush was almost as becoming as Sarah's.

Exhaustion flooded him and he stood to leave before it overwhelmed. "The doctor gave her some prescriptions. If you can get her to take a Valium, I think she'll sleep easy."

"Don't you worry about her. I can handle Sarah." She tilted her face up and Randy kissed her forehead.

* * * * *

Randy arrived at the station, ignoring the sidelong glances from other officers as he made his way down the corridor to lockup. Chris, wearing an orange prison jumpsuit, lay on his back on a narrow cot, arms folded behind his head. He stared at the ceiling, his eyes void of any expression.

"He's lawyered up," the officer on duty said. "Want me to call the guy?"

"No," Randy said. "I just wanted to see the prisoner."

Chris jumped up and moved to the front of the cell. He leered at Randy, his eyes now wide open, whites showing all around. "What are you doing here, you overgrown excuse for a cop?"

"Detweiler," the guard said. "Are you sure—?"

Randy shot the guard a look, one he usually reserved for uncooperative suspects. "If Mr. Westmoreland wants to talk without his lawyer present, that's his business."

The guard shook his head and busied himself with paperwork.

"Oh, I want to talk to this guy," Chris said. "She's mine, you know. You thought she loved you, but she loves me. She married me. Sealed with a kiss."

Randy heard the contempt in Chris' voice and his stomach churned at the thought of Chris' lips touching Sarah's. He clenched his fists and concentrated on the pain of his nails digging into his palms. He forced himself to remain silent until his jaws throbbed.

You're a lying, worthless piece of shit. You're lucky you've got those bars between us.

Randy yearned to grab the monster by his neck and squeeze the life out of him.

Chris licked his lips. All Randy could see was a snake.

"You should have seen her in that wedding dress." Chris sighed. "She was beautiful. And when I carried her across the threshold and she was cold, it was me who warmed her, not you. I took off her wedding gown. You know she has the most succulent—"

Randy lunged toward Chris, his control snapped in two.

"Hey, what's going on?" He heard Kovak's voice and several strong arms pulled him away. He looked into the faces of his partner and the guard.

"Nothing," Randy mumbled. "Chris wanted to talk. I didn't say a word, as I'm sure this officer can attest." He worked free of Kovak's grasp and bolted down the hall.

Kovak followed, half a pace behind and shut their office door behind them. "We've got him, big guy. Don't blow it."

Randy picked up his coffee mug and threw it against the wall, watching the shards fall to the floor as if in slow motion.

"Feel better?" Kovak said.

Randy sat for a moment. "No. Not really. Give me the damn arrest report. Give me whatever damn paperwork you've got."

Kovak handed Randy a thick folder. "He muttered something about being married, about how everything would be right now and then he lawyered up."

"I didn't ask him any questions, you know. He volunteered everything he just said."

"What's really the problem? She's all right, isn't she?"

Damn, could everyone on the planet read him now? "Something happened. She's not talking." He tunneled his fingers through his hair. "I should have known better. People, things I care about get hurt and I'm always too late. Easier not to care."

"Easy to say. But losing the lows mean you lose the highs, too. Give it time."

"Maybe. For now, I want to read this report."

"Understood." Kovak slipped out the door and eased it shut behind him.

Randy worked through the pages, feeling more and more frustrated. Evidence collected—videotape, torn and dirty wedding dress, bottle of ether, champagne bottle with traces of blood. Whose blood? Bed sheets, partially empty box of condoms. Randy rubbed his eyes. Wastebasket had crumpled tissues, two disposable razors, seven Big Red gum wrappers and two toothbrush packages. But no used condoms. That told him absolutely nothing. Chris could have used one and flushed it. He slammed the folder against the table. The evidence wasn't talking.

He found the statement Sarah had given at the hospital and the medical report. She was bruised, but the rape kit would go straight to the state lab. Had she been raped? Her bruises said he'd tried. But no signs of forcible penetration. Had she gone along to keep from getting hurt? Or had she escaped before he got that far? The doctor's notes said something about denial, dissociation. Was she blocking the memories? He pushed the folder aside.

Someone knocked on the door. Randy looked up, waiting for it to open, but it remained shut. What was it with everyone pussyfooting around him? He closed his eyes, inhaled, exhaled, then said, "Come in."

Laughlin opened the door, stepped inside and closed it behind him. Randy wondered if this would be worse than the usual summons to the chief's office. "Sir?"

"She's all right?"

He nodded. "At home."

"Good work. I think we mentioned your vacation surplus. You're going to use up some of that starting immediately. I don't want to see you until Monday. And then, it'll be in my office, oh-seven-thirty. Sharp."

Randy looked up, but at a point above Laughlin's head. "Yes, sir."

The chief gave him a brusque nod and left.

Randy gathered his belongings and put them in his truck. Chief had said he was on vacation, but he didn't say where he had to take it. He went back to the courthouse in time to watch Chris appear before the judge. When he entered the courtroom, there were few empty seats. Pine Hills didn't see this kind of crime often. A cluster of his colleagues already sat on the spectator's benches. He started to join them, but he found he couldn't deal with the curious expressions he read in their faces. Instead, he gave a polite nod and found a place to stand at the rear of the room near the door.

Chris, in his orange jumpsuit, stood beside his attorney, handcuffed, his head bowed. Randy listened with numbed detachment as the judge read the charges. His fury was gone. The lawyers were in control now. The District Attorney listed all the ways she would prove that Chris was guilty. Chris' attorney opened his mouth in protest.

"Your honor, my client is an upstanding member of this community with no prior record. I see no reason not to release him on his own recognizance."

The judge glanced at the sheets of paper before him. "I seem to be looking at an awful lot of reasons, Mr. Gordon."

"But your honor, there are explanations for all those misunderstandings."

"Save them for the trial. I'm sure you know the procedures."

The gavel slammed, the judge said, "Bail set at two million dollars." Randy watched Chris being led out of the courtroom in defeat. Instead of elation, Randy felt completely drained. All he wanted to do was to get out of there.

Avoiding his colleagues, he worked his way out of the building, to his truck and drove home.

He went straight for the music room. Chopin's *Fantasie Impromptu* required his full concentration and its complexity drained him of his tension. He found himself playing the love songs and ballads people had requested during his nights playing in lounges during his college years. Each one reminded him of Sarah. He played "Bridge Over Troubled Water" and he was sitting in the dark with her again.

He stretched. He'd go for a run, burn off some of the nerves. But first, he retrieved a dust-covered box from the top shelf of the closet. Inside, he found the photographs of his grandmother, hidden away after she died, when the memories were too painful. He placed his favorites, a black and white picture of her as a young woman and a more recent portrait taken a few years before her death, beside the rest of the family pictures on the piano. He ran his fingers over her smile and touched the image of her brooch. "Welcome back."

Chapter Thirty-Two

Sarah awoke to bright sunlight and the smell of coffee. She lay in bed, muddle-headed and tried to get her bearings. Her own bed. She groaned past a thick tongue and looked at the clock. Quarter to eleven. She raised herself to her elbows and the room spun for a moment.

Memories of heart-pounding nightmares, of Maggie making her take a Valium, came back. She staggered to the bathroom and let the hot steam of a shower clear her head and ease her aching muscles. The bruise on her cheek had faded to a pale yellow and purple and the swelling on her lip was barely noticeable. A little makeup and she'd be presentable.

On the kitchen counter, she found a basket of fruit and a bag of bagels, along with a note and a set of car keys.

Hope you got enough sleep. Don't worry about anything. I'll be taking care of your shop. I took the bus — you can use my car if you feel up to going in. Love, Maggie.

Up to going in? Of course she was. She knew once she was at work, everything would get behind her. Still, she lingered a little longer than she needed to over a bagel and coffee.

She'd hurt Randy yesterday, but the unfamiliar sensation at his touch had surprised her. Not the revulsion she had felt with Chris, but not the tingle she expected. Because she couldn't express her own feelings, not even to herself, much less to him, she'd sent him away. She told herself she'd deal with it later, chalked it up to exhaustion and emotional overload.

Sarah parked in the alley and entered the shop through the back door. The customers she'd had after the robbery were

Finding Sarah

nothing compared to the bustling business she saw now. Maggie was in three places at once, smiling, bubbling and aside from wisps of red hair that clung to her forehead, seemed perfectly in control. Sidling her way through the milling customers, Sarah worked her coat off and put her things in her office, anxious to get back to her life.

* * * * *

The next two days passed in a blur. Sarah was where she belonged and despite Maggie's not-so-subtle hints about support groups at the Women's Center, she didn't need anyone, or any drugs, to help her. A little time, that's all she needed. During the lulls in the shop, Sarah paced the floor, fighting to control unbidden tears and trembling fingers. She had to relax. She was fine. Nothing had happened.

At closing time, she'd stare at the register receipts and have no recollection of some of the sales. Another look confirmed that the merchandise had indeed been sold. She'd hyperventilate, afraid she was losing her mind.

Home was little better. Countless hours of Mahjong did little to quell the nightmares. Chris and Randy kept swirling until she couldn't tell who was who. She'd reach for Randy, but he would dissolve into Chris, or disappear, before she got close.

On Friday, after locking the shop door, she went through her closing routine on autopilot, unable to ignore the tears that fell from her cheeks onto the counter. She picked up the phone. "Maggie? Tell me about that support group again."

Half an hour later, Maggie delivered Sarah to a cream-colored room at the back of the Women's Center. Orange and blue plastic chairs were set in a circle, filled with women from a somber young girl barely into her teens, to a gray-haired woman with a crinkle-eyed smile. A tall redhead stood up when Sarah entered the room.

"Linda, this is Sarah. I know she's in the right place." Maggie squeezed Sarah's hands. "I'll be back for you at seven-thirty."

"Welcome, Sarah," Linda said. "Let me introduce you to the group."

* * * * *

Randy spent the next few days wallowing in his own misery. Feeling like a first-class idiot, he'd even gone to Thriftway and bought a gallon of Peach Blossom shampoo, only to pour it all down the drain after he'd used it once. Countless hours at the piano, endless miles of running and still, he found no peace. Some inane sitcom blared from the television. Starsky and Hutch mewed from the floor.

"You feel like shit, too, guys? I'm sorry. I can't seem to get it right, can I?" He picked them up and sat on the couch with them, feeling their quiet purring resonate though his lap. "If I hadn't been watching the damn game, you'd be able to jump up here on your own. Hang in there. Doc says you'll be as good as new in a week or so."

Would Sarah? She needed time, needed space and he vowed to give it to her, although vowing and doing were at odds. Since Laughlin had virtually banished him from the station until Monday, Randy picked up the only tie to Sarah he had—the report from Dobs. What the hell. He was on his own time and the case was closed.

After settling the cats in their bed, Randy grabbed his keys and headed to the Polk County Highway Patrol office.

It took him nearly an hour to match all the evidence in the boxes against the inventory list. Remembering what Dobs had told him about the conditions, he wondered what would have been collected if it had been an easy scene. Photos showed the car balanced precariously on a tree before it slid the rest of the way down into the ravine. He whistled in appreciation of the investigators who'd braved the elements and the danger to pick up bits of broken glass, candy and gum wrappers, Burger King drink cups and a collection of hairs and fibers. According to the report, they'd collected about fifty fingerprints, none of which showed up in AFIS. Then, Darnell had decreed it a suicide and it didn't look like anything else had been processed.

He stared at the evidence, stared at the photos and stared at the reports until his eyes burned, but nothing popped. Nothing he could take to Oregon Trust to reverse the verdict. But something grabbed him and wouldn't let go. He went to find the property room officer.

All the protocols followed, which seemed to stop just short of a pint of blood and a promise to relinquish his firstborn, Randy hefted the box to his truck. Maybe it would make more sense in the morning.

It didn't.

By Monday, Randy was more than relieved to be back at work. He signed the box into evidence and verified that the chain of custody hadn't been broken. "Just hang onto this. I keep getting the feeling I'm missing something." Of course he was. Sarah.

Laughlin had been understanding, but Randy knew the chief would be watching. He tried to lose himself in his job. Why, when he needed to work, had the citizens of Pine Hills become so law-abiding? He dug through the cold case files, even closed a couple.

After two weeks, he stopped eating at Sadie's for most of his meal breaks. After three, his heart no longer raced in anticipation when the phone rang. That Special Something seemed to have customers in it whenever he passed by and he felt glad for Sarah.

The emptiness inside wasn't gone, but it didn't ache so much anymore. He gave in to the urge to review the evidence from Sarah's kidnapping. And as he reread the reports and examined what had been collected, his pulse quickened. He signed out the evidence from David's accident. How had he missed it? Nothing conclusive, but it was a place to start.

Slowing down enough to follow procedure, he secured everything and went to find Connor. "How fast can you get a DNA analysis on this?" he asked almost before he was inside the lab.

Connor looked up, wary and defensive. "On what? Why?"

"Chill. I'm together." He handed Connor an evidence envelope. "It's a piece of chewed gum. Found in David Tucker's car the day he died."

"And you need DNA because—?"

"Because I think the gum might have belonged to Christopher Westmoreland. They found the same kind of wrappers at the cabin."

Connor looked like he was going to protest, but he backed off. "I'll see what I can do. State lab usually takes two to three weeks. But even if you've got Westmoreland's DNA, how will that help you? It won't show when he was in the car, only that he was."

Randy stopped. "Lord, I don't know for sure, but I've got to do something. Please? Anything to convince Oregon Trust to reverse the suicide."

"Kovak know you want this? It was his case."

"Just do it, dammit. I'll get Kovak to sign." He went back to his office, unable to concentrate on anything for the rest of the day.

Now that he had something to wait for, the waiting became unbearable. If his interrogation techniques had become more brusque, nobody questioned him and he was closing cases. He immersed himself in paperwork, grabbed more than his share of the calls and pretty much had everyone giving him a wide berth. Even Kovak.

Five days later, Connor poked his head through Randy's office doorway.

"Got a sec?" Connor waved a file folder. "I think you might be interested in this."

Randy set aside the report he was writing. "Sure. Come in. You get results on the Horton TA already?"

"Yes on the traffic accident. No on the Horton."

Randy looked more closely. The glint in Connor's eyes said he'd found something good.

"Remember Sheila?" Connor said.

"Sheila, as in 'legs to her neck and hooters like cantaloupes' if I recall your description correctly?"

Connor grinned. "That's Sheila. She's also married and six months pregnant now, but I suppose that only enhances her hooters. Anyway, she works at the state lab and she called me with some DNA test results."

Randy's pulse tripped. "Are you talking about my request? I thought you said two to three weeks."

"Sheila moved it to the front of the line and babysat it through the process. I guess she still has fond memories of a certain weekend in Seattle." Connor reversed the chair beside Randy's desk and straddled it. His expression shifted to pure scientist.

"The DNA from the gum matched Westmoreland's. That puts him in the car. Only trouble is, that won't put a date on it. But I'd taken the liberty of including a hair for testing, too. They found a couple on the body that didn't come from Tucker and I didn't think you'd mind. They matched the hair to the gum."

Things clicked into place. "So he must have been in the car or at least with David the day he died. Not likely a hair would be there the next day, or the next week, assuming the guy showered and changed his shirt."

"That's how I read it. I don't know if it's enough to reverse the suicide, but I thought you might be able to convince the insurance company. Or get the Highway Patrol to look again. You've been very—convincing—lately."

"You're damn right." Randy reached for the file folder. "Report's in here?"

"Yes, but there's one more thing. When they ran Westmoreland's DNA through CODIS, it matched an unsolved case from eight years ago in New Jersey, near Rutgers."

Randy leaned across the desk. "Tell me more."

"Unsolved case. A hooker, beaten. Dead. Nothing to go on, nobody talking, but the DNA from under her fingernails went into CODIS and that's what hit when Westmoreland's came through the system."

Too stunned to speak, Randy sat back in his chair and tried to absorb everything.

"Umm, I guess I'll leave you the report and get back to the Horton investigation," Connor said.

"Yeah, right. Wait." Randy got up and reached for Connor's shoulders.

"Hey, you're not going to kiss me or anything, are you?"

Randy burst into uncontrolled laughter. "Not on your life. But if you want, we can go to the Wagon Wheel and you can have the biggest steak on the menu."

"You're just saying that because you know I'm a vegetarian, right?"

"Go. Thanks. Really. Let me get going on this and we'll all celebrate. My treat."

Connor retreated and Randy tried to keep from running as he went to Laughlin's office.

Chapter Thirty-Three

Even before he could see her clearly, Randy knew it was Sarah leaving the DMV office in the Municipal Building. Her walk, the tilt of her head, the way she tucked a wayward lock of hair behind her ear. He could almost smell the peaches, even though she was still thirty feet away. She dug through her purse and for a moment, he thought about ducking to the back entrance. He took a deep breath and strode the other way, down the hall toward the police department offices, burying the desire to approach her.

She had her insurance check, he knew, although he'd made the Polk County Highway Patrol the good guys. He didn't want her coming to him out of gratitude. Kovak had done all the follow-up on her kidnapping. The fact that Chris was now a murder suspect had been all over the papers. He'd seen her on the news one night after that one hit the fan. She looked composed, like she'd finally made peace with David's death.

It had been almost two months since she'd sent him away and he'd dealt with the pain. Or so he'd thought. Without knowing exactly why, he stopped, turned and looked back.

She looked up from her purse, right at him. He saw the hesitation in her stone blue eyes, the eyes he saw in his dreams every night and he could see her trying to find an escape route. Her face was as transparent as ever. Damn, he didn't know if he wanted to shake her or hug her. Only his promise to give her space kept him from doing either. He gave her a polite nod and a quick smile. Waited.

"Hi, Randy." She stepped toward him. Looked at his chest, not his eyes. At least she wasn't looking any lower.

"Hi yourself. You look good." But not happy, he thought. Shadows under her eyes and she was still too thin. Definitely hug, not shake. He dug for control.

"Started working out."

"Good for you." He saw the gears spinning before she spoke again.

She shifted her purse from one shoulder to the other. "Will you call me? I'd like to talk."

"I can spare a few minutes." He motioned to some seats in the lobby.

"Can't. Jennifer's waiting." She hurried past him toward the door. He watched her stop, look over her shoulder and his mouth went dry.

"Call me, please?" she said, extending her thumb and pinkie to her face, mimicking talking on a phone.

So she could tell him it was over for good? He gave her another nod and walked down the hall. He felt empty inside, despite the big lunch he'd just finished.

* * * * *

When Randy didn't call that night, or the next, Sarah wanted to pick up the phone, to explain, but every time she reached for it, something pulled her hand away. She had tried rehearsing the words, but her voice kept breaking. If she couldn't speak them aloud in an empty room, how could she say them to him? It wasn't right. She'd sent him away. She should make the first move. But was she ready? The memories she'd blocked had come back and she was dealing with them. What if he couldn't cope with someone who spent way too much time as an emotional basket case? Her support group said give it time. How long would it take? Even the money from the insurance settlement hadn't helped. Being her own Sarah didn't feel the way she thought it would.

Finding Sarah

When she'd bumped into Randy the other day, her first instinct had been to race up to him and bury herself in his chest. But he'd looked so distant. Did he care?

Sarah sat on the edge of her bed and looked at the pile of clean laundry in the basket in front of her. Somehow, she'd managed to pair all her socks without regard for color or style. She had dumped them onto the floor to start over when he called.

"Is this a bad time?" His voice was guarded.

"No. It's fine." Darn, she was already breathing too fast. She listened to the silence on the other end of the line. "How are you?" she finally said. Dumb, but a start.

"I'm okay. Busy. Sorry I didn't call sooner."

"Randy, this is hard for me. Please, bear with me, okay?"

"Always, Sarah."

This time, she heard compassion in his voice and something loosened inside. "I'm going to a support group. It's helping, but I'm still confused." She took a deep breath. "Whenever I think of you, everything comes rushing back and I don't feel the same inside and I want it all to be like it was, but it isn't and I don't know how long it will take, or if—" The tears started to flow and she couldn't speak.

"It's all right. Let me be there for you. Please."

"I want to." She wondered if he could hear her she could barely get the words through the lump in her throat.

"Let me in, Sarah. I'm here for you."

She sniffed. "I do want to, honest."

"Open your door."

Sarah walked to the door and peered through the peephole. Across the hall, cross-legged, leaning against the wall, sat Randy, talking into his cell phone. That lock of his hair still hung into his eyes. She longed to brush it back. She went to release the deadbolt, but her hand shook. Weak-kneed, she sank to the floor. "Not yet," she whispered.

315

"Then I'll stay here. What did you want to talk about?"

"You. Me. Us."

"I like the sound of the last one best."

"That's what scares me. I thought I knew *us*, but now I'm not sure. Every *us* thought has Chris in it. We never did any normal get-to-know-each-other stuff, did we? It was always the case. Even going to a play turned into the case." She rested her palm on the door, leaned her forehead against the cool wood. "What if we don't like each other when there's no case?"

She heard a deep sigh. "Would it help if I said that I never thought of you as part of a case? That I couldn't wait for it to be gone so that we could be together?"

"I don't know. Maybe."

"Open the door, Sarah. Let me tell you face-to-face that I love you. That I'll do whatever you need. That I understand you need time and space, but it won't keep me from loving you."

Heart pounding, Sarah pulled herself up and unlocked the door. Randy must have heard the deadbolt release, because when she opened it, he was standing at her door, the phone still to his ear.

"I hope you'll invite me in. We can continue on the phone if it makes you feel better," he said. "I'll sit on the couch and you can go into your bedroom."

She managed a smile and clicked off her phone. "Stay. You're here. I've been avoiding you and it isn't fair. You didn't do anything wrong." She considered the couch, then sank into one of the armchairs. "I got the insurance money, but you know that don't you? And about Chris murdering that woman—and David?"

Randy put his phone in his pocket and sat in the chair opposite hers. He nodded.

"Did you have something to do with it?"

He compressed his lips, but didn't answer.

"You did, didn't you?"

"I just lit a fire or two. What's important is the truth, not who found it."

"Why didn't you say something? I mean, one day, I get this check from the insurance company and a form letter that says that based in new evidence, the Highway Patrol no longer considered the case a suicide."

"If I told you I had anything to do with it, I thought you might feel like you owed me. You said you needed to work it out for yourself. I didn't think my part in finding the truth needed to be part of the mix."

"You know what was the worst? It wasn't finding out Chris murdered David. That made me furious for a while, but then, everything fell into place. I'd made my peace with David's death and finding out he didn't kill himself—well, that kind of outweighed the anger. The worst was finding out Chris killed that woman when he was at school."

Her voice started to tremble and she couldn't look at Randy. She almost picked up the phone again, but instead went into the kitchen and turned off the overhead light. "Turn off the lamp," she said. Randy clicked the switch and she returned to her chair, hiding in the twilight's semi-darkness.

"It took a while for all the memories to come back. Chris didn't rape me. He couldn't. He tried to...consummate...the stupid marriage, but he couldn't perform. He told me he wanted it to be true love, not like it had been with his bad girls. I figured he was talking about prostitutes and he said that with us, there shouldn't be hitting. But when he couldn't get an erection, he started hitting me. I tried being submissive, but he was too angry. That's when I fought back and got away, but now I keep thinking he could have killed me, too." She choked back something between a laugh and a sob. "Funny, isn't it? I'm safe now, but I'm more scared than I was when he had me in bed with him."

"You've been having nightmares, haven't you? Flashbacks?"

Although it was a question, she knew he was telling, not asking. She met his eyes for an instant before lowering her gaze. Took refuge in the familiar. "You want some hot chocolate?"

"Sounds good."

She went to the kitchen and saw Randy head toward the stereo. "Bridge Over Troubled Water" shimmered through the room. He stood at the edge of the kitchen, singing along softly. When the song finished, he whispered, "I'd like to be that for you. Your bridge."

Silent tears trickled down Sarah's cheeks. She handed Randy a mug and took hers back to her chair. He followed, two paces behind her and settled into the other one.

Sarah closed her eyes and tried the relaxation techniques she'd been learning at the Women's Center. A deep breath in through her nose to a count of three, an exhale through her mouth to a count of eight, her mind focused on a peaceful beach. When her heart stopped drumming against her rib cage, she spoke.

"I'm going to try to explain something I don't understand myself. I need you to stay where you are and not interrupt, okay?"

"Take your time."

"When I sent you away before…it was—" She swallowed and tried again. "When you brought me home, when you touched me, it didn't feel the same. No tingles. Not like with Chris, but strange.

"Before all this happened, when you took me in your arms, I felt like nothing bad could ever happen to me. I was afraid I wouldn't feel like that again. I needed to find some way to separate you from Chris. I didn't know how I could explain that to you without hurting you. But I think hiding from it hurt you even more."

Even in the dim light, she saw his brown and hazel eyes fixed on her. "I was so sure I could do everything on my own. But I couldn't. I felt like a failure and I didn't think you would want me anymore."

"Remember when you showed up at my place?" Randy said. "After Starsky and Hutch? You came to offer help. I accepted. There's no shame in that. Neither is getting outside help. I've been there."

"You? When? Why?"

He inhaled, his eyes lost their focus and Sarah knew he was finding a place deep inside him where the memories were buried. When he spoke, there was no inflection in his voice.

"Ten years ago. I was still pretty green. Uniform. There was a robbery. Guns. I did everything by the book, but firing my weapon at another human being, even one who would have killed an innocent bystander— You always wonder if there might have been another way. One where no one would have to get hurt."

"Oh, God. That must have been horrible. Did he... Was he... How did you—?"

"I killed him. I saved a woman, but I took a life."

"I'm so sorry." She looked up at him, her eyes stinging with tears.

Randy blinked back his own. "It's part of the job. We have mandatory counseling. It helps, but I know what the nightmares are like."

She wondered if he'd slept with the lights full on the way she had for a week. She thought of how long it had been before she could take down the trash without Maggie coming along. She leaned forward to set her mug on the coffee table and Randy reached to help her. When his fingers brushed against hers, a tingle, faint but familiar, made her quiver.

"I liked making love with you," she murmured. "I don't know what I'd do if it couldn't be the same. Would you want to be with me forever if the pleasure never came back?"

He set her mug down with a clunk. "You can't think I'm in this just for sex. If that's all you thought, we can say goodbye right now."

"No!" Her response was automatic and its vehemence surprised her.

He pressed his fingertips to his temples, slid them down to his chin and exhaled a shaky breath. "So, does that mean you still have feelings for me?"

She hesitated. Images of Randy and Chris swirled through her mind. Then there was only Randy. "Yes. I do. But can you undo a relationship and start over? Pretend we're meeting for the first time? I don't think so."

"Why don't we try? Dinner and a movie tomorrow? That's a pretty normal thing for two people to do on a first date, isn't it?"

Even in the dim light, she saw the hope behind the uncertainty in his face. And hope rose in her. Get back to a normal routine, her support group had said. This looked like as good a start as any. "Yes, but instead of the movie, would you teach me how to drive a stick shift? That's a normal thing, too, isn't it?"

Randy's brows lifted. "I guess so, but why that?"

Sarah took a sip of her cocoa and some of the knots inside untied. "The first time I got away from Chris, I found his car, but it was a stick shift and I didn't know how to drive it." She paused. "Well, it didn't start, but if it had, I might have gotten away."

"These days, manual transmissions won't start unless you depress the clutch all the way when you turn on the ignition. But sure, I'll be happy to teach you."

She smiled. "Good. And one more thing."

"Name it."

"I'd like to take some self-defense classes, too. It might be locking the barn door after the horse got away, but I think I'd feel better."

"The department offers classes. I'll look into it for you." He grinned. "I might even be able to show you some moves myself. I'd still like the dinner and a movie, though."

Sarah smiled as a warm glow crept through her insides. Her heart tried to escape her rib cage again, but this time it was a positive feeling. She rose from her chair. Randy's gaze locked onto hers. When she crossed to him, he sat there, motionless. Letting her make the first move. She closed the distance between them, brushed her mouth against his forehead, heard the sharp intake of his breath. When she stepped between his legs and put her hands on his shoulders, he raised his head, his lips parted, inviting, but not insisting.

Without conscious thought, she accepted his invitation. Their lips met, barely touching. And then she was sitting on his lap. Without hesitation, she ran her hands through his hair and pulled him to her. As the kiss grew in intensity, her bones dissolved and her insides puddled. "Don't stop," she gasped. She kissed him deeper and deeper and absorbed his kisses as they sent flames raging through her.

When it was time to breathe again, she leaned away. "Oh, I missed us so much. Thanks for waiting."

"As long as it takes."

"Enough talk," she said and drew him to her.

Why an electronic book?

We live in the Information Age—an exciting time in the history of human civilization, in which technology rules supreme and continues to progress in leaps and bounds every minute of every day. For a multitude of reasons, more and more avid literary fans are opting to purchase e-books instead of paper books. The question from those not yet initiated into the world of electronic reading is simply: *Why?*

1. ***Price.*** An electronic title at Ellora's Cave Publishing and Cerridwen Press runs anywhere from 40% to 75% less than the cover price of the exact same title in paperback format. Why? Basic mathematics and cost. It is less expensive to publish an e-book (no paper and printing, no warehousing and shipping) than it is to publish a paperback, so the savings are passed along to the consumer.
2. ***Space.*** Running out of room in your house for your books? That is one worry you will never have with electronic books. For a low one-time cost, you can purchase a handheld device specifically designed for e-reading. Many e-readers have large, convenient screens for viewing. Better yet, hundreds of titles can be stored within your new library—on a single microchip. There are a variety of e-readers from different manufacturers. You can also read e-books on your PC or laptop computer. (Please note that

Ellora's Cave does not endorse any specific brands. You can check our websites at www.ellorascave.com or www.cerridwenpress.com for information we make available to new consumers.)

3. *Mobility.* Because your new e-library consists of only a microchip within a small, easily transportable e-reader, your entire cache of books can be taken with you wherever you go.

4. *Personal Viewing Preferences.* Are the words you are currently reading too small? Too large? Too… ANNOYING? Paperback books cannot be modified according to personal preferences, but e-books can.

5. *Instant Gratification.* Is it the middle of the night and all the bookstores near you are closed? Are you tired of waiting days, sometimes weeks, for bookstores to ship the novels you bought? Ellora's Cave Publishing sells instantaneous downloads twenty-four hours a day, seven days a week, every day of the year. Our webstore is never closed. Our e-book delivery system is 100% automated, meaning your order is filled as soon as you pay for it.

Those are a few of the top reasons why electronic books are replacing paperbacks for many avid readers.

As always, Ellora's Cave and Cerridwen Press welcome your questions and comments. We invite you to email us at Comments@ellorascave.com or write to us directly at Ellora's Cave Publishing Inc., 1056 Home Avenue, Akron, OH 44310-3502.

Cerridwen Press

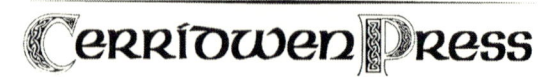

Cerridwen, the Celtic goddess of wisdom, was the muse who brought inspiration to storytellers and those in the creative arts.

Cerridwen Press encompasses the best and most innovative stories in all genres of today's fiction.

Visit our website and discover the newest titles by talented authors who still get inspired—much like the ancient storytellers did...

once upon a time.

www.cerridwenpress.com